FINE IN LINGERIE

Lingerie #11

PENELOPE SKY

Contents

ONE

Mia

I sat on the couch in my sweatpants and t-shirt, careful to look as unappealing as possible.

But that didn't seem to make a difference when Carter walked around in just his sweatpants all the time. I tried to seem as unattractive as I could, but since he showed off his godly figure all the time, it was impossible for me not to think of him in that way.

He had a bottle of scotch on the table and helped himself to it all night while he watched the evening news.

I couldn't understand a word of it, so I lay there under the blanket and tried to pick up on the language. Small luxuries like TV weren't important to me anymore because I'd lived without it for so long. Egor kept me in a dark room constantly. I wasn't even left at liberty to pee.

Carter picked up the remote and changed the channel. "I have a few American channels. You like comedies?"

"I like English."

He turned on a popular sitcom in America, a show I used to watch growing up. The second I heard English, I felt a little better, a little closer to him.

He tossed the remote on the table and returned to drinking. The large window behind him showed the grounds around his house, all cast in darkness with the exception of the evening lights that made the yard visible from the inside.

He hadn't tried to make a move on me since that moment in the kitchen. The second I said no, he listened, which was surprising since he accused me of lying about what I really wanted. But I still had power in this situation.

Power to say no.

It was the most exhilarating feeling in the world, to say something and actually be heard. I missed my former life. I missed everything about how perfect it was. I missed the small freedoms I once had.

All those things had been taken from me.

But Carter gave some of them back.

If I really tried to escape, I was taking a gamble. If I just left it alone, I could have a comfortable life here. I was a prisoner, but at least I had some liberty. If I crossed him, he would make good on his threats and change the dynamic. I wouldn't have the same power I did before. As long as I remained cooperative, my life could be bearable.

I would settle for it if I could…but that wasn't possible.

"Would you like something to drink?" He picked up the bottle for me to see.

"No thanks." I'd never been into hard alcohol. A glass of wine with dinner was nice, but nothing more than that. Carter drank all the time, starting after lunchtime. I'd noticed he hadn't left the house much, seeming to do all of his work from home.

He refilled his glass and kept drinking.

"You drink a lot but never seem drunk."

He set his glass down and looked at the TV. "Because I'm always drunk. You've never seen me sober."

"Is it healthy to drink that much?"

He shrugged. "Is it healthy to worry?"

I could be quiet and watch TV, but I found him more interesting. He was an enigma, his motives unclear. He wanted to fuck me, but he wouldn't actually go through with it until I gave my consent…unless I broke his rules. He allowed me to visit most of the house, to eat whenever I wanted, and enjoy his pool. Never did he speak down to me or raise a hand to me. He seemed like a very sexy roommate. "Do you have a girlfriend?"

He turned back to me, his right eyebrow arched so

high it nearly jumped off his face. "No. If I did, I wouldn't be pressing my dick into your ass."

"So, you don't have a girlfriend *right now*."

"I've never had a girlfriend. Do I strike you as the romantic type?" His eyes bored into mine, like he was offended by the question. "My sex life is one meaningless lay after another. Good sex with beautiful women is my game. Nothing more."

"So you're just like every other handsome man out there?"

"Meaning?"

"The good ones never settle until the last minute. They have too many options, so they can't make up their minds. But once they turn a certain age and their looks fade away, they find someone they like and finally settle down."

"Close," he said. "But I genuinely have no interest in settling down."

"Not ever?"

"No." His eyes moved back to the TV. "I have a sister who will have children, so my family line will continue. My cousin carries my last name, and he has a kid on the way, so my surname will outlive me. I don't need to have children."

"You don't like children?" I asked, unsure if I wanted to hear the answer.

He shook his head. "I wouldn't say that. I just don't want any of my own. My cousin is about to have his first child, so I'll be an uncle. That's enough for me."

I stared at him, pitying him. I could understand a man not wanting to settle with one woman, but not to have children was heartbreaking. Having a family was a blessing. Having someone to love with your whole heart was...indescribable. "It's a shame."

"I disagree." When he looked at me, it was with a twinge of hostility. "Don't judge me. Don't think you're better than me. I know what I want out of life. You were the one stupid enough to get captured."

Within the snap of a finger, the peacefulness I felt sitting there with him faded away. I used to tolerate him, even like him, but that comment hurt far too much. He sliced a knife over a scar that hadn't healed yet. He stabbed me in the heart even though my heart was already broken.

He must have realized what he said, because he winced slightly then sighed, his eyes on the TV.

I kicked off the blanket and stormed up the stairs, no longer interested in talking to him. Maybe I'd misjudged him. Maybe I shouldn't have assumed he had some good qualities. I should have assumed he was an asshole—just like my gut told me.

He followed me a moment later. "Mia—"

I reached the top of the staircase then turned around to look at him. "I'm not the one who bought some woman with cash to boost my ego. I'm not the one who keeps her as a prisoner even though she deserves to be free. I'm not the mama's boy who pretends to be a good man, only to turn around and

5

keep an innocent person against their will. Yes, I am better than you, Carter. I'm so much better than you."

He paused halfway up the staircase, listening to my speech with unblinking eyes. When he stepped up the stairs, his muscles shifted and moved under the skin. His eyes were full of pity, as if he genuinely cared about the way he made me feel.

"A real man doesn't need to force a woman on her back. He should be able to bed her without force."

"And have I forced you?" His deep voice echoed against the vaulted ceiling.

"But you force me to live here without a purpose."

"You cook and clean—"

"Go fuck yourself." I turned around on my heel and stormed into my bedroom. I slammed the door behind me, hoping he wouldn't follow me inside. I would rather stare at the wall in my room then look at his handsome face another second.

The door opened a second later. "Mia—"

"You should be fucking yourself. I gave very specific orders." I sat on the floor at the foot of the bed, my back against the wooden frame.

"I'll do that later tonight before I go to sleep." He lowered himself to the spot on the ground beside me, keeping a few feet in between us.

I hated myself for feeling slightly hot at that information. I even pictured him going to town on himself, sitting up against his headboard while he rubbed lube up and down his dick. I imagined him picturing me, not watching porn on his computer.

"I take back what I said. It was an asshole thing to say."

"Because you are an asshole." With my arms crossed over my chest, I stared straight ahead at the wall in front of me. I could smell him beside me, a mixture of shampoo, shaving cream, and cologne. He had a distinct scent, like leather and oak.

"I don't disagree with that. I just hate it when people get on my case about not wanting a family."

"Who gets on your case about it?"

"My mother." He faced forward, looking at the same wall. "She says I'm getting old. Instead of fucking around, I need to focus on finding a nice woman who will put up with me, who wants me for me and not my money. And she wants me to have my own family… because having me is the greatest joy she's ever known." He shook his head slightly. "My father and I have a different kind of relationship. We're close, but we talk about other things like guns, sports, work, stuff like that. But when my mom talks to me about stuff, she has this special way of making me feel guilty. So when I tell her I don't want a family…she looks so heartbroken. Now you're giving me shit about it, and I just get defensive. Doesn't give me the right to say that to you…so, I'm sorry." He didn't look at me, not the way he did earlier. Sometimes he was aggressive and intense, filling the entire room with silent hostility. At other times, he seemed like a nice guy…like now.

"I wasn't judging you. I just wanted you to know that having children is a wonderful experience. You shouldn't write it off as something you don't want…not when you don't understand how great it can be."

"Women always think having children will be this wonderful experience. Well, I can tell you that my mother had one hell of a time raising me. Stealing the car in the middle of the night, sneaking girls up to my room, taking my father's gun without permission… I did a lot of crazy shit when I was growing up. Nearly gave my mother a heart attack a few times."

I kept staring at the wall, doing my best to keep my breathing under control. Tears burned deep behind my eyes, making my throat constrict painfully. My hands came together, and I rubbed my palms against one another, fidgeting in place so I would have something to do. Heartbreak welled up inside me, and it was almost enough to make me fall apart.

Carter kept looking forward, oblivious to the emotions that raged deep inside me.

I couldn't sit with him anymore. I couldn't pretend to be okay when I wasn't. Now there was no possibility of me staying here. Even if Carter's apology was sincere, I had to get out of here. Regardless of the consequences, I had to escape. I belonged somewhere else. Just because I'd been unlucky enough to be captured didn't mean I should remain a prisoner forever. Even if I died trying, I was going to get out of here.

I had to.

NOW THAT I'D made my decision, I searched for every opportunity.

Carter woke up at the same time every day, whether it was by an alarm clock or naturally. He had his coffee and breakfast in the dining room, read the newspaper, took some phone calls, and then he went for a run around his property before he hit the gym near the garage. That was when he turned off the alarm system.

When he was in the garage, I did a quick sweep of the house, searching for weapons taped underneath the tables or hidden behind picture frames. I searched every corner of the house, taking advantage of the times when I knew he would be distracted.

But he wiped the place clean.

The only weapons in the house were the knives in the kitchen. Before I slipped out, I would take the biggest steak knife I could find. I didn't want to use it on Carter, but if he didn't give me a choice, I would stab him right in the heart.

This was about survival. I wasn't going to stop until I was the victor.

I had a phone that couldn't do anything besides make phone calls to Carter, but it did have a camera. I purposely set it up on the kitchen counter behind one of the crocks that held the spatulas and spoons. I hid the other part of the phone behind the salt and pepper shakers, allowing the camera a full view of the alarm pad. After charging the phone all night and making sure it had enough battery, I kept the camera on and recorded everything in the kitchen.

Then I did my best to pretend it was a normal day.

I made pancakes, bacon, and scrambled eggs. I slid everything onto the plate just when Carter walked into the kitchen. Shirtless and barefoot, he walked inside with his kissable tanned skin. His hair was messy from running his fingers through it. Deep brown eyes looked into me, looking me up and down with obvious interest. After our fight the other evening, he'd returned to normal, not disguising the things he wished he could do to me. "Can I get you anything?"

He grabbed the coffee pot and refilled his mug. "More coffee."

I faced forward again, sprinkling the powdered sugar on top along with the maple syrup. The alarm pad was behind me, the buttons lit up with blue light. The camera was tucked away on the counter, hidden behind the kitchen gear. The red light was on in the front, but I put a piece of tape over it to hide the glow. A part of me felt guilty for what I was doing, but the guilt also made me feel worse.

I shouldn't feel guilty.

He turned around and leaned against the counter, sipping from his mug while he watched me.

I could feel his stare at the nape of my neck, feel his desire fill the room. He had a natural way of occupying the entire space with his intensity, of bringing an invisible cloud into the room. It was suffocating, like high humidity in the middle of August. "I'm almost done."

"Take your time." He kept sipping his coffee, one hand resting on the counter.

I continued to wear the same stoic expression, focusing on my hands. I arranged the pieces of bacon along with the eggs. Normally, he took egg whites and fruit, but today, he seemed to splurge a little more.

My heart was beating so fast. I could hear the pounding in my ears, and I hoped he couldn't hear it too. I wasn't just unnerved by this beautiful man's stare. I was unnerved by the possibility of him discovering my plan. If he did, all of this would be over.

I cleared my throat and carried his plate into the dining room. Instead of following me, he stayed behind. I set down his silverware and hoped he would join me, but he never did. I breathed a little harder, afraid he'd noticed the phone hidden behind the crock. I turned around and walked back into the kitchen, seeing him at the counter still, over six feet of carved muscle and tanned skin.

His eyes followed my movements.

What was going on? "I just put your breakfast down."

He sipped his coffee again.

Now I really was terrified. Did he know what I was doing?

He held his mug at his waist, licking his lips as he looked at me.

I tossed the garbage, doing my best to ignore him. If I acted innocent, then he would have no reason to be suspicious of me.

He finally headed toward the dining room. "I want you to join me." Then he walked out, his footsteps growing quiet as he rounded the corner.

When he was gone, I finally released the air I was storing in my lungs. When he was intense like that, hovering and staring, I didn't have a clue what he was thinking. All I could do was wait and hope my paranoia was the only threat in the room.

I put food on my plate then joined him in the dining room.

Instead of looking at his phone like he usually did, all of his attention was focused on me. He sat at the head of the table, his elbows resting on the tablecloth. He stabbed his eggs before placing them in his mouth, but he didn't watch his movements because he was looking at me so intently.

"Yes?" I kept my eyes downcast, refusing to meet his gaze and solidify the connection between us.

"I didn't say a word."

"But you're staring at me."

"I have to look at something, right?" He placed

another piece of food into his mouth. He chewed it with his strong jaw, the muscles in his face working together as he moved. Even the cords in his neck shifted at the movements. He made the most rudimentary movements undeniably sexy.

"There's a window right there." I nodded to the large window that overlooked the front of his house. "And a beautiful landscape to boot."

"True." He glanced outside at the lawn before he looked at me again. "But I prefer this beautiful landscape." He returned to eating, watching me with his searing gaze that could melt panties right off a pair of hot legs.

The hair on the back of my neck stood on end, but I brushed off his comment. "What a line."

"I don't have lines. I say what I want. Sometimes it gets me laid. Sometimes it doesn't."

"Are you trying to get laid?" I countered.

He set his fork down and sent me a harder expression than he had before. "I've been trying to get between your legs from the second I bought you, the instant I saw your naked body on that stage. Your tits are unbelievable. Your face becomes even more beautiful when you're pissed at me. I wonder how beautiful it looks when you're coming around my fat dick."

My nipples hardened under my shirt, and I did my best to remain indifferent to his words. My fork stabbed the eggs on my plate, and I kept my gaze averted, trying to play the part. But my breathing quickened noticeably.

My thighs tightened together under the table, but thankfully, he couldn't see that. This beautiful man made me feel the kind of desire I hadn't felt in years, but I refused to act on it.

"Mia."

I stared at my plate as I chewed.

"Mia." He repeated my name, this time with a deeper tone. Whenever he said my name, it sounded innately sexy on my ears. "Look at me, or I'll make you look at me."

I finally lifted my gaze, pretending not to care about anything he said.

"Let me have you."

I held his gaze, doing my best to look angry rather than aroused. When I couldn't hold his stare any longer, I turned back to my food. "I don't sleep with men who buy women like livestock...at least, not voluntarily."

"Then why do you want to fuck me?"

"Who said I did?"

"Not your mouth. But your eyes certainly say you do."

I didn't care if he was right. I didn't care if he was sexy and confident. This man was standing in the way of my freedom, and I wouldn't let him become an obstacle. If I did sleep with him, he would only hold on to me tighter. It would make it harder to escape. It would make it harder for me to want to escape. Living with him had been a vacation compared to the hell I was used to. It would be easy to get comfortable and never leave. "You're confusing arousal with hatred."

"Who says you can't have both?" He leaned closer to me over the table, invading my personal space as usual. His hand slid to the back of my elbow where his fingers lightly touched me. He glanced at my lips before my eyes, his desire dancing on the surface of his eyes.

I pulled my arm away, getting away from his touch. "You could bed any woman you want. Don't waste your time with me."

"I don't want any woman. I want you."

I turned back to him, seeing the sincerity written around his muscular jaw. He wanted to kiss me again, this time not on the neck. He wanted to kiss me every-where, to explore my body with his mouth. "Why?"

"Why what?"

"Why me?" I asked.

The corner of his mouth rose in a smile, like the question amused him. "Look at you." His hand moved into my hair, his fingers lightly tucking the strands behind my ear. He was gentle with me, just like the last time he touched me. Unlike Egor, he didn't possess evil cruelty. He glanced at my lips again. "Those soft lips. The sass that flies out of them." His eyes moved to my right cheek. "These rose petal cheeks." He dragged the backs of his fingers across my skin. "The little freckles I would love to kiss. Those brown eyes…like my hot coffee in the morning." His hand moved to my neck next, gripping me delicately. "That thick hair I want to

15

fist. You're exquisite, Mia. Fucking exquisite." His fingers moved to my chin, and he directed his gaze on me. "You've got a backbone made of steel. I don't know anyone else who would jump out of a speeding car and run. I don't know anyone else who would dare insult a man like me. I don't know anyone else who could have endured what you have but still hold your head high. I'll say it again…fucking exquisite." He dropped his hand but kept his grip on me with his eyes. "Those scars on your back… I'm not going to lie. I like them. The idea of hurting you gets me hard. I know you can handle it, which makes me want you more."

His touch aroused me, and I hated the way he could make me feel just by looking at me. Egor had done terrible things to me, and even though Carter admitted he wanted to hurt me, I knew the two men weren't comparable. If Carter really were cruel, he would chain me up and do whatever he wanted. But he never crossed that line…always giving me the power to say yes or no.

Right now, he wanted me to say yes.

I respected him for giving me rights. In the cold world we lived in, any form of kindness was appreciated. My expectations of men had declined over the years. Despite the fact that Carter had bought me, he exceeded my expectations.

"Let me hurt you." His eyes focused on my face, taking in my features with authority. He continued to give me a choice even though he didn't want to. It was like he hated himself for giving me any kind of rights.

"You want to hurt me," I whispered. "I want to be free. Let's make an exchange."

He sat back in his chair, withdrawing his heat. He cocked his head to the side slightly, prepared to listen to my pitch.

"I'll be what you want me to be…if you let me go."

He released a quiet breath with his nostrils flared.

"I'll do what you want. I'll let you do what you want. Whatever it is. If you let me go when you're finished." I didn't want to be whipped until I bled. I didn't want to be choked until I passed out. I didn't want to be in pain anymore. But with Carter, it was a sacrifice I was willing to make…to be free.

He said nothing, his jaw clenched tightly.

"Carter."

"I told you I would never let you go."

"And I'm never going to fuck you…willingly."

His eyebrows slowly furrowed, his anger filling the room. A shadow passed across the window, making it darker in the room. His rage was palpable. Like a king who had just been defied, he was planning the best execution.

"This is the only way you get what you want. Just let me go. You're going to get bored with me eventually. I won't tell anyone you bought me…if you'll just let me be free."

He shook his head slightly. "There is one other way."

"What?" I asked, confused.

"If you try to escape. If you break your rule, I can break mine too."

My heart started to race again.

"I'm not stupid, Mia. I know you'll make your move eventually. Take this as a friendly warning. When you try, you won't get away. I'll be as cruel as your previous master. I will open those old wounds and drain you of all your blood. But if you take me now…I'll be kind. I'll be gentle. You'll always have the power to ask me to stop, to ask me to be gentler. I'll make you come—all night long. You will enjoy it as much as I do. You may be strong and smart… but you'll never match me. I'm an opponent you can't defeat. So, think about it…and make the right decision."

CARTER WAS RIGHT. I had underestimated him.

He gave me another option, but since that option didn't give me what I wanted, I couldn't take it.

Despite the threat he'd unleashed, I couldn't let it deter me. I had to get out of here.

I retrieved my phone from behind the crock in the kitchen then carried it into my room to take a look. I played the video and fast-forwarded it to the moment when Carter entered the code into the alarm system.

I got it.

I got all five numbers and the pound key.

I had the code to escape this place.

A light of hope shone from my heart, and it was the first time I'd felt excitement in the last three years. I'd accomplished something I didn't think was possible. I had the code to turn off the alarm. If I left while he was asleep, I would be hours ahead of him. He wouldn't notice until the following morning, and by then, I could be anywhere.

And if I took one of his cars and crashed it into a lake, he wouldn't even know where to begin to look for me.

I could run and disappear. Once he stopped searching for me, I could reveal myself again.

But then I remembered one little flaw in my plan.

The tracker.

It was embedded in my ankle, deep underneath the scar tissue.

I didn't have any other choice. I would have to cut it out.

There would be so much blood, so much pain. It would be disgusting, staining the bed all the way down to the mattress. I didn't know how to do stitches, and even if I did, I doubt he had the supplies. I would have to bandage it up as best as I could before I fled.

I didn't want to do it.

But I had to.

I had to do whatever was necessary to get out of there.

And finally go home.

I made dinner that night, a mixed green salad with chicken and rice. Carter had someone drop off groceries at the house, and I was told to make meals based on what was brought. I worked in the kitchen, roasting the chicken in the oven while I perfected the rice on the stove. I used to cook at home all the time. It was a regular part of my life. When I was stuck with Egor, all those everyday luxuries were taken from me. It was nice to be in the kitchen, nice to cook a meal I could actually enjoy.

Carter was in the living room, watching TV, shirtless like always. He enjoyed his scotch, a nighttime ritual he'd done every single evening since I'd arrived. If he didn't have such a strong hold on his faculties, I would be concerned by how much he drank. He could hold his liquor better than anyone else I knew, even Egor.

I eyed the sharp steak knife sitting on the counter. With a razor edge and made of stainless steel, it was the perfect instrument to remove the tracker from my ankle. It would be painful, but since I'd found a stash of bandages in the downstairs bathroom, I should be able to make it work.

I just had to sneak it into my room.

Carter had stopped locking me in my bedroom a week ago, confident that the tracker and alarm system would be enough to keep me inside. His bedroom and office were locked, so there was no way I could get to him.

Unless I burned the house down.

That wasn't the worst idea...except I didn't want to kill him.

I shouldn't care about granting him mercy just because he wasn't evil like Egor. He wouldn't rape me, but he wouldn't give me my freedom either. There might be different degrees of evil, but at the end of the day, it was still evil in its most basic form.

It shouldn't matter that I found him attractive... despite everything I'd been through.

But I still couldn't do it.

I finished dinner then set the plates on the coffee table in the living room. In the morning, Carter liked to sit at the dining table, but in the evening, he liked to sit in front of the TV. For most of the day, he was either on the phone, working out, or taking care of things in his office. I hadn't seen him leave once, with the exception of a family emergency.

I wondered if he would ever leave.

It would make my plan easier. I could do all of this when he was out of the house, rather than if he was asleep. But since I had no idea when that would happen, I didn't want to wait a day longer than I had to.

Carter's eyes watched my movements as I set the plate in front of him. "This looks good."

"Thanks." I sat on the other couch with my plate,

enjoying a glass of wine since I would need it for the pain I was about to self-induce.

Instead of digging in, he kept looking at me. Egor always infected my space with his disgusting touch. Carter could do it with just a look. An intense and deep gaze that made my skin prickle and form bumps.

I ignored him, pretending his penetrating stare didn't affect me as much as it really did.

He finally turned to his food and started eating. Even when he was hunched forward over his food, his stomach was still rigid with his tight abs. His tanned skin was firm everywhere, covering thick and powerful muscles. He cut into his food and took a bite. "Tastes as good as it looks."

"Thank you."

"I wonder if you taste as good as you look."

I refused to look at him, telling myself this would be my last night with him. Even if a part of me wanted to stay here, to have a comfortable life cooking and cleaning, I couldn't stay. I had a life waiting for me.

"Hopefully, I won't have to wonder for long."

I took a bite and chewed. "You know what I think?"

"Tell me." He drank his scotch. "I find that smart mouth as appealing as the rest of you."

I brushed off his words, annoyed with myself that I found his asshole comments charming. "I think you only want me because you can't have me. I'm just an object, a prize. Another notch on your belt. I'm something you can collect, something that can boost your ego. Since I don't want you, it shakes your confidence. Now, getting between my legs is a matter of pride. Why else won't you force me? Because it's a game to you. The point doesn't count if you cheat."

Instead of being angry about what I said, he released a quiet chuckle. "Your rejection doesn't shake my confidence. And your rejection doesn't make me want you more. Regardless of your attraction to me, you've suffered a great deal. Why would any woman who's experienced those things want to spread her legs ever again? No, the reason I want you is simply because I want you, because I admire your fire, your bravery, and your endurance. From head to toe, I find you beautiful. From the scars on your back to your perfectly soft lips, I think you're a very desirable woman. Trust me, I'm not the kind of man who goes for women in this situation. I may pay for sex from time to time, but that's only because whores are kinkier. I never thought I would be attracted to someone like you, when I've bedded all kinds of women—from virgins who wanted me to be their first, to women who wanted me to fuck them in the ass. You don't fit my palate at all. I've never been into slaves. But that doesn't change anything. I want you, Mia."

I believed every word he said because his actions proved it. He wouldn't respect my rights otherwise. But there was something missing from his explanation. "I'm not a slave. I'm a prisoner—big difference. And if you don't like prisoners, why did you buy me?"

He turned back to his scotch and took a long drink. "I already answered you."

"Just to piss off someone?" I asked incredulously. "Sounds like more work than it's worth."

"I don't know about that… I get to look at you every day." He picked up his fork and started to eat again. "You cook for me. You clean for me. And I think I'm going to start having you wear lingerie while you do all those things."

"I'm not wearing lingerie."

His authoritative gaze turned back to me. "Pick your battles, sweetheart. Because you won't win them all."

The threat was clear, and I knew he would make good on his word if I pushed him. If I wanted to keep my legs closed, I would have to comply in other ways. My temper naturally flared, but I kept it reined in, knowing it was better to remain silent.

He went back to eating, his eyes turning to the TV.

I hoped the hostility for the evening had departed. A few hours after he was asleep, I would make my move. I would cut out the tracker from my ankle, turn off the alarm, and take off in one of his cars.

I would be free.

So I shut my mouth and ate my dinner in silence.

I DID the dishes and cleaned the kitchen before I went

to bed. Carter walked up the stairs before me, so I slipped the knife into the back pocket of my jeans and covered the handle with my shirt. I walked up the stairs a moment later, seeing his bedroom closed at the end of the hall.

I walked into mine and shut the door behind me.

I'd done it.

I pulled out the knife and slipped it under the sheets of my bed. There was no lock on my bedroom door, not from the inside. So I quickly stashed the knife away just in case Carter came back to say anything else.

I passed the time by lying in bed with the knife beside me, staring at the ceiling as the night deepened. Carter had never burst into my bedroom in the middle of the night, but I wanted to play the part just in case his behavior was different. The more I rejected him, the more he pursued me. He might take it a step further and come into my bedroom unannounced, naked and hard.

There was a clock on my nightstand, so I kept glancing at it, waiting for the time to pass.

Waiting until three a.m. seemed to take a lifetime.

Carter was usually awake before eight in the morning, so he had to be asleep by one at the latest. But I waited a few extra hours to make sure he was asleep before I made my move.

When three a.m. arrived, I finally got to work.

My heart was beating hard in terror. Panic was heavy in my throat, and my breath came out shaky despite how hard I worked to stay calm. My hands were shaking, both from fear and excitement. The thought of breaking free tonight gave me a kind of high I couldn't come down from. It was what I wanted more than anything in the world. I couldn't let this opportunity slip away from me.

That wasn't an option.

I pulled a stack of towels to the bedside and prepared for the first step.

Removing the tracker.

I'd never done anything like this in my life. My fingers felt exactly where the tracker was under the skin, the definitive shape it made when I pressed my fingers down. It wasn't very big, so it should be easy to remove —if I cut myself in the right way.

I was scared of what might happen, but I reminded myself I'd been through worse—at Egor's hands. He'd whipped me until I bled all over the bed. He'd punched me in the face when I resisted him. He even broke my leg when I slapped him. There was nothing I could do to myself that would hurt more than that.

So I held my breath and did it.

It hurt like a bitch. There was blood everywhere. But I kept calm and finished the procedure, setting the small tracker on the bed beside me. I bandaged myself up and ignored the pain shooting up my leg. There was a possibility of an infection, but when I was free, I could visit a doctor to get what I needed.

Now, I had to move.

I placed the pillows under the sheet to make it look like I was still sleeping there. I placed the tracker there too, just in case he checked my coordinates randomly. I tossed the bloody towels into the bathroom then crept into the hallway.

His bedroom door was still shut.

The hallway was dark because all the lights were still out. I didn't risk turning them on and gripped the wooden rail to guide myself down to the bottom floor. Without breathing and with small movements, I descended without making the wooden steps creak. When I reached the first floor, I made my way to the kitchen.

The alarm pad was outlined in blue light, each of the buttons easily visible in the darkness. I'd memorized the five-digit code he entered yesterday, so I typed in the code without having to check twice. There was always a possibility he'd changed it since yesterday, but I took the gamble.

The alarm gave a slight beep before it was turned off.

Yes.

I knew where his garage was even though I'd never been inside. My inspection of the house had left me empty-handed in regard to his car keys. I had no idea where he left them. They were nowhere in the house, and unless he took them to his bedroom, there was only one place they could be.

In the garage.

I opened the door and stepped inside the large garage. I flicked on the lights, revealing six different sports cars. Two were black, two were red, one was blue, and another yellow.

I grinned, tasting freedom on my tongue. I didn't even notice the pain in my ankle or the blood dripping down my foot. Now that I'd gotten this far, there was nothing that was going to stop me.

The hardest part was over.

I hit the garage button, so the large door slowly rose and revealed the front driveway.

I could see the stars. Could feel the breeze. Could smell summer in the air. It was so quiet I could hear myself breathe, hear my loud heartbeat. My hands shook slightly, either from the loss of blood or from the rush of excitement.

On the wall hung six different sets of keys.

Perfect.

All the cars were in a row, one next to another, so I needed the keys to one of the last two, the two farthest from the house so it would be quieter. They were all the same make, so I couldn't figure out which key belonged to which. Based on the order in which the keys hung, either the first set of keys was to one of the last two cars, or it was the opposite.

I grabbed the last set of keys and hit the unlock button.

The horn sounded and the lights flashed. It was the last car in the row, the one closest to the driveway.

Thank god.

The sound was a bit loud, but since Carter was on the other side of the house with the door shut, I doubted he heard it. I opened the driver's door and got inside. The keys didn't slide into the ignition because everything was electronic. I hit the start button and pressed the brake, waiting for the engine to roar to life.

Nothing happened.

I tried a few more times, knowing I was doing everything right.

It still didn't work.

"What the hell?" I started to hit everything, to put my foot on the gas instead. No matter what I pressed, the engine never came on. It couldn't be this difficult to start a car, but nothing I did worked.

Shit.

Taking off in the car made more sense, but if that wasn't an option, I would go on foot.

I'd made it this far, and a stupid car wasn't going to stop me.

I opened the door and got out.

A hand flew out of the darkness and grabbed me by the neck. I was pushed up against the car, my tits hitting the door. My hands smacked against the windows, and the air was squeezed from my lungs.

My hands were yanked behind my back, like a police officer arresting a fugitive. One of his large hands held my wrists together, while his other hand continued to grip the back of my neck. His powerful chest pushed against me, his hard dick pressing through his sweat-pants and into my jeans. He breathed into my ear, his words menacing. "You broke your rule." He squeezed my neck a little tighter, making me struggle to breathe.

I stared at the wall of the garage, the adrenaline pounding in my ears. I hadn't seen him in the garage. I'd had no idea he was coming. I really thought I'd outsmarted him, that I was just minutes away from free-dom. It was a mistake to defy him, to think I could actu-ally outwit him on his own property.

But I didn't regret it, regardless of what happened next.

His lips brushed against the shell of my ear. "Now I get to break mine."

He was too heavy and strong for me to fight. My hands were compromised, and my throat was at his mercy. My ankle continued to bleed, and now the pain was excruciating. All the hope that had once burned in my heart was now gone. I'd never felt so defeated, felt so much self-loathing. Escape had never really been an option. It had always been a fantasy. "Please let me go. You're a good man."

"I've never given you a reason to believe I am. I wanted you to break your rule, tricked you into thinking you could actually get away. Would a good man do that?" He kept talking into my ear, his thick dick pressing right against my ass.

"Please…" This couldn't be the end. I would never

stop trying. Never stop trying to get back to where I belonged.

"I told you this once, and I'll tell you again." He yanked on my hands, forcing my shoulders to stretch back uncomfortably. His arm circled across my throat, and he put me in a one-arm chokehold, having complete control over my body. "Never. I'll never let you go."

TWO

Vanessa

I stood with Carmen at a high-top table in the bar. It was a Friday night, and after the long workweek, people were celebrating the arrival of the weekend. Music played overhead, the bass thudding in the background. I was in a purple dress with black heels. Carmen looked like a supermodel in a blue dress cut low in the front.

"So what did Griffin and your dad talk about?" Carmen stirred the ice in her drink with her straw. We'd both finished our drinks, and Griffin had left for the bar to get us refills. It was a packed night, so he probably wouldn't be back for a while.

"He didn't really say."

"Does he ever really say anything?" she teased, glancing at him behind me.

I chuckled. "Not with his mouth, no. He usually conveys his thoughts with a look."

Her eyes moved over my shoulder again, seeing him

in the background. "I think I know what he's trying to say right now…"

I didn't turn around. "He's probably staring at my ass." I could feel his piercing stare against my back, feel him surrounding me even when he was fifty feet away at the bar.

"He's staring at all of you, hon."

I finally glanced over my shoulder to look at Griffin. He was leaning against the bar waiting for service, and he killed time by staring at me like the most possessive man in the universe. He staked a claim all the way on the other side of the room, keeping the boys away with his brooding confidence. Just as he did when we were alone together, he wasn't afraid to give me that look… the same look he showed when he was on top of me, driving my body into the mattress underneath him.

"The hottie beside him practically has her ass cheeks popping out, and he doesn't even notice her."

A woman in black heels was next to him, wearing a short red dress, the hem of which had risen throughout the night. Now the bottom part of her ass cheeks were visible, and her thong wouldn't be far behind. Bones seemed oblivious to her, watching me like I was the only thing that mattered. "She's not his type." I turned back around, unable to wipe the smirk off my face.

"What's his type?" she asked.

I shrugged. "Me."

Her eyes softened. "I've never seen you so happy, Vanessa. Not even before you met him."

"No. I didn't discover the meaning of happiness until now."

She glanced at the bar again. "Still staring at you."

"He'll be doing that all night."

"Is he like that at home?"

"Yes. Every second of every day."

She sighed, her eyes moving to the ceiling. "That's one hell of a man. He's the kind of man who doesn't make you jealous with other women...but makes all women jealous of you. He's possessive but not mistrustful. He's built like a brickhouse. He'd take a bullet for you or anyone you love in a heartbeat." She sighed again. "He knows how to handle a real woman. He's so bad that he's good. I hope I find a man like that someday...but I suspect he's one of a kind."

I'd been with a few men, and none of them came close to Bones. "He's *definitely* one of a kind."

"Does he have a brother by chance?"

I chuckled. "No. Sorry."

"Damn," she said. "Maybe I need to walk the streets late at night and hope I witness a crime..."

"Carmen, you better be joking."

"Worked for you, didn't it?" she teased.

"You'll find the right man, Carmen. I don't know when or how...but you will. Conway was never the kind of guy to be a husband and a father...until he met Sapphire. So you'll meet a guy and turn him into the man you want him to be."

"I don't want to turn him into a man. I want him to turn me into a woman. Catch my drift?"

I chuckled. "Good point."

"I'm sure Griffin was already a man when you met."

"Yep. All man."

She scanned the bar, seeing the crowd of men and women. "I don't mind being single. It's fun. I have my independence, I have my shop, and I'm still young. There's no rush. But all those first dates, awkward bad sex, and clingy men are getting old. Seeing what you have with him makes me want that too. But I know I can't rush it. I have to wait for Prince Charming to walk in the door."

"You know what I've learned?"

"What?" she asked. "You have it all figured out."

"You don't want Prince Charming," I said. "You don't want a vanilla gentleman. I liked Antonio, but he was too plain for me. He was too safe, too boring. I never would have been happy with him, not like I am with Griffin."

"So you're into the bad boys?"

"Griffin is a man, not a boy. And no, that's not my type either. I just realized I wanted a strong man who wasn't intimidated by my sass or strength. I wanted a strong man who was powerful enough to make me feel safe, even though I don't need a man for anything. Griffin does all those things…makes me want things I didn't know I needed."

Her eyes glanced up, following someone through the bar. "Incoming."

I smelled him when he was feet away. His cologne mixed with his aftershave and body soap filled my nostrils. I could feel the heat his body generated before he actually touched me. He set the drinks on the table, two drinks for us and one scotch for him. He moved to the spot beside me and rested his arm on the surface, his fingers gripping his glass. His gaze burned right through my skin.

"Thanks for the drink." Carmen sipped hers through the straw.

He didn't look at her, his eyes on me. "You're welcome."

I was used to him staring at me like that all the time, but everyone else wasn't. "Stop."

He knew exactly what I was referring to, but he lifted his glass and took a drink without directing his gaze elsewhere. "No."

Carmen smirked. "Let the man do what he wants. He's earned it." She looked at the crowd again, giving us some privacy.

The corner of his mouth rose in a smile. "She's my favorite Barsetti."

"You've said that before." I gripped my glass but didn't take a drink.

"I'm saying it again."

"Aren't I your favorite Barsetti?" I took a drink, letting the cool alcohol move down my throat.

"You won't always be a Barsetti." He drank his scotch, drinking like an alcoholic even though he'd already cut back.

I kept my face controlled and didn't react to what he said, but his words hit me right in the heart. We'd talked about getting married before. He said if my father approved of him, he wanted to get married, but since we'd been back together, the conversation hadn't come up. I never mentioned it, not wanting to rush him. As long as we were together, I was happy. Whether I was his wife or not, the connection we had was unbreakable. After everything he'd been through, he could take all the time he wanted. I wanted him to be my husband, but if he never was, it wouldn't change anything.

He held my gaze then took another drink, unashamed of what he said.

"So, for now, I'm your favorite."

He moved closer to me, his head bent down so he could bring his face closer to mine. "For now." His hand moved across the deep curve in my spine, his fingertips spanning my entire back. His palm was warm, heating the fabric right against my skin. He didn't show public affection very often, not with his hands, at least. But now he was, hinting at the things he wanted to do with me when we were back at home.

Carmen turned back to us after she was finished surveying the room. "Griffin, you got any guys to set me up with? Since I'm your favorite?" She smiled at him, her long brown hair framing her shoulders perfectly.

"I'm looking for the strong and silent type, someone like you. You know, bad but not too bad…"

Bones finally took his gaze off me to look at my cousin. "No."

"You don't have a single guy?" she asked incredulously.

He drank then set the glass down. "No."

She cocked an eyebrow. "No friends or what?"

"I have a few," he answered, his voice deep. "But none that are good enough for you."

"Aww." She stirred her drink. "That's sweet of you to say."

"What about Max?" I asked.

Bones shot down the suggestion immediately. "No."

"What about the other one?" I asked.

"No," he repeated, stirring his drink.

"Looks like you're on your own," I said to Carmen.

"Oh well." She looked into her drink just as a man walked up to the table. With a drink in his hand, he came to Carmen's side.

"I like your dress." He looked her up and down, a handsome man in a fitted t-shirt. He was confident. A little too confident.

"Thanks." Carmen smiled. "I'm Carmen—"

"Boy." Bones stared down the man who joined us, giving him a terrifying glare that would make anyone piss their pants. He spoke in a rich baritone, his powerful voice deeper than the bass that played overhead.

I stilled at his unexpected aggression, and Carmen nearly jumped out of her skin.

The guy turned to him, his glass starting to slip due to the sweat that had formed on his palm.

"Men only," Bones barked. "No boys. Leave."

The guy didn't stand up to Bones and walked back into the crowd, not saying another word before he disappeared into the groups of people that were shoulder-to-shoulder in the packed room.

Carmen turned back to Bones, her eyebrow raised. "What was wrong with him?"

"Yeah?" I asked.

"He was drinking Jack and Coke."

Carmen and I stared at each other, having no idea what that was supposed to mean.

"One, how did you know it was Jack and Coke?" I asked. "And two, what does that matter?"

"I can tell by looking at it." He turned his gaze on me again, just as possessive as before. "And it fucking matters. If a guy has to dilute his drink with cola, he's not a man. He's a boy. And that opening line was pathetic. He'd last two minutes in bed before collapsing on top of you. Barsetti women belong with real men, not pathetic little boys pretending to be men." He downed the rest of his scotch until the glass was empty before he marched back to the bar to get a refill.

Carmen watched him go, and when he was out of earshot, she smiled. "He's intense, huh?"

"Always."

"Kinda territorial."

"It's because he likes you."

"He's territorial because he likes me?" she asked, tilting her head to the side.

"Yeah. You're his favorite, so he wants the best for you."

"Well, that's sweet…even though I don't need another overprotective brother." She stirred the contents of her glass before she took a drink.

"I didn't think I needed another protective man in my life either." I'd never needed a man to take care of me, to keep me safe at night or keep me warm when the heater died. I'd never needed a man to walk me home, to lift heavy things to make my life easier. "But now I can't imagine my life without that overprotective, psychopathic, territorial caveman."

AFTER WE WALKED CARMEN HOME, we headed back to our little apartment above the gallery. It was strange to walk down the cobblestone streets with him beside me, after I'd walked these streets alone for so long. It was a warm summer night, and the breeze licked the sweat off the back of my neck. My heels were starting to kill my feet because I'd been wearing them for nearly five hours. I didn't think we needed to walk Carmen home, but Bones insisted, so that was an extra mile I had to spend in the shoes.

Bones walked beside me, wearing a gray V-neck that stretched across his powerful chest and thick arms. Over a foot taller than me and possessing the menace of a gargoyle, he kept the path ahead of us clear with just his presence. His powerful arms swung slightly by his sides, and he stared straight ahead, his eyes scanning for danger that didn't exist.

I sighed under my breath, the heels becoming too much. I didn't care how dirty my feet got from walking barefoot. No way in hell could I walk three more blocks like this. I stopped and slipped them off.

Bones stopped at the exact same moment, in tune with me completely.

"I can't wear these anymore. They're—"

He scooped me into his arms and cradled me against his chest before he walked up the street again. Like I weighed as much as a pile of feathers, he carried me down the street under the dimly lit street lamps.

I held my heels with a single hand, letting them dangle past his shoulder. "I could have walked."

"I don't want your dirty feet against my chest."

I watched his side profile as he moved in and out of the beams from the streetlights. His hard jaw was tight and covered by a slight beard, and his blue eyes faced forward as he carried me home. There wasn't a sign of exertion, not a twinge of pain from his healed gunshot wound. "You already know how you're going to fuck me when we get home?"

"I always know."

I moved my arm around his neck, my heels dangling from his other shoulder. My mouth slid to his neck just below his ear, and I kissed him gently, dragging my soft lips over the cords in his neck. "Maybe I know how I want to fuck you." I kept kissing him, my hot breaths falling on his ear.

He crossed the street and kept going, his body not indicating his enjoyment. We were in public, so he was prepared for an attack from every direction. After everything he'd seen, he was always paranoid. If he enjoyed my kisses, he only enjoyed them so much.

"Don't care."

I circled my other arm around his neck, my face resting against the side of his head. "You don't care how your woman wants to fuck you?"

"No. Tonight, I want to do all the fucking."

I closed my eyes, aroused within seconds. Just a moment ago, all I could think about was the pain from my heels, but now all I could think about was the powerful muscles that were holding me up effortlessly, the way my man told me he would take me the second we were home. I liked being surrounded by him, his massive body dipping into the mattress and protecting me from the horrors of the world. I liked feeling him enjoy me, take all of me like a prize he'd won. I spoke into his ear. "Get me home."

He turned his head my way and brushed a kiss over my hairline. "Yes, baby."

He carried me up the stairs, got the door unlocked

with one hand, and took me inside the apartment he'd bought for me. My shoes hit the ground, thudding against the hardwood floor along with his heavy footfalls. He whisked me away into the bedroom and dropped me on the covers. He yanked his shirt over his head then moved for his bottoms, moving as quickly as he could because he wasn't in the mood to take it slow. Even if I asked him to make love to me, he probably wouldn't do it. His boxers and jeans hit the ground, and he stood in the darkness, all muscle, ink, and power. His narrow hips led to a broad chest that was flanked with enough definition to make him look like a Roman soldier. The black ink contrasted against his fair skin, a fresco all over his body. His eight-pack was hard as concrete, and his shoulders were chiseled with so many individual muscles, he seemed to be carved from marble.

I stared at him, my thighs aching and my pussy burning.

His knees hit the mattress, making all the gravity shift because of his weight. His hands moved up my short dress, and he gripped the lace of my panties before he yanked them down my long legs. Once he pulled them off my feet, he pressed them into his nose and took a deep breath, his eyes locked on mine.

Oh god.

He tossed my panties onto the floor then shoved my dress above my hips. Normally, he stripped off every piece of clothing before he enjoyed me, but tonight, he wasn't in the mood to wait an extra thirty seconds.

He grabbed both of my hips, his fingers spanning across my ass, and lifted me until my body was level with his. He held me in place as he shoved himself into me, getting his big cock inside me with a single thrust.

"God…" My hips were in the air, and my shoulders were against the bed. I clutched his wrists and watched him pound into me, taking my pussy like he owned it.

He fucked me fast, hitting me hard with every thrust. All the muscles of his core tightened and shifted as he used his stomach, ass, and back to shove himself inside me over and over.

"Griffin…" My head rolled back, and I enjoyed this man, enjoyed everything he gave to me.

He moved one hand to my throat, gripping me while he held me. "Eyes on me."

I turned my gaze back to him, his hand still around my neck.

"This. Pussy. Is. Mine."

"Griffin…"

"Say it." He squeezed me a little tighter, his thrusts never faltering.

"My pussy is yours."

"No." He dropped my hips and repositioned himself, his arms moving behind my knees. He buried himself between my legs, going balls deep. He started to fuck me again, this time deep and hard. "It's not yours, Vanessa. It's mine now. Say it again."

I knew I was going to come a few times that night. He was perfect between my legs, so big and deep that I would agree to anything he told me to say. "This pussy is yours."

He angled his neck down and gave me a hot kiss, full of tongue and longing. "Yes. Yes, it is."

LIKE EVERY MORNING at seven a.m., I woke up to Bones helping himself between my legs. He always turned me on my back, spread my knees, and shoved his dick inside me without even waiting for me to wake up. He rocked me into the mattress, hard enough to make the headboard tap against the wall, but not nearly as aggressive as he was at night.

My eyes remained closed, and I felt him bury his face in my neck, fucking me in a lazy way. One hand fisted the back of my hair, and he clenched his ass as he buried himself deep inside me. My hand gripped his tight ass, and I widened my legs farther, still not waking up fully.

First thing in the morning, he always wanted to come inside me. It was the only time when he was selfish in bed, using me to dump his come somewhere. But he always made me come anyway, whether that was intentional or not. His hard body rubbed against my clit, and his warmth and smell made me convulse all around him. He usually came in that same moment, finishing within five minutes of when he started.

He pulled himself out and left me there, my eyes still closed because it was way too early to wake up. It didn't matter what time Bones went to bed, he was always up insanely early. And it didn't matter how early I went to bed, I was never up before nine.

The mattress shifted when he left the bed. I heard him walk around, pull on his sweatpants, and then walk out.

I fell back asleep before he reached the kitchen.

Two hours later, I woke up and picked up his abandoned shirt from the foot of the bed. He'd been wearing it the night before, so it still smelled like his soap and cologne. The cotton was soft against my skin, all the way down to my knees. I wiped the sleep from my eyes before I walked down the hallway into the living room.

He was sitting at the dining table, his laptop open with a cup of coffee beside him. He was shirtless, the muscles of his body cut and defined. His shoulder blades moved the muscles of his back every single time he breathed. His ink covered his battle scars, acting as an artful bandage to hide his old wounds. The hair on the back of his neck was clipped short, merging into the short strands on his head. His knees were wide apart as he sat in the chair, a large man taking up every single inch of space.

It was a view I could wake up to every single day.

A view I would never get tired of.

I came up behind him and rested my palms against his shoulders, feeling his hard muscles under his scorching hot skin. My hands slid down his chest as I bent over to embrace him. My arms wrapped around his shoulders, and I pressed my face into his neck. "Morning."

His arm covered mine, just the way he did every morning. "Good morning, baby."

I kissed his neck before I released him. As I walked away, he gave me a playful smack on the ass.

When I looked at him over my shoulder, he was already looking at his laptop again. "You want anything?"

"No."

"You already ate?"

"Two hours ago."

I narrowed my eyes as I looked at the time on the clock. "Shit, it's ten?"

He chuckled, never taking his eyes off the screen. "Yes."

I rubbed my eyes before I made myself a bowl of cereal. "I should get to work downstairs, but I need to get out to the house. I haven't seen Conway in a while, and Sapphire is about to pop."

"I would offer to help, but I think I would scare off all your customers."

I rolled my eyes because he had no idea how wrong he was. Women all over would flock inside to look at him, not my artwork. "I want you to come with me

48

anyway." I carried my cereal to the table and started to eat.

Bones didn't make an argument. He scrolled through a document on his computer then typed an email. I didn't know what he was working on, but it probably had something to do with Max and his crew.

"You want to come along?"

He drank his coffee, his eyes focused on the screen. It was the only time of day when he didn't drink scotch. And it was the only time of day when he didn't stare at me as often as usual. He took care of business in the morning and didn't get distracted. "If you want me there."

I didn't expect Bones to immediately get along with my family, even after receiving a long overdue apology, but I hoped he would get closer to my family naturally. My father was here a few days ago, but Bones never elaborated on that afternoon. Since he was a man of few words, it was impossible to get him to say anything. "I always want you there." I scooped my spoon into the bowl and kept eating.

Silence passed. The morning light filtered through the windows of the apartment. The artwork on the walls was visible, looking beautiful in the natural light. There were a few images of Bones, images that captured the intense way I loved him.

"I'm sure my father wants to see you again. The two of you were out for a long time the other day."

Silence.

I waited for him to say something and gave up when words never came. "So, you guys just got something to drink and talked?"

He sighed and finally withdrew his gaze from the screen. It was the first time he'd really looked at me all morning. "I haven't left my job yet, baby. I have work to do. Can we talk about this later?"

He never bothered me when I was painting, so I knew I had to respect his request. "Of course."

He turned back to his computer, dismissing me.

I stared at him, enjoying my breakfast while letting my eyes be entertained by the man across from me. I watched the way his head shifted slightly when he was thinking, the way his eyes remained still and focused when he was reading. Sometimes, he rubbed his fingers along his jaw, deep in contemplation.

After fifteen minutes of that, Bones flicked his eyes up and looked at me.

I held his gaze, unflinching despite being the recipient of that powerful look.

"Yes?" he asked, his voice deep.

"I can stare at you all I want. No questions asked."

His eyes turned slightly playful before he looked at his screen again. "No questions asked…"

THREE

Bones

I watched her finish her makeup in the bathroom mirror, applying mascara to her long lashes. She wore a yellow t-shirt with dark denim shorts that were ripped all over the place. They were exceptionally short, showing her gorgeous legs and stopping just below her ass. Her dark hair was straight today, thick and framing her face.

She hadn't noticed me yet.

I leaned against the wall with my arms crossed over my chest. Once I was finished reading the mission statement Max sent over to me, I'd returned to my favorite pastime—staring at my woman. I already knew she was stunning, knew she was even more stunning when I was fucking her, but I never got tired of studying her, watching the way she rubbed her lips together after putting on lipstick.

I would have to leave soon, and I was dreading it. I

didn't want to be away from her again, not so soon, and I didn't want her to be scared the entire time I was gone. She would probably stay at the apartment by herself instead of going to her parents'. Staying with her father was the last place I wanted her to be.

It was humiliating.

I wanted to be the one to protect her every night, not the man who raised her.

At least this wouldn't be forever.

She put her makeup back in the small bag before she zipped it up. Her eyes returned to the mirror, and this time, she noticed me lurking in the background, still as a statue in the bedroom doorway. There was a slight reaction of surprise in her eyes before she recovered from the shock. "I'm ready."

"Good." I came up behind her and pressed my chest against her back. My hands gripped the counter on either side of her, keeping her boxed in like frightened prey that might scurry away.

Her breathing picked up immediately. It always did the second I was near. I made her heart race without touching her, made her afraid and aroused at the same time.

My mouth moved down to her neck, and I kissed her hard as my hand undid the front of her shorts. I pushed them down with a tug, and they fell the rest of the way. I breathed into her ear before I turned her face toward mine and kissed her, getting that lipstick off her mouth and onto my tongue. My hand slid underneath her panties, and I cupped her sex, my fingers feeling the arousal that leaked from her tight little slit. "Fuck, you are ready." I yanked her panties down her ass and thighs until they fell to the ground on their own. I kept kissing her, feeling her kiss me back with the same enthusiasm.

I lifted her legs and positioned her on the bathroom counter before I dropped my pants and thrust myself inside her.

"God…" She breathed into my mouth, her lips immobile after the violent way I'd forced myself inside her.

"I'm not your god." I watched her reaction in the mirror as I fucked her. "I'm your man."

I WAS behind the wheel of the truck while Vanessa sat beside me. Her long legs were sexy in the cutoff shorts she wore. Yellow was a perfect color on her, especially with that gorgeous Tuscan skin. My hand gripped the inside of her thigh, feeling the tight muscle of her slender leg.

We drove through the fields of Tuscany, approaching the house where she grew up. The last time I was there, I screamed at her father. He said he would take the memory to the grave—and I believed him. I had serious dirt on him, the kind of dirt that would make Vanessa look at her father in a whole new way.

I didn't like him, but I didn't want her not to like him too.

She had both of her arms wrapped around mine, her hands resting in the crook of my elbow. One single arm of mine was bigger than both of hers put together, but her slenderness didn't undermine her strength. She might be small, but she was resourceful. It was one of the things I loved about her, her fiery combustion.

"So, what did you and my father talk about for two hours?" She kept pressing this topic, her curiosity impossible to withstand.

"You."

"Be more specific."

With one hand on the wheel and the radio playing lightly in the background, I kept my eyes on the road. "I can't remember."

"Bullshit. Why won't you tell me?"

"It was a conversation between two men, baby. That's all."

"I like the idea of you two having your own rela-tionship, but I'd like to know the context."

"He said he wanted to get to know me better, to try having some kind of relationship with me."

"Really?" she said, her voice suddenly quiet. "That was sweet of him."

Sweet or not, I still didn't like him.

"It means a lot to me that he's trying...it really

does."

A part of me was touched that Crow Barsetti was trying to move forward with me, and me alone. He wasn't bringing Vanessa into it. He had the courage to face me head on and look me in the eye while he told me how he felt. He was honest, never apologizing for what he did but admitting he wanted the future to be different. At any point in time, he could have walked out of that bar and abandoned the attempt, especially with the harsh things I said, but he stayed.

I didn't think we could move forward and have any kind of relationship.

Just tolerance.

But he seemed to want more.

I didn't want to tell Vanessa how I really felt, that I disliked her father as much now as I did in the beginning. He took her away from me when he had no right, and as a result, she could have ended up with that perfect painter. How could I forgive a man for interfering with my life so much? It'd been over six months of cold brutality from the Barsetti clan. A simple apology and a glass of scotch couldn't erase all of that.

She turned her gaze up at me, watching me for a moment. "I appreciate that you're trying too."

I kept my eyes on the road, refusing to let the guilt suffocate me. She wouldn't be happy if she knew I stormed onto her family's property and insulted them after peace had been established. I could have ignited her father's wrath all over again.

But I wouldn't have let him take her away from me again.

I would have kidnapped her if it came down to it.

We pulled into the driveway a few minutes later. I parked in the gravel of the roundabout, taking the same spot I always took. I still remembered the day I showed up here and handed over the fully loaded shotgun. Maybe to Crow, it seemed like a lifetime ago, but for me, that just happened yesterday.

Yesterday, he called me trash.

Yesterday, he called my mother a whore.

We got out of the car and walked to the front door, the sweltering heat apparent the second the engine was turned off. It was humid on a clear day, and the summer breeze wasn't enough to combat the scorching temperatures.

Vanessa led us inside, and we greeted her parents in the entryway.

Pearl's eyes softened the second she looked at me. Instead of greeting her daughter first, all of her focus was on me. She looked at me differently from the way she used to, respecting my presence every time I stepped into the room. She used to regard me with a cold and guarded expression, anticipating an attack at any point in time. She was always stuck between disdain and contempt. But now, she didn't look at me that way. Her expression was warm and inviting, the same look she gave when she saw Vanessa or Conway. "Hello, Griffin. It's so nice to see you." She extended her arms to me and hugged me, holding me for an extra second like I was another son to her. She patted my back before she pulled away, her blue eyes full of friendliness. "How are you liking Florence?"

I still wasn't used to the change in our relationship. Before I saw her at the hospital, she'd been unforgiving toward me. But now, she was a whole new person. "I'm not used to the humidity and the smaller space, but I like it. Wherever Vanessa is, that's home to me." My woman was my home, my everything. Whether I was buried deep inside her or watching her eat her cereal in the morning, it was where I was meant to be. I would rather be in Lake Garda or Milan, but I'd been living in both places alone, and with Vanessa gone, they never felt like home again.

"Good," she said. "I'm glad you're liking it. Crow and I are so happy that you both are so close."

I noticed the way she chose her words, always including me in everything she said. Before, she would have no problem excluding me, indirectly telling me she wished I weren't around. I didn't know what else to say to her, so I just nodded. I'd never been good with words. I barely talked to Vanessa as it was.

Pearl turned to Vanessa next and hugged her for a long time. Her hand cupped the back of Vanessa's head, and she held her close, treasuring her daughter like they'd been apart for months rather than weeks. Pearl closed her eyes, the pained look of motherly affection written all over her face.

I watched her, thinking of my own mother. I didn't remember her that well, but I always remembered the way she made me feel. She loved me with her whole heart, would have made any sacrifice to take care of me. Sometimes it was hard to believe she'd been gone for over twenty years.

Crow walked up to me, wearing the same stern expression he usually wore. Unless he was emotionally moved or particularly angry, he always looked the same, displaying a constant expression of indifference. "Griffin." He extended his hand to shake mine.

I paused for a moment before I took it. I shook hands with my biggest enemy, a man I'd vowed to kill just a year ago. Now I stood in his house, welcomed into his family. I held his gaze as I squeezed his hand.

He did the same. "Can I get you a drink?"

"Scotch."

He nodded before he turned to the dining room. "Come with me."

I followed behind him then glanced at Vanessa over my shoulder, where she was whispering words with her mother. It wasn't until I stepped into the dining room with Crow that I noticed he hadn't even greeted his own daughter, giving me all of his attention.

He poured two glasses then handed me the drink.

I brought it to my lips and let the alcohol coat my throat.

He did the same before he set it down. "How was the drive?"

"Fine." It took twenty minutes to get there. It wasn't like it was a long trip.

Crow stared at me, looking confident but obviously pressed to have a conversation with me. "What have you been doing to keep busy? While Vanessa paints?"

"Work out. When I'm not doing that, I watch her work."

He leaned against the table while he held the drink in his hand.

Even after the two-hour conversation we'd had the other day, it was still awkward between us. Though we were a lot alike, we had nothing in common except the brutal past we both shared, along with the one woman keeping us bound to each other.

"I'm glad you're here," he said to break the silence. "Lars is making a nice dinner. You like steak?"

I kept the smile off my face, hiding my amusement at his struggle. He was desperate to make me feel welcome, and he clearly didn't know how to do that, not like his wife. He never went out of his way to talk to anyone, not even his brother, but he was bending over backward to engage with me. "I eat anything—except Vanessa's cooking."

He chuckled, a true smile coming over his face. "She's a smart girl…but she never caught on to that."

"It's fine. I usually do the cooking."

"You cook?" he asked in surprise.

"Yeah. Chicken, fish, stuff like that. I was pretty much forced to when Vanessa and I got together. It was either that or eat pizza every night…and a man like me can't eat pizza very often." Vanessa pigged out and ate whatever she wanted, but she still had curves I loved to grab on to. For me, I couldn't be this muscular without eating a lot of protein, and I couldn't be this cut if I ate too much shit. It took a lot of discipline. The only reason we had cereal in the house was because Vanessa bought it.

He chuckled again. "My wife learned throughout our marriage, but when we met, she wasn't the greatest either."

You mean, when you kept her as a prisoner. Since Vanessa was around, I kept that insult to myself. There were a lot of things I wanted to blurt out, but since I wanted to make her happy, I was on my best behavior. But there would never be a time when I looked at Crow without feeling a twinge of pain in my shoulder. "How's Conway?"

He took another drink before he answered. "Much better. He's moving around a lot more. They're looking for a house before the baby comes, but since she's due in a month, I'm not sure how likely that is to happen."

"So all the Barsettis are congregating here?"

"Except Carter. He's been busy lately with work, but he calls Conway to check in."

That was a lot of Barsettis for one postal code.

He stared at me for a while, probably wanting to say more but unable to think of something.

I refused to make it easier on him. I'd tried talking

to him many times, especially at the winery, and I was always met with hostility. I should be the bigger man for Vanessa, but this was as big as I was willing to be. She should be grateful I was standing in that house at all, let alone drinking her father's scotch.

He studied me for a moment longer, his features slackening into a focused look. "There's something I want to talk to you about. But I'll wait until after dinner."

I didn't care what he wanted to discuss. I didn't want to stay in that house any longer than necessary, especially for another hour after dinner. Sitting with the Barsettis for an entire meal seemed impossible.

Vanessa walked into the room. "Father? Uh, thanks for saying hi…"

"Sorry, *tesoro*." He set his glass down and wrapped his arms around her. "Just got sidetracked." His hand cupped the back of her head as he held her, his eyes soft in a special way just for her. His chiseled arms tightened noticeably while he gripped her, his body stiffening protectively for her. It was like he couldn't breathe, couldn't appreciate the moment enough. "How are you?" He kissed her forehead before he pulled away.

"Good. I'm hungry."

He smiled at her, a look of pure happiness on his face. "You always say that when you walk in the door."

"Because it's true. All I eat is cereal all day."

"Yes, Griffin mentioned that," he teased.

She turned to me. "You told him I couldn't cook?"

I shrugged. "It's not like it's a secret, baby."

She smacked my arm playfully. "You—"

I grabbed her wrist and yanked her into me, pressing my mouth on hers. I gave her a kiss, right in front of her father because I didn't give a damn. I pulled away and fixed my authoritative look on her face. "You what?"

She melted right before my eyes, not caring about her father either. "You...wonderful man."

I pulled her in for another kiss. "Good answer."

I PULLED out the chair for her before we sat down to dinner.

Vanessa did a double take, shocked by what I'd just done. I'd never been the kind of man that showed manners. I didn't open the door for her, I didn't pull out the chair before dinner, and I never gave her any indication I was a gentleman.

But I had it in me...once in a while.

She smiled before she took her seat.

I pushed it in then sat beside her.

Her parents sat down, along with Conway and Sapphire. Conway made small talk with me about Florence and his sister's artwork, but he didn't go out of his way the way Crow did. But Conway's behavior was definitely an improvement over to the hostile way he treated me before.

Sapphire was nice, like always.

The women in this family were a lot more understanding, with the exception of Pearl. They were the kind of Barsettis that I liked, the kind that were logical enough to look past their hatred and see me as my own man.

I'd been sitting there for less than a minute when the memory came back to me.

This was the very chair I'd sat in. The very chair Vanessa handcuffed me to. I recognized it because of the cuts in the wood, the cuts the metal from my handcuffs had caused. The shotgun had been placed on the table, and Crow checked the barrel to make sure it was loaded. Both of the Barsetti brothers had stared at me with utter disgust. They called me trash. They called my mother trash. They said I was worthless then ordered me to get out of their house. I shouldn't have expected them to react in any other way, especially with our history, but there was something I would never let go…

The way he insulted my mother.

My dead mother.

I stared at my empty plate while the Barsettis talked among themselves. Bottles of wine sat on the table, along with burning white candles. Everyone helped themselves to the freshly baked bread in the baskets, along with the extra virgin olive oil and freshly churned butter. The smell of dinner wafted in from the kitchen.

But my mind was a million miles away.

I wasn't an innocent person. I admitted I wanted to

kill every single person in this room at one point in time. But I dropped that vendetta because I loved a very special woman. Crow could never drop that vendetta. It wasn't until I took that bullet for him that he started to see me as a real person.

As something more than trash.

All I had to do was sit there in silence and let Vanessa visit with her family. I didn't have to talk unless spoken to. When the food arrived, all I had to do was eat. I wanted to make Vanessa happy by allowing her to have both of us, her family and me at the same time.

But I wasn't ready for it.

It was too soon.

I pushed the chair back and rose to my feet. Everyone watched my movements, including Vanessa. "I'm going home. I'm sure your father can give you a ride back when you're finished, baby." I tossed the napkin on the table and turned away.

Crow looked indifferent. Pearl didn't hide the surprise in her eyes. Sapphire looked down at her plate, the intensity too much for her to address. Conway stared at his father, waiting for him to do something.

Vanessa couldn't believe what I said. "What's wrong? You were fine ten minutes ago."

"I wasn't fine ten minutes ago. I can't sit here with your family and pretend everything is fine. Your entire family treated me like fucking trash until I took a bullet that almost killed me. All I ever wanted was you, but my love wasn't good enough. I know I should leave the past where it belongs…but it's too soon." I didn't want to look at Vanessa a moment longer, so I walked out. I knew my way through the maze of the mansion and let myself outside. It was dark out now, but the heat hadn't dropped by much.

Vanessa emerged a second later, her light footsteps hitting the gravel. "Griffin—"

I turned around. "I didn't mean to ruin dinner. Just go back inside."

She marched up to me, still looking beautiful even when she was upset. "You didn't ruin anything. Just come back in—"

"No."

Her mouth shut.

"You know I'll do anything for you. I've proven that already. I'm glad we're finally together and your family doesn't want to murder me anymore. I'm happy—really. But I can't sit there and pretend none of that shit happened. I busted my ass for six months, but your family continued to insult me, continued to call my mom a whore who deserved to die a whore's death. I understand they despise my father and always will. No contest there. But my mom was innocent. I was innocent." I pressed my hand over my chest. "I'm just not ready, Vanessa. Spend time with your family all you want. I'll live in Florence. I'll move in down the street if that's what you want…but I'm not ready for this. You know what chair I was just sitting in?"

She crossed her arms over her chest, keeping several

feet in between us.

"It was the chair you handcuffed me to, the chair where your father pointed that shotgun at me."

"That was a long time ago—"

"Maybe for you. Not for me." My nostrils flared. "You're mine now, and I'll never let anyone take you away from me. But they did take you away from me… for a long time. I don't believe in soul mates or any of that bullshit, but something tells me we're supposed to be together. I know that doesn't make sense, not with our history, but it doesn't make it untrue. You've healed me in ways I can't explain."

Her eyes started to water. "Griffin…"

I hated watching her cry. It killed me inside. "I went through hell for those three months."

"I know…I did too."

"No, you don't know," I said coldly. "You don't know how hard I fell. You don't know how violent I became. You were the best thing that ever happened to me, and then you were gone. I can't sit in that fucking chair and pretend that didn't happen."

"I'm here now. We're together now."

"Only because I jumped in front of your father and took a bullet that would have killed him. Vanessa, that gun was pointed at his damn face. He would have—"

"Stop." She closed her eyes, the tears moving down her cheeks. "Please don't do that…"

I knew I would always share her heart with her family, especially her father. They would always have one half, and I would have the other half. I would never have it all, not even after what we'd been through. "It's been less than a month since I was in the hospital. I need more time. I need more time to move past this."

"I understand." She opened her eyes and looked at me again. "I never meant to rush you. You didn't tell me any of this—"

"Because I want to make you happy. I thought I could put up a front for a few hours...but I can't. Not sitting in that damn chair at that fucking table." I hated being this far away from her, hated watching the tears stream down her face without doing anything to stop them. I was the reason this was happening, and I hated myself for hurting her. The last few days had been spent fucking and being happy. The second we got here, the bliss was over. "I understand what your family means to you, so I'll share you. But...don't expect me ever to be close with them. Don't expect me to be the man you've always dreamed about, a man who will be another son to your father. I know that's important to you, but you have to deal with reality. That guy isn't me."

She wiped at her tears. "You are the man of my dreams, Griffin. Exactly as you are, no matter how difficult it gets. Whether you love my family or hate them... you're the only man that I want. I never meant to rush you. When you're ready...if you're ever ready...we'll try again."

I stared at her, relieved that she was patient with me. It would be ridiculous if she weren't. Her father was making an effort to move forward, and her mother was kind to me. But no matter what they did to start over, it could never erase the past. I couldn't forget what happened…and I hadn't forgiven them for it either.

I moved into Vanessa and cupped her cheeks before I kissed her. It was a soft kiss, full of remorse and self-loathing. I wiped her tears away with my thumbs then kissed her forehead. I didn't say a word before I turned around and walked to the truck. I didn't need to tell her I loved her every time I said goodbye.

Our love was so real that she always knew.

"Griffin." Crow's deep voice came from behind me, his boots crunching against the gravel.

I was trying to get away from the Barsettis, not engage with them. It would be easy for me to get in the truck and drive off, ignoring him like he deserved. But something stopped me. Something kept me from crossing that line.

I turned around, seeing that Vanessa had walked back into the house.

Crow walked up to me, dressed in all black like usual. He was slightly shorter than I was, and with green eyes like Vanessa's, he reminded me of hers in some ways. They were both fearless and hard, but they also loved openly. He stopped in front of me and rubbed the back of his neck. "I heard what you said to Vanessa."

"Of course you did." I leaned against my truck and crossed my arms over my chest.

Crow ignored the insult. "I can't apologize for the way I behaved before. I love my daughter and—"

"You've said all of this already. You did your best, Crow. Give yourself a pat on the back and just let it go. I don't like you—never will."

This time, he actually looked pained by what I said.

"I didn't mean to ruin your night. Honestly. Spend time with your family." I turned around.

Crow grabbed my shoulder and forced me back toward him. "You are family, Griffin."

I pushed his hand down. "Don't touch me again. The only reason why I won't cross the line and actually punch you is because of Vanessa. But don't push me." I leaned back into the truck again.

He ignored everything I said. "You are family, Griffin. You are part of this family, and it would make us all very happy if you came back in and joined us."

"I don't care about making you happy." I turned back to the truck and opened the door.

He pushed it shut.

I faced him. "You don't think I'll break your nose?"

Crow didn't flinch at the threat. "Then hit me, Griffin. We both know I deserve it. If that will make you feel better, by all means." He dropped his hands to his sides. "Do it. I'm serious."

It was tempting. Very tempting. But it would break Vanessa's heart. I would never do anything that would cause her that kind of pain. When I talked about that gun in her father's face, it brought her to tears. "No."

"Come on." He egged me on with his hands.

"Hitting you is like hitting Vanessa. I won't do it."

He dropped his hands. "Then what's it going to take? How are we going to move forward?"

"We can't move forward," I snapped. "There's too much pain here. Vanessa will be part of our lives forever, and I will always take care of her. But it will always be divided. I'm not taking her away from you, and you aren't taking her away from me. So let's just be happy with that."

He stepped back and ran his hand through his hair, sighing through his flared nostrils. "You don't get it. I want you to be part of this family simply because it's what I want. Yes, I get to see my daughter whenever I want and have a close relationship with her. But all I care about right now is having a relationship with you." He shook his head slightly as he looked at me. "We both have shit that haunts us. We both have done terrible things to each other. We're both guilty of horrible crimes. We both need to let it go."

"I agree. But I'm not ready."

He moved his hands to his hips, his shoulders stiff with frustration. "I'm sorry for what I said about your mother. It was uncalled for...even then. I mean that."

I looked at the house, refusing to meet his gaze.

"You're right. She was an innocent person. It was low...even for me."

My mother was the only family I had. She'd been dead for nearly as long as I'd been alive, but she was all

I had. I had to defend her. I had to defend her the way Vanessa defended her father. It shouldn't make a difference if she was dead or alive. "She's all I have. I don't remember her very well, but that was the only time I celebrated a holiday or had a home...until Vanessa. I listened to you insult her because I was doing whatever I could to keep Vanessa...but I haven't forgotten it."

He took a deep breath, his eyes filling with sorrow. "I'm sorry, Griffin. I didn't mean what I said. I was just angry. I was trying to get you away from my daughter. We all say things we don't mean."

"Yeah...maybe." I turned my gaze back to him.

He stared at me for a long time, his hands still on his hips.

I didn't know what else to say. The rest of his family was inside, wondering about this conversation as we had it.

"I know you love my daughter." He dropped his hands before he crossed his arms over his chest. "I see it written all over your face now. I see it in the way you cried when you got her back, a man like you moved to tears. But I want you to prove it to me one last time."

"You've got to be kidding me..."

"I'm not," he said seriously. "I need you to do this for me."

I moved my hands into my pockets, unable to believe this asshole was actually asking me for something.

"Griffin?"

I stared at the vineyards in the background for a second, doing my best to lower the rage in my blood. I needed to concentrate on the breeze, to clear my mind, before I looked at him again.

"I want you to come to the winery three times a week. I want you to help me run the place."

That was the last thing I'd expected him to say. "Free labor?"

"No. Not free labor. I'll pay you."

I was so disgusted I spat on the ground at his feet. "I don't want or need your money, Crow."

"Fine. Then just come. Three days a week."

"Why?"

"No questions asked. Do that for her."

"What does this have to do with Vanessa?"

He took a long time to articulate his next response, his jaw clenching hard before he finally gave me an answer. "Because it would mean the world to her if you gave me a chance. Please give me a chance."

"I just told you it was too soon. It was less than a month ago when you threatened to kill me."

"I'm not asking for our relationship to change, Griffin. I'm only asking for a bit of your time."

If I couldn't sit inside that house and eat dinner, then I couldn't go to the winery and pretend that would be okay. "All I want is to not see you or hear from you for a long time. You want a chance to make this right?" I got closer to his face. "Then disappear. Fucking disappear."

FOUR

Vanessa

I sat on the couch in the living room with a glass of
wine in my hand. My mom rubbed my back and
consoled me, handing me tissues so I could wipe away
the tears and fix my makeup.

I wasn't the kind of person that cried, but seeing
Bones in that much pain killed me inside.

It killed me that we would never overcome this.

He would always be an outsider. He would never be
part of my family.

The worst part was, I didn't blame him.

My father came back inside, whispered something
to my mother, and then took the seat beside me when
she left. It was just the two of us in the large living room
with the vaulted ceilings and the fireplace. It was the
same room where we put up our Christmas tree, where
we opened gifts on Christmas morning.

Something Bones would never experience.

My father sat beside me, his knee almost touching mine.

I didn't ask how his conversation went. Based on Bones's hostility, he wouldn't listen to anyone, not even me.

"*Tesoro*." He placed his hand on my back, resting it between my shoulder blades. "I'll find a way to make this work." He peered into my face, his cologne surrounding me. He held a glass of scotch in his hand and placed it on the table.

"I'm sorry…about all of this." I stared at the coffee table, avoiding my father's look of pity.

"You don't need to apologize, *tesoro*."

"He didn't mean to be rude and ruin dinner. He's just—"

"Really, it's fine. I understand. This is hard for him…I don't blame him." He lowered his hand from my back and rested it on his thigh. His black wedding ring sat on his left hand, where it remained always. I'd never seen him without it, not when he worked or when he was in the pool.

"I know you wanted me to be with someone who could be a son to you… I don't think that's possible with Griffin."

"Vanessa, that doesn't matter." He rested his hand on mine. "He's the man you want, and we'll make this work. I don't care how difficult or complicated he is. You love him…so we love him."

I turned my gaze on my father, my eyes soft. "Thank you...that means a lot to me."

He squeezed my hand before he pulled away.

"He never told me what you guys talked about last week. He said a few things...but not much."

He gave a slight nod. "He's a man of few words."

"What did you talk about?"

He shrugged. "In a nutshell...he doesn't like me."

I sighed in disappointment, but I wasn't surprised.

He rubbed his palms together, his callused skin chafing together. His eyes were on his movements. "I didn't realize this until your mother pointed it out to me, and now that I've spent some alone time with him, it's all I can see. All he's ever wanted is somewhere he belongs...a family. He doesn't have anyone but you, and when I took you away, it was like losing his mom all over again. Your absence hurt him...but I was the one who killed him. I'm not better than the man who murdered his mother. He resents me for the power I have over him. And he's hurt by the things I said about his mother. He's a powerful man who's perfectly capable of taking care of himself and you...but he needs more. He needs a family."

I nodded, knowing he was right. "He's always resented me for everything that I have, for the beautiful childhood home and the wonderful family that loves me. He says that life should have been his...but you took it away from him."

"And then I did it again...when I took you away."

He kept staring at his hands. "I'm trying to make this right, *tesoro*. I'm trying to connect with him, to move forward on a different foot. I've never apologized for protecting you. I still stand by my decision. But I want things to be different as we move into the future. But he's not willing to meet me halfway, not anymore."

"He's very stubborn…" He was the most stubborn man I'd ever known.

"And angry."

"Yes…that too."

"It would be easy for me to let it go. Griffin has said that's what he wants, to put on a show for you and pretend everything is fine. We can pretend to like each other when we see each other, but we don't need to stand in the same room together longer than we have to. That would save me time and work. But after what he did for us…I can't settle for that kind of relationship. He didn't have to join the fight and save all of us. He could have easily looked the other way and let us all die…and then took you when we were gone." He rubbed the back of his neck, his eyes still on the table. "So I have to make this right."

I moved my hand to his shoulder and rubbed my palm across the cotton of his shirt. "Thank you…I want him to be part of us. I want him to be happy."

"Me too, *tesoro*. So I need you to help me."

"How?"

"You need to ask him to meet me halfway. You need

to ask him to come to the winery three days a week. We'll work together, spend time together, and maybe in time, some kind of relationship will form."

I had a lot of power over Griffin, the power to make him do almost anything. He was ruthless and bossy, but I could get my way if I asked for it.

"He wouldn't agree when I asked. But he will if you do." He turned back to me, his hands coming together.

It would be the easiest solution to the problem. Even if Griffin didn't want to do it, he would do it because I asked. He loved me, would give me the world if I asked for it. "As much as I want to do that…I can't."

His eyebrows furrowed.

"He's done so much for me. He told me he needed time, and I can't rush him. After everything he's done for me, how loyal he's been to me, I can't ask him to keep trying. I understand his pain. I understand his anger. It would be selfish of me to ask for anything more. I'm sorry…but I can't." I'd asked him to try to win my family over in the beginning, and he put up with my father's and uncle's bullshit every single day. He handed a loaded weapon to his enemy while he agreed to be chained to a chair. He worked at the winery every day, moving heavy crates and being insulted at the same time, just for a little bit of my father's attention. And then he took a bullet for my father…almost died because of it. "You have to do this on your own. I can't choose sides. I have to respect what he wants. I won't

use my power over him, even if I could get what
I want."

My father didn't hide his disappointment, but he
didn't argue with me either. "I understand, *tesoro*."

I wrapped my arm through his and rested my cheek
against his shoulder. "Please don't stop trying. I know
you—you can do anything. If anyone can make this
happen, it's you." I wanted my father and Bones to get
along. I wanted them to like each other, to trust each
other. I wanted us all to be one family…more than
anything else.

"In most respects, that's true," he whispered. "But
I've never been in this kind of situation before. You
know I'm not good with words. Even having deep
conversations with your mother is a challenge for me."

"I know you can do it, Father."

"You have a high opinion of me…"

"Yes. But I also know how much you love me…and
you'll do anything to make me happy."

He sighed before he looked at me, his eyes soft in a
special way. It was a look he only gave me, his only
daughter. I had a special hold on his heart, a grip that
even my mother didn't have. "Yes…anything."

FATHER DROVE me home and parked on the street.
Despite my insistence that I could make it inside on my
own, he walked me up the stairs to the door.

"Thanks for driving me back."

"I didn't mind in the least." He pulled me into his chest and hugged me, pressing a kiss to my forehead. "Good night."

"Good night, Father."

He gave me another soft look before he walked down the stairs and got into his car. He waited there, not turning on the engine until he saw me go into my apartment.

I unlocked the door and stepped inside.

I set my purse on the entryway table and walked into the living room. It was almost ten o'clock, the time we usually went to bed. The TV was off, and Bones lay on the couch, wearing nothing but his boxers. The size of a horse, he took up every inch of the cushions, his feet dangling over the edge. He'd taken a few pillows from the bedroom and rested on them now.

I stopped near the coffee table, spotting the open bottle of scotch and the empty glass beside it. There were a few drops at the bottom of the glass, amber liquid from the alcohol he'd downed for the last few hours.

I knew he wasn't asleep, so I stood there and waited for him to say something.

He kept looking at the ceiling, comfortable with the never-ending silence.

I walked to the couch and stood over him, seeing all his muscles and tattoos. When I looked down into his face, I saw his eyes meet mine in the darkness. Light from the streetlamp outside flooded the apartment, casting shadows in the corners.

He held my gaze, his look unresponsive. He was far too stubborn to utter a single word.

So I folded. "What are you doing?"

"Sleeping."

"You look wide awake to me."

"Well, this couch isn't made for a man like me."

"Then why aren't you sleeping in the bedroom?" I assumed he'd drunk until he passed out in front of the TV. But now that I noticed the pillows and his sobriety, I knew this choice had been purposeful.

"Isn't this what couples do? The man does something wrong, so he gets stuck on the couch?" He sat up then ran his hand through his hair, his eyes sleepy even though he hadn't slept for even a minute. His hair was messy from fingering it for the last few hours. He leaned back against the couch, a man comprised of endless power. He glanced at the bottle of scotch on the table but didn't pour himself another glass. He stared straight ahead, not looking at me.

I stared at his hard outline, from the broad shape of his shoulders to his enormous chest. He was a beast more than a man, his tattoos only heightening his intimidating presence. The black ink hid some of his beautiful skin, but it also hid the battle scars he'd been carrying for the last ten years. His jawline was hard, casting a shadow down his neck from the gentle light coming through the window. He hadn't shaved in a few days, so his beard was starting to get thick. His blue eyes were the only gentle feature he possessed. The rest of him was all man.

I gripped his shoulder then straddled his hips, sitting on him as he leaned against the couch. My arms hooked around his neck, and I looked him in the eye, seeing him slowly soften now that I was on top of him.

He glanced at my lips before he looked me in the eye. His hands automatically moved to my waist, his fingers sliding underneath my shirt so he could feel my soft skin with his fingertips.

I pressed my mouth to his and gave him a soft kiss, just our lips touching together. It was long, our breaths coming in deeper the second we touched. I felt the same electric shock as I did when he was inside me. A simple touch from this man was all I needed. I pulled away and looked into his eyes. "For as long as we live, you're never sleeping on this couch." I pulled my shirt over my head then unclasped my bra. The bra fell to the cushion, revealing my bare tits.

His eyes moved to my rack, the arousal instantly coming into his gaze. Within the snap of a finger, his cock hardened underneath my shorts, pressing right against my clit. His fingers dug into me tighter before he moved his face into my neck. Like an animal, he kissed me hard, dragging his lips against my warm skin as he rose from the couch and carried me with him. "Baby." His mouth moved over mine, and he crushed me with his embrace, whisking me down the hallway and into our bedroom. "I love you so damn much."

THE FOLLOWING DAY, I got up early and headed to the gallery. I hadn't been working much over the last few weeks. Sometimes my gallery wasn't open for days at a time. I purposely left the front door wide open, that way pedestrians would know I was open for business.

I had a pile of emails to catch up on. My regular clients were inquiring about new work, especially after recommending me to their friends and family. I took several photos of the artwork I had in stock, uploaded it, and sent it to each client I thought would like it. It took up most of the morning, and by the time I finished up, it was past noon.

I hadn't even gotten to paint.

Heavy footsteps sounded from the entryway, and I looked up to see Bones walk in. In jeans and a t-shirt that fit snugly over his chest and arms, he was a behemoth of a man. He was so hard in comparison to the softness of my artwork. His eyes scanned the pictures as he stepped inside, every footstep a loud echo because of his immense weight.

Then he turned his gaze on me.

And just like that, everything stopped. No man had ever looked at me the way he did, to make my lungs stop needing air, to make my heart stop needing blood. He was all I ever needed.

I rose from behind the white desk. This was the first time he'd ever been in my space, at least with me at the same time. I'd left the apartment early that morning, so I hadn't shared our regular routine of me eating cereal while he worked on his laptop. "Hey."

He didn't speak, regarding me with his stare instead of with words.

I came around the desk and moved into his chest. I rose on my tiptoes and kissed him on the mouth.

He kissed me back, gripping the deep curve in my back with his large hands. "Baby."

My hands slid down his chest as I pulled away, loving the way he called me that. No other man could pull it off the way he did.

He dropped his hands then took a look around the gallery, examining my pieces with obvious interest. He stopped in front of each one, taking his time as he took in the colors and lines.

I stared at his back, watching the strength of his body as he moved. Dinner at my parents' place had been terrible, and we hadn't spoken of that incident since yesterday. I came home, and we went straight to bed.

There might not be much to say anyway.

My father told me he wouldn't give up, that he would keep trying until he and Bones could have a new start. All I wanted was for everyone I loved to be under one roof. I wanted Bones to spend time with my brother and father, to become another Barsetti with a different last name. I wanted him to see my father as a father figure, and if not that, at least a friend. But those things took time. And with Bones, it would take a very long time.

He finished looking at the paintings before he came back toward me. "I like them."

"Thanks."

His hand moved to the back of my neck, and he kissed me on the forehead.

I closed my eyes, treasuring his affection. I could never get enough of it, get enough love from this man.

"I'll let you get back to work. Just wanted to see you for a bit."

"What are you doing?" My hands moved up and down his muscular arms.

"Just working on a few things."

I knew he would be leaving for a hit soon. Whenever he worked on his laptop, it meant he was doing research. His departure was usually shortly after that. I was dreading it, dreading it before he even mentioned it. I had to remind myself it would be over soon, that he would be retiring to live a quiet life with me. He would marry me and start a family with me. I would love to have a son who looked like him to inherit those pretty blue eyes and his natural power. "Alright."

He gripped my chin and lifted my gaze. He looked

at me, reading my emotions, and then kissed me on the mouth. "Love you."

"Love you."

He released me then walked out.

I stared at his powerful frame as he left, following him with my eyes until he walked past the windows and disappeared from sight.

WE DIDN'T EVEN GET through dinner before he threw me on the table and made love to me. He knocked over my wineglass, and it shattered on the hardwood floor. The bottle rolled across the table and met the same fate, but that didn't stop him from thrusting inside me, his hand deep in my hair and his gaze possessive.

I didn't give a damn about the mess.

He came inside me then carried me into our bedroom, ignoring the dirty plates and spilled wine that we would worry about in the morning. We got into bed, side by side, with our faces together. My leg was hooked over his hip, and his large hand gripped the back of my thigh. He'd shaved that morning, so his face was clean. I could see his hard jaw better, study the prominent line that separated his chin from his neck.

I could feel his come inside me, feel the hefty weight and warmth. At any given time, I had his essence inside me. When I was at work, I could feel it. When I slept at night, I could feel it. Only rare times in the middle of the day did I not feel it.

He watched me, his chest still sweaty from the way he took me earlier. His eyes were on me like that last session hadn't been enough. He always seemed to want me, no matter many times he took me. This lifetime wasn't enough. A thousand lifetimes wouldn't be enough.

My fingers moved over his chest, sliding across the sweat and the muscles. His black ink was vibrant in contrast to his fair skin. I was dark in comparison, my Italian blood giving me an exotic appearance. My fingers rubbed over the black ink, touching a date he had inked along his ribs. "What does this mean?" I never asked him about his tattoos. I studied them every time we were in bed together, staring at the different artwork that formed a fresco over his body. He never used colored ink, always sticking to black. There was a skull in one place, a snake on the other side of his stomach, a gravestone above his heart. Images were separated by vague symbols. I wondered if every single image meant something to him, or if the only purpose was to hide his broken skin underneath.

He didn't look at my hand to see what I was pointing at. "The day my mother was killed."

My fingers trembled against his skin, the jolt of pain slamming in my heart. "Christmas Eve."

"Yes."

My fingers moved over his heart, feeling the steady beat. "I'm sorry, Griffin."

His eyes shifted back and forth slightly as he looked at me. He studied me with the same intensity he always regarded me with, claiming me and watching me at the exact same time. "I know, baby. She was a good woman."

"Yes, she was. What do you remember about her?"

He paused as he considered my question. "Not a lot. I vaguely remember the way she smelled, the way she would whisper when she was truly angry. I remember the way she made me feel…like I was loved, no matter what. When I became an adult, I learned more about my parents. My mother didn't love my father. She was a concubine he'd claimed as his own. He knocked her up, but he had no idea she was ever pregnant. My mother loved me anyway, didn't care that I was the result of a horrible night. We lost everything, but that didn't make her give up. She kept going… doing the best she could. I would do anything to have her here now, to take care of her so she would never have to worry about anything ever again."

My heart throbbed once more, hearing the regret in his voice. "She'd be proud of you."

"Proud of what exactly?" he whispered. "I kill people for a living."

"You never cared that she was a prostitute. Why would she care that you kill people?"

He watched me, silent.

"She'd be proud of you because of what you just said to me…that you wish you could take care of her. You take care of me. You love me with everything that you have. I sleep well at night because you're beside me. I've never needed a man for anything, but I need you for everything." I moved my face into his chest and kissed the skin over his heart, feeling his heart pound against my mouth. When I pulled away, he was still looking at me, his eyes even more focused than before.

"There's nothing that turns me on more than hearing you say that."

"That I need you?" I whispered, my fingers moving down his hard stomach.

"Yes."

"I mean it." I kissed his heart again. "I'll always mean it."

His hand slid up my thigh until he reached my ass. He gave it a firm squeeze. "Baby." He pressed his face into mine and kissed me, a hot kiss with tongue, passion, and heavy breaths. He pulled my bottom lip into his mouth and gave it a gentle nibble before he released it. "I'll always make you need me."

"Good…because I like it." I'd spent three months without him, and I'd needed him every single second we were apart. He was my happiness, all my joy. My hand moved to his shoulder, feeling the tight muscles that shifted under my touch. "You've never told me about your tattoos."

"Because there's nothing to tell."

"I disagree. Which one was your first?"

He pointed to his right side, indicating the skull.

"And you've been getting them ever since?" I hadn't seen him get new sink since we'd been together. His ink was smeared in places where he'd been shot, from when I'd put a bullet in him as well as the one meant for my father. He would have to touch those up eventually.

"Yes."

"Are they just to cover your wounds? Because you have them all over the place."

"I got most of them in my early twenties. I had nothing else better to do."

"So, they don't mean anything to you?"

"Some do. Some don't." His hand trailed over my hips until he cupped my right tit. "I think you'd look sexy with some ink." He moved to my right hip. "Right here." He dragged the backs of his fingers over the skin, his eyes following his movements.

"And what should I put there?"

He shrugged.

"Let me guess…you name?"

He didn't crack a smile at my comment. "I don't need to brand you with my name to prove you're mine. Any idiot with eyes can see that you're my woman. Because my eyes are always on you, and your eyes are always on me."

It was true. Anytime I went out in public, men never hit on me. Bones always lingered in the background, acting as the strongest bug repellent a girl ever needed. I didn't even need to wear a large diamond ring to keep the gnats away.

"A man brands his woman in the bedroom. A man doesn't need to hold her hand or wrap his arm around her waist in public, not when his come is sitting inside her at all times. You never forget you belong to me, not when you can always feel me between your legs." His hand moved down my stomach until he reached the apex of my thighs. He played with my clit a little bit before his fingers moved inside my slit, feeling his come sitting at the entrance. He kept his eyes locked on me, his possessive gaze burning into my skin. "You like feeling me between your legs. It helps you sleep at night."

"Yes." I loved his come. I'd never let a man come inside me before. I always used condoms. He had the first honor, and I was glad I'd waited until I met him. "But I think I need some more…"

His fingers froze against my entrance, his own come on the tips of his fingers. He stilled as he looked at me, his nostrils flaring slightly in arousal. There was nothing he liked more than listening to me ask him for more sex. He thrived on it. "I want you to do something for me first."

"Yes?"

He grabbed my hand and placed it against my clit. "You fucked yourself when I was gone?"

For the first month, I was too depressed to feel aroused, but as time passed, my pussy ached for the sex

I used to get on a daily basis. "Yes." I swallowed the lump in my throat and refused to be ashamed of it. A woman was just as sexual as a man. I needed sex as much as he did. After the explosive and passionate relationship we had, I couldn't get by on nothing.

"You thought of me." He didn't ask it as a question, already knowing what my answer would be.

"Always."

"Show me."

"No." I kept my fingers between my legs but didn't rub my clit. "I don't want to pretend, not when I can have the real thing."

He repeated the command. "Show me and I'll show you."

I pictured him touching himself, and my skin immediately flared with heat. With his big hand and big dick, it'd be sexy to watch the vein in his neck pop while he pleased himself, watch his breathing pick up as his balls tightened against his body. "Okay." I turned on my back and let my knees fall apart before I rubbed my fingers against my clit in a circular motion. I could feel his come inside still, so touching myself immediately made me moan.

He licked his palm before he circled his fingers around his length. Then he started to jerk himself hard, moving from his head to his balls.

I watched him, seeing the fluid ooze from the top of his head. My fingers worked my clit harder, and my back arched with the pleasure. My hard nipples pointed to the ceiling, and I pulled my knees against my waist, widening my legs as I imagined his cock moving inside me.

He jerked himself harder, his breathing filling the quietness of the room.

"Griffin…" I wasn't going to last much longer like this, not watching him jerk himself off. Everything he did was sexy, but watching him touch himself was even sexier. "I'm gonna come. But I wanna come around your dick instead."

He moved on top of me immediately, shoving his fat dick into my soaking pussy. "Fuck." He pinned his arms behind my knees and thrust hard, his balls tapping against my ass. After a few pumps, he brought me to a climax.

"Yes…" My toes curled, and I dragged my nails down his back. "Now give it to me." I loved having an orgasm when I felt him throb inside me at the same time. I loved taking his come as I rode my high, feeling his seed fill my entire cavity.

He came right on cue, filling me up with his come. He claimed me just the way he vowed to, by stuffing me with so much come that I always felt him inside me. When I went about my day, I always pitied the young women I came across, knowing they didn't have what I had. They didn't have a powerful man fucking them like it was the first time, every time. Bones always took me like it was a new experience, one he couldn't get enough of. I always felt like the sexiest woman he'd ever seen, like there was no other woman in the world he'd rather be with.

He spoke against my ear when he was finished. "Is that enough come, baby?" He started to soften inside me, but I was still stretched apart because of the size of his dick. There was plenty of come inside me, plenty of his seed that would last through the night.

I gripped his shoulders and locked my ankles around his waist. "No. Not even close."

FIVE

Crow

Cane drank his scotch and rolled his eyes at the same time. "Just let it go. The guy doesn't like us, and he's not gonna change his mind. His family and the Barsettis are like oil and water—they don't mix." He set the glass down on the table in between us, his jaw tight with annoyance. "Leave it alone."

Button sat beside me, her legs crossed underneath her dress. She wore a deep blue dress that stopped above her knee. With her hair pulled back and her diamond earrings exposed, she had the grace of a queen.

My queen.

She'd aged like a fine wine, becoming more graceful and potent as the years wore on. Her confidence only heightened her beauty, and those sharp blue eyes never faded despite the decades of stress we'd both endured.

She turned her gaze on me, silently beckoning me to address what my brother just said.

It would be easy to give up—but not for me. "I'm not gonna stop. Not until water and oil finally mix."

"But they *can't* mix," Cane spat. "They always separate."

"Well, I'll make it happen."

He shook his head as he refilled his glass. "Dumbest thing I've ever heard you say. And you've said a lot of dumb things over the past few decades…"

Button narrowed her eyes on his face, her lips pressed tightly together. "Not nearly as many as you."

I couldn't hide the slight grin that formed on my face. She was my wife, the person at my side forever. She always defended me even though I didn't need her to do it. But she was also a member of this relationship, a sister to Cane who fit perfectly. We'd defeated Bones Sr. together, saved each other's asses more times than I could count. It was the kind of bond that allowed insults to fly all the time.

Crow swirled his glass before he shrugged. "True. But this is still stupid. You've made your attempt. We've got to move on. If he doesn't want to be the bigger man, then whatever."

"Be the bigger man?" I set my glass on the table, my hands coming together. "He always was the bigger man. Despite the shit we put him through, he warned me about Conway. On top of that, he put his neck on the line and saved all of us." I pointed between him and me. "We'd be dead right now if it weren't for him. It would have been easy for him to ignore that information. I bet you he considered it for a moment. All he would have to do is wait for us to be killed off before he took Vanessa. We'd be out of the way for good, and he would get exactly what he wanted—Vanessa and the rest of us dead."

My brother held my gaze, still slightly swirling his drink.

"He already was the bigger man." My eyes moved to the table between us. "He proved it a million times over. I'm in debt to him for the rest of my damn life. I don't even give a shit about my life that much, not compared to my only son."

"And mine?" he asked in offense.

"You know what I mean," I spat. "He saved my son. He saved my daughter-in-law. He saved my grandchild. It's my turn to be the bigger man. It's my turn to put up with his bullshit until I finally earn his respect."

Cane leaned back against the leather chair, his drink sitting on his thigh. A sigh erupted from his lips and filled the room.

Button nodded. "Crow is right. We have to keep trying until we make it right."

"But he doesn't want anything to do with us," Cane said. "That's the part you don't understand. All he wants is Vanessa. He wants to be left alone. You trying to make this right is only annoying him. If you really want to respect him, just stop bothering him."

I shook my head. "No. I get that he's angry at us, particularly me, but this needs to be mended. He's a strong guy, but he needs more in life. He needs a place where he belongs. I never thought I would try to be a father figure to him...but that's what he needs. That's what Vanessa wants me to be for him."

"A father?" he asked incredulously. "The guy is thirty years old. He doesn't need a father."

"My son needs me," I countered. "When he was taken, I stepped into the open and prepared to die to save his life, just for the slim chance he could get away. When he didn't know what to do about Sapphire, he came to me for advice. When he raises his kids, he's going to come me. He needs me as much now as he did when he was a child, just in different ways. Carter and Carmen need you too."

Cane fell silent and drank his scotch.

"Sometimes I think I make some progress with Griffin, but then we take ten steps back." When I met him in the bar, it seemed like he was slowly opening up to me. It seemed like his walls were coming down. But then he came over for dinner, and that trigger went off and pushed him away all over again. "I asked Vanessa to ask him to meet me halfway, but she refused. She said she can't ask any more from him, which I understand. So, I'm on my own."

Carter stared into his glass, swallowing his annoyance. "I hope I don't go through anything like this with

Carmen. I always make jokes about putting her in a nunnery, but Jesus, I'm serious now."

My only daughter dating my biggest enemy was the worst heartache I'd ever experienced. There was so much hate in my veins, so much frustration. It would have been so much easier if she'd just settled down with Matteo or Antonio, two fine gentlemen, either of whom would have made her happy. But she chose someone else, a man hard like me. "It's not so bad, Cane. I know he would do anything for her, and that's enough for me."

"If Carmen dated someone like him…" Cane shook his head. "I don't even want to think about it."

"As much as I hate to admit, she found someone like me." Griffin and I looked nothing alike, but we were similar in our hostility and mannerisms. He was fearless, strong, and passionate. With very little to say, he announced his presence in silence. After Button pointed out the similarities, I couldn't stop seeing them. "Carmen might find someone like you."

Cane scoffed. "Over my dead body."

Button looked at him. "As much as we don't want to admit it, Barsetti blood is tainted with blood and violence. We have a specific palate when it comes to our partners. We don't want an average person. We need someone like us. Carmen probably wouldn't be happy with an average man. She'll likely always want an extraordinary one."

"That's why the nunnery is such a good idea." He

downed the contents of his glass before he set it on the table. "Because my daughter is so damn beautiful. She looks like Adelina, but with Barsetti eyes and height." He shook his head. "I wish she were ugly…"

Button chuckled. "No, you don't."

"Yes, he does," I said. "I've been there. But now that I know Vanessa's going to spend her life with Griffin, I'm not worried about her. She has the perfect man to protect her. I never have to worry about her…and that's all I wanted."

Cane shrugged. "I don't think any man out there will ever be good enough for my daughter."

I nodded. "I know what you mean."

Cane refilled his glass before he changed the subject. "I know you're trying to kiss Griffin's ass right now, but we've got to do something about the Skull Kings. I haven't heard a peep about them, but after ordering a hit like that, I don't think it will end quietly. If they're anything like the way I remember, they're insanely ruthless. I'm sure killing the entire team they dispatched made them realize they underestimated us… but I don't think it's over."

It'd been on mind for the last few weeks. Their quiet surrender sounded too good to be true. Things like that never dissolved into nothingness. "Neither do I." Now that my son was going to be a father in just a few weeks, this war needed to be dead and buried for good. I didn't want my grandbaby to come into the world in the midst of a battle. They should only know peace.

"Griffin has some kind of relationship with the Skull Kings," Cane said. "Based on what Conway said about the Underground. He was there one night, whether he was buying a woman or staking out the place. He might be able to help us."

"Perhaps he can talk to them about dropping this feud," Button said. "We aren't even certain what instigated this provocation in the first place. Conway doesn't seem to know what the problem is."

"They must have realized that Conway was buying and freeing the slaves," I said. "Maybe someone ratted on him. That's the only thing that makes sense. They probably don't appreciate the fact that Conway was making a fortune of their products."

Cane nodded. "Probably. And I don't think that's something we can discuss calmly. The Skull Kings aren't calm. They're psychopaths."

"Griffin might have something that could help." He was a powerful man with a lot of connections. Maybe he had a special relationship with them and could arrange a peaceful negotiation. "Outright attacking the Skull Kings is the only other choice—and it's a terrible choice. We'll be fighting that war for three more generations."

"I don't like that idea either," Button said. "Not when we only want peace."

"Griffin will help if you ask, right?" Cane asked.

I felt pathetic asking him for help after what he did for my family. He didn't owe us anything, not any longer. I hated to admit that I needed him, but I definitely did. "Since this concerns Vanessa, yes. I prefer to wait until Griffin and I have established a better relationship because I don't want him to think I'm only behaving this way because I want something…"

"Well, you're going to have to get over that," Cane snapped. "Because we don't have time for that shit. We need to pull him in now." He tapped his fist against the table. "We've already wasted enough time."

"I agree," Button said. "Griffin is a smart man. I'm sure he understands that these are two separate issues. Since he loves Vanessa, I'm sure he wants to bury this as much as we do. He craves the same quiet life that we do…with our daughter."

I'd hoped I could make progress with Griffin before I asked him for a favor, but that didn't seem possible. Right now, protecting my family was the most important thing. I didn't just have Vanessa, but a son, a daughter-in-law, a niece, and nephew…and so much more. "I'll talk to him."

"When?" Cane pressed.

"I'll make the drive tomorrow," I answered. "Ask him out for a beer or something."

"Should I come along too?" Cane asked. "So we can get to work right away?"

"No." I was the one who ruined everything with Griffin in the first place. I was the father of the woman he loved. It had to be me. "I should go alone."

SIX

Bones

_____

My life was the same few variations on repeat.

It was simple. Predictable. Tame.

But I loved every second of it.

I used to work constantly, pick up women at a bar for dirty threeways, and get off on the corpses I would dump in the lake. My life was never the same, full of adrenaline and the unknown.

I traded all of that for Vanessa.

With no regrets.

I woke up at seven every day because I liked to get my workout finished before Vanessa woke up. She was usually cuddled into my side, her hair all over the place and her arm draped across my chest. It was easy to roll her onto her back, move between her legs, and fuck her quickly before I started my day. She moved with me slightly, her eyes barely open and her nails deep in my hair. Every morning, I woke up with a hard-on, and I liked to take care of that before I continued on my day. Before her, I would jerk off before I hit the weights. But now, I preferred her, whether she was really conscious to enjoy it or not. She climaxed most of the time, so her body was obviously aware of what was happening even if her mind wasn't. I put my come where it belonged, deep inside that slit I paid for with my blood, and then left her there and went about my day.

There was a gym down the street that I went to. I didn't like sharing my space with the public, which was why I had a private gym in my homes. But for now, it would do. Vanessa was obsessed with my body, aroused by the way I'd thickened over the last three months, so I increased the weight to keep my size. I didn't need it for a battle. I just liked making her forget she ever bothered with that boy painter.

I returned home, showered, and then sat at the dining table with my laptop. It was another sunny day in Florence, and the sunlight filtered through the apartment. When I scouted this piece of real estate, I thought it would be the perfect place for her. I bought it under the assumption she would never share her space with anyone, not even me. So it was smaller than I preferred.

I finally finished the mission statement Max sent over to me. I completed all the case studies I needed against my hit. I'd be heading to Egypt in a few days, something I hadn't mentioned to Vanessa. She knew it was coming. She always knew.

Vanessa woke up thirty minutes later, parading around in my t-shirt. She looked sexy in the lingerie I picked out for her, but never quite as sexy as she did in my clothes. She leaned over me with her arms wrapped around my shoulders and kissed me on the neck, the same way she always greeted me in the morning. "Good morning."

"Morning, baby." When she walked away, I smacked her ass—like clockwork.

She helped herself in the kitchen, making a bowl of cereal. Her long, tanned legs poked out from underneath my shirt, two legs that looked like pure sex. She ran her fingers through her hair before she carried her bowl to the table.

My eyes were glued to her, focused on the one woman who captured my complete focus the second I met her. She was such a woman that she made me, a man incapable of love, fall so deeply that I sacrificed everything to keep her. I gave up promiscuity for monogamy. I gave up death for life. I'd been a man a long time, but I'd never met a woman who could match me, a lady so strong and fierce that she reminded me of myself. Once she put that bullet in my shoulder, I was gone. I watched her shoot me with determination, and the second she pulled that trigger, I was harder than I'd ever been my entire life.

Every day I couldn't stop staring at her like this, like it was the first time I'd laid eyes on her. She was used to my constant looks that bordered hostility, but she had no idea what I was thinking. She had no idea that I was thinking about how much I loved her every single second of those stares. Sometimes, I wanted to fuck her. Sometimes, I wanted to grab her by the neck and pin her into the mattress, just to remind her that she belonged to me—even though I would never let her forget. My love was sometimes so possessive, it was violent. My love was so physical that I wanted to fuck her ass and mouth just as much as her pussy. My love so intense that it made everyone in our vicinity uncomfortable. But she was such an extraordinary woman that she could handle it.

Since the moment I met her, I could honestly say no other woman ever caught my attention the way she did. I didn't fantasize about other women. I didn't miss the threesomes, the handcuffs, and the strippers.

Never once did I doubt what we had.

That it was the greatest thing that ever happened to me.

She ate her cereal while these thoughts passed through my head, the corner of her mouth raised in a smile. She could feel my stare, and even though she should be used to it by now, it still distracted her. She turned her face toward me. "What?"

I didn't waste my time telling her every thought I had. I didn't describe the way she made me feel, the way she turned me into a stronger and weaker man at the same time. All those words seemed like too much work, the feelings impossible to translate into a spoken language. So I held her gaze, my eyes conveying everything I didn't have to say. "You already know."

VANESSA WAS downstairs at the gallery for the day, so I stayed in the apartment and watched TV on the couch. It was tempting to go downstairs and watch her work, but I knew my hostile presence made people uncomfortable. She needed more customers, not fewer, so I stayed out of her business.

She came upstairs in the middle of the afternoon and stood in front of me, blocking the TV with her petite frame. Her eyes locked on to mine before she undid her jean shorts and pushed them down her long legs. Her panties came next, landing on top of her jeans on the rug.

My arms rested along the back of the couch, and I didn't move despite the way she silently paraded into the apartment and demanded sex from me. Instead of staring at the area between her legs, I kept my gaze locked on hers, seeing the way she wanted me.

She pushed down the front of my sweatpants, revealing my cock that had hardened just thirty seconds ago. She lowered herself on top of me, gasping as she felt me stretch her deep and far. When she was sitting on my balls, she gripped my shoulders and breathed into my face. "Oh…yes." She pressed her feet against the cushions and held herself in a squatting position.

My hands moved underneath her thighs, carrying most of her weight so she could ride my dick with ease. I helped her up and down, making her sheathe my dick over and over again. The white cream built up at the base of my dick. I could practically smell her hormones in the air, feel her horniness between her legs.

My bare feet pushed against the rug as I thrust inside her, hitting her hard like she wanted me to. Her sexy ass cheeks were in my grip, and I pushed her up and down at a faster pace, making her ride my dick fast.

Her green eyes were focused on mine, her sexy lips parted from the sexy moans she made. Her fingers pressed into my shoulder, digging into my old wound. Even if it caused me pain, I still wouldn't mention it.

I loved kissing her, but I also loved fucking her without kissing her. I liked the connection between our eyes, the way we both smoldered and burned for one another in mutual passion. We made love, but we also fucked like two people in love—and that was my favorite. We didn't screw each other because we had to. We fucked each other hard like it was the hottest one-night stand of our lives.

I spanked her ass. "Hit me."

She kept moving up and down, her pussy making the sexiest noises as it rode my cock.

I spanked her ass again. "Hit me."

She listened this time, slapping me across the face with her palm. She didn't give me a sissy hit like most women did. She slapped me like she meant it, striking the side of my face with a hard palm. She put her weight into it, using those sexy muscles in her arm.

Her hand stung when it collided with my face, making the surface of my skin burn and the blood underneath boil. I loved the pain she caused me, the way she delivered the hit without hesitation. She knew I was a man who could handle anything, so she hit me with the kind of brutality I craved.

My cock throbbed inside her, my balls tightening because I wanted to come. I loved her fearlessness. I loved the momentum she could unleash with that arm. A strong woman like Vanessa probably intimidated most men, but she turned me on like crazy. "Hit me again when you come. Hard. Hard as fuck, baby."

She bounced on my dick for another thirty seconds, her pussy slowly tightening around me as she prepared to explode around my throbbing cock. Her breathing deepened, and she bit her bottom lip as she enjoyed the preliminary pleasure, the buildup before the blow. She closed her eyes for a second right before the explosion hit. Then she screamed in my face, her pussy clenching my dick with an iron grip.

As I'd asked, she slammed her hand against my face as hard as she could, hitting me with enough momentum that nearly made my head turn. With precise aim and powerful strength, she struck my cheek with the force to shake a mountain.

I fucking loved it.

I came inside her instantly, pumping her with more

PENELOPE SKY

come than I usually did. I tugged on her hips and kept her right on my lap, making sure I gave her every drop of come as deep as possible.

We finished together, our bodies twitching and clenching together. Her pussy soaked up every ounce of come I gave her, inhaling it like a vacuum. My eyes watched the sexy performance hers gave me, and she looked so damn beautiful I thought I could come again.

When she finished, she got off my lap without giving me a kiss. She didn't ask if my cheek was okay, even though it was probably bright red and slightly puffy. She turned around and bent over to grab her panties from the floor.

My eyes immediately went to her pussy, seeing some of my come seep out of her slick slit.

She pulled her panties up her long legs then pulled on her jean shorts. Then, like nothing had happened, she walked out of the apartment without saying good-bye. Not a single word was exchanged between us. She only wanted me for one thing, for a midday fuck because she'd been horny thinking about me down-stairs. The door shut behind her, and only the sound of the TV remained behind, my sweatpants still down and my wet dick against my stomach.

Vanessa wanted what she wanted, and when she got it, she disappeared. With no apologies and no explana-tion, she did whatever the hell she wanted.

"That's my baby."

I WAS JUST ABOUT to head downstairs and check on Vanessa when someone knocked on the door

It obviously wasn't Vanessa, especially since she marched in there just hours ago and fucked me without preamble, so it was someone else stopping by for a visit. If it was a friend of Vanessa's, they would have noticed she was downstairs in the gallery.

That meant they were here to see me.

And the culprit could only be one person.

Crow Barsetti.

I opened the door in a pissed-off mood, not wanting to spend any extra time with her father. I'd just told him off a few days ago. He barely gave me a break before he made another move.

When I opened the door, I came face-to-face with him. In dark jeans and a gray V-neck, he stood with his hands in his pockets. He used to regard me with an innately hostile expression anytime he looked at me. Now that coldness was gone, but warmth didn't replace it. He looked at me with a subdued expression, a look that was full of remorse.

I clenched my jaw as I kept one hand on the door. I was tempted to slam it in his face. Something stopped me from doing it, and I wasn't sure if that something was Vanessa. "Vanessa is downstairs."

"I saw her."

My nostrils flared. "You better not be here for me."

"You know I am."

I leaned my arm against the doorframe, shirtless with my tattoos obvious in the light. He knew I was marked with ink before because my arms were covered with it, but now he knew I had tattoos everywhere, from chest to my narrow hips. "It was less than a week ago when I told you I needed space."

"I remember. But I don't think space is going to accomplish much."

Why were the Barsettis such pains in the ass? "You're an asshole. You know that?"

He shrugged. "So I've been told. Are you going to invite me inside?"

"No." I kept my body in the way, not letting this man step onto my personal property. Technically, Vanessa owned it because I signed the papers in her name, but it was bought with my money—so it was mine.

Crow didn't seem offended by the cold response. "Then let's get a drink."

"No." I didn't owe him anything. I went out with him once, and I'd spoken to him outside his house. I'd already given him plenty of my time. "Leave. Don't make me ask you again."

Crow held his position, standing on my doorstep with no intention of going anywhere. He was one of the only men who was never intimidated by me. I'd made men shit their pants, but Crow was made of something stronger than everyone else. "This isn't going to stop, Griffin. You may as well give me a chance."

"I don't owe you a damn thing. I earned Vanessa by saving your ass. We're even."

"We're never even," he said quietly. "I will never be able to repay you for what you did."

"You want to repay me for what I did?" I demanded. "Then disappear."

He stayed on the doorstep, his arms crossing over his chest.

Whether Crow Barsetti hated me or liked me, he was just as infuriating.

Footsteps sounded in the background, and then Vanessa appeared up the stairs. In those same denim shorts and t-shirt, she was just as cute as she was earlier. She still wore the same panties as she had on earlier, and my come was probably sitting inside them now.

She stopped beside her father, and her disappointed look told me she saw the animosity on both of our faces. She didn't say a word as she walked past us and headed into the house. She moved behind me and wrapped her arm around my waist. Her warm lips pressed against my back, right between my shoulder blades. Soft like a rose petal and full of the love she didn't need to speak out loud, her kiss was a sheath to my anger. Her touch brought my inferno to a simmer. She pulled her arm away and disappeared into the apartment.

And just like that, all the rage I felt was gone.

She never asked me to spend time with her father. When I walked out on dinner, she didn't beg me to come back. When I asked for space, she said I could have as much of it as I wanted. She loved her father and wanted us to have a close relationship, but she never made me do anything I didn't want to do. All she had to do was ask me to have a drink with him and I would listen—but she didn't do that either.

Crow stared at me with the same expression, not reacting to the affectionate way Vanessa greeted me when she came home. His eyes were still on me, like he didn't care about his daughter at all.

I was the only thing that mattered.

"Just one drink."

———

WE RETURNED to the bar we'd visited the previous week. We ordered the exact same thing. Scotch—neat. The bar was busier than it was last time since it was closer to the evening, but we got a booth in the corner —away from unfriendly ears.

Like every other time we interacted, it was tense in the beginning. Neither one of us was certain where to start since we started over so many times. It didn't matter what words were exchanged, it didn't change the context of our situation.

Crow swirled his drink before he brought it to his lips. "What happened to your face?"

My left cheek was still red and puffy from where Vanessa had slapped me a few hours ago. I considered telling him the truth, to teach him a lesson about asking questions. But I figured that would scar him, so I kept it to myself. "I'm fine. Thanks for asking."

Crow didn't press it. "Pearl wanted me to tell you she says hello."

I stared at him and enjoyed my drink. I was beginning to realize that being with Vanessa meant I would have to be with her parents too. These people would never disappear. Crow would constantly try to connect with me, whether he was doing it for himself or Vanessa. This would be an uphill battle, and the more I fought it, the more it would grow.

"How are you?" Crow Barsetti wasn't much of a talker, but he forced a conversation with me anyway.

"Never better." I woke up to Vanessa beside me every morning. I went to bed with her there too. There was nothing else I needed. "What about you?"

He shrugged. "I've been better."

"What's got you down?" I blurted the question out before I could stop myself. His family was safe, so there was nothing that could be keeping him down.

"There's something I need to talk to you about, but I hope you understand it's separate from the relationship I'm trying to establish with you."

I cocked an eyebrow.

"I don't want to ask you for anything. You've done enough for my family. But you're the best person to turn to, and since it involves the safety of my family, I can't keep you out of it."

I set the glass on the table and leaned forward, the blood pounding in my ears. "I'm listening."

"I need your help with the Skull Kings."

The Skull Kings were a group of thugs that made their fortune in lots of ways. They kept their power because of their unpredictability. Even their most loyal followers could be cut down without notice. Equally emotional and logical, they balanced on the edge of a knife. They weren't the best men to do business with because you had no idea how they would feel the following morning. "What about them?"

"They're the ones that ordered the hit on Conway."

"I'm aware."

"It's been quiet on the front for the last month," Crow said. "But I don't think it's going to stay that way forever. I need to shut down hostilities before they grow again. My son is finally back on his feet, and I don't want another war to break out. All my family wants is peace."

"And what does this have to do with me?" I'd already saved Conway once. Now my only concern was the woman waiting in my apartment.

"I know you have a relationship with the Skull Kings."

"Every criminal does."

"Is yours any different?" he asked, his head cocked to the side. "Is there any information you can give me that might help? Should I approach them head on? Should I do nothing? I have no idea what move to make."

I'd visited the Underground for entertainment. I'd never bought a woman, but I liked the drinks from the bar and the connections with the other men who participated in the bidding. I had a relationship with Tony, one of the main Skull Kings. They'd commissioned me for work in the past. "I know them well enough. They've hired me to take out a few of their enemies."

"Good to know." He drank from his scotch. "If I have to hit them hard, I will. If I have to round up as many men as I can find and hit them when they aren't expecting it, I will. But the last thing I want is a war. I don't want bloodshed. All I want is peace. If there's a way to establish that, I'd prefer that."

"You know the Skull Kings aren't big on peace."

"Unfortunately."

"My guess is they figured out what Conway was doing with the slaves." The Skull Kings cared about money above all things. The fact that Conway was making a bigger profit off their hard work must have infuriated them. "On top of that, it may have pissed off their buyers. These women were taken for revenge, but then the revenge never took place. If you meet with the Skull Kings and offer to make up the difference that Conway profited, that would be a strong way to start the meeting. But for that second part...I'm not sure how you can make amends for that."

"Neither can I." Now that we were deep in conversation, Crow turned bitter and sour. The stress etched into his features as he thought of the situation in front of him, the problem looking him right in the face. None of this was his fault, especially since Conway was a grown man, but he loved his son too much not to be involved. He had to protect his family as the patriarch. "Fuck, I don't know how to handle this." He rubbed his hand along his jaw, his eyes dark with sorrow.

It was one of those moments that made me like Crow again, the way he sacrificed anything for his family. His worry came from love, the overwhelming devotion he had to his family. His love for Vanessa was the reason he got rid of me. He got his hands dirty when he didn't want to because his family was more important than his discomfort. It reminded me of myself. I was determined to take down my mother's killer at any cost—even though she was already dead and gone. That didn't stop me—and it wouldn't stop Crow.

"Do you think it's possible for you to get a meeting with them?"

"I can ask. But I don't know if I'll be successful. As far as I know, they have no idea how we're connected. I'm very private about my personal life, so they may not know I'm seeing Vanessa at all."

"I hope they don't."

"If they ask, we should say we've done business together."

"Agreed," he said quickly. "Now comes my next question…are you willing to do that?"

The Skull Kings were known for being erratic. I had no idea how they would react once I broached the subject. I was getting tangled up in a potential mess, a mess that wasn't my problem. But when I pictured Vanessa as my wife, wearing my ring on her hand every single day for the rest of her life, I knew her family would always be my problem. I would have to protect every member of her family for the rest of my life.

But it was a price I was willing to pay—for her.

"You know my answer, Crow." I stared at him head on, my hand gripping my glass. "My love for your daughter has made me loyal to your family. I will spill my own blood for a Barsetti—every time."

He tilted his head down, severing eye contact. He swallowed the lump in his throat before he drank from his glass. "I was so fucking wrong about you." He lifted his gaze again to look at me. He rubbed his hand along the back of his head, his eyes hardening in frustration. "So damn wrong."

CROW LEFT without saying goodbye to Vanessa, and I walked into the house to smell burned dinner.

There was smoke in the kitchen, and she had the windows open to air it out.

I kicked off my shoes and pulled my shirt over my head. "Need help?"

"No." She placed the pans in the sink then soaked them. There was no food inside, so I assumed she'd already dumped it into the garbage can. "Unless you want to pick the place we're going to order from."

I didn't tease her for her inability to prepare a meal. It was the one thing she wasn't good at. But if you put a gun in her hand, she could hit her target with perfect aim. I walked into the kitchen, came up behind her, and pressed a kiss to her neck. "How about I take you out?"

She turned off the water and looked at me over her shoulder. "As nice as that sounds, I prefer to stay in."

"Why?"

"Because we can have sex on the dining table in the middle of dinner."

I pressed another kiss to her ear. "Very true, baby. You've convinced me."

She turned around and arched her back against the sink while the swell of her tits rubbed against my bare chest. Her wet fingers moved up my shoulders, and she tilted her chin up to look at me loom over her. "How'd it go?" Despite how much pain this situation caused her, she continued to seem indifferent about it, doing her best not to put any pressure on me. But the desperation was deep in her eyes, the undying hope.

"Fine." My hands gripped her slender waistline, and my thumbs dug into her stomach. Whenever I looked at this beautiful woman, all I wanted was to make her happy. She was my woman, and that never felt more real than when she was in my arms, my hands right over her ribs.

"Just fine?" she whispered.

"I didn't shoot him."

Her eyes narrowed, and she gave me a playful slap on the arm. "Don't say things like that."

I rubbed my nose against hers, apologetic for the crass thing I'd just said. "We just talked. Even when we spend hours together, when I walk away, I feel like nothing was accomplished. The man and I are just too different."

"You're exactly the same," she whispered. "Identical."

I tilted my head as I looked at her, seeing the sadness in her eyes.

"Why do you think I love you so much?" She moved her arms around my neck and pressed her face closer to mine. "My father is very stubborn, just like you. He wouldn't be making this effort if I asked him to. Even if my mother asked him, he still wouldn't do it. He's doing this because it's what he wants. So the next time he tries to talk with you, keep that in mind. The man is on your side. He's loyal to you forever. You have someone who's willing to be rejected and insulted over and over again just to have a drink with you." She gave me a simple kiss, her eyes still wide and on mine. "I get that you're angry…but just remember you have someone who cares about you."

"Cares—"

"Yes." She gave me a fiery look, refusing to let me override her. "He cares about you very much."

I DIDN'T TELL Vanessa what Crow and I discussed. It seemed like something that would only upset her. She was calm in the most stressful situations, but I wanted to let her believe peace continued to reign in our lives.

So when she was at work, I drove to Florence and approached the Barsetti manor, the three-story mansion that overlooked the acres of land that had been in their family for generations. Ivy grew up on the walls, and the olive trees surrounded the property, bearing fruit.

I knocked on the front door, feeling strange standing on the doorstep without Vanessa. When I was here a few days ago, I marched out and drove home without eating the meal they prepared for me. This house pricked at my anger, made me feel resentment and rage. While Vanessa and Conway grew up in a mansion with a butler, my mother and I were just trying to survive.

I knew I shouldn't blame the Barsettis for that. My father wasn't a good man, and he got what was coming to him. If he thought he could rape Crow's wife and get away with it, he was mistaken. I admired Pearl for killing him herself. After what she'd been through, she deserved the honor.

But my mother and I were innocent bystanders. We

didn't deserve to be homeless because of his sins. She and I were good people. Good people didn't deserve what we'd been through.

Sapphire answered, her stomach even bigger than it was the last time I saw her. "Hey, Griffin." She turned her stomach to the side so she could move into my chest and hug me.

It was strange to hug a woman besides Vanessa, so I patted her on the back and waited for her to move out of the way. She was the same height as Vanessa, petite despite the weight she carried from her pregnancy.

She stepped away, still smiling. "Please come in."

I stepped inside, feeling anxious the second I walked into the home of the Barsettis.

She turned to me, her hand resting on her stomach. "They're in the dining room."

"You doing okay?" I asked, looking at her stomach.

"I'm a little uncomfortable," she said with a laugh. "My fingers are so swollen I can't wear my wedding ring anymore. But any day now, our little one will be here."

"You don't know if it's a boy or girl?"

"Conway and I decided to be surprised."

That was the extent of the conversation I could offer. The only other Barsetti I was genuinely comfortable around was Carmen, but it was unlikely she would be there. She reminded me of Vanessa in a lot of ways. She was fiery, sassy, and candid. There was no bullshit when it came to her.

After an awkward pause, Sapphire guided me to the dining room.

Not that I didn't know exactly where it was. "Thanks."

I stepped inside, seeing Crow sitting beside his wife next to the windows. Cane was across from him, along with Conway. The last time I was here, I stormed off and made a scene. The time before that, I had a loaded shotgun pointed at my chest from five feet away. This place was like a prison cell to me.

Crow's eyes darted to mine the second I entered the room. "Griffin, thanks for coming." He rose to his feet instantly and came around the table to shake my hand. He moved quickly, not wanting me to wait a second longer than necessary. His grip was firm, and he gave me the respect of eye contact. "Can I get you anything?"

"Just a glass of scotch."

"Already waiting for you." He nodded and stepped aside so Pearl could move in next.

She hugged me, her cheek pressing against my chest as she wrapped her arms around my torso.

I felt uncomfortable touching her, especially after what my father did to her. It seemed innately wrong that we were this close together, but I didn't detect a hint of unease from her. Her touch was maternal and loving, the same kind of affection she gave to her children. "Thank you for coming, Griffin. We're all very grateful you're here." When she pulled away, she gave me an affectionate look with her eyes. I was the subject of her endearing expression, and she gave me that same look she gave to Conway sometimes, like she was proud of me.

Pearl reminded me of Vanessa, but she also reminded me of my mother in some ways. The soft sound of her voice was similar to my mother's. Sometimes the memory of my mother's features faded, but I never forgot the sound of her voice. They were also both strong women, both victims of my father's cruelty. But neither woman had ever succumbed to his brutality. They never stopped fighting. They never gave up. I respected her in a way I didn't respect Crow and Cane. There was definitely a soft spot for her in my heart. "Thank you, Mrs. Barsetti." I never addressed Crow by anything other than his first name—because he didn't deserve my respect. Pearl was different.

Like she understood the significance of my words, she smiled. "How's my daughter?"

"Good," I answered. "She's at the gallery today."

She patted my arm before she stepped away.

Conway came next, looking nearly as good as new. The bruising was gone from his face, revealing handsome features that were clearly visible. With a hard jaw like his father's and masculine cheekbones, he possessed the distinct appearance of a Barsetti. He regarded me with kindness and shook my hand. "Hey, man. How are you?"

"Good. You?"

"Never better. Ribs are pretty much back to normal, and my wife is about to start our family. With the exception of the context of our conversation, life has treated me well." He stood close to me, speaking to me like I was a friend rather than some unfortunate acquaintance. "I've been to your apartment in Florence. It's nice. The second I saw it, I thought it was perfect for my sister."

"That's why I bought it." The Barsettis were going out of their way to make me feel comfortable. It was an interesting experience after they'd been so cold to me. But I appreciated the gesture because everything seemed genuine. "We'll be moving in to the countryside soon. It's too cramped for someone like me."

"Yeah," he said with a chuckle. "I can imagine." When he moved out of the way, Cane came next.

Cane and I had never had a positive experience. He didn't visit me in the hospital room. He'd been even more vicious to me than his brother. I saw the stark differences between the two brothers. While Crow was pragmatic most of the time, Cane was passionate and emotional. He could be impulsive, making rash decisions in the blink of an eye. He sighed before he extended his hand to shake mine. "I know this is long overdue…but I'm a bit of an asshole."

I didn't take his hand. "I've noticed."

His nostrils flared in annoyance when I didn't reciprocate. "I know I was a jackass to you before. It's just hard for me to trust people."

"Same here." These people expected me to forgive them for what they did, to trust them when they never trusted me. I didn't want them to forget that.

It was a testament to Cane's sincerity when he didn't blow up. "I can't think straight when it comes to my daughter. My son is a powerful man who can hold his own, but my daughter…she's my little girl. I know I shouldn't have made a big scene when you spoke to her, but I couldn't help it. If I could lock her up in a nunnery, I would. When you're a father, you'll understand."

I'd spent some time with Carmen, and she certainly wasn't a damsel in distress. "Carmen is a strong woman like Vanessa. She's not naïve. She's highly intuitive and instinctive. You don't need to worry about her all the time. She can handle herself."

Cane lowered his hand, his eyes concentrating on my face. "That's quite a compliment."

"I like your daughter. I've spent time with her and Vanessa in Florence. It's hard to believe she's your daughter because she's pragmatic and easygoing."

Crow chuckled. "Ouch."

"Whenever we're together, I look after her." I didn't tell him I scared off the boys that weren't good enough for her. No father wanted to picture his daughter being hit on in a bar. "I always walk her to her door and make sure she gets inside. I'd give my life to protect her— because I respect her." Cane had threatened to kill me if I came near his daughter again, but I was the best person to keep an eye on her. I could get to her in two minutes if she ever needed anything. That was a lot more than Cane could say.

For the first time, Cane was speechless. He stared at me in silence, having no idea what to say.

I held his gaze, wanting him to feel like shit for the way he treated me. Everything he ever said to me was hypocritical. Crow told me Pearl was a prisoner when he fell in love with her. I imagined Cane's story with Adelina wasn't much different. These men were hypocrites, out of touch with reality. They only trusted each other—and no one else. But they'd been wrong about me.

Cane cleared his throat and extended his hand again. "I don't expect you to like me. Not very many people do…"

"Including me," Crow said.

"And me," Pearl added.

Cane rolled his eyes as he kept his hand extended. "But I've got your back, Griffin. You have my loyalty and my trust. If you're ever in a jam, I'll fight by your side until your enemies are dead. You have my word."

I didn't need his pledge of loyalty. I didn't need anything from him or the rest of the Barsetti clan. But I shook his hand anyway, knowing I needed to move forward instead of live in the past. "I don't want anything from you. The only thing I want is now mine." Once the handshake was completed, I dropped my palm.

Cane gave a slight nod. "I respect that. I admire a man who wears his heart on his sleeve." He turned back to the table.

Now that the greetings were over, we sat down at the large wooden table. The men were drinking scotch, while Pearl enjoyed a glass of wine. I sat on the other side of Conway, leaning back against the wooden backboard of the chair. I remembered how the cool material felt against my skin when I was handcuffed there.

Crow started the conversation. "Griffin told me he's done work for the Skull Kings before. He has a closer relationship with them than any of us. I think we should have him attempt to establish a meeting with them. None of us is looking for increased hostilities. Even if we have to apologize and pay back everything Conway made, I'm fine with that."

"If this were thirty years ago, I'd say we take them out," Cane said. "But you're right. If these hostilities continue, our kids will be fighting this war long after we're gone."

Conway sat in silence, his arms crossed over his chest.

"So how should we do this?" Pearl asked. "Maybe we should try calling instead. Less invasive."

I shook my head. "No. That's pussy shit."

The men turned their gazes on me.

"They don't respect cowardice," I continued. "It'll only agitate them even more."

"A phone call isn't cowardly," Pearl said.

"It is," I said. "If you really want them to take you seriously, it needs to be face-to-face. If a man is truly powerful, he has no problem walking onto their turf. If you're too scared to do that, they think they can run you over."

"We defeated their entire team," Cane said. "I think we have more credentials than that."

"You asked for my help," I snapped. "I'm giving it to you. Don't be stupid and not take it."

Cane didn't take offense to the comment. "Then what do you suggest?"

"I walk into the Underground first and talk to Tony. Tell him you want me to broker a peace treaty. I'll listen to what he says. If they agree, I'll call you and you'll walk in. If they don't, we'll need a backup plan. We'll have to threaten them."

"No." Crow set down his glass. "I don't want to escalate the situation."

"If they don't cooperate, you have no other choice." Showing fear wasn't an option. "You need to prove that your peace offering is one of convenience. You're doing it because it's in your best interest, like you may want to do business with them in the future. If you say you're just looking for a quiet life in the countryside, they won't respect that. And if they choose to be hostile, you need to give them a threat that gives them pause. Then they'll see that peace is more convenient, and they'll go for it."

"I've been involved with the Skull Kings in the

past," Cane said. "Trust me, you don't want to threaten them."

"And if you really know them, then you'll know that threatening them is the only option," I countered. "Holding your respect in the conversation is vital. Backing down is just as bad as pulling the trigger."

After a pause, Cane nodded. "He's right."

"What kind of threat?" Crow asked. "Thirty years ago, we could pull off something spectacular, but now, we don't have many tricks up our sleeve."

"They care about the auction more than anything else," Cane said. "It's their biggest source of income, and it's easy to manage. If we disturb that convenience, it could hit them where it hurts."

"Yes," I said in agreement. "We could threaten to tell their enemies exactly what they're doing and where to find the girls. If they take a diplomat's daughter, all we have to do is tell that diplomat and the government where the girl is being held. If we do that enough times, they'll have more enemies than they can handle. The Italian government won't be able to look the other way anymore, not when potential war is standing on their doorstep. They could threaten us in return, saying they'll kill everyone we've ever loved, but that threat won't be fulfilling, not when we've disturbed something they care so much about."

"Sounds tricky," Pearl said. "I'm not sure how I feel about it."

"And I don't want to drag you into it," Crow said.

"You have nothing to do with this. You shouldn't risk getting involved."

I didn't want to dance with the Skull Kings either, but I wanted to eradicate this threat. This situation affected Vanessa, and in order to keep her safe, I needed to fix the problem Conway caused. "This situation directly affects Vanessa. I have to make sure it's addressed properly. Since you took out the entire team that was supposed to execute Conway, they already recognize you as a serious threat. If you walk in there with me, they'll know you have more allies than they realize. They respect me immensely. Having me by your side is only going to help you fix this mess."

"Are you sure you want to do this?" Cane asked. "You aren't obligated."

"Yes." I wanted to make sure this was done right. I didn't want anything to ever take Vanessa away from me again. "So I'll go in first. Once I get their agreement, I'll bring in the next person. Not everyone can step inside that meeting. It'll be considered aggressive if we bring the entire clan." If all the Barsettis marched in there, it would be too claustrophobic. And there certainly couldn't be any women.

"I'll go," Crow volunteered instantly, stepping up as the patriarch of the family. "I'll wait outside, and you call me in. I'll handle the Skull Kings, hand over the money, and hope for the best."

"I will too," Cane said. "The three of us."

"No." Crow turned his forceful stare on his brother. "You can't come, and you know exactly why."

A silent conversation passed between them, and Cane didn't press his argument.

"Then I will come," Conway said. "I'm the one—"

"No." Crow didn't look at his son, as if the idea of bringing him along disturbed him. "Out of the question. You have a pregnant wife who needs you."

"Father," Conway pressed. "This is my mess and—"

"You aren't coming." Crow finally looked at him. "That's final, Conway." He silenced his son with his authority, his darkened eyes adding to his volatile persona.

Conway clenched his jaw tightly, clearly pissed off that he wasn't getting his way.

"Your father is right, Con." Pearl moved her hand to Crow's thigh under the table. "You need to stay here with Sapphire."

"That's bullshit." Conway couldn't keep his anger back even though his father had just silenced him. "I'm the one who fucked everything up. I'm the one who should pay the price. It shouldn't be Father—"

"That's how it's going to be." Crow turned furious again, his rage filling the entire room. "I told you how important it was to live a quiet and peaceful life, to earn an honest living and not to provoke the demons that surround us. But you didn't listen to me. Now we're in this mess, and I will not let anything happen to you. You're my son, and I would rather die than bury you in the cemetery next to my mother and father. You will be a father tomorrow or the next day or the next day…and that's when you will understand this." He grabbed his glass and took a long drink, like he needed the booze to calm his shaking hand. "That will be your punishment. To watch your father risk his life for you—again."

Pearl's eyes moved to her husband's face. "Crow…"

I watched this man come apart right before my eyes, saw the love and anger dance across the surface of his eyes. He was selfless, loving his family so much that he put himself through hell to keep them together. His kids were the most important thing to him, so important that he would continually stand in the middle of gunfire and sacrifice himself—over and over.

As much as I hated to admit it, I respected him.

And I understood why he worked so hard to keep me from his daughter.

Conway lowered his gaze, hurt by his father's words.

I let the silence soak into my flesh, felt the tension seep into my bones. The Barsettis weren't that complicated to understand. The two brothers constantly worked together to protect the families they'd made. Crow wouldn't allow Cane to help him with this, knowing he needed one brother to survive to protect the rest of the family.

Now I wanted to do this alone. I wanted to protect the Barsetti family—and not just because I loved Vanessa. "Nothing will happen to you, Crow. I promise you that."

Crow turned his gaze back to me. "That's a promise you can't make, Griffin."

"Actually, I can."

I'D JUST WALKED out the door and headed to my truck when Pearl called my name. "Griffin."

I turned around, my shoes digging into the gravel beneath my feet.

She caught up to me, her long dress nearly touching the ground beneath her feet. Her hair was pulled back into a loose bun, revealing the sharp angles of her face as well as her pretty eyes. She wore a wedding ring on her left hand, a simple button molded into the metal.

Now that I knew their story, the button made complete sense. "Yes?"

She walked with me to the truck, her perfume potent the second she was close to me. "You said you can guarantee my husband's safety… Could you elaborate on that?" She was normally confident when she spoke to me, but talking about Crow shook the foundation beneath her feet.

I stopped at the truck, the waning afternoon sunshine starting to become less bright. "I know a lot of people, Mrs. Barsetti. I've been hired by the most powerful men in the world. I've done favors in exchange for loyalty instead of money. I know everyone in the underworld. My boys and I have made men indebted to us forever. If I ever need help, they'll be there. At the Underground, I'll be surrounded by men who will intervene if it comes to that. And I've done favors for the Skull Kings myself, harbored secrets I've vowed to take to the grave. I'm the last person they want to cross—and I'm willing to cash all that in if necessary."

Relief flashed across her eyes as she took in a deep breath. She placed her hands over her face, covering her expression for a second so I couldn't see her reaction. In front of her husband and children, she was always poised and strong, but the second they were gone, she showed her true anguish. Vanessa was the same way, only dropping her mask when we were alone together.

"I'm the silent king. I rule with both loyalty and fear. The Skull Kings respect me, and if I ask them to drop this, they will. But it'll make it a lot easier if Crow presents some peace offering, like the money that should have been theirs. Then their egos are left intact, and they won't feel like they lost anything. I don't cash in my favors very often, but I will do it this time. It's in my best interest to make sure your husband gets back here in one piece."

She dropped her hands, showing her wet eyes and trembling lips. "I'm so sorry for what I did to you, Griffin…"

I wasn't expecting an apology. I was expecting gratitude, especially since she'd already said these words to me.

Fine in Lingerie

"I'm so sorry that I took my daughter away. I'm sorry I didn't trust you. I'm sorry I hurt you so much…" She wiped her fingers underneath her eyes to remove the tears and fix her smeared makeup. "You're so wonderful, and I should have loved you from the beginning, not banished you. I judged you for the sins of your father instead of getting to know the man you truly are. I was unfair and cruel. You've done so much for my family when you didn't have to. You love my daughter as much as I do…as much as Crow does… and that makes me so happy." She moved into my chest and hugged me, her tears smearing against my t-shirt.

I let her hold on to me for a moment before I rested my hand against her back. I felt strange touching her, felt strange touching someone other than Vanessa. Once Vanessa was mine, I didn't even shake hands with another woman. My body was hers and hers alone.

When she pulled away, her eyes were no longer swelling with tears. "I don't expect you to forgive me—"

"I do."

Her eyes moved to mine, heavy with surprise.

I didn't know why I blurted out those words, not when I'd been harboring anger for so long. But something about Pearl softened me. Maybe it was the similarities she shared with Vanessa. Maybe it was because she was a woman. Or maybe it was because she reminded me of my mother. I'd always had a soft spot for strong women, for women who only broke down into tears out of love for someone else, not because of self-pity.

"Will you have dinner with me? There's a cute little place just down the road." She looked at me with hesitation, like she wasn't sure if I would agree to something so unorthodox.

"Just you and me?"

"Yes."

"I don't want to make Crow angry." There had never been a time when he'd allowed me to be alone with his wife. When I first came to the winery, he made sure I never had direct access to her. He was always around, watching over her like a guard watching a prisoner.

"You won't," she said. "He trusts you, Griffin."

I DROVE us to a little restaurant ten minutes away. It was in a small village, a village so small I wasn't sure what the name was. We sat inside the small building constructed of cobblestone and had a small table in the corner. The chair was a little small for my size, and I hoped the legs wouldn't give out on me.

Pearl ordered a bottle of wine for the table and looked at the menu. "Crow brought me here when we were first getting to know each other. The waitress was making subtle moves on him, and I got extremely jealous." She smiled at the memory, still scanning her menu.

Had she still been a prisoner at the time? I looked at the menu and picked out the first thing that looked good. I'd never sat across from Vanessa's mom like this, just the two of us without another Barsetti around.

It was strange.

The waitress returned, and we both ordered.

I was glad the waitress was being quick with our service. I didn't hate Pearl, but this situation was too intimate for me. I never dined with anyone but Vanessa. Even if I had a woman in my life, we didn't go out to dinner. It was all straight to business—fucking. Pearl was the only woman I'd been out with besides Vanessa.

She stared at me, a slight smile on her lips and affection in her eyes. "Let me pay for dinner tonight. It's the least I can do…"

That was even stranger, but I didn't make an argument against it.

My phone started to vibrate in my pocket. I fished it out and saw Vanessa's name on the screen. I'd slipped out while she was at work, so she had no idea where I was. If it had been someone else, I would have ignored the call. I answered. "Hey, baby."

"Where are you? Are you picking up dinner?" I liked the slight anger in her voice, the disappointment she felt when she didn't see me on the couch when she walked through the door. Possessive like I was, she wanted me all the time. When that didn't happen, she got angry.

"Sorta."

"Meaning?" she asked, growing angrier.

I couldn't stop the smile from spreading across my lips. "I like it when you get mad." When I spoke to Vanessa, I forgot about her mother altogether, who was listening to the conversation.

"I'm not mad," she said defensively. "I just want to know where you are. You didn't tell me you were going anywhere."

"You don't tell me where you're going, and I never ask," I reminded her. Vanessa did whatever she wanted without asking for my approval or permission. If she wanted to see Carmen at the flower shop, she didn't mention it to me. If she wanted to go out, she did that too.

Vanessa was quiet, knowing I had her cornered.

"Just admit that you hate when I'm not home." I leaned back in my chair, enjoying the anger simmering in her silence.

"I just wanted to know where you were…that's all."

"Sure, baby."

She sighed into the phone. "So are you going to tell me where you are?"

"Are you going to admit I'm right?" I countered.

More silence.

Pearl smiled as she listened to the conversation.

Vanessa caved. "Fine. I don't like it when you aren't home…"

"There's my woman. Possessive. Obsessive."

She didn't disagree with the statement.

Now that she'd fulfilled her end of the deal, I fulfilled mine. "I'm at dinner with your mother."

"What?" she blurted. "You are? How did that happen?"

"I'll tell you when I get home."

"Alright," she said. "When do you think that will be…?"

I couldn't stop smiling, loving how clingy she was. She used to be the opposite, trying to prove to herself and to me that she didn't need me. But now she laid all her cards on the table, needing me like she needed air. "Two hours."

"Okay. Love you."

I usually said it first when we got off the phone, but she was quick to jump in before me, missing me because she was in that apartment by herself. She took me for granted, and the second I wasn't there, she was caught off-balance. "Love you too."

She hung up.

I put my phone back in my pocket.

Pearl was still smiling. "Vanessa is a different person with you."

"Yes, she's a bit clingy."

"But you like that, clearly."

I shrugged. "She wasn't like that in the beginning.

But now she's a little bossy and gets angry when she doesn't get her way. When her man isn't around...she gets mean. For the longest time, she refused to allow herself to need me, to rely on me for her happiness. But she stopped that production and now wears her heart on her sleeve the way I do. It's fun to watch."

"I bet. You conquered an unconquerable woman."

"Conquered her?" I asked. "No. I claimed her." I grabbed my scotch and took a drink, refusing to feel guilty about my candor. Vanessa was irrevocably mine now, so I could say whatever I wanted.

"Crow is the same way. I think being married for nearly thirty years has made him worse, actually. I thought he would be less intense after our children changed my body, but that also made him worse too. He admired my scars and the pain my body had to endure to give birth to his son and daughter."

"Because that's how a man should be. He should love his woman more every day, not less. He should admire the sacrifice she made to continue his line. He should be turned on by her scars just the way a woman is turned on by a man's battle scars. It's the exact same thing."

She smiled. "You have a point. Does that mean kids are in your future?"

Vanessa hadn't given me much of a choice. If I had it my way, the answer would be no. But she put her foot down and gave me an ultimatum. It was the only thing she wanted more than me, so I would do it. "Yes.

Vanessa made it clear we couldn't be together unless I had a family with her."

"You didn't want one before?"

"No." I didn't grow up with a family, so I had no idea how to have one of my own.

"Crow was the same way. Had no interest in kids. But when he got me pregnant by accident, everything changed. He became a father the very minute I told him about Conway. I see how much he loves his kids every day, and it's hard to believe he didn't want a family in the beginning."

"You're suggesting that will be me?"

"Yes."

I never thought I could love a woman the way I loved Vanessa, so anything was possible. "We'll see."

The waitress brought our entrees, and we started to eat. Pearl ate with perfect manners the way Vanessa did. Crow shared the same kind of grace. Cane, on the other hand, ate like a pig.

With the food in front of us, there was less pressure to fill the silence with mindless conversation. When I spent time with Crow, he always filled the silence with something. Pearl didn't do that as much.

"When are you guys going to head to Milan?" she asked, switching the conversation back to the matter at hand.

"After I get back from my next mission. I leave tomorrow."

She finished chewing her pasta before she raised her

eyebrow. "I didn't know you were leaving so soon. Vanessa didn't mention that to me."

"Because I haven't told her." The second I told her I was leaving, she would be in a state of constant worry until I was back home. It made sense to tell her at the last minute, to spare her the pain as long as possible.

Her eyes filled with disappointment. "I see…"

"I only have two more, and then it'll be over. But I can't pull out now. It would be a betrayal to my guys."

"I understand," she said. "But she's not going to take it well."

"No, she won't." There would be tears.

I hated the tears. It was the worst feeling in the world, to watch my woman cry because of me. I hated putting her through the pain, hated being the reason she was in pain at all. I should be the one fixing her, not hurting her.

"Will she stay at the apartment?"

"I don't know. That's up to her."

"Well, she's always welcome with us."

I didn't want to send my woman off with her parents. That made me feel like less of a man. But I couldn't tell her what to do. I'd never been that kind of guy, and I wasn't going to start now.

"I'm really happy you're leaving that line of work. Not just for Vanessa, but for me."

I could see the sincerity in her eyes, see the way she cared about me. She was alone with me ten minutes from the house, and she wasn't scared at all. My father had raped her and beaten her, but she didn't view me in the same light. To her, I was a completely different man.

"Crow is happy too. All he wants is for all of us to live a quiet life."

"My life has never been quiet. I wonder how I'll adjust."

"As long as you have Vanessa, you'll be fine."

I would never forget what it was like not to be with her. Those three months changed me, broke me in ways that hadn't fully healed yet.

"I understand that it's difficult for you to bury the hatchet with Crow, but he's trying very hard to make things right with you. He's grown to respect you immensely, and he would love to have his own relationship with you."

I should have known this would come up.

Pearl waited for me to say something, and when I didn't, she continued on. "It takes a lot to change my husband's mind about anything. He's stubborn and intense. Doesn't know how to take a joke. But he views you in a completely different light now. He's come to admire you…something neither one of us thought was possible."

"Yes, he's said this to me."

Her eyes fell in sadness. "I'm not trying to pressure you. I'm just trying to…I don't know. My husband is in pain every day over this. Whenever he comes home from visiting you, he looks worse and worse."

"He should have seen me during those three months," I jabbed.

She picked at her food and took a few more bites.

I did the same, trying to dismiss the tense conversation.

"Griffin, my husband is the best man I know. I know you're angry, but I hope you can see that eventually."

Sometimes Crow said things that changed my opinion about him, like stepping up in his son's place— twice. He loved his kids more than himself. He showed a level of selflessness I couldn't match. "He has a lot of great qualities. I see the way he talks to Vanessa, the way his eyes soften uniquely for her. He doesn't show that look with you. I listen to his tone change, addressing her in a way he doesn't with anyone else. I saw the way he stepped into combat, knowing he would be shot down just for the slim possibility of saving his son. I see the special way he looks at you, the way he constantly places himself in front of you whenever he feels threatened. You're right. He's a selfless man who always puts his family before himself. And anytime his family is threatened...he turns into a different person. He viewed me as a threat to his daughter, and the second that happened, his entire life became dedicated to her protection. I understand."

"Then could you let this go?" she asked quietly. "Leave it in the past?"

It wasn't that long ago I was in mortal agony. It was just a couple months ago when I was drinking myself

146

into a stupor. I'd never known that kind of depression, not even when I was living on the streets as a young boy. "She almost ended up with someone else. If he was just some guy she was fucking to stop thinking about me, I wouldn't have cared." I didn't care about censoring myself. When I first introduced myself to the Barsettis, I was transparent about who I was. I was myself— completely. "But she had a connection with that guy. They shared artwork. They bought each other's paintings. That guy was the biggest threat I'd ever come across. That wouldn't have happened if Crow hadn't taken Vanessa away from me." I stared at my food and kept eating.

She set her fork down. "I understand that, Griffin. But even if she got together with him, it wouldn't have changed her feelings for you. You could have walked back into her life at any moment, and she would have left him for you."

"Or even worse, I never could have walked back into her life. If Conway hadn't pissed off the Skull Kings, none of this would have happened. I wouldn't have taken that bullet in my shoulder, and we wouldn't be sitting here right now. If the opportunity to prove myself hadn't arisen, none of this would be possible."

Pearl said nothing, knowing there was nothing she could add.

"I came to the winery every day, I gave your husband a loaded shotgun with my hands cuffed to a chair, and I put up with his bullshit for months trying to prove myself to him. But we both know he never really gave me a chance. It didn't matter what I did, Crow was going to have the same answer. Only when I was willing to die for the Barsettis did he think that was good enough. It forced his hand. And trust me, I don't believe in soul mates or any of that bullshit. But I know Vanessa is the only woman I could ever love. She's it." I placed my hand over my heart. "How easy could it have been for me to lose her for good? That's why I don't forgive him. That's why I don't like him."

Pearl watched me, her blue eyes showing her sadness. She didn't challenge me or try to change my mind. After the speech I'd just made, there was little she could do to turn it around. "If that's the case, why have you forgiven me? I was blinded by my hatred as much as he was."

Crow was the operator of the family, the man who made all the final decisions. He had a lot more power, control over everything. But if she really wanted to, she could have changed his mind before things got so bad. She didn't insult me the way Crow did, but she didn't defend me either. I was gentler on her for a reason. "Because you remind me of my mother."

THE SECOND I stepped through the door, Vanessa was all over me.

She jumped into my arms without giving me any

notice, completely naked and ready for me. Her arms wrapped around my neck, and her ankles locked together around my waist as she sealed her mouth over mine.

Fuck, this was nice.

My arms scooped under her thighs and ass, and I held her in the doorway, taking her sexy tongue and giving her my own. "Jesus Christ, you missed me."

"Yes." She breathed against my mouth, her eyes wild. "And I'm pissed."

"Good. I love it when you're pissed." I carried her down the hallway and into our bedroom.

She slapped me across the face then kissed me again.

Shit, she was driving me crazy.

I dropped her on the bed and pushed off my jeans and boxers. My cock sprang free, hard the second she jumped into my arms.

She turned on her hands and knees and looked at me over her shoulder, her slick pussy staring at me too.

I didn't bother taking off my shirt before my knees dropped and hit the mattress. My head aimed right for her opening on its own, and I slid inside her, pushing through the arousal she'd released before I walked in the door. I moved all the way inside until my balls were pressed right against her body.

I grabbed both of her wrists and pulled them from under her body, making her face shift forward and hit the sheets. Her ass moved higher in the air, and I gripped the back of her neck so I could keep her in place. My other hand pinned her wrists together against her lower back, treating her like a prisoner rather than the woman I loved. "Still pissed at me, baby?" I thrust into her hard, hitting her with deep thrusts that smacked right against her body.

She groaned as she shifted forward. "God…"

"I asked you a question." I fucked her harder, pounding into her pussy.

She breathed against the sheets, her hair stretched out around her. "No…"

"That's what I thought."

SEVEN

Carter

Mine.

She was officially mine.

I gave her a way out to avoid this avenue. All she had to do was be a cooperative prisoner, and this wouldn't be happening. But she carved the tracker out of her ankle, figured out the passcode to the alarm system, and attempted to steal one of my million-dollar cars.

She deserved to be punished.

My bedroom was already prepared. I had the hand-cuffs hooked to the headboard and the whip on the nightstand. I'd never wanted to hurt a woman so much, and now I couldn't wait to turn her skin bright red. I wanted to douse her fire with my authority. I wanted her to scream in pain and in pleasure. I wanted this fantasy, a fantasy I never knew I had until she came along.

I dragged her back into the house and up the stairs. She fought against me the entire way, using all the muscles in her body to get herself free. She pushed against the floor and tried to throw my body into the wall, but she was no match for my size.

"Carter, you're better than this." She tried to twist her wrists out of my hold, but my grip was too strong. "Come on. Please—"

I squeezed her throat, stopping the words before they could pour out of her mouth. "Begging and pleading won't do anything, sweetheart. It only makes me want you more. If you didn't want this, you should have just gone to bed." I dragged her down the hallway and made it into my bedroom.

She kept fighting me, bucking her hips and trying to kick me.

I pushed her onto the bed then got her wrists in the cuffs. Once the steel was closed in place, there was nowhere for her to go. I would have paused to take off her shirt, but I would be able to just pull it up over her body.

"Carter, don't do this." She tried to yank on the headboard, but the wood was too strong to even sway.

My shirt was already off, and my jeans hit the floor. My cock was throbbing in anguish since I'd wanted to fuck her for weeks. I hadn't picked up another woman in that time frame, so of course, I was losing my mind. I didn't want another woman when I could have this one instead. I dropped my boxers next.

Mia went quiet, her eyes converging on the sight of my big dick. Her eyebrows rose as she looked at it, her surprise written all over her face. It was enough to make her stop fighting, for at least a few seconds.

When I grabbed the condom from my nightstand, she started to get worked up again.

"You aren't this guy, Carter," she said. "I know you aren't."

"You don't know me, sweetheart." I ripped open the packet and rolled it on, my cock twitching in my hands because I was excited to have her.

"You're better than this."

"No." I grabbed the whip from the nightstand. My fingers gripped the handle, excited to add more scars to the surface of her skin. Logic was long gone as desire took over. I wanted to make her cry, bring her to tears so I could watch her sob as I fucked her.

When she saw the whip in my hand, her protests only increased. "Don't..."

I undid her jeans and pulled them down her beautiful legs.

She kicked hard like a horse, throwing her hips into it. The fight was futile, but she didn't give up. "No. Don't do this to me."

"If you'd never tried to escape, this wouldn't be happening." I grabbed her thong next and pulled it down. The second I saw her slit, my cock twitched again. I hadn't seen pussy in weeks, and hers was exceptional.

She kicked again, but once her panties were gone, she finally gave up. "I would have hated myself more if I didn't try. I deserve better than this, Carter. I deserve to be free. I deserve to say no. Don't be this guy. You may not care now, but someday, you will. Someday, you'll remember this and will hate yourself for it."

I moved on top of her, bringing our faces close together. I looked her in the eye, not feeling an ounce of shame for what I was about to do. "Maybe. But someday isn't today." I moved off her, grabbed her hips, and flipped her over.

"Carter!"

I secured her ankles to the chains then grabbed the whip again, my cock sheathed inside the latex condom. "Cry if you want. The louder you are, the more I'll enjoy it."

She had enough slack on the chain to hold herself up on her elbows. She was suddenly quiet, suddenly still. Perhaps her silence was a form of protest. But after ten slaps across the back, she would start to whimper. By the time I was done with her, she would be screaming.

I dragged the edge of the whip from her left shoulder down her back, letting the leather graze against her skin. I'd done some kinky things with the women I bedded, but never this. I savored the moment, savored the violence and arousal in my blood. I never knew how much I could enjoy this. The BDSM lifestyle was something I'd never given any thought to. But once she came into my life, I obsessed over it. "Since it's been a while, we'll start with twenty." I tapped her ass before I stepped back and readied the whip.

She was still, her perky ass round like a nectarine. The skin along her ass and legs was perfect and unblemished. She had a sexy curve in her lower back, so deep and prominent, a basketball could fit in the dip perfectly.

I gripped the whip so tightly my knuckles turned white. Her silence was a challenge, and that challenge only turned me on more. I would make her cry before I was through. I'd watch the tears stream down her face as I fucked her.

But then she said something that changed everything. "You know what's sad? I did want to sleep with you. You're the first man who's made my panties wet in…years. After everything I've been through, I didn't think it was possible for me to even think about sex again. But with you, I thought about it. If we'd met under different circumstances, I would have fucked you. I probably would have even done this willingly because it turns you on. But instead, this is how it is…"

My hand slackened on the whip. I stared at her naked body with a little less desire. Instead of wanting her violently, I pictured a different outcome for our relationship. I remembered the way she'd let me touch her, let me get near her. I remembered the way she would look at me when she thought I wasn't watching. There was chemistry between us. It'd been there since the day we met. I knew she wasn't lying, some manipulative game to get inside my head.

I held the whip between my fingers, but my resolve was slowly slipping away. I wanted this woman so much that I didn't care how I had her. I'd justified my behavior by making an arbitrary set of rules for her to break...and then I tricked her into breaking them. Instead of being a real man who seduced a woman, I took advantage of her situation and the power I had over her. Instead of putting in the time to get between her legs, I got lazy and took a shortcut.

She was right. I was an asshole.

I tossed the whip on the ground and unlocked the cuffs around her ankles.

"What are you doing?" she whispered.

I walked around the bed and unlocked the cuffs that bound her wrists to the headboard. Once the chains were off, I tossed the key on the floor next to the whip. "You're right, Mia. It is sad." I sat on the edge of the bed, the condom still on my softening dick. I kept my back to her and rested my arms on my knees. "You can go." I stared at the fireplace across the room. The logs were old because it'd been months since I'd lit a fire. I looked at the blank TV on the wall and waited for her to walk out. When she was gone, I would clean up and shower. I was in such a sour mood, I didn't even want to jerk off.

She sat up behind me but didn't get off the bed.

Instead, she lingered there, not even putting her clothes back on.

I could vaguely see her movements in the reflection of the TV, but I couldn't distinguish her features. My head tilted down, and I stared at my hands.

She scooted closer to me before she pressed her hands against my back. She was probably at a loss for words, grateful I'd changed my mind. But she also probably thought I was weak. If I ever made another threat, she wouldn't take it seriously. Her fingers explored my back, giving me a soft massage with a womanly touch. Her hands moved up again, and her fingers glided through my hair.

The touch was so nice, I closed my eyes.

Her thighs moved to either side of my hips, and she wrapped her arms around my shoulders. Her soft lips pressed against my neck, giving me a kiss with a slight bit of tongue.

I kept my eyes closed, savoring the way her plump tits felt against my back. Her nipples dragged against me, pointed and round. I thought it would be a single kiss, a sexy way for her to show her gratitude.

But the kisses continued.

The embraces were soft in the beginning, but then she kissed me harder, dragging her tongue over the cord in my neck. Her fingers dug into me gently, showing her arousal and her desperation. Her warm breaths entered my ear, the sexy noises filling my brain and making my cock hard again.

If she didn't want me, she should stop. Because I was seconds away from turning around and pinning her against the mattress.

Her fingers grabbed my chin, and she turned my face toward hers. Her coffee-colored eyes looked into mine with mutual desire. Without blinking, she pressed her soft lips directly against mine and kissed me.

Kissed me slowly.

Kissed me softly.

Kissed me good.

My hand moved to the back of her head, and I cradled her there, my mouth moving with hers in the perfect rhythm. Her tongue felt perfect against mine. Her breaths filled my lungs, urging me to devour her. Her nails continued to scratch at me as she pulled me closer into her. "Fuck me."

I sucked in a breath between my teeth, and my cock twitched at the same time. My fingers dug farther into her hair, and I pulled her closer to me. The words were even sexier because I hadn't expected to hear them. I'd just chained her to the bed with the intention of making her bleed. Now she wanted me inside her, but on her terms.

I'd take it.

I turned around and guided her back to the bed, our slow kiss still continuing. My hands explored her, from gently touching her neck to grasping one of her firm tits in my palm. My thumb flicked over her nipple, and I exhaled in her mouth because it felt as erotic as I imagined.

Her hand cupped my cheek then slid into my hair, fisting the short strands as she hiked one leg around my hip.

My hand slid down her leg and explored her thigh, moving all the way until I gripped her hips. I liked these slow and intense kisses, but my mouth naturally began to speed up. I kissed her harder, giving her more tongue as my cock thickened. Kissing her was better than I imagined it would be. It was better than kissing any woman. Maybe it was because I'd wanted her for so long or because I'd been celibate for weeks. I didn't know what the explanation was, but I knew I wanted to kiss her and never stop.

Her hands explored my body the way I'd just explored hers. She felt the solid muscles of my chest, and her fingers outlined my frame, feeling the riverbeds between my abs and the sex lines over my hips. She touched the small happy trail beneath my belly button then reached my balls. She fingered them gently, her soft fingers incredible against my sensitive sac.

I moaned into her mouth, loving her gentle hands.

She didn't touch my dick, probably because it was sheathed inside a latex glove. But she explored my balls for a few more moments before she gripped my tight ass next, her fingers digging into the muscle.

My hand moved between her legs, and my fingers found her clit. I rubbed her gently, treating her pussy with the same delicateness she treated my balls. My fingers moved in a circular motion, lightly stimulating her.

She moaned into my mouth the second I touched her, like a man had never touched her in that special spot before. She breathed into my mouth before she kissed me harder, her nails being more aggressive than they were before. "Fuck me gently." She spoke into my mouth as she kissed me. "It's been a while…and you have a big dick."

My cock twitched as I listened to her instructions, listened to her preferences. This was really going to happen. I finally got to fuck this woman. I didn't need to tie her down to enjoy her. She was giving herself to me, spreading her legs so I could enjoy her. It seemed like I'd earned it, and that made it sexier. "Yes, Mia." When I said her name, all the muscles of my body tightened.

She folded her other leg, giving me room to move between her thighs. Her hand gripped my ass as she guided me.

My hand moved away from her clit, and I felt her slit with my fingers, checking to see that she was ready for me. Before my finger even moved inside her, I felt the pool of moisture that seeped right from her cunt.

Fuck, she wanted me.

She wanted me bad.

She wasn't just fucking me in gratitude. Her pussy wanted my dick. My fingers moved inside her because I wanted to feel her wetness all the way to my knuckle. Several inches deep, I could feel the sticky residue that lined her walls.

I slowly pulled out, my breaths shaky against her lips. My cock was throbbing so much, it actually hurt. I was anxious to be inside her, more anxious than I'd been in my entire life. Even with this condom on my dick, I was excited.

My arm hooked around the back of her knee as I positioned her underneath me. My lips turned immobile for a moment, wanting to focus on her expression as I slid inside. My head found her opening, and I pushed past her tight entrance. Being a slave for years hadn't changed her perfect anatomy. I sank inside her, moving inches at a time as I entered her. I could sense the tightness of her slit, feel the moisture surround me everywhere. I sank deeper until there was nowhere left to go.

Her eyes brightened visibly, and instead of showing that constant look of hatred, her expression was soft. Her fingers caressed my hair, and she breathed against my mouth, her pants light and sexy. Her hand gripped my hip, and she bit her bottom lip when she felt me completely. There were no more smartass comments from her lips, no more pledges of hostility. Now she was just a woman, giving in to her attraction for me.

I kissed her bottom lip and gently pulled it into my mouth. "You're more beautiful than I imagined." I could walk out of the house right now and find a beautiful woman in Milan. She wouldn't be a victim of trafficking or abuse. She would be normal. But being with Mia showed me that I didn't want normal, at least, not right now. I wanted a woman made of something stronger, a woman with battle scars that destroyed her skin but not her mind. I'd always been attracted to all kinds of women, from blondes to redheads. But I'd never been this attracted to anyone but her. There was something about her…and I knew it had to do with her past. I didn't just want to hurt her.

I wanted to bow to her.

I gave her hard and even strokes, my body hitting her deep and tapping against her clit at the same time. Instead of kissing her, I kept my face above hers, watching the sexy reaction she had.

Her fingers explored my chest, digging into the muscles underneath my tanned skin. She'd started to moan the second we began, unable to keep her lips closed because the moans continued indefinitely. Her tits shook with my thrusts, her nipples hardening until they were sharper than blades.

I could feel her pussy change around my dick, feel the walls constrict. I could feel the increased moisture, the way her body prepared for the climax she was about to receive. Her lips started to tremble, and she couldn't hide the short instance of surprise from entering her features.

"I promised I would make you come." Sometimes, I worked hard to satisfy a woman. Sometimes, I didn't care about her pleasure at all. But this time, it was my main focus. Mia told me she didn't think it was possible to want a man, not after what happened to her, but she wanted me…had wanted me since she first looked at me. I shouldn't care about her suffering, not when I was going to return her in a very short amount of time, but I wanted her to feel good, to feel good because of me.

"I just…" She breathed harder and bit her bottom lip as she felt the climax approach. "I just didn't think it would happen so fast."

My hand moved into the back of her hair, and I fisted the strands hard. My gaze bored into hers, seeing this beautiful woman come apart for me. She took my dick as deeply as I gave it to her, enjoying it like every woman before her. "I'll make it faster next time." I rubbed my nose against hers before I kissed her again, this time fucking her a little harder. I pounded into her, driving her into an orgasm she didn't expect.

"God…" She stopped kissing me so she could scream in my mouth. "Carter…"

I'd never loved hearing my name on a woman's lips so much, not like I did right now.

"Carter."

I pounded into her harder, making her scream louder. She tightened around me so much, it felt like my dick might snap in half. I pressed my forehead against hers and concentrated on her, making sure she enjoyed every single second of the long climax. I wanted her to live in the moment, to ride the high as long as she could. I focused on her, keeping my body in line so I wouldn't finish too soon. Keeping myself in check had never been difficult, not when I got pussy on a regular basis, but it'd been weeks with no action. It was the hardest thing I'd ever had to do…to be a gentleman and wait for her to finish.

When she stopped screaming in my face, I knew she was finished. Her pussy released my cock after it finished bruising it, and then she kissed me again. She kissed me hard, giving me a deeper affection than she had before. This time, it was full of gratitude, thanking me for making her feel such an incredible rush of pleasure. "Carter…your turn." Her lips paused as she looked me in the eye. She focused her gaze on me, her tits still shaking from my thrusts. She grabbed my hips and directed me inside her, pulling me as far as she could before wincing in pain.

With my eyes locked on hers, I thrust until my dick exploded. I shoved my dick as deep as I could go as I released into the condom, watching the satisfaction in her eyes as I hit my threshold. I dumped my come into the tip of the condom, pretending it wasn't there at all and I was inserting my seed right inside her.

The climax was good, so good that I would never forget it. I loved feeling her thighs around my hips, feeling her tits drag against my chest when I moved. I loved being buried deep inside her, just a man and a woman. I'd had more adventurous sex with more unin-hibited women, but plain vanilla with this woman was far more satisfying. It was exactly what I wanted, the perfect ending to my obsession.

When I finished, I stayed on top of her, letting my dick soften inside her.

The arousal was still in her eyes, despite the satisfaction I just gave her. Her fingers glided along the back of my neck, and she looked at me with nothing less than affection. She pulled my lips to hers and kissed me again, her ankles coming together at my back.

Once I finished, I usually rolled off and hopped in the shower right away. But her kiss was exactly what I wanted. Watching her want me inflated my ego, gave me another boost of confidence I didn't think I needed. Conquering this woman made me feel like a king.

She gave me a bit of her tongue before she pulled away, her lips just an inch from mine. "Could you do that again?" She begged with her eyes, asking me to satisfy her just like that once more.

All the muscles in my body tightened at her request. I'd never heard a woman say something so sexy, ask me to please her again because she enjoyed it so much the first time. This woman hated me, but that hatred didn't affect our mutual attraction. There was a distinct line drawn, separating the two. We both understood the difference. "Sweetheart, I'll do it as many times as you want."

EIGHT

Mia

I lay beside Carter in his bed, the sunshine starting to come through the windows because dawn had arrived. The night had been filled with terror and pleasure, and the time moved so quickly that I didn't notice the night was gone until morning light appeared.

Hot and sweaty, we lay several feet apart. His chest shone from the moisture that coated his skin. With his eyes closed, he breathed deeply as his body returned to calm. The sheets were kicked away, so most of his naked body was revealed, from his chiseled torso to his muscular thighs. His dick lay on his stomach, smaller than it was before but still impressive in size. His guard was down, creating a perfect opportunity for me to strike.

But I continued to lie there.

When I came on to Carter, I wasn't thinking about

my actions. I was living in the moment, my emotions and empathy dictating my actions. My limbs were secure in chains, and Carter's hostile arousal filled his bedroom. He wanted to hurt me so bad, wanted to fulfill the dark fantasies every man had—whether they admitted it or not. I had absolutely no power in the situation. I forfeited all my rights when I tried to escape.

But my words changed his mind.

Somehow.

They made him rethink his actions, made him wonder what kind of man he wanted to be. Knowing that I'd ever wanted him made him question his behavior. What kind of man forced a woman to submit? A real man convinced her to submit. That truth hit him hard and made him reexamine everything he wanted.

Then he let me go.

I couldn't believe it.

He unlocked every chain and set me free. Then he sat at the edge of the bed, his anger and desire subdued.

I could have just walked out and returned to my room, but I didn't. I admired his decision. I admired him for listening to me. Egor never cared for my pleas or tears. He never cared about me as a human being. Carter might have darker aspects, might not be a gentleman, but he certainly had compassion.

He had a heart.

He was a good man…in his own way.

I hadn't been treated with any kind of respect for

years, but Carter was good to me. His heart was pure and easily swayed. He didn't have blood lust in his veins, not like other men. He wasn't evil.

Not at all.

And that made me want him, made me want to give him something. Sex was on my terms, and that made me want to feel him between my legs, to enjoy him when I never allowed myself to.

I did enjoy it—immensely.

This was a new beginning for us. Whether he let me go the next morning or not, we had a connection now. If I just let it be, he would let me be free eventually. If I asked enough times, he would do it.

There wasn't a single doubt in my mind.

Carter Barsetti was a good man.

So I lay beside him in the darkness, not interested in slitting his throat while he slept. He was kind to me, and now I wanted to be kind to him. He pleased me in a way I hadn't felt in a long time. Actually, I'd never been satisfied like that. I'd never been with a man who had Carter's raging masculinity, had his level of confidence. Seeing him want me so much, despite the fact that I was a victim of rape and torture, made me feel beautiful for the first time in years. He didn't care where I'd been, about the men who took me before he laid eyes on me. Most men would be disgusted by it, judge me for the horrible things that were done to me on a regular basis. Not Carter.

Since he had a soft spot inside his chest, I knew I would be able to get away eventually. If we continued to sleep together and his heart softened even more, he wouldn't be able to resist my request. Just as my earlier words made him drop the whip, he would do it again.

I could try to escape, but that might provoke his anger. Right now, he was kind and gentle, fucking me in a way Egor never did. If I let the peace continue, I would get my way eventually. Cane wasn't a psychopath like the others. He had a heart underneath that concrete chest. It beat with compassion, understanding, and empathy. He would let me go.

I knew he would.

Neither one of us crossed the divide between us, not snuggling together like lovers after lovemaking. I watched his breathing return to normal as he slipped off into sleep. His hand rested on his stomach, slowly rising and falling with his deep breaths. When he was unconscious, the hardness of his face relaxed, and his jawline softened slightly. He looked handsome either way, but with his guard down, his true nature seemed to be more visible.

I couldn't help but consider myself lucky, to appreciate the man beside me. After sleeping in chains and being whipped until I bled, Carter was a godsend. He was handsome, charming, and compassionate. He still kept me against my will, so I shouldn't be too fond of him, but I was. I felt my heart soften the way his did for me.

I actually liked him.

And I liked the way he pleased me, caring about our mutual pleasure instead of his own exclusively. He gave me the greatest sex of my life, sex so good I didn't think it was possible. When my ankles were locked around his waist, I didn't think about the last three years of my life. All I thought about was the two of us, a man and a woman, doing something natural and beautiful.

I didn't think sex could be beautiful anymore.

I knew he wouldn't want to sleep with me, so I maneuvered to the edge of the bed and sat up. My skin smelled like sweat and sex, and my hair was tangled from the way he'd fisted it. He fucked me like I was the only woman he wanted for the rest of his life. Did he fuck every woman like that?

When my feet hit the rug, I stood up, doing my best to move stealthily so I wouldn't disturb him. When I took my first step, he heard me.

With a deep voice that sounded perfectly awake, he commanded me. "Get back here."

"I'm going to bed."

"Then lie down." He opened his eyes and turned his head my way. With rich brown eyes that complemented the depth of his soul, he stared at me with powerful hostility. He patted the bed beside him.

"I thought you'd want to sleep alone."

"No." He patted the bed again, this time harder. "When I wake up, the first thing I'm going to do is fuck you. So get back here."

A wave of desire ran through me, making me feel beautiful again when I didn't think it was possible. He didn't get tired of me after he had me. He wanted to keep taking me. I moved back onto the bed and tucked myself under his sheets.

He turned his gaze to the ceiling again and closed his eyes.

"You aren't afraid I'm going to kill you?" There was bound to be a gun in here somewhere. All I had to do was point it at his face while he slept, and his life would be over.

He sighed like he was too peaceful to really care about the question. "No, sweetheart. I'm not afraid of anything. In fact, I hope you try. Just gives me a reason to punish you."

———

IT WAS noon when I woke up the next day.

Carter was already awake, scrolling through his phone and checking his emails. The sheets were bunched around his waist, showing his chiseled stomach and sexy, tanned skin. His short dark hair was slightly messy from the way I'd gripped it last night.

When he realized I was awake, he tossed his phone on the nightstand. "Morning, sweetheart."

"Morning." I turned on my side and faced him, the sheet pulled to my shoulder.

He opened his nightstand and pulled out a condom.

He ripped through the foil quickly then rolled the latex onto his hard dick. He pushed the sheets back, revealing his monster size and thickness. He was the biggest man I'd ever taken, putting Egor to shame. "Right to the point, huh?"

He positioned himself on top of me and rolled me onto my back. "I warned you last night." He separated my thighs so his hips could slide through. The muscles of his chiseled physique shifted and moved under the skin. His narrow hips had deep lines in between the muscles, making a prominent V that turned his body into the perfect shape of a triangle. "I went easy on you last night." He held his face above mine, his lips taunting my mouth with their proximity. "Not again."

This man helped himself to me like I was a station on a buffet line. He was nice enough to at least let me wake up first, but the second my eyes were open, he went for the kill. My palms immediately pressed against his pecs, my favorite feature. They were two slabs of powerful muscle, hard against my hands. "Really? Because I enjoyed it a lot…" My eyes shifted to his lips before I looked into his gaze again.

He held his body still on top of mine, his brown eyes looking into mine with that same aggression. His cock twitched slightly in response. I could feel the latex rub against my thigh with the movement. His hard jawline tensed a little more, and he seemed angry with himself for being moved by my words. He got off on my plea-sure. Maybe it was because he was a gentleman. Or maybe it was because it inflated his already fat ego. "You like it nice and slow?"

"I like how you gave it to me…" My fingers dug into his shoulders as I waited for him to slip inside me. I couldn't believe I was saying these words to a man who kept me as a prisoner. Instead of being a slave, I felt like a woman he'd brought home for the night. For just a moment, it was a different kind of fantasy, one where I could pretend I was free.

He pressed his forehead against mine and inhaled deeply, a slight moan coming from his lips. His cock twitched again before he pressed his lips against mine, giving me a slow kiss like he did the night before.

The chemistry was there the second we touched. The air left my lungs as soon as our warm bodies combined. My fingers moved into his hair, and I kissed him like he was the only man I ever wanted. I loved his kiss, loved the way his soft lips moved against mine and claimed them. When he gave me his tongue next, my thighs squeezed his hips.

Without realizing what I was doing, I ground my hips against his body, feeling his length rub against my throbbing clit. I panted into his mouth, my fingers digging deeper into his hair. This man ignited my sexual desire, made me feel like a woman again. I forgot how wonderful sex could be, even if it was meaningless. He brought me back to life, made me feel pleasure for the first time in years.

He pushed on the shaft of his length, then slipped

inside me, fitting through my tight opening and sinking until his fat dick was completely inside me, his warm balls hitting my ass. His powerful arms held his weight on top of me, kept me squished against the mattress while he weighed me down. I was smothered by his hot skin and sexy muscles. I was enveloped by his kisses. He was an enormous barrier that separated me from the horrors of the world. For that moment, I felt safe underneath him, that nothing could interrupt this pleasurable peace that he gave me.

I never thought sex could heal me.

Not after it had destroyed me for so long.

He thrust inside me just the way he did last night, hitting me in the right spot at the perfect pace. I could probably handle something more intense, but since last night felt so good, I wanted that again. It was my favorite item on the menu.

I'd already fucked him once, so I wasn't ashamed of how much I enjoyed him. My nails clawed at his muscular back, and my pussy soaked his fat length wrapped in the condom. His name escaped from my lips, like I was with a lover rather than my keeper.

He moaned every time I said his name.

I didn't want this to end. I wanted it to keep going forever. My mind shut off, and I didn't think about anything else except the fire between my legs. Like last night, he brought me to a climax instantly, the size and shape of his dick hitting an invisible button inside my body. My thighs squeezed his hips, and I bucked against him in response, my body working on its own and inde-pendent of my mind.

"Looks like I broke my record."

I kept my face pressed against his as I finished, my pussy still convulsing around his length. I rode the high until I was completely finished, the arousal seeping between my legs even more than before. "Make me come again…"

He smiled against my mouth. "I'd be happy to."

I PREPARED LUNCH, making sandwiches and salads. Carter jumped in the shower once we were done, so I had some time to myself. I brought everything to the table, along with two glasses of iced tea.

I sat down and stared out the window, unsure how to feel about my new situation. I'd slept with Carter because I was attracted to him, but I kept bedding him because the sex was good. Not just good, but extraordinary. The list of men I'd slept with wasn't very long, but I hadn't experienced anything like what I had with Carter.

He was a professional.

Being in his captivity was starting to feel more like a vacation than imprisonment. If I didn't have someone waiting for me, I would just settle for the comfortable life he offered me. No one would judge me for it. And if they did, then they simply didn't understand the kind of torture I'd endured. It was a miracle my mind hadn't shattered like the rest of my body. If I didn't have so much to live for, I would have thrown in the towel a long time ago.

Carter came into the dining room and joined me, shirtless in his sweatpants—as usual. He sat down, didn't say a word, and started to eat.

Once he was beside me, I helped myself to the meal I prepared. We'd skipped breakfast because we woke up too late for that. It was midday, and the scorching sun burned the golden fields outside the window. The cooling system in his house kept us comfortable, but I could tell it was insanely hot outside, not to mention humid.

He watched me as he chewed, more entertained by my appearance than the Italian landscape around us. He hadn't shaved for the last two days, so a thick line of hair was beginning to cover his jawline. His eyes were dark brown, the color beautiful and deep. When they were directed on me, it was like being under the scrutiny of a microscope.

I didn't smell like him or hot, sweaty sex anymore since I'd showered. But I suspected my pores would slowly start to soak up every single molecule, and it wouldn't matter how many times I showered, the smell would become permanent.

I kept my eyes on my food, ignoring him. I should get used to the stare, but I still hadn't. Our routine was exactly the same as it was every single day. We sat together, and he watched me like I was a TV screen.

He broke the silence with a question. "Why did you sleep with me?"

Despite the candidness of his question, I didn't stop chewing my food. I finished it before I sipped my iced tea.

He stopped eating, focused on me completely as he waited for an answer.

"I think the answer is obvious."

"I'd like to be sure. So, what is it?"

I looked out the window, trying to think of the right way to phrase it.

He grabbed my chin and forced my stare on him, his fingers digging into the skin of my jaw. "What is it?" He lowered his hand after he had my attention.

"It's not that complicated. I was attracted to you, and I was moved that you listened to me. I realized you weren't the evil man you wish you were. Without thinking, my hands were on you, and my lips wanted to feel yours. One thing led to another, and it just happened."

"No other reason?" he asked.

"What reason are you looking for?"

"I wasn't sure if you did it out of gratitude…since I didn't hurt you."

I wanted to look away, but I knew he would just grab my chin again. "I guess I wanted to reward you for being better than most men out there. You restored some of my faith in men. I guess I wanted to honor that."

He must have been satisfied with that answer because he looked away. "I still want to hurt you. But I won't."

"I know." I knew he wouldn't do anything I didn't want him to do. "You're a good man, Carter."

"A good man should never want to hurt a woman," he said coldly. "I'm not a good man, and I have no interest in being one. Maybe I'm not evil, but there's a lot of room between good and evil. I fall somewhere in the middle."

"Still an improvement from what I'm used to…"

He turned back to me, his eyes still cold. "You like fucking me?"

I rolled my eyes. "That's obvious."

"I want to hear you say it."

"I already said it when I asked you to make me come again." He wanted to listen to me say these words because it only made his ego grow bigger—and his cock.

A slight smile formed on his lips. "I like fucking you too, sweetheart. Very much."

"I picked up on that."

"And I intend to keep fucking you." He set his fork down, and he watched me with his intense expression, as if challenging me not to say a word in response. "I'm having a doctor come to the house today to check you."

"Check me?" I asked. "For what?"

"That you're clean."

I stopped myself from rolling my eyes. "I want the same from you."

"I am clean."

"I don't care," I snapped. "I refuse to make it this far and catch something now."

He leaned back in his chair. "I'm not trying to sound like an ass, but you're the one we should be concerned about."

"He checked me for the same thing, meaning he was clean. And you're the one who sleeps around."

"Who said I sleep around?" he demanded.

He'd never actually said those words, but it was obvious. "Are you saying you don't?"

He didn't say anything at all.

I proved my point.

"Fine," he said. "We'll both do it. Then he'll give you some birth control."

I held my tongue and kept my silence. I didn't need birth control, but a part of me didn't want to tell him that. I hated saying the words out loud because that made them more true. Egor took away the most important thing to me…the ability to have children. "I don't need anything."

"I'm not wearing a condom. I hate that shit." He drank from his glass, enjoying something besides scotch for once.

"That's not what I mean." I couldn't look at him as I said the truth. I didn't even want to say the words out loud because I would hear them. "I can't have chil-dren...so you don't need to worry about that."

He regarded me in silence, his head slightly cocked as he examined me. He didn't say anything for a long time, like he didn't know how to tread in this difficult conversation. His fingers rested against his glass, and he sighed quietly under his breath. "I'm sorry."

I didn't say anything. There was nothing I could say to that. "My previous master...had my tubes tied. Didn't want to put me on birth control so just went straight to the source." I refused to cry, especially in front of someone. I didn't want his pity, and I didn't want to pity myself either. I wanted to pretend it never happened. I knew it was possible that I could get preg-nant again with medical intervention, but it wouldn't be natural and it would be difficult. Egor took away the most important thing to me...something so beautiful.

He sighed and bowed his head, like he couldn't think of a response to match the horrible thing I'd just said. Carter wasn't a sensitive guy, a man of few words. He listened to my pleas, but that didn't mean he cared about other things.

I concentrated on my food and waited for the tense moment to pass. Tears burned behind my eyes, but I refused to let them fall. One day, I would kill Egor for what he did to me. I would kill him for the way he made me suffer. I would kill him for what he did to my family. I didn't know how or when...but I would figure it out.

Carter reached his hand across the table and

grabbed my hand. He held it, his fingers gently squeezing mine. He looked at me with sad eyes and a tense jawline, the unspeakable pain written on his face. "Sweetheart…" Unable to find the words to soothe the situation, he said nothing else.

Feeling his hand in mine was comforting. He'd never touched me that way before, gave me the kind of affection two friends would share. It'd been years since I'd felt something real, like a hug or an embrace. I'd been fucked and smothered with sex, but that wasn't the physical contact I needed.

This was what I needed.

I squeezed his hand back, silently telling him I appreciated his sympathy. I knew it was real. If it weren't, he wouldn't have done anything at all. I understood Carter better now than I did before, and I knew he had a heart. He had compassion. And I knew he cared.

He scooted his chair closer to me and wrapped his arm around my shoulder while his hand continued to grip mine. The food was abandoned, and we sat together in front of the window, the world outside peaceful. He brushed his thumb over mine, consoling me quietly. His hand rubbed down the middle of my back. "I'm sorry, Mia." The sincerity was in his voice, potent and real.

"I know."

He pressed his forehead against the side of my head and pressed a kiss to my hairline.

I closed my eyes at his touch, his affection reminding me what it was like to be loved. It reminded me of a kiss from an old lover, affection between a man and a woman who loved each other. It reminded me of the way my mother would comfort me after my father died. The embrace was so simple, but it meant so much to me. "Thank you, Carter." This man was slowly putting me back together without even realizing it. He was proving that there was some good in the world. He was proving that not all men were like Egor. Egor made me barren, but Carter would never do something like that. He wanted to be evil, but he simply couldn't.

And that was exactly what I needed.

***

CARTER WORKED in his office all day and didn't come out until dinnertime.

I spent my free time at his pool, lying in the sun in a bikini Carter had given me and floating around on the inflatable swan when it got too hot. I helped myself to his bar and made myself Long Island Iced Teas while I soaked in the sunshine.

Since the sun didn't set until after nine, I lost track of the time.

Carter stepped onto the pool deck in his t-shirt and jeans. With his arms crossed over his chest, he watched me float around in the pool, my drink in the inflatable cup holder. "No dinner tonight, then?"

"What time is it?"

"Eight thirty."

"Oh…guess not." I was in the middle of the pool, so he couldn't get me unless he jumped in. Like a princess in a castle surrounded by a moat, I was safe.

"What am I supposed to eat?"

I shrugged. "You did fine before I came along."

"Yes. But having a maid has been nice."

"Well, this maid has taken the day off." My sunglasses were still on the bridge of my nose even though the sun was about to set.

"You look cute as hell right now."

"Why, thank you. Good thing you can't get to me."

"Can't get to you?" he asked, amused. "You think water could stop me?"

"It's pretty cold."

He accepted my challenge and pulled his shirt over his head.

"You don't have any swim trunks."

"Don't need them." He pushed his jeans down along with his boxers.

Letting his monster cock hang out.

He took the stairs into the water then walked toward me, his feet hitting the bottom because he was over six feet in height. He grabbed the inflatable swan and dragged me toward the shallow end of the pool. "That was easy."

"Damn…"

He rested his arms on the raft then leaned over to

kiss my shoulder and arm. The affection was meaning-less, but it felt nice at the same time. He kept his eyes on me, watching my reaction to his touch.

I was floating across the pool with a beautiful man kissing my shoulder. The landscape was beautiful, and my stomach was full because I could eat whenever I wanted. I'd never been on a vacation before, but this felt like the closest thing to one. "How was work?"

"I'm going to have to head to the offices soon. I've got to get started on production for the next line."

"What will you do with me?"

"Leave you here. Unless you'll miss me too much." He smiled playfully, showing a slight, boyish charm to complement his hard masculinity.

I chuckled, knowing I would miss him—just a little. "What if I run for it?"

"You won't." His confidence didn't miss a beat.

"You're so sure about that?"

"You live in a beautiful mansion with anything you could possibly want, and you have a sexy man to bed you every night. Where exactly are you going to go?"

If I didn't have someone so important in my life, I would probably stay. "You make a good argument."

He kissed my shoulder again, his scruff rubbing against my arm. "I've changed the security system. It's activated by my thumbprint now. So unless you cut my finger off, you don't have a chance."

I knew he wouldn't be stupid enough to trust me completely.

"By the way, you probably shouldn't be in the pool with a cut like that."

I shrugged. "I've been through worse."

He gave me an affectionate look, as if he admired me. "I'm impressed you cut that tracker out of your ankle. That took balls."

"I don't have balls, so it took guts."

"Yes." He smiled. "Guts. A lot of them."

"It hurt like a bitch."

"If you weren't careful, that could have been bad."

"The adrenaline outweighed the fear." I sipped my drink. "How did you know I was going to escape that night anyway?"

"If the tracker deviates from the average body temperature, I get a notification. The second you carved that thing out of your body, I knew. And my cars are designed with a specific security system, so it'll only turn on with my thumbprint. You can't even hot-wire it."

I never had a chance. The only possibility of getting out of there was by killing him.

He watched my reaction. "Sorry, sweetheart. I feel bad for letting you think you really had a chance."

"Even if I knew otherwise, I still would have tried."

His affection only deepened. "I know. For some reason, I admire you more."

Carter was a regular guy in life, not a psychopath like Egor. When he made comments like that, I could see the goodness behind his eyes. He showed affection instead of hatred, gave sexy caresses instead of slaps across the face. Never was he violent with me. He detained me when he had to, but that was only to get me under control. "Then why don't you let me go?"

Instantly, the tenderness in his eyes evaporated. He broke eye contact, sighed, and the comfortable companionship was gone. As if he was annoyed by the question, he pulled away from me.

"Did you ever consider letting me go and, you know, asking me out on a date? You know I would say yes." I watched his expression even though he wouldn't meet my gaze. This was the part of our relationship that I still didn't understand. If he didn't possess the kind of cruelty that Egor did, why didn't he let me go? He continued to keep me—even though it made no sense.

"I'll take to out to dinner if that's what you want."

"If you pick me up at my house and drop me off when we're done."

He rubbed the back of his neck, getting drops of water in his hair.

"Carter."

He wouldn't look at me.

"Carter." I grabbed his chin and pressed a kiss to his lips. Instantly, he softened. He took a breath when he felt me, and the muscles in his neck relaxed as he turned my way. He didn't give in to my command, but he gave in to my affection. I pulled away, my fingers still on his hard chin. "You aren't this man. We both know you aren't. Letting me go isn't a sign of weakness. Letting me go and bedding me as a free woman is far more impressive."

He looked at me, his eyes unblinking. "You'd want to still see me?"

Before I'd slept with him, my answer would have been no. But since the sex was so good and our chemistry was so hot, I knew I'd want to keep seeing him. I knew he was kind and compassionate, not a threat to me at all. I could forgive everything in the past if he gave me a new future. "Yes."

He stared into my gaze, looking for the sincerity of my words.

"You know I'm not lying, Carter." My hand ran up his chiseled forearm. "I doubt I'd want to see you forever. I doubt I'd want you to be my boyfriend or husband. But I wouldn't mind hooking up for a while." That was exactly what he wanted anyway, just hot sex with no strings attached. "So, there's no reason to keep me. You can have what you want—and I can have what I want." I hoped I would say the right thing to change his mind, to realize that keeping me as a prisoner wasn't in his best interest anymore.

I must have said the wrong thing because he pulled away from the float and climbed back up the stairs. His bare ass was fit and tight, and the rest of physique moved like living stone. "I'll make dinner tonight." He grabbed the towel off the chair and dried himself off before he walked inside.

I continued to drift in the pool now that he wasn't

keeping me centered anymore. He said he bought me to piss off someone else, but he'd already accomplished what he set out to do. What was the reason he continued to keep me?

I knew I was missing a piece of the story.

I just didn't know what it was.

NINE

Carter

I hung up the phone then walked back into the dining room where Mia was sitting. I'd made salmon and rice for dinner, something light after all the booze I'd had that day. We hadn't said much to each other since she asked me to let her go.

I didn't know what to say, so I said nothing.

I didn't want to keep lying to her.

From her point of view, there was no reason for me to keep her as a prisoner anymore. Sex was consensual, and she said she would keep sleeping with me if I let her go. I knew she meant it. It wasn't just a trick to escape.

So I had no reason to keep her.

Now that I knew what Egor did to her, I hated the bastard even more. I had never cared about Mia's mistreatment because I'd purposely tried not to connect with her. I steered away from personal questions. It was smart not to get attached to her so I could hand her over to that demon without feeling guilty about it. But the second we screwed, all that went out the window.

She came on to me.

She kissed me. Fucked me. Came for me.

The attachment I tried to avoid had already happened.

Egor took away her ability to have children...which was so despicable I wanted to murder him. It was worse than rape and torture. It was just cruel.

Now I had to give her back to him...in just a few days.

Fuck.

She kept asking me to release her, and if she kept this up, she might figure out the real reason I didn't.

I couldn't let that happen.

But could I really return this woman to the cruel life she'd just escaped from?

There was so much money on the table, money I'd already collected. If I pulled out of the deal and wired the money back, there would be bloodshed. Egor would never accept that betrayal. He would come after me and my entire family.

I didn't have a choice anymore.

I would try to enjoy the last days I had with her, fucking her and making her feel good, before I returned her to the master that would never let her go. Now that I was sleeping with her, I understood Egor's obsession.

She was magnificent.

"Are you alright?" Mia's pretty voice interrupted my thoughts.

My gaze shifted to her face, her beautiful coffee-colored eyes and her full lips. With long brown hair and a curvy body, she was a fantasy. She deserved to be with a man who would protect her from the world, who would put her on a pedestal and worship her. She was too good for that asshole. "Yeah."

"Your face is pale." Her eyes shifted back and forth slightly as she looked at me.

Because I was a terrible person. I bought women from the Underground and returned them to safety. That's why I didn't feel bad profiting from the exchange —because I was doing a good thing.

But now, I was doing a bad thing.

I hadn't known the context of the situation when I'd agreed to do the deal, but that didn't change anything. I was sending this woman back to a life of horror. She would eventually die in his captivity…or take her own life.

And unfortunately, I was starting to care about her.

Dammit. "That was the doctor. We're both clean."

"Oh." She drank her glass of wine. "Not surprised…"

I should be hard at the thought of fucking her that night without a condom, but I wasn't. I felt too guilty for what I was about to do. Mia wouldn't even see it coming. I would slip a syringe into her neck and put her to sleep before I made the exchange. She would have no idea what happened until she woke up with Egor beside her. He would pick up where he left off—and she would know giving her back was part of my plan all along.

And she would hate me.

I'd done terrible things to her before, but she forgave me. She saw the good in me despite the bad situation. I held a whip in my hand and chained her to the bed, but she had the power to talk me out of it. And she'd still wanted to sleep with me anyway. She accepted me for who I was…and my money didn't seem to impress her.

She still wanted to leave.

She wanted to be free…but keep sleeping with me. That meant she didn't want anything from me…only me.

"I thought you would be thrilled about that," she whispered.

"I am. I just have other stuff on my mind."

After she did the dishes, we went upstairs to my room. She immediately assumed she would be sharing my bed with me for the foreseeable future, and she was right. I wanted to fuck her before I went to sleep. Then I wanted to fuck her again the second I opened my eyes in the morning.

When she stepped into the room, she saw the black lingerie sitting on top of the bed. Black, lacy, and sexy, it was the perfect piece of clothing to place on that beautiful body. She eyed it on the bed before she turned to me, a question in her eyes.

I felt like an asshole for asking her to do anything, not when I was going to betray her in a few days. If she knew what my true intentions were, she wouldn't stop until she killed me. But since she saw me as harmless, her guard was down. A part of her probably believed I would let her go eventually, just as I changed my mind about whipping her.

She couldn't be more wrong.

She picked up the black thong and held it between her fingertips. "You want me to put this on?"

I held her gaze, standing in my sweatpants near the foot of the bed. This was wrong on so many levels. Now I was dressing her up for my desire. She wanted to be the recipient of my kisses and thrusts…but not if she knew the truth. "Yes."

"And this?" She picked up the see-through bra.

Just picturing her wearing that turned me on. "Yes."

Without a protest, she walked into my bathroom and changed.

I dropped my boxers and sweatpants, my cock already hard thinking about how she would look. I got on the bed with my elbows propping up my body. My hard dick lay against my stomach, eager to feel her bare pussy surround me. With skin-on-skin, I would be able to feel her warm and soft flesh. I would be able to feel her squeeze me even harder. I would be able to drop my come deep inside her, where it would sit until morning.

I moaned to myself because I was horny as hell. All the guilt I felt was muffled by the hardness in my dick.

Just like every other asshole on the planet, I stopped caring about morals the second sex was involved. Now that I was about to get laid, I didn't care that I was screwing her over.

I just cared about screwing her.

She stepped out of the bathroom, the lingerie fitting her hourglass frame perfectly. She fixed her hair with her fingertips, making it frame her face and her shoulders. The bra pushed her plump tits together, and her long legs moved gracefully across the floor. The dark color was sexy against her flawless skin. Her brown eyes were on me, watching my reaction to her.

"Jesus Christ." I loved a woman in lingerie, but not quite like this.

She crawled onto the bed, on her hands and knees. Her tits filled out the bra, and her back arched as she moved. Her eyes were directed on me as she came closer, the mutual desire in her gaze.

She wanted me as much as I wanted her.

She moved on top of me and straddled my hips, her hair dragging against my chest as she positioned her face over mine.

I watched this beautiful woman sit on me, her tits about to fall out and her sexy thighs parting over my hips. She stared at my lips as she leaned down to place her mouth over mine. My cock twitched against her panties just before I felt her lips.

Fuck.

The second our mouths were combined together,

my hand dug into her hair, and I kissed her hard. My lips ached for something deeper, something more intense. My tongue darted into her mouth right away, and I ground against her, my cock eager to feel the arousal that was seeping from between her legs that very moment. If she was as wet as she was last night, my cock would be very happy.

My fingers dug into her panties, and I rubbed her clit, the pads of my fingers becoming soaked in the slickness right away. I forgot to breathe for a second, my body pausing in excitement. Like I was a teenager who treasured every moment of sexual activity, this felt brand-new. I touched her pussy like it was the first time I'd ever gotten any action. Something about this woman made me feel brand-new, like this was the first time sex actually mattered. My fingers slid into her slit, and I explored her, feeling her moan against my mouth. "So fucking wet." I used two fingers to move inside her, to feel her tight pussy as it prepared for my big dick. Being inside her was heaven, whether it was my fingers or my dick.

Her fingers dug into my hair as she kept kissing me, her kisses turning just as carnal as mine. When she was with me, she didn't think about anyone else. She didn't think about the horrible things Egor did to her. When our bodies moved together, there was no one else.

It was just us.

I would love to watch her ride my dick, but I was so anxious to fuck her that I craved the control. I rolled her onto her back and pulled her wet panties off her legs. She'd barely had them on for fifteen minutes before the lace became soaked with her arousal. She opened her legs for me the second the material was gone, her hands running up my back at the same time. With parted lips and heavy breathing, she was ready to take me, even more eager than she was last night or this morning.

This time, I wasn't gentle. I pushed my swollen head into her entrance and gave one hard thrust, sliding inside her instantly. "Jesus fucking Christ."

"God…"

I rested my face against hers as I got used to the sensation between her legs, the wetness and the tightness. It drove me wild, made it impossible for me to think straight. It was so good…so damn good.

"Carter." She clawed at my back as we lay idle together, getting used to the feeling of our bodies combined. She was insanely wet, and I was harder than I'd ever been my entire life.

"Fuck." I hadn't even started to move yet, and I was on the verge of exploding. The idea of filling her pussy with my come was too much to even think about. I'd fucked women without a condom before, but there was something about her cunt that did a number on my dick.

She cupped the back of my head as she looked into my eyes. "You feel so damn good…"

My gaze was locked on to hers, my cock stretching

her far apart. I'd never seen a more beautiful woman underneath me, a woman so passionate and erotic. She shouldn't succumb to this desire, not the same way I did. She deserved better, deserved better than me. But the innate chemistry between us dictated our behavior, controlled our reactions to one another. Neither one of us could fight this; we were both in so deep.

I hadn't even started, and I knew I didn't want to stop.

She didn't want me to stop either.

"All I can think about is coming inside you." I wanted my dick to explode like a rocket, shooting my seed as deep as it could go. The instinct was unshakable. I wanted to claim her as mine in the most animalistic way possible. I wanted to make this pussy exclusively mine. The idea of letting Egor have her back pissed me off, especially when I was deep inside her like this. I wanted to fuck this cunt every single night and again in the morning. I didn't want to share it with anyone.

"Me too…" She grabbed my hip and tugged me inside her. "I'm almost there…"

"I haven't even started, sweetheart."

"I know." She squeezed her thighs around my waist. "I can't help it…"

I watched her close her eyes and felt her dig her nails into me harder, fighting the explosion that was about to happen between her legs. "Looks like you have a new record."

I would normally chuckle, but I was far too invested

in this moment. I gave her three thrusts, moving slowly and rubbing against her clit every time I touched her. Somehow, I could feel her impending climax between her legs, and she could feel mine. We were moving as slowly as possible, but just enough for both of us to get off.

"There…" She breathed against my mouth as she cupped my cheeks, coming just from the feeling of my dick inside her. I'd never made a woman come that quickly, and I knew it didn't happen now because of my skills. She'd wanted to come before I was even inside. She was aroused the second she put on that lingerie. And when she felt my hardness inside her, that was all she needed. I turned her on in a special manner, made her feel arousal in a whole new way.

Her cunt constricted around my dick as she came, moaning in my face as the desire swept her away. "Carter, give it to me…"

I was already holding on as best as I could, and once I had her permission, all the fight left my body. I moaned in her face as I filled her, dumping all my seed into her pussy instead of the tip of a condom. All the muscles in my body burned with the exertion, and I kept my dick deep inside her so she would get every last drop. Tonight, I would give her so much, she couldn't keep it all. And for the last few days she was in my captivity, she would always be full of my come.

Until I had to give her back.

IT WAS the middle of the day when my father called.

I was sitting in my office, taking some privacy away from my prisoner.

I wasn't even sure if I should call her that anymore. She seemed like a sexy roommate that I was constantly fucking. When I dated women, sometimes they would stay at my place for the weekend, but their stay never lasted longer than that.

Mia had been there for an entire month.

From the day she arrived until the present moment, our relationship had changed so drastically.

It was hard to believe I'd ever chained her up in a room to begin with.

I cleared my throat. "Hey." I'd been avoiding speaking to my family for a few weeks. Only Conway knew about my situation. Since he was so loyal to me, he would take the secret to the grave. But I felt awkward talking to my family, especially my parents. My father was a very candid man, speaking his mind with such bluntness, people thought he was an asshole most of the time.

Well, he was an asshole.

"Hey?" he asked. "We haven't spoken in two weeks, and that's all you have to say to me?"

"Hi?" I asked sarcastically. "Is that better?"

"Same shit, different word."

"Alright, what do you want me to say?"

"I don't know," he snapped. "But a lot more than that."

He turned aggressive when he was emotional. He wasn't good with words, and he was even worse with feelings. The response turned him into an asshole… even more. I hadn't understood any of that until my mother explained it to me. "Alright. How are you?"

"Pretty pissed off since we haven't spoken for two weeks."

I rolled my eyes. "We're talking now."

"I haven't seen you in almost a month. I know you're a hotshot with your cars and shit, but don't forget where you come from."

If only I could tell him the real reason for my absence. "I'll be done with this project in a few days. Then I'll be all yours."

"That's more like it."

"I'll take a trip down there. Sapphire is gonna have the baby soon anyway. I'll help out at the winery, see Mom for a bit, and see what Carmen is up to without me. I'll stay for a week."

"Make it two."

I tried not to grin. "A week and a half."

"Two and a half." All my father wanted was to spend time with me. Conway had been around a lot, so he was probably jealous he wasn't spending as much time with his own son.

"Two."

The victory in his voice was obvious. "Two, it is. Can't wait to see you. Your mother and I miss you."

"I know. I miss you too."

"Maybe you should think about moving to Florence. Conway and Sapphire are doing it. You work from home a lot, and you can just fly out there when you need to. Makes sense to me…" My father would do anything to get me back to Tuscany. Carmen was still there, but that wasn't enough for him. He wanted both of us.

Not having Conway around had already affected me. I used to see him all the time, but now that he was married and living five hours away, I missed him. He was my closest friend, not just my cousin. "I'll think about it."

"Great. Your mother would be so happy if she got to see you more often. And remember—"

"You won't always be around." He said the same thing to me all the time, for the last decade. "Yeah, I know. I said I would think about it."

My father finally backed off, knowing he'd made his point. Now he just had to hope that I would take his words to heart and move there. I was the last Barsetti who wasn't living in that vicinity. Being isolated from the herd had never bothered me because Conway was here, but without him as a neighbor, I really did feel separated from my family. I would think about it more seriously when I had time. Right now, I still had Mia to deal with. "Anything else new?"

"Actually, that's the reason why I'm calling. Well, the main reason." His tone changed, simmering down to a serious coldness. "Your uncle and I had a chat with Griffin."

I'd come to accept that Griffin was a part of our lives now, as strange as that seemed. "Yeah?"

"This issue with the Skull Kings isn't buried yet, so Griffin and your uncle are going to take a trip to the Underground to have a conversation."

I sat up straighter in my chair, the muscles hugging my spine tightening.

"We killed the men they hired to take out Conway, but we have no way to know if the war is actually over. Instead of taking that risk, we want to bury it. Crow will meet with them to establish peace, to present them an offering to make them forget about us."

"What does Griffin have to do with this?" Conway and I were the ones that started this mess. It didn't seem right that my uncle had to take care of it.

"He has a close relationship with them," he explained. "They've hired him for work in the past. Griffin also knows a lot of people, a lot of men at the Underground. He's done favors in exchange for loyalty instead of money. He's as close to untouchable as possible. He offered to intervene because it gives the Barsettis a lot of credibility."

Griffin was the reason I still had all the members of my family. He had managed to take down all the enemies surrounding them. My father and uncle were the strongest men I knew, but Griffin was made of something else. "I should come too. I'm responsible for all this—"

"No." My father's cold tone silenced me instantly. "Crow and I have already talked about this. There's no room for negotiation."

"Father, Conway and I are both adults—"

"Who were stupid enough to get mixed up in this," he snapped. "Now your fathers are cleaning up your mess."

"We never asked you to—"

"Be grateful that you don't have to ask. Be grateful that your fathers are willing to sacrifice their lives for you. Be grateful that we would do anything for you, even walk into the monsters' den and risk our necks."

I stared at my desk, seeing the pile of bills and documents that needed to be addressed. I was just scolded by my father, and as much as it angered me, I knew I deserved it. "What about the money?"

"We can talk about that later. It's not important right now."

If we had to pay back the Skull Kings for the profit we made, it should come out of our pockets, not Crow's. "When is this happening?"

"As soon as Griffin gets back from his mission."

"He's still doing that?" I asked incredulously.

"He's quitting. He just has to finish two more before he can be done."

I knew Crow wasn't happy about that. He wanted a

simple and peaceful life. Griffin wasn't fitting the bill at all right now. "Let me know if there's anything I can do." I should probably tell him about Mia, but if she was leaving before the deal even went down, I didn't see why it mattered.

"You know what you can do?" he asked coldly. "Learn your lesson."

"I have." More than he could possibly understand. The woman I was holding captive was actually an exceptional human being, someone who deserved better than the fate she would be forced to accept. I was ignorant and got myself into a bad situation, blinded by the greed the cash instilled in me.

I'd definitely learned my lesson.

TEN

Mia

_____

Carter sat beside me on the couch with his arm wrapped around my shoulders. My legs were pulled over his thighs, and we cuddled on the couch together like a couple enjoying their evening together. His hand rested on my thigh, and his bare chest rose and fell gently with his even breathing. Instead of focusing on the TV, he glanced at me from time to time.

It felt so normal.

It didn't seem like I was a prisoner anymore. It seemed like I was just a woman with her man. We'd already screwed on the couch, and now we were just enjoying each other's company. He drank his scotch while I had my wine. I pulled my panties back on so his come wouldn't drip down my thighs and onto the fabric of his furniture.

If I didn't have a life to get back to, I would actually want to stay there.

My life had been stressful since I was young. A lot of stupid decisions put me in bad situations. Every day was a struggle, and I constantly worked to have a better life. Being a guest in Carter's home showed me a luxurious life I'd never imagined. There was no such thing as stress, not when a man like him took care of me.

But it didn't matter how much I loved being there. It couldn't compare with the life waiting for me.

The true place where I belonged.

His phone vibrated in his pocket, and he fished it out to see the name on the screen.

Ever since I came into his captivity, I always looked for an opportunity to escape, to gain more knowledge about Carter and his behavior. So naturally, I looked at the screen even though I didn't expect to see anything relevant.

But the name on the screen was very relevant.

Egor.

Carter immediately repositioned the phone in his hand to hide the screen. "I have to take this, sweetheart." He left the couch and headed up the stairs, his black sweatpants hanging low on his hips.

Was that a coincidence?

What were the odds that he would be in contact with the same Egor?

It seemed unlikely, but that didn't chase away the dread that settled in my heart. Carter and I had just experienced an evening of peace and quiet, but all of that faded away the second that phone rang. My body became heavy with terror, and my heart thudded with palpitations.

It couldn't be the same Egor.

It just couldn't.

The only way I was going to find out was by asking him or spying on him. If it really was the same Egor, Carter would probably lie about it. This whole situation had been a lie. The only true way to get my answer was to eavesdrop, to hear the conversation myself.

I sprang off the couch and sprinted across the rug until I reached the hardwood floor in front of the staircase. I was careful with my footfalls, making them quiet as I ascended to the next floor as fast as possible. When my feet hit the rug in the hallway, I moved quickly again, the sound muffled by the thickness of the rug. I stopped in front of his office door, which was closed. His voice was immediately audible.

"Friday, then?" Carter's deep voice was calm as usual, borderline indifferent. He was quiet as he listened to the person on the other line. When he spoke again, it was nearly a minute later. "Yes, I'll bring her. We'll make the exchange at the border."

My heart dropped into my stomach like a heavy stone. He never said my name, but his words were all the evidence I needed. Carter worked for Egor, and he was bringing me back to him like he planned.

Everything had been a lie.

Carter had never bought me for himself.

I ran away from Egor, throwing myself into the

arms of crueler men in the hope I would be able to get away. But of course, Egor tracked me down, had someone else buy me, and now I was returning to him.

How could I have been so stupid?

I panicked in front of the door, the perspiration immediately marking my brow and palms. The adrenaline was so intense it knocked the energy out of me. I felt weak in the knees, felt my fingertips go numb, and lost all sensation in my lips. I couldn't feel anything, but I could also feel overwhelming pain.

I thought Carter was a good man…but I'd been so wrong.

So fucking wrong.

He'd lied to me every single day, making up excuses for why he was keeping me. He was just babysitting me until Egor returned from one of his complicated business trips. Now he was back in the country, and he was ready to claim me.

I couldn't believe I'd slept with Carter.

I couldn't believe how fucking stupid I was.

Carter must have finished up the conversation because nothing else was said. His footsteps were audible on the other side of the door as he approached the hallway.

A part of me wanted to stand there and confront him, to scream at him for this terrible betrayal. But then I remembered my words wouldn't matter because Carter didn't give a damn about me. He'd been lying to me every single day. The time for conversation was over. I knew what I had to do.

I had to kill him.

That was the only way out of this nightmare.

I would kill him, use his thumb to unlock the security system, and then use it again to start one of his cars.

Then I would get the hell out of there—and disappear.

I sprinted down the hallway without worrying about the loud sounds I was making. I took the stairs rapidly and then made it into the kitchen. The knives were on the counter, so I grabbed the biggest one I could find, gripped the handle as tightly as possible, and then prepared to butcher my captor.

Even without a weapon, he was a serious opponent. Bigger and stronger than me, he would be able to take me down if I made the wrong move. I had to slice him across the throat or stab him in the heart. My movements had to be precise. The only comforting thought I had was my invincibility. Regardless of what I did, he wouldn't kill me.

Egor wanted me alive.

I stepped out of the kitchen and spotted him at the bottom of the staircase. With the knife gripped in my hand, I was prepared to slice that beautiful skin until he bled out and died on the elegant Turkish rug. He had been a man I was fond of, someone I even liked, but now, he was just my enemy. I should have killed him in his sleep when I had the chance.

I wouldn't make that mistake again.

He turned his gaze away from the couch, where he'd been searching for me. The instant his eyes settled on me, seeing the large knife in my hand, he knew exactly what had transpired. He saw the rage in my eyes, the intent of murder. He stared at the knife for a moment, not showing a hint of fear even though he was the one unarmed. When he lifted his gaze to meet mine, the same look of calmness was settled there. "Sweetheart, I don't want to hurt you."

I gripped the knife tighter, wanting to slice his heart out and watch the light leave his eyes. "You can't hurt me when you're dead."

He stepped closer to me, his thick arms remaining by his sides. All the muscles of his body were tense in preparation of the fight about to ensue, but his handsome features remained as stoic as ever. "Even if you cut me, it's not going to slow me down. And you're more likely to cut off your hand in the process." His brown eyes narrowed in hostility. "So just put down the knife down, sweetheart. I mean it when I say I don't want to hurt you."

"You mean it?" I asked coldly. "You expect me to believe that? You've been lying to me this entire time. I thought you were some kind of good guy, but now I know you're just Egor's bitch."

His eyes narrowed even more as both of his hands tightened into fists. "Be careful, sweetheart."

"I will," I hissed. "The only way I'm getting out of here is by killing you. And I'm not gonna stop until——"

He charged me. His lean but ripped physique came at me quicker than a bullet. His heavy feet pounded against the hardwood floor as he propelled himself with a formidable momentum.

I barely had a second to react.

I steadied the knife and sliced at him, but my blade only hit air. I pointed the blade right at his heart, ready to claim his life. I was prepared to make the ultimate sacrifice for my freedom—by taking someone's life.

I missed.

Carter moved with stealthy speed. He grabbed my wrist, slammed it hard onto his knee, and forced me to drop the blade on the floor.

"No!"

He kicked it away then shackled both of my hands behind my back with one of his. Without the same gentleness he showed me before, he shoved me against the wall and pressed his chest into my body, keeping me in anchored in place.

Just like the last time he pinned me down, I could hardly move.

I was completely at his mercy.

He breathed heavily in my ear, his massive hands so strong I couldn't even flinch. "You never had a chance, sweetheart."

"I'll make another chance." My cheek was pressed against the wall, and I felt his hard-on through his sweats. My loss fueled him in many ways. "I'm not going back to him. I will never stop trying to kill you, asshole."

He gripped the back of my neck, keeping me in place so easily. "I'm sorry you had to find out that way."

"And I'm sorry for sleeping with you. I'm sorry for thinking you were a good man. You're no better than him…"

He kept his mouth pressed to my ear. "You don't have the full story, sweetheart."

"I don't care about the full story." I tried to buck off him with my hips, to catch him off guard with my words. "I hate you, Carter. You can't send me back to that monster. You have no idea what kind of shit he does to me."

He pressed his forehead to the back of my head. A quiet sigh escaped his mouth. "Trust me, I don't like this."

"If you meant that, you would let me go."

"It's not that simple. My hands are tied."

"No," I hissed, bucking against him again. "*My* hands are tied."

His hands loosened on my wrists, and he forced me to turn around. Pressing my back against the wall with my hands pinned beside me, he looked into my face. With a clenched jaw and remorseful eyes, he didn't seem like the monster he'd just revealed himself to be. "I hate this, sweetheart. I mean that."

"No, you don't. You would let me go if you did."

He clenched his jaw. "I can't."

"You can do anything, Carter. If you really give a shit about me, do the right thing. Be a good man." A slight jolt of hope moved into my heart when I saw the sadness in his eyes. His feelings seemed sincere, as if he didn't like the situation we were in.

"I can't." This time, his voice emerged as a whisper. "If I let you go, Egor will come after my family. I can't allow that to happen. They've already been through enough."

"And you don't think I have a family?" I hissed. "Why is your life more important than mine?"

"I never said it was. But my family's life is more important to me than yours." He cocked his head to the side slightly, his eyes narrowing in pain. "I have to choose—and I have to choose them. When I bought you, I had no idea what I was getting myself into."

I listened to every word, wanting an explanation for our situation. How did Carter get mixed up with Egor in the first place?

He sighed before he continued. "My cousin and I buy trafficked women from the Underground. We've been doing it for years. Their families pay us to get them out of the situation. We pretend to be genuine buyers. Once the money is transferred, we keep them for a while to avoid suspicion, and then we return them, untouched by us, to their families."

It was so selfless and sweet, I could hardly believe what I was hearing. "What…?"

"When Egor asked me to buy you, I'd already retired from the business. My family and I decided it was too risky. But he gave me an offer I couldn't refuse, more money than anyone had ever offered me before. He told me he was your brother…and I believed him."

Fucking asshole.

"It wasn't until I had you in my captivity that I realized he was lying. He had business to attend to, so he asked me to keep you for a month before I handed you over."

It'd been almost a month since I'd arrived here. That meant I only had days left.

"Here we are now…" He sighed as he looked at me, his jaw tight. "I tried to interact with you as little as possible. I didn't want to get attached to you, especially since I've been attracted to you since the moment you jumped out of my car. You're like a lamb that's about to be slaughtered…I shouldn't make you a pet. But of course, that didn't happen. I wanted an excuse to have you, to keep it violent and nonconsensual so there would be no emotion involved… That didn't work. I wanted to be a bad guy for once, to live out a fantasy since the situation was perfect. But I couldn't go through with it…and here we are."

My hands were still pinned to the wall with his

strength. Even though I wasn't fighting him, he never relaxed his hold. He knew I would do anything to escape, and this story wouldn't change my objective.

"I'm not as evil as you think I am. I just made a mistake." He moved in closer to me, his lips close to mine. "I never would have bought you if I'd known. I should have been smarter. I should have been less greedy. I shouldn't have cared about the money, especially when I don't even need it."

Now everything made sense. He didn't strike me as an evil guy. I would know since I was always in the company of the cruelest men in the world. His love for his family suggested he had empathy and compassion, and judging by the fact that he wouldn't rape me, it indicated he had a soul under that hard chest.

"I'm sorry, Mia." He looked me in the eye as he said it. "I hate this. It makes me sick to my stomach to hand you back to him. You deserve better than that. You deserve to be free... I've always thought that."

I could feel his sincerity in his touch as well as his words. I could feel the remorse, the overwhelming sadness.

He bowed his head and stared at the ground for a moment, his fingers relaxing around my wrists. "If I could let you go, I would. But Egor is the kind of man I don't want to cross. My family is in the middle of some serious shit with the Skull Kings. My cousin almost died because of it. If I provoke Egor, I'll drag my family into another war...and we can't fight on two fronts." He lifted his gaze and looked at me again. "I'm sorry. I mean that from the bottom of my heart."

I looked into his gaze and somehow found comfort in the look. I knew he was at war with himself, wanting to protect me as well as his family. He was in a difficult situation, and no matter what he decided, he lost.

But I shouldn't feel bad for him, not when I had to worry about myself. "I believe everything you said…but you still have to let me go. I know you need to protect your family, but I have a family too. I can't go back to him. I won't go back to him."

He released my wrists, assuming I was subdued. "There's no other way, Mia."

"I will kill you, Carter." I looked him in the eye as I unleashed my threat. "I don't want to, but I will. Nothing is gonna stop me…not this time."

He gave a slight nod in understanding. "Then I'll have to chain you up until it's time—not that I want to do that. I was hoping we could enjoy each other a little longer…that you could be happy for a little longer."

"You think I'm happy?" I asked coldly.

His eyes shifted back and forth as he looked into mine.

I'd never told Carter the truth about my life because I was too afraid he would use it against me. But now that his true colors were revealed, I knew exactly who he was. "You have to let me go…because I have a son."

Carter stiffened noticeably at the revelation, his eyes stilling as they focused on me. His arms rested by his sides, but his shoulders were tight with the revelation. He took in a deep breath, like the information pained him.

"He's eight. I haven't seen him in three years, not since Egor captured me. There were times when I wanted to kill myself in Egor's captivity. The only reason why I didn't was because of my son…because I have to survive for him." My eyes watered as I remembered my darkest times, when I thought about hanging myself in my own prison cell. The temptation rose several times. Death sounded so sweet, sounded so wonderful. My little boy was the only reason I resisted. "Please help me, Carter. My son needs me. You love your mother…imagine life without her. Even as a grown man, you still need her."

He bowed his head, unable to look at me.

I grabbed his chin and forced him to look at me.

He complied, but his eyes were still full of self-loathing.

"Please," I whispered.

"Why didn't you mention this before?"

"And risk you using him against me?" I whispered. "Egor threatened to do it all the time, but he never did because I always complied with his demands."

He pushed my hand away, forcing my fingers off his chin.

"Carter, do the right thing. My son doesn't have a father. All he has is me. I don't want him to grow up and forget about me…" Tears built up in my eyes until they started to fall down my cheeks. "I want to raise my son into a man. I want to go to his soccer games. I want to be there every day, to make up for all the time I lost. I can't do that unless you help me. So please help me."

He stepped back, his hands moving to his hips. "You know I would help you if I could. But if I set you free, he'll come after me and my family. My family is innocent. I can't involve them in this."

"And my son is innocent," I said. "I'm innocent. You said you would help all those women… Now help me."

"It's not that simple."

"Doesn't matter. My only crime was being in the wrong place at the wrong time. Egor spotted me in a bar, and in that moment, he decided I was his and he would never let me go. I had no power to stop him. He put a bag over my head as soon as I walked outside, and his men threw me in the back of a van. How can you let him get away with it?"

He rubbed the back of his head. "I won't change my mind, Mia. My family is everything to me."

"So is mine…"

He dragged his hands down his chest, his movements accompanied with a sigh. "You're asking me to make a sacrifice I can't make. I'm very sorry that you're in this position. I'm sorry that your son is out there somewhere without his mother. I really wish things were different…I mean that. But you're asking for more than I can give."

I crossed my arms over my chest, knowing the knife was too far away for me to reach. "If you do this for me, I will do anything for you. I will be your maid and your fantasy. I will do whatever you ask…for the rest of my life. I would be eternally bound to you…always."

He crossed his arms over his chest, intrigued by the request.

"I will let you whip me whenever you want. I will let you do whatever you wish. I will be obedient and grateful. I will make your house spotless and put dinner on the table every night. I will be your servant for as long as you want. Just give me back my son…give me back my life."

He dropped his gaze again, remaining silent.

I took his silence as a good sign. Instead of rejecting me right away, he actually considered my request. I was giving him something he wanted, a dark fantasy he wanted to fulfill. He wanted to ruin my skin with more scars. He wanted to make me cry as he fucked me. He could have all of those things, turn me into his private whore, if he made this sacrifice for me. It was something I would gladly give…in exchange for my son.

He shook his head slightly. "It doesn't change the problem. I'll never be able to enjoy you if I'm constantly at war with Egor."

"Then figure out a way to avoid the war."

"How so?" he demanded.

"Pretend I killed myself."

"He's going to want to see proof."

"Then give him proof," I said. "Make it happen. Do something."

He sighed again, frustrated to his core. "You're simplifying everything."

"No. I'm giving you solutions."

He rubbed the back of his head. "It's still a risk I'm taking."

"If you give me back, you're still taking a risk."

He dropped his hand, his eyebrow raised. "How so?"

Carter wasn't evil the way Egor was. The second he handed me over, the guilt would eat him alive. Knowing my son would always be alone in the world would be a burden he would have to carry. He would have to live with the fact that a mother and son were permanently separated. "Because you won't be able to live with yourself."

ELEVEN

Vanessa

I was used to morning sex—even if I wasn't really awake at the time. Bones took what he wanted when he felt like it, pretty much the same way I did. He didn't explain his behavior or make apologies for it either. He just went for it.

Now it was part of our daily routine.

But that morning, it didn't come.

When I opened my eyes, it was almost eight. Bones usually woke me up the first time at seven in the morning. He moved between my legs, got off, and then headed to the gym. I assumed there was something wrong because our routine never changed.

I sat up and looked around the room, not seeing anything unusual. I pulled on his t-shirt and walked into the living room, expecting to see him at the dining table with his morning coffee. He was usually shirtless, his ink vibrant against his fair skin.

Instead, I saw him sitting on the couch, fully clothed in black jeans and a t-shirt. His bag was on the floor beside the coffee table. His elbows rested on his knees, and his chin was tilted toward the floor, his eyes downcast instead of on the TV or me.

I knew what that meant.

I knew he had two more missions to do. This was the first one.

I'd convinced myself I could do this. It was just two more, and it would be over for good. Bones was a strong man who was capable of anything. He would come back to me. He was powerful, fast, and experienced, and there was nothing he couldn't handle. There was nothing that would stop him from coming back to me.

But no matter how many times I whispered those assurances to myself, it didn't change anything.

It didn't heal my broken heart.

I stared at his black bag on the floor then took a deep breath, doing my best to be calm about the situation. Getting emotional wouldn't change anything. It would just make it harder for both of us. I knew he waited until the last possible moment to limit my suffering.

But now, I would suffer every single moment he was gone.

Bones sighed before he rose to his feet. "Baby…"

I crossed my arms over my chest and refused to look at him.

He faced me, the couch between us. "Only two more."

All it took was one bad mission to take him away from me. All it took was one stray bullet. I'd lost him once, and now that my life was complete, I couldn't bear that pain again. I'd finally found the man I wanted to spend my life with, to sleep with every night, and I wanted to hold on to that so tightly that it never slipped through my fingers.

When I turned my gaze back on him, I saw the structured way he held himself, his muscular arms hanging by his sides and stretching the sleeves of his t-shirt. He watched me with his hard gaze, waiting for me to say something about the horrible situation we were in.

But I didn't have anything to say. It was just too horrible to address.

He sighed when I remained silent. "I'll be gone three days. Short trip."

"For you…" I turned away again, not wanting to look at him.

"It'll be over before you know it."

"Again, for you…"

He moved around the couch and approached me, his footsteps heavy in his boots. "Baby, you're stronger than this."

"Stronger than this?" My neck nearly snapped when I turned my head. "You think I'm weak for not wanting you to go? You think I'm weak because I want my man to stay here with me, to live the quiet life he promised me? You think I'm weak because I don't want to sleep alone? Griffin, I'm stronger when you're here. I'm braver when you're here. Because I know I can do anything as long as you're beside me. If that makes me weak…then, fine. Guess I'm weak."

He bowed his head slightly, visibly regretting his words.

"I don't understand why you have to go. There are three other men who want to be part of this. They'll have to manage without you then, so why can't they manage without you now?" Maybe I was being selfish, but I didn't want to live without Bones ever again. I'd already paid my dues with my suffering.

"Because." He lifted his head, his intense gaze staring into mine. "They had my back when I saved your family. They didn't have to do that. They weren't obligated. They didn't even want to until I asked. These guys are family to me. I owe them everything. I'm not turning my back on them—not even for you."

I was suddenly overwhelmed with embarrassment, feeling selfish for making my demands. Bones did some-thing unforgettable for my family. I forgot that his men made the same sacrifice.

"Just as you didn't turn your back on your family when it came to me. We both have loyalties to other people—loyalties that we both respect."

I tightened my arms across my chest. "I hate this." I closed my eyes for a brief moment, and that's when the tears started. "I can't lose you, okay? I don't want to feel that agony again. I'm so damn happy, and I never want to not be happy again."

"I'm happy too, baby. This is the only time I've ever been happy—when I found you."

My eyes softened, just the way they always did when he said something like that.

"Two more times." His massive shoulders tensed with the words. "That's it."

Getting upset wouldn't change what was about to happen. I had to tuck my chin and prepare for the hit. A part of me wished someone would put me in a coma until he came back, just so I wouldn't have to suffer the stress.

"Then I'll never leave again."

"Okay…"

He crossed the distance between us and moved his palms up my cheeks until his fingertips reached my hair. He tilted my chin up, forcing me to look at him. Instead of kissing me, he gazed into my eyes with the love that thudded deep in his look. His thumb brushed across my bottom lip, and he sighed as he looked down at me. "Where are you going to stay?"

"I don't know…probably here. I stayed here alone when you were gone."

His eyes shone with a hint of approval. "You'll be safe here. Max will around if you need anything."

"Alright."

He bent his neck down and gave me a soft kiss on the lips. "I need to make love to you before I go."

"I didn't get morning sex today…"

He scooped me up in his powerful arms and cradled me against his chest. "You'll get it now."

AFTER BONES WAS GONE, I went back to bed to cry into the sheets. The bed smelled like him, so it was easier to pretend he was still there. My imagination ran wild, and I thought about things I didn't want to think about…like him being shot between the eyes.

I lay there for a few hours, forgetting about work and the life waiting for me outside the front door. If I stayed in bed until he returned, time would only move more slowly. I was making myself suffer needlessly instead of breathing fresh air and being productive. I reminded myself he only had two missions left. Once they were completed, I would never have to feel this anguish again. We could live a peaceful life, the one we promised to each other. We would find a house close to my parents, get married, and raise a family.

I finally had the courage to go down to the gallery and get some work done. I wasn't in the mood to paint, so I sat behind the counter and waited for customers to walk inside. Sometimes I would get foot traffic, but most of the time, I was addressing emails from current clients. They contacted me when they wanted to decorate their second home or redo their living room. They already had a few of my paintings, and once they became fans, they preferred to contact me when they wanted something new. Most of the time, tourists only came inside to see Italian craftsmanship. That was fine with me because it was always nice to meet new people and ask how they felt about Florence.

In the late afternoon, my father walked inside.

I wasn't the least bit surprised. I'd assumed he would show his face after Bones left. I was sure he knew everything about it and wanted to check up on me. I left the chair behind the desk and came around to greet him. "I'm fine." I blurted out the phrase without bothering with a hello.

He stopped in front of me, a foot taller than me with dark Tuscan skin. He wore the same affection in his eyes, just as he wore his heart on his sleeve. His entire life was devoted to me and Conway; he was a lot more than just a parent. His intelligent eyes scanned mine, seeing the despair written all over my face. "It's okay if you're not fine, *tesoro*. I know this is difficult for you."

I shrugged it off, trying to be strong like Bones asked me to be. "Just trying to keep busy…"

He glanced around the gallery, seeing that it was completely empty. "How's that going?"

"It's been a pretty slow day…too hot."

He examined the new paintings I had on display, pausing in front of each one to take it in. My father wasn't an artistic person, but his natural curiosity for everything I did made him seem like an art collector. "This one is my favorite in the batch." He pointed to an image of a sunset, one Bones and I had seen about a week ago.

"Thanks."

He walked back to me, his hands sliding into his pockets. "I always want to buy your paintings, but then I realize I would be hogging all of your work…and you wouldn't have any other clients."

I knew he was being sincere. "True."

"You want to get some coffee? Have lunch?"

"Father, you don't need to check on me every time he's gone." I appreciated the concern, but I was a grown woman. Bones fell in love with me because I was tough and fearless. When he wasn't around, I had to be that same person. I didn't need a man before he came along. I shouldn't need one when he was gone.

"*Tesoro*, you know I'll always check on you. Even when you're forty and I'm almost eighty, I'll still be here…checking on you."

I smiled. "When you're almost eighty, I should be the one checking on you."

He grinned back. "That's what your mother is for."

"I'm sure she has better things to do."

He chuckled. "Yes, she does. So, are you going to stay here until Griffin returns? You know you're welcome at our place."

I'd stayed at that apartment when Bones was gone.

It didn't make sense for me to leave now. "I'm fine here. It's a nice place. Quiet."

My father didn't try to convince me otherwise. "The offer always stands if you change your mind."

"I know."

"So, how about lunch?" he asked. "Since I'm here, we may as well spend some time together."

"Sure."

Father and I went to the café down the road, a place with great coffee and deli sandwiches. We both got the same thing along with two coffees. It was the same place Antonio liked to go to, but I didn't care if I saw him. I was too upset about Bones's absence to care about anything else.

Father scanned the café and the events occurring outside the window, always on alert for anything that might happen. It was a hot day in Florence, with scorching temperatures and insane humidity. When October arrived, it would start to cool off again. "I've been trying with Griffin, but it doesn't seem to be getting better." He looked out the window as he spoke, his sadness obvious in the tone of his voice.

"I know…he's very stubborn."

"Your mother told me he forgave her…because she reminds him of his mother."

Griffin never told me that, and I couldn't stop my eyes from softening. "That doesn't surprise me. She's a pretty great mom."

"But with me, I'll always be the man who came

between you. I'll always be the reason you almost ended up with that other young man." He drank from his coffee, his black wedding ring contrasting against the whiteness of the cup. "I can't change the past, so I'm not sure what I can do at this point. I guess we'll just have to deal with it." He kept his look indifferent even though the pain was deep inside him.

"There's still hope. He'll come around."

"What makes you say that?" He lifted his gaze and looked at me again, his hand gripping the handle of the coffee cup.

"He's a very stubborn man. He was even more stubborn when we met. But when love looked him in the face, he softened. He softened more and more…until there was no hatred left. He was committed to killing our family for his revenge, and nothing was going to deter him from that. But after enough time had passed, he dropped his pain and turned into a new man. The same thing is happening now. Each time you talk to him, you make a dent in his armor. It gets bigger and bigger every single time. Eventually, you'll break through it. Trust me."

He held my gaze without blinking, and after several seconds, he gave a nod. "Then I'll keep trying."

"I know you will. I told him you cared about him."

"I hope he believed you…because I do. I used to hate him so much, but now I admire him. When I asked him to help with the Skull Kings, he immediately agreed. He's committed to doing right by you, protecting the family he vowed to execute. His love for you has turned him into someone different, but not someone weaker. I wish I'd seen it sooner…things would be so much different if I had."

I hated seeing my father in regret since it was something he rarely did. He stood by his decisions and didn't think twice about them. But now he would give anything to erase the past, to accept the man I loved far sooner. "Our separation only solidified our love. It only brought us closer together. In time, he will forgive you. I know he will—and not just for me."

"I hope you're right, *tesoro*. It gives me hope that he's forgiven your mother."

"She's the one who killed his father, so that speaks volumes. You'll be next."

"Hopefully." He drank his coffee then looked out the window again. "Three days, huh?"

"Two and a half," I said with a sigh. I'd been counting down the hours since he left. I spent most of my days down at the gallery, so we weren't always together, but knowing he was in danger every single second until he returned is what killed me. It made every hour feel like a lifetime.

My father gave me a slight smile. "He'll come back. He's the strongest man I've ever met. It would take an entire army to take him down."

"I hope he never crosses paths with any army…"

"He'll be fine. Only two left, and it'll be over."

I had to focus on that, to remember that this would

be over for good eventually. "You asked for his help with the Skull Kings. What does that mean?"

My father sighed before he explained the plan to me. "Griffin has a pretty solid relationship with them. My goal is to pay them off, basically. End the war before it can escalate. Conway is about to be a father, and Griffin is getting out of that life of crime. I want to settle our debts so we can never think about it again."

"And you're going with him?" I asked, slightly afraid.

He nodded. "But it'll be alright, *tesoro*. I've been in worse situations."

"When is this happening?"

"Once he gets back."

So Bones would return to me but then take off on another mission. This nightmare would never end.

My father gave me a look of pity. "I wouldn't have asked him if I had any other choice. He was eager to get on board because he wants to make sure this is done right. He wants all the Barsettis to have peace…since you're a Barsetti."

"Now I understand the need for a simple life…what you've been talking about all these years." I wanted to leave my front door open without fear of who might walk inside. I didn't want to look over my shoulder and expect to see someone following me. I wanted my family to live freely under the sun, unafraid of the past.

My father gave a slight nod. "And we'll get it, *tesoro*. I promise."

TWELVE

Bones
_____

I set it up to look like an accident.

An overdose on opioids put him in cardiac arrest.

But in reality, I slipped something into his drink and put the pills where they belonged. He collapsed on the floor of his office, foam pouring out of his mouth and his heart giving out on him.

I watched the whole thing—to make sure it was done right.

Then I slipped out and headed to the airport. Egypt was warm this time of year. I headed through the poverty-stricken streets until I found my bike in the alleyway. I kicked it into gear and sped to the airport at the edge of the city, just fifty miles away from the iconic pyramids.

Max spoke in my ear. "Everything went according to plan?"

"Yeah."

"No witnesses?"

"They won't even notice he's dead for a few hours."
His guards remained outside the dining room and
surrounded the entire block, but they hadn't noticed me
slip inside from the roof.

"Good."

"Tell Vanessa I'm getting on my flight." I pulled up
to the terminal and left my bike in the parking lot.

"Sure thing."

"How has she been?"

"Spending time with her father. He's come to
Florence every day to hang out in her gallery."

It wasn't clear if he was doing that just to spend
time with his daughter or give me peace of mind that
she was safe. Maybe it was both. He'd been trying to
earn my forgiveness, and the best way to do that was
through Vanessa. I liked knowing she wasn't alone, that
she was distracted instead of counting down the hours
until I returned. "Good to know."

"I'll let her know you're on your way back."

"Thanks."

"You're one of the best in the group. I'll miss
working with you." Max never hid his displeasure at my
decision. We'd decided it would be the four of us until
we were too old to do this anymore. It wasn't difficult to
find someone who could kill people for money, but it
was nearly impossible to find someone who could be
trusted. It would be impossible to replace me. Instead of

finding a fourth man, they would manage with three instead.

Words escaped me, and I didn't know what to say. A part of me wanted to keep working with Max, but I knew that wasn't possible anymore. Shane stayed in the business, and as a result, Cynthia wouldn't live nearly as long because of the stress. Vanessa wanted to raise a family with me. I couldn't do that if I was gone all the time. Once she became my wife, she would be the center of my universe—even more than she was now. My place was beside her, keeping her safe day and night.

Not killing men for money.

I finally responded to his words. "I'm going to miss it too, Max. But we both know it's time for me to move on."

He didn't say anything for a long time, like he'd turned off his mic. But then his voice came through. "Yeah, I know. Doesn't make it easier for me to accept."

MY PLANE LANDED in the middle of the night, and I arrived at the apartment past three. But the late hour didn't fool me. I knew what would be waiting for me the second I walked in the door.

I stepped inside and set my bag on the hardwood floor next to the door. In the darkness, she moved toward me. Dressed in nothing but my t-shirt, she moved into my chest and wrapped her arms around my neck. "Thank God you're home."

God had nothing to do with it. I walked through that door because nothing was going to stop me from coming back to her. I scooped her into my arms so we could be at eye level with each other. Her soft hair formed a curtain across half of her face, the strands grazing against my neck with their gentle touch. My large hands felt her ass cheeks, the soft pieces of muscle I loved to spank. "I promised I would come back, baby. You know I keep my promises." I kicked the door shut behind me and didn't worry about locking it. With me in the house, there was nothing that could bother either one of us.

"I missed you…"

"I know, baby." I carried her down the hallway and into our bedroom, feeling my woman shake in my arms. She'd counted down the hours until I returned, stayed up late at night because she couldn't stop worrying about me. She didn't need a man to be happy, but I was an exception. She needed me for everything, from protection to love. She allowed me to take care of her because I was the only man qualified for the job. "I'm here now." I dropped her onto the bed then moved to pull her panties down her legs.

But she wasn't wearing any.

She undid my jeans and pushed them down with my boxers, getting them over my ass but not any farther. She didn't remove her t-shirt but pulled it up around her waist so I could move between her legs. She grabbed my hips and yanked on me hard, pulling my length inside her.

She gasped when she felt me, like she somehow forgot how I felt.

I held myself on top of her, my jeans below my ass and my shirt pulled up to my waist. We were both still partially clothed, but undressing seemed to be too much effort. I held her gaze as my cock felt her, was welcomed by the overwhelming wetness between her legs. She was ready for me long before I walked in the front door. Without telling me how she felt about me, she showed me she loved me every day. With tears in her eyes and desperation in her fingertips, she acted like it'd been three months since she'd seen me last, like this was the first time she was getting me back. Our love was so intense, it was almost too much for me to handle. But she was the kind of woman who could handle anything —even me.

Her hand slid up the back of my neck and into my hair as her legs wrapped around my waist, securing me inside her. "Griffin." She spoke into my mouth, begging me to never leave her again. Her lips touched mine, but she didn't kiss me. "I can't do it again…"

I settled between her legs then started to move, surrounded by the slick arousal that coated my dick. "Yes, you can. I know you can."

"No." She held onto my shoulder and moved with me, her hips shifting as she took my length over and over. "I missed you so much…I couldn't sleep. I worried the whole time."

"I know, baby. I could feel it." I could feel her turmoil even when we were thousands of miles apart. I brushed my lips across hers before I finally kissed her. "But we can do it one more time. One more time and it'll be over."

"Two more times…" She stopped moving and looked me in the eye. "I know you're going to talk with the Skull Kings."

Her father had obviously told her. I'd been waiting, wanting to tell her the truth at the last minute. "We'll get through that too."

She growled in my face, a weak sound because she couldn't mask the pleasure between her legs. "You better marry me when all of this is over. Because that's what I want…to live in a nice house in the middle of nowhere…just us and our family." Her fingers grazed my hair, lightly fisting it as she took my big dick with ease.

I stopped thrusting so I could look down at her, seeing her beautiful hair cascade around her. With bright eyes and a seductive part to her mouth, she was the sexiest thing I'd ever seen. She hid her thoughts from the rest of the world, but with me, she wore her heart on her sleeve. She didn't just want me, she demanded me. She wasn't afraid to tell me what she wanted, unashamed to love me with all of her heart. "You bet your ass, I will."

IT WAS good to be home, even though I would be leaving again in a short while. My woman was there with me, taking my dick first thing in the morning before she was even truly awake. I moved around the kitchen and made breakfast and coffee before I sat down at the dining table.

I hadn't been inside the apartment for that long, but it felt like home to me. Decorated with Vanessa's artwork and the furniture that was picked out for her, it was her haven. It absorbed her spirit, made her love heavy in the fabric of the couches and carpet. Even when she wasn't in the room, I could feel her presence everywhere.

Crow's name popped up on my phone.

It was the first time I wasn't annoyed to see his name, knowing this was just business. I answered without saying a word, unsure how to greet this man.

He wasn't affected by my poor manners. "How did your mission go?"

"Fine. Killed the guy and left." My line of work wasn't as exciting as people thought. I did my job then went home. There was no emotion attached to it. When my head hit the pillow, I went to sleep immediately.

"I'm sure Vanessa is happy you're home."

But she was miserable I had to leave again. "She is."

Once the pleasantries were out of the way, he got to

the heart of the matter. "Are we still doing this tonight? You need more time?"

I wanted this over and done with soon as possible. I had no idea what the Skull Kings were planning. Once the threat was neutralized, it was one less thing I had to worry about. The Barsettis always seemed to get themselves into trouble. Carter and Conway got mixed up in this bullshit, and Vanessa walked home alone and ran into me. Must be a family trait. "I'm ready."

"My daughter can spare you for the night?"

Despite the tears she shed when I left, she was a tough woman who could handle anything. "She'll be fine. I'll meet at your place in a few hours."

"Will you tell the Skull Kings you're coming?"

"No. Dates aren't really their style."

"You'll catch them off guard."

I chuckled. "They're never caught off guard." I finished up the conversation with him just as Vanessa walked into the room. In my t-shirt and with messy hair, she was the queen of my castle. She was also the prisoner in my four walls. She constantly hovered between both, balancing between royalty and servitude. Even if she wanted to leave me, she couldn't. Her commitment was the price she paid for her father's life.

Her hand snaked over my bare shoulders as she looked down at me, a sleepy look in her eyes. "How'd you sleep?"

"Never better." The bed we shared was too small, but I'd never been more comfortable. My hand moved up under her shirt to the soft skin of her belly. She'd put on some weight since I'd returned, but I liked seeing the extra inches around her middle. I preferred a healthy woman over a depressed one.

"Me too." She smiled down at me. "I hadn't slept in days."

Pain pulled at my heartstrings, the guilt killing me inside. What kind of man hurt his woman like that? What kind of man made his woman sleep alone? I didn't like who I was when I was still in this line of business.

She caught the sadness in my eyes. "You're leaving tonight, aren't you?"

I didn't hide the truth from her. "In a few hours."

A heavy sigh escaped her lips. "Here we go again…"

"This won't be nearly as dangerous as the other stuff I do."

She cocked her head to the side. "Is that supposed to make me feel better?"

I'd shoved my foot in my mouth. "It'll be fine, baby. I promise you."

"Don't make promises you can't keep."

I grabbed her hip and dragged her into my lap, placing her across my thighs. "I keep all my promises, baby. I promise you, your father and I will be fine. And I'll be fine on my last mission too."

She rested her forehead against mine. "It doesn't matter what you say or do. I'll never feel peace until it's all over. I'll never relax or truly be happy until you walk in that door for the last time, until I sleep alone for the last time."

No one had ever made me feel as low as Vanessa. Her love for me raised me up, but it also crippled me at the same time. When she needed me, it gave me a greater purpose in life. Leaving her side for a job seemed ridiculous. I had more money than I would ever need, more money than she would ever need. I certainly didn't need more of it. I just needed more of her. "It'll happen soon enough."

I'D JUST SAID goodbye to Vanessa a few days ago, and now I was doing it again. We stood in front of the door, my bag over my shoulder. It was packed with my rifle, shotgun, and pistol, along with ammunition. It was black leather, sleek and smooth. Anytime Vanessa saw that bag, she knew what was inside it. And she knew that meant one thing.

She couldn't keep the pain out of her eyes. "Call me the instant it's over."

"I will."

She stood in front of me without touching me, unable to keep the misery out of her expression. Vanessa had hardly shown her emotions to me when we first got to know each other, but now she wore them out in the open. She tried to hide them now, to the best of her ability. "I hate the way you make me feel. I've turned into one of those women who worries all the time…who stay up all night waiting for the front door to open."

"You mean, you hate that I made you fall head over heels for me."

She shook her head. "Now isn't the time for your arrogance."

"I'm always arrogant. And I love seeing you this way…even though it makes me an asshole."

"You love seeing me miserable?" she whispered.

"No. I love seeing the way you love me, the way you can't live without me. When I told you I loved you, you tried to run away. But now you're so hung up on me that it's hard to believe I said I love you first."

She shook her head again. "Arrogant."

"No. Just proud. Proud that I earned the love of such a woman." I cupped her face and leaned down to kiss her, to feel the emotion in her lips as she embraced mine. I didn't want her to cry, not after I'd seen her shed so many tears for me. My fingers touched her hair, and I felt her petite frame against me. It was nearly impossible to leave this place, to leave the home I made with this extraordinary woman. My heart would always remain behind, even if my body took me somewhere else.

"Please be careful," she whispered against my mouth.

I kept my eyes closed, not wanting to see the sorrow

etched into her features. "Always." I turned away before I could look at her again, not wanting to see the heartbreak I caused. When I was gone, she would let her tears fall, but I didn't want to see upcoming heartbreak. I hadn't even been home for a day before I had to walk out on her again.

I made it to my truck and pulled onto the road, doing my best to focus on the next task at hand. My emotions had to be left behind so I could remain pragmatic for the evening. As far as I was concerned, Vanessa didn't exist. I had to be calm, cruel, and sinister. I had to behave like I had no one to live for but myself.

But when everything was said and done, I had to marry her.

Officially make my woman mine.

WHEN I ARRIVED at the Barsetti home, they were gathered outside. Crow was dressed in all black, his dark hair matching the color. Pearl was in high-rise jeans and a white blouse. With her hair pulled back, she looked elegant, the opposite of her husband. Cane and his wife were there too. Cane had a gun in his holster and a shotgun across his back, even though he wouldn't be participating in the meeting.

I left my truck parked in the gravel and joined them. Lately, I'd been spending more time with the Barsetti clan than Vanessa. I talked to her father as much as I talked to her.

It was becoming a pain in my ass.

Pearl smiled when she laid eyes on me, and when she walked up to me, she didn't just greet me with a hug, but a kiss on the cheek—the way she greeted her son. "How are you, honey?"

Honey. That was the first time someone had called me that. "Good, Mrs. Barsetti. How are you?"

She squeezed my arm and smiled. "You can call me Pearl, Griffin."

"I prefer Mrs. Barsetti." It was a sign of respect that she'd earned.

She smiled but didn't press me on it. "I'm sorry you had to leave Vanessa again."

I didn't want to think about what she was doing at that moment. Probably lying in bed next to the phone. "When all of this is over, I'll never leave her again."

She gave a nod. "I know."

Crow came up to me next. "Griffin. Thanks for coming." He shook my hand.

I followed the movements, my heart not truly invested. "Let's bury this once and for all."

Cane came next. "I really think Conway and I should back you up, somewhere outside the city. If we're five hours away—"

"No." Crow had made up his mind, and he wouldn't change it. "If something goes wrong, you need a head start. There will be time for you to evacuate everyone. If you don't get the call from me…assume the worst."

Pearl held her gaze steady, but her eyes started to water in terror.

Cane's face remained stoic, probably because he'd been in these situations so many times. The possibility of death didn't unnerve him anymore. "Alright."

"Nothing is going to go wrong," I said. "It'll be tense, even difficult, but nothing will go wrong, not when you're walking in there with me."

Crow turned to me. "Arrogance turns your strength into weakness."

I held his gaze, unaffected by the insult. "A man without confidence becomes a human target."

Crow didn't back down.

"The Barsettis may have a respectable name, but I'm a respectable man. I'm not the kind of person you want to cross. I have connections everywhere from being in the game for so long. The Skull Kings need me. It will be in their best interest to establish peace, at least when it comes to me." I turned back to my truck, dismissing the conversation. I wanted to get this over with. The sooner we got there, the sooner we could leave. The sooner this would be over and I could make that call to Vanessa to tell her we were both okay. I lived for that moment, looked forward to that moment with everything I had.

Crow said goodbye to his family, holding his wife the longest. It was one of the only times I saw him be affectionate with her, at least in front of me. He cupped her cheeks with both hands and rested his forehead against hers. They didn't seem to say anything to one another, just holding each other.

I turned away, feeling like I was infringing on their privacy.

When they were finished, Pearl walked up to me. With tears in her eyes from saying goodbye to her husband, she hugged me next. "I need you to come back too, Griffin. Not just for my daughter's sake…but for mine." She squeezed me around the waist before she let me go.

The maternal love wrapped around me, made me think of my own mother, the woman whose face I could hardly remember. I never needed anyone until I met Vanessa, but now I felt a strange connection to the woman who killed my father. Vanessa filled the hole in my chest, but Pearl kept my mother's spirit alive. "I will." I pulled my arms away from her, uncomfortable touching her when Crow was standing right there.

We got into the truck and pulled onto the road. I was behind the steering wheel, and Crow was in the passenger seat. I'd screwed Vanessa in this truck a couple times, so it was strange to have her father sit there, but I pushed the thoughts from my mind so it wouldn't be awkward.

It would be a long drive, and I wasn't looking forward to spending so many hours with this man. I still resented him for what he did to me. I still hated him for the pain he caused. It was strange to respect his wife so much but have so little for him.

Crow didn't say anything, and I hoped the tense silence would continue. I preferred the quiet over forced conversation.

The first hour was spent driving through the countryside without sharing a single word. We left Tuscany and headed north, taking the shortest path to Milan instead of the most scenic route. He spoke. "If you had it your way, we wouldn't say anything the entire time?"

I kept one hand on the wheel while my other arm rested on the windowsill. "Yep."

He shook his head slightly and kept looking out the window. "I'm not much of a talker either, but that sounds boring."

"I like boring."

He sighed from his side of the truck. "Fine. We'll do it your way." He rested his elbow against his windowsill and propped his head up, enjoying the scenic views in silence. He didn't try to talk to me again, allowing the silence to become the loudest sound in the truck.

It was exactly what I wanted, for it to be so quiet that I could pretend he wasn't there at all.

Twenty minutes later, his phone rang. He dug it out of his pocket and looked at the screen. Once he saw the name, he immediately took the call. With the phone pressed to his ear and his gaze focused out the window, he addressed the person on the phone. "*Tesoro*."

My body stiffened slightly when I realized Vanessa

was on the other line. I kept my eyes on the road and my hand on the wheel, but my mind became distracted, focused on the conversation they were having.

"Hey, Father." Her words were audible through the phone, her beautiful voice filling the truck. There was anguish in her tone, tears in her voice. "Are you busy right now?"

"No. Griffin and I are in the truck. It'll be a few hours before we get there." He had a distinctly different tone when he spoke to his daughter. Affection mixed with protectiveness, he addressed his daughter like an adult. But there was always an undertone of childlike gentleness, something he didn't use with Conway. Crow balanced between the two different approaches, treating her like a young princess and a grown adult at the same time.

When she spoke again, her voice was brimming with emotion. Like rising water about the burst from a dam, she was barely holding on. "Please be careful…"

He swallowed the lump in his throat and struggled to keep his composure even though she couldn't see his face. But he kept his voice stoic, a mask of strength that was forced. "I'll be fine, *tesoro*. Don't worry about me."

"I need both of you to come back, okay? I can't live without either of you."

The fields passed me on the left, but I wasn't paying attention to the open road or the setting sun. The sky was starting to blend with the colors of pink, purple, and blue, but I didn't care about the beauty of the land right in front of me. All I could do was focus on the pain in my woman's voice, the heartache she couldn't contain anymore.

"We will," Crow said, keeping a strong front for his daughter. He refused to show any kind of vulnerability, giving her the reassurance she needed to hear. "Griffin and I are both experts. You have absolutely nothing to worry about."

"Okay, I hope so."

Crow lingered on the phone even though there was nothing else to say.

"I love you so much. You're my best friend…"

I gripped the steering wheel a little tighter, feeling my heart ache for the words she was saying. I wished I could do this on my own and keep her father out of it to give her peace of mind.

"I love you too, *tesoro*. And you're my best friend as well."

I didn't expect to witness such a heartfelt conversation. It made me uncomfortable because their connection was so deep. Now it didn't surprise me that Crow did everything he could to keep me away from her. And it didn't surprise me that Vanessa worked so hard to get his approval, and when that approval didn't come, she couldn't stay with me.

"Please come back," she said. "Both of you."

"We will." Crow took a deep breath as his eyes remained focused out the window. "I should get go. I'll talk to you soon."

"Okay...talk soon."

He hung up and dropped the phone on his thigh. He purposely turned his head away and focused his gaze out the window so most of his reaction wasn't visible. He never showed an expression besides annoyance or anger, at least that I'd seen. But when Vanessa was around, it was a different story. She stripped away his hardness and made him softer than a cloud. He purposely hid his face from me, and if he could, he would have walked away to have this moment to himself.

But since we were stuck together, there was nowhere for him to go.

WE ARRIVED in Milan and left the truck at the curb outside the Underground. Hours had passed, and it was deep into the night. At midnight on a Monday, there was no one out. People had retired to bed long ago.

We sat side by side.

Crow turned to me, most of his face hidden in shadow. "Let's do this."

"Alright. I'll go in first. If I don't come back, leave without me."

"You really think that's a possibility?"

I faced forward again. "It's unlikely, but I like to prepare for the worst."

"Armed or unarmed?"

"Unarmed." I opened my door. "I'm gonna offer the cash Conway profited from their operation. Bring your laptop to make the transfer."

"Alright."

I stood in the street with the door open. "I told your wife I wouldn't let anything happen to you." I wouldn't protect him just for Vanessa's sake. I saw the way Pearl looked at her husband, the way she always defended him. There was nothing but love between them—and undying loyalty. "I'm a man of my word, Crow." I shut the door before he had the chance to say anything.

I walked to the back entrance and entered the Underground. I was stopped by the guards for a quick pat-down before I stepped inside. The auction wasn't starting for a few hours, so I was early—and there was hardly anyone there.

I headed to the bar, watched the blonde behind the counter smile at me, and I ordered a drink.

A few minutes later, Tony appeared. Dressed in black and gray, he was a man ten years older than me, with his nose pierced and tattoos up and down both of his arms. He leaned against the counter and fist-bumped me. "It's been a while since I've seen you. Got a big hit list?"

"Very."

He chuckled then ordered a drink. "Life is more fun when business is good." He downed his drink in one gulp. "And there's blood on your hands." He patted my back then turned to the rest of the room where the empty tables sat. "Why are you here so early? Heard that we have fresh meat tonight?"

"Not exactly." I drank my glass in one gulp, matching his thirst. "I have business to discuss with you and Rush."

"Business, huh?" he asked. "We're usually the ones coming to you, not the other way around."

"I think you'll be interested in what I have to say."

He grinned, like this was all a joke. "You are an interesting man…" He drifted away and spoke to one of his men. They exchanged a few words before the guy disappeared down one of the hallways. He came back to me, the tattoo on his neck more visible when he turned the other way. It was an image of a naked woman in chains, her wrists and ankles bound together. "Rush is finishing up. Be here in a second."

I leaned my back against the bar and kept up my indifference even though my heart was pounding more than usual. Normally, I didn't have anything important on the line. Before Vanessa, even my own life didn't matter. But now, I had to make sure everything went well, that Crow made it back to his family. "Business has been good for you?"

"It's always good. And it has extra perks…like playing with the goods." He winked.

I'd paid for sex a lot in my life, but I'd never paid for a slave. A woman submitting of her own will was far sexier than forcing her to. Vanessa wanted me constantly, used me for sex all the time. Seeing the way she needed me was the biggest turn-on in the world. Sometimes I wanted to tie her up, but watching her bounce freely on my dick was the sexiest thing of all.

Rush joined us a moment later and greeted me with an embrace. "It's been a while, Bones. My bar sales have gone down."

I gave a sly grin. "Looks like that's about to change."

"Good. My bartender missed you too." Rush was the leader of the Skull Kings at the Underground. Of course, he had a man above him. And that man had someone above him in a different place. The Skull Kings were a widespread group with many different connections. It was why they were so formidable. "So, I hear you have a business proposition for me."

"I do." I ordered another drink, getting rounds for all of us first.

Rush grinned before he took a drink of his scotch. "Always the gentleman."

I leaned against the counter again and looked him straight in the eye, showing the same fearlessness I was known for. "I know you've got beef with the Barsettis. You tried to take them out, and it went to shit."

Rush's endearing smile immediately faded away, the scar underneath his eye becoming more noticeable. When he frowned, he seemed innately hostile. "We originally called you for the job, but you turned it down."

"Had other obligations." They had no idea I was

the one who killed most of their men—since there were no survivors to tell the tale. "The Barsettis are pretty formidable. Have a lot of contacts in a lot of places. Their allegiances are unknown, and that's what makes them unpredictable."

"What's your point?" Rush asked, flustered by the compliments I showered his enemy with.

"I've done work with Crow Barsetti in the past. Pretty ruthless guy. He was informed of the attack on his son's life and the bloody massacre that followed. The streets outside the opera house are still stained with blood."

Rush's eyes shifted back and forth as he stared at me. Tony did the same.

Having their full attention, I continued. "Crow's got a business deal going down soon. Doesn't need any distractions. Contacted me to intervene in the situation. He has a peace offering for you, if you're willing to hear it."

"A peace offering?" Rush asked coldly.

"His piece of shit son undermined our operation," Tony spat. "You think there will be peace when some asshole crosses us?"

"If it's convenient for both of you," I said. "And I think it is."

"We don't give a shit about convenience." Rush's voice lowered, turning sinister. "That asshole under-mined us, took a cut of our profits that belong to us exclusively. He may have wiped out our team, but that doesn't mean the war is over. It just means they won the battle."

This was worse than I thought. The Skull Kings had a serious vendetta against the Barsettis, because of Conway's and Carter's stupidity. It was fortunate they hadn't struck again in the last few weeks. "What if I told you Crow Barsetti wants to make an offer?"

Rush raised an eyebrow. "What kind of offer?"

"To pay back the money Conway profited. Plus interest."

When Rush didn't shoot down the offer right away, I knew there was hope. Tony listened to every word too, not detesting the offer put on the table.

I continued. "It's money you didn't have to work for. He'd transfer it into your account right now. In exchange, he wants this issue to vanish. He has a big business venture he's planning overseas, and he doesn't have time to address this at the same time. But if you don't agree, he will switch his focus to the Skull Kings." I couldn't tell them the truth, that the Barsettis just wanted to disappear. If I made them seem weak, the Skull Kings would try to take advantage of their exhaustion. The Barsettis had to maintain the front of strength, that they could keep fighting forever.

Rush finally turned to Tony, their eyes having a private conversation.

It was good news they didn't say no right away. "Obviously, Conway Barsetti would never come near the Underground again. None of the Barsettis would.

You're both worthy opponents. If the war keeps going, you'll both lose men and resources over the next decade, but neither one of you will be the victor. Take the deal."

"Why did he bring you into this?" Rush demanded.

"Because I'm an objective third-party negotiator," I said simply. "You trust me. He trusts me."

Rush pulled Tony to the side, and they spoke quietly for a few minutes. Neither one of them raised their voices, so that was a positive sign. After a few minutes, they returned to me.

"What have you decided, gentlemen?" I asked.

"He's outside?" Tony asked.

I nodded.

Rush snapped his fingers. "Bring him in."

"Does that mean you accept the deal?" I asked.

Rush narrowed his eyes. "I said, bring him in."

"Rush." I gave him a firm look. "Cross him, and you cross me. And we both know you don't want to do that. If you think you can take the money and kill him, that would be a mistake. Because there would be hell to pay."

"Are you threatening me?" Rush asked, stepping closer to me.

"Depends on your intentions," I said calmly. "But yeah, I'm threatening you."

It was a testament to his unpredictability, because he grinned. "Bones, I've always liked you." He clapped me on the shoulder. "Bring him in—only him."

I was convinced that Crow wasn't walking into a danger zone, not after I reminded the Skull Kings they were also declaring war on me if something sinister happened. I knew that changed their tune pretty quickly. I pulled out my phone and made the call. "They're interested in the deal. Bring your shit."

"Alright." Crow hung up as quickly as he answered.

I stood at the bar and waited, my eyes on the door.

A minute later, Crow made it past security with his satchel over his shoulder. He walked toward me, appearing tall and confident despite the antagonistic air in the room. He headed for me, his eyes on Rush and Tony. For a man who had everything on the line, he seemed oddly unaffected. I admired him for his bravery, for wearing his heart on his sleeve when he spoke to his daughter, but now for appearing as unemotional as a rock. He set the bag on the counter then turned to the three of us.

Silence.

Hostile silence.

Rush stared Crow up and down, the rage deep in his eyes.

Tony stood with his hands in his pockets, detesting Crow with the same enmity.

I didn't speak, knowing I had to let Crow take the stand on his own. It wasn't like he needed me anyway. I laid the groundwork. He could handle the rest.

"I have the account set up." He spoke with a strong voice, his back straight and his muscular shoulders rounded. "All I need is your information, and we can get this shit over with. All the funds will be transferred in less than five minutes. Then we can move on."

Rush was silent as he stared at him.

When Crow didn't get a response, he opened his bag.

"Asshole." Rush rested one arm on the counter as he stared at him.

I stood between them, ready to intervene if it came to that. I could take a bullet and survive. Crow was too old for that.

Crow turned back to Rush, his green eyes vibrant with hatred.

"Where's my apology?" Rush demanded.

Crow's eyes shifted back and forth as he looked at him, the fury no doubt simmering deep in his gut. He was too proud to apologize to a tyrant like Rush, but he had to respond in some way. He couldn't bend and look weak. But he couldn't fight either, not when that would escalate the already tense situation. "The only thing I will apologize for is the stupidity of my son. I thought I raised him to be smarter than this, not to be so greedy, not to profit off a woman's life like she's livestock. He's better than that—better than you. That's the only apology you'll get from me." He turned back to the counter and pulled out the laptop.

It was a smart thing to say, an acknowledgment but not a pussy move.

Rush was silent, which was a good thing.

Tony crossed his arms over his chest.

Crow set up everything on the laptop then slid it down the bar toward them. "Enter your account information, and I'll begin the transfer."

Rush turned to the screen and typed in everything, having memorized his banking information instead of writing it down. He finished and pushed the laptop back, his jaw tense.

Crow turned to them before he finished the deal. "We have an understanding, gentlemen? I never want to hear from you, and you'll never hear from me. If you cross me, I'll make sure your operation crumbles beneath your feet."

I had to hand it to Crow. He knew how to hustle pretty damn well.

Rush raised an eyebrow. "No one could pull that off."

Crow turned back to them. "I already have men in Hungary, Russia, and Romania, your main ports of operation. I know you funnel the women through those channels. If I pay the right money and tell the right people, your entire operation will be undermined. I'll retrieve every woman you sell, distribute all your secrets to your enemies, tell all the authorities where you auction your women. This income is easy for you to streamline, and all I'll have to do is interrupt the food chain. Yes, I can pull it off, asshole."

I tried not to grin.

It was the first time I'd ever seen Rush speechless.

Crow didn't blink. "So, do we have a deal?"

Tony glanced at Rush before he nodded. "If every cent is put in our account, then yes, we have a deal."

"Good." Crow turned back to the laptop, typed in the information, and then hit the enter button. He stared at the screen and waited for the funds to be transferred. It took almost a full minute for the transfer to go through because of the size of the funds. When it was completed, he turned back to Rush. "Check it."

Rush pulled out his phone and logged in to his account. "It's there."

Crow immediately packed up his laptop into the bag. "It's been a pleasure." Like nothing happened at all, he turned his back to Rush and Tony and walked out, leaving his back exposed as he left the Underground.

I stayed behind, wanting to make sure this was really settled. "Sounds like a fair trade."

Tony looked at Rush's phone before he met my gaze. "He paid up. That's all that matters."

"We've got more important things to do than chase him around," Rush said in agreement. "Let the Barsettis disappear. They must be scared of us if they paid us all that money."

"And you must be scared of him," I reminded them. "As you should be."

WE DIDN'T SAY a word to one another until we were outside of Milan. The light shone in the rearview mirror, and then we were on an empty road leading to the south of Italy. Crow kept up his indifferent persona, like he wasn't relieved that the tense confrontation was now behind him.

When we were far away and certain no one was following us, the conversation began.

"They won't be a problem," I said. "They're happy with what they got and ready to move on to the next thing."

"That's the impression I got too."

"And you said all the right things. Defused the situation without sounding like a pussy."

He looked out the window. "Not my first time."

"It just sucks that you're out that much cash…it was a lot."

"I don't care about the money," he said honestly. "I'm just glad this is over. I'm grateful my son can have his child without looking over his shoulder, that my wife isn't scared about our kids. And besides, Conway and Carter are paying back every single dime. I cleaned up their mess, but I won't pay for it."

I grinned. "That's fair."

It was late into the night, so Crow rested his head against the window and closed his eyes. "I know I should call my wife, but I don't want to. She'll cry…I hate listening to her cry."

"She didn't cry when you left."

"She always tears up when I tell her I'm okay," he said quietly. "She holds her breath the entire time I'm gone, and once I'm back, she releases all her pain. Instead of feeling it at the beginning, she feels it at the end. Her tears don't annoy me, they just hurt. I hate it when she hurts."

I understood that feeling all too well. I pulled out my phone and called Vanessa, my elbow resting on the windowsill. She answered before the first ring finished.

"Are you both okay?" she blurted, breathing hard like she'd been marching around the apartment with her phone clutched tightly in her hand.

"Yes. Both of us."

"Oh..." She breathed into the phone, her eyes probably closed as she stood in the middle of the living room. "Thank god. I'm so happy to hear that...you have no idea. I haven't been able to sleep. I've just been staring at my phone all night."

I felt the same pain Crow described, feeling like shit for scaring her. "We just left Milan. We'll be home in a few hours."

"And it went well?" she asked with hesitation.

"It went better than I expected. They took the money. There were a few bumps and some hostilities, but your father handled it well. We both parted on good terms. They stopped thinking about us the second we walked out...which was what we wanted."

"Good...I'm relieved. When will you be home?"

"Not for at least five hours. I've got to drop your father off first."

"Oh…"

"Go to sleep, baby." She was probably exhausted from stressing all night, from being upset for almost an entire week.

"I want to see you when you get home."

"I'll wake you."

"Promise?" she asked. "Don't let me sleep. I would much rather see you right away."

I should feel awkward with her clinginess in front of her father, but strangely, I didn't. I didn't care at all. I loved her and she loved me. There was no reason to be embarrassed about it. "Promise."

"Alright, I'll let you go," she said. "Love you."

"Love you too, baby." I hung up and returned the phone to my pocket, not looking at her father's reaction to the conversation I'd had with his daughter. I didn't care about his opinion anyway.

After a long stretch of silence, he addressed it. "Thank you for making my daughter so happy." He didn't look at me when he spoke, staring straight ahead. "You've put up with me, my brother, a bunch of bull-shit…never gave up on her. I don't care how much you hate me. Even if you always hate me, that's fine with me. Regardless, I'm grateful she has you. It's all I've ever wanted, for my little girl to have the right man." As if he hadn't just said something heartfelt, he called his wife and told her he was fine.

As he predicted, she cried on the phone a bit.

Like a real man, he listened to it. Consoled her. Told her he would be home soon. Gave her a shoulder to cry on even though he wasn't there for her in person. After several minutes, he got off the phone with her and got comfortable, prepared to sleep for the rest of the drive.

I kept thinking about his conversation with Vanessa, how she loved her father so deeply, called him her best friend. They had a close relationship, remaining loyal to each other regardless of what life threw at them. I never wanted to come between them, but I knew I already was.

How could I hate a man who loved Vanessa as much as I did? Who would do anything for her, even risk turning her against him? Crow always had his daughter's best interest at heart, and I had to admit I was the worst possible guy for any man's daughter. It was unrealistic to expect him to behave in any other way. I wouldn't make excuses for the hurtful things he did and said, especially when he got carried away, but when I witnessed their tender relationship with my own eyes, I knew I couldn't be a wedge between them.

I could bring them closer together.

Nothing would make Vanessa happier than to see me build a relationship with her father, to become part of her family in a meaningful way. After everything I put her through, it was the least I could do. Vanessa and I were going to spend the rest of our lives together and start a family. Holding on to this hatred for Crow wasn't realistic.

I should let it go.

There were better people to hate besides Crow Barsetti, people who deserved it more. I respected this man in a lot of ways, the way he could walk in there so calmly and establish peace, the way he took his son's place without thinking twice about it, the way he listened to his wife cry and carried her pain with him. I admired this man because he'd raised a strong daughter, the perfect woman to spend my life with. Without him, I never would have found her. I would have spent my entire life alone, never knowing love. I didn't believe in soul mates, but I certainly believed in that.

I had a terrible past, but perhaps everything was meant to happen...to lead me here. My forgiveness would bury the past for good. The blood war that had continued for three generations would be buried in the past like the dead. I would never be a Barsetti, but my children would have Barsetti blood.

Our bloodlines would fuse together and become one.

CROW WOKE up when I pulled onto the gravel. He ran his fingers through his hair then wiped the sleep from his eyes. He looked at the front door, the large wooden slab that reached the ceiling of the first floor.

The lights in the windows turned on as everyone in the house woke up. Before Crow got out of the truck, the front door flung open and Pearl stepped out first.

Crow got out and watched his wife run to him in the darkness, her bare feet crunching against the gravel with her movements. She jumped into his arms, her legs and arms hooking around his torso.

I stared at them, immediately thinking of Vanessa and me. She greeted me in the same way, with overwhelming affection. Regardless of who was watching, she loved me openly, showing the depth of our romantic relationship.

Pearl cupped his face and kissed him, like a young couple still passionately in love.

I got out of the truck next and saw Conway and Sapphire on the front steps. Conway had his arm around Sapphire, but he wasn't watching his parents. With his gaze averted to the ground, he found something else to look at.

I heard Pearl and Crow talking as he held her.

"Our babies are okay?" she whispered, her forehead against his.

"Yes."

"It's over? You're sure?"

"Yes." He kissed her on the mouth as he carried her closer to the front door. "Everything is alright, Button. Our simple life is safe. Our children are safe. I'm safe." He held her against his chest as he carried her to the front of the house with ease. He set her on the concrete so her feet wouldn't have to touch the gravel again.

She was in the same clothes she'd been wearing earlier, but her hair was messy from lying down until we came home. She cupped his cheeks one more time before she stepped back so he could greet their son.

He kissed the inside of her palm before he dropped her hand. He looked at his son next. "Con—"

Conway embraced his father, hugging him tightly. "I'm glad you're home, Father. I'm sorry about everything."

Crow stilled before he hugged his son back. Whatever he was going to say didn't seem important anymore, not when his son said those words to him. He hugged him tighter and closed his eyes, holding his son even longer than he held his wife. "I'd do it again...a million times." He cupped the back of his head and kissed his forehead. "I love you, son. So damn much."

"I love you too, Father. I'm so sorry—"

"Forget it. It's over." He pulled away and looked his son in the eye. "It's time for us to be happy. To live quietly. To welcome the new Barsetti that will be here any day. I just hope this is the last lesson I have to teach you."

Conway stared at his father, his eyes starting to water. "I will always need you to teach me things, Father..."

Crow's eyes watered in return. "Then this better be the last mess I have to clean up."

"I can't promise that either," Conway said. "Sapphire and I are going to need you to babysit and change diapers…"

Crow blinked the emotion away and chuckled. "I don't mind cleaning up after my grandbaby. But I'm not cleaning up after you anymore."

"Deal," Conway said. "Carter and I will pay back every dime you gave them."

Crow gripped his son by the shoulder. "I know you will. That's how I raised you." He moved to Sapphire next and embraced his daughter-in-law, delicately hugging her because of her enormous stomach.

Pearl came to me next, tears still in her eyes. She moved into my chest and hugged me. "Thank you for everything, Griffin. You've been such a blessing to this family. We love you very much."

Love. They loved me. "Thank you, Mrs. Barsetti."

"I don't want to hog you too much," she said as she pulled away. "I know Vanessa is probably waiting by the door as we speak. I was sleeping on the couch in front of the window, waiting for the lights from your truck."

"I told her to go to sleep. I'll wake her when I get back."

She smiled. "I promise you she's wide awake."

I smiled back. "You're probably right."

She kissed me on the cheek before she pulled away. "Good night, Griffin. Hope to see you soon." She walked inside with Conway and Sapphire, leaving Crow behind.

Crow turned to me and extended his hand. "Thanks for everything…again. I'm sure that would have gone quite differently if you weren't there to lay the groundwork. As my wife just said, you've been a blessing to this family…definitely not a curse. I'm sorry I ever said otherwise."

I didn't take his hand, letting it hang between us.

When Crow realized there would be no reciprocation, he lowered his hand, his eyes filling with disappointment. "Good night, then."

"I forgive you."

He flinched in place, his eyes widening when he heard the words I said. He regarded me with focused eyes, as if he didn't believe the words that came out of my mouth. Perhaps it was part of his imagination. Perhaps he'd misheard what I said. He didn't say anything, unsure how to proceed.

"You're a great father. I think a man isn't only judged by his strength and success. He's judged by the way he takes care of other people, even if those people don't deserve it. I see the way you respect your wife, treat her like a queen, and put her before yourself. I see the way you love your children, the way you've been a great example of what Vanessa should expect in a man. She's a picky woman, only falling in love with a man who's strong enough to handle someone like her. And you've been a great example to your son, to make him follow in your footsteps."

Crow tilted his head to the ground, seeming to be overwhelmed by the praise he'd just received.

"When I hear you talk to Vanessa, I understand how much you love her. I can hear it in your voice, see the way you react to the sound of hers. You're different, softer. I know you would do anything for her, even keep her away from me because you thought she deserved better. How could I hate a man who refused to let his daughter settle for anything less than the perfect man? You taught her loyalty, how to throw a mean punch, and how to take care of herself, not wait for a man to do it. If you hadn't had her, hadn't raised her to be so damn perfect, I wouldn't have found the woman to spend my life with. There's no other woman out there who would have brought me to my knees the way she did, who would have softened my rage and anger the way she has. She's turned me into a better man, a man I'm actually proud of. So instead of hating you...I should be thanking you."

Crow lifted his gaze again, his hard expression gone. He took a deep breath, his eyes softening in the way they did for Vanessa and Conway. He didn't erect any of his walls around himself. He allowed me to see a more vulnerable side to him...since I'd showed him a different side to myself. "That means a lot to me, Griffin."

"And it means a lot to me that you raised the perfect woman. I respect her so much. She's not the kind of woman to wait for a man to save her. She saves herself.

I've never seen anything like it. She's half my size but manages to put me in my place…over and over. I didn't realize I wanted a wife and kids until I found her. I didn't realize what kind of man I wanted to be until I found the right woman."

A half grin formed on my face.

"I was really wrong about you, Griffin. I'm sorry for that."

I shook my head. "You wanted the best for her. I understand that now."

"I never thought I would say this, but…I'm glad all of this happened. I'm glad the Skull Kings attacked us and all these events were put into motion…because my daughter never would have found the right man…since you're the right man." He stepped closer to me. "You're a part of this family, Griffin. Whether you're married to my daughter or not, you're a son to me. You'll always be a son to me."

I never knew how much I wanted to be part of something until I had it. Vanessa was family to me, and now the rest of her family was too. They didn't accept me because they had to. They accepted me because they wanted to. I could see the sincerity in Crow's eyes, the way he admired me the way I now admired him. On the surface, I was a dangerous guy covered in tattoos who had been shot more times than any other man. But underneath that, I had a heart the same size as his.

He extended his arms and moved into me, pausing before he touched me to gauge my reaction.

I didn't move away.

He was an inch shorter than I was, and he closed the gap between us and wrapped his arms around me. He hugged me the way he hugged his son, with the same kind of grip and the same kind of affection.

My arms moved around his body, and my chin moved to his shoulder. I held my greatest enemy in my arms, embraced a man I'd plotted to murder. But now there wasn't a hint of rage inside my chest. Now I embraced this man as a friend...as a father.

He cupped the back of my head—just the way he did with Conway. "When my time comes, I know you'll take care of my wife. I know you'll take care of Vanessa. I can rest in peace knowing you're there...and that is the greatest gift you could have given me."

PEARL WAS RIGHT.

When I walked in the door, Vanessa was wide awake.

Judging by her tired eyes and flat hair, she hadn't closed her eyes—even for a few minutes. The sun had already risen about twenty minutes ago, so the night had passed. She stayed up the entire time, waiting for the moment she would see me in person.

"Griffin." Relief washed over her face when she saw me with her own eyes. Just the way Pearl broke down when she saw Crow, Vanessa did the same with me. She buried herself in my chest, her fingers exploring my body to make sure I was okay. "I'm so glad you're home." She kept her face against my chest, the tears from her eyes soaking into my t-shirt. "I couldn't sleep…"

"I'm here now." My hand cupped the back of her head, and I watched her lean on me like a crutch. "Everything went smoothly. Nothing to worry about."

"You don't think they'll be a problem again?"

"No." I scooped her into my arms and carried her to bed. "They got their money. That's all they care about." I set her on the bed then stripped my clothes off so I could get into bed beside her. It was one of the rare times when I wasn't in the mood for sex. There was something else deep inside my chest, a satisfying feeling that completed me. I didn't want anything more.

She was already in my t-shirt, so she got under the covers with me. She was happy just to hold me, to feel me beside her as the sun continued to rise and fill the bedroom with sunlight. "I'm glad this is over. I know how much my father worries about these sorts of things. Mama too."

"They're both happy. Relieved."

"Good. I'm glad to hear that." She rested her hand on my stomach while her leg was tucked between mine. With her face on my shoulder and her hair spread out everywhere, she was the perfect sleeping companion.

She was light, soft, and beautiful, and there was no one else I'd rather share my bed with—along with everything else. She closed her eyes, finally finding peace now that I'd returned home.

I watched her, entranced by the woman who'd captured my heart. She was my reason for living. It used to be cash and violence, but now both of those things didn't matter anymore. She was my purpose, my world. "Baby?"

"Hmm?" She kept her eyes closed, more comfortable in my arms than in any other position.

"I forgave your father."

Her eyes snapped open, her fatigue instantly wiped away. "You did? Why? What happened?"

"When I listened to your conversation over the phone, I realized that he loves you as much as I do. And how could I hate someone who would do anything for you? We have the same thing in common, the biggest thing in common."

Her eyes softened.

"He was just doing the right thing for you. He stood up for you when most men would have backed down. He was never afraid of me, never afraid of making me a worse enemy. All he cared about was protecting you, regardless of the consequences to himself. He risked turning you against him by rejecting me, but he did it anyway. Maybe he didn't handle it the best way, but there's no doubt that your father would do anything for you, even the hardest things. Then I saw the way he treated your mother and brother, the way he selflessly protects his family. Maybe we got off to a bad start… but he's definitely a respectable man. I decided to let it go…since his blood and my blood will be mixing to start a family. How could I hate a man you love so much? Someone you consider to be your best friend? So I let it go, knowing it was the right thing to do."

"Griffin…" She rubbed my chest as the emotion grew in her eyes. "You have no idea how happy that makes me…how happy that must have made him."

"It did make him happy. He hugged me."

"Aww…" She cuddled into me closer, her face moving into my neck.

"And he said I was a son to him."

"Because you are." She squeezed me tightly. "This is what I wanted for so long, and it's finally happening… I can hardly believe it."

My arms moved around her waist, and I cradled her against me, her size dwarfed by mine. She was a petite woman, but her spunk made up for her stature. Plus, she didn't need to be big when she had a big man for strength. "There are better people I should spend my time hating. Your father isn't one of those people."

Also by Penelope Sky

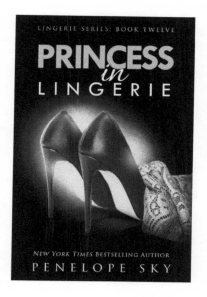

Order Now

Praise for Marc D. Angel's *A New World* . . .

I don't know whether Rabbi Marc Angel's mother was right in assuming that "we could learn almost everything we need to know about human nature from our own extended family," but I would go as far as to claim that we could learn almost everything we need to know about Sephardic ethos and way of life from Rabbi Angel's reminiscences. And we certainly should. For our own sake! Out of many faces that Judaism developed, the Sephardic one still radiates as the most "equilibric" one.

— Dr. Eliezer Papo, Chairman of the Moshe David Gaon Center for Ladino Culture at Ben-Gurion University of the Negev

This memoir of growing up in a close-knit Sephardic immigrant community is poignant and a pleasure to read. It's also sharp and provocative. It pushes us to figure out how, in our vexed, complicated world today, we can provide our children with a natural sense of belonging and joy.

— Jane Mushabac, CUNY Professor of English, author of *His Hundred Years, A Tale*

A beautiful family memoir and an unforgettable contribution to Sephardic-American letters… a window on the little-known world of Seattle's Sephardic Jews.

— Jonathan D. Sarna, Brandeis University and author of *American Judaism: A History*

Rabbi Angel's absorbing memoir of growing-up in Seattle, Washington, is an ode to the Ottoman-Sephardic culture and Judeo-Spanish language in which he was raised. Though it has gradually faded among subsequent generations, its beauty and lasting meaning, too valuable to lose, is the main thrust of the book. In each chapter—whether he has recounted an event, religious tradition, folk remedy, humor, adages, even food and music—the author points out a life lesson, a human value, and a relevance for today.

— Rachel Amado Bortnick, Founder of Ladinokomunita

In a creative blend of narrative, nostalgia and personal memoir, Rabbi Marc. D. Angel transports us back to the once-upon-a-time world of the Ladino-Sephardic community of his upbringing in Seattle, where Sephardic immigrants seamlessly blended religion, family traditions from the old country and modern-day values to create a joyous and uplifting Jewish way of life, one that could still serve as a model to emulate for our communities today.

— Rabbi Daniel Bouskila, International Director of the Sephardic Educational Center

A New World

An American Sephardic Memoir

MARC D. ANGEL

Albion
Andalus
Boulder, Colorado
2019

"The old shall be renewed,
and the new shall be made holy."
— Rabbi Avraham Yitzhak Kook

Albion-Andalus, Inc.
P. O. Box 19852
Boulder, CO 80308
www.albionandalus.com

Design and composition by Erica Holland Leitz
Cover design by D.A.M. Cool Graphics
Cover image of Marco and Sultana Romey (author's maternal grandparents) with their children.

Manufactured in the United States of America

ISBN-10: 1-7336589-2-0

ISBN-13: 978-1-7336589-2-8

*We thank the Institute for Jewish Ideas and Ideals
and the Sephardic Educational Center for their
support of this publication as part of their
"Sephardic Initiative."*

Contents

Preface

Transitions.

Things stay the same, but not really. Things change, but not totally.

My grandparents were among the 30,000 or so Sephardic Jews who came to the United States during the early 20th century. They were born and raised in Turkey and the Island of Rhodes. They had little formal education, little money, but a lot of courage.

They brought the "old country" with them to the new world. Their language was Judeo-Spanish. Their culture was the traditional Sephardic Judaism of Ottoman Jewry. They settled in Seattle, Washington, and were part of a vibrant Sephardic enclave with large extended families.

My grandparents were of the "old world" and they sought to transmit their ideals and values to their children. Their children were of the "new world." Life in America was very different from the tradition-centered life of the Jews in Turkey and Rhodes. The children's generation respected their parents; but this new American generation was restless. They wanted to adapt fully to American life. How much of the "old world" could they carry with them? How much of it had to be left behind?

By my generation (I was born in 1945), the Americanization process was well advanced. We loved and admired our grandparents and their generation; but we were full-blooded Americans, many of us with American-born parents. The "old world" was remote, somewhat exotic. It didn't define who we were.

Our children and grandchildren are further removed from the "old country." Most have never heard a conversation in Judeo-Spanish. Most have not had personal contact with members of my grandparents' generation.

The Americanization of our family over the past hundred years has brought many changes. We are far better educated than the immigrant generation. We are generally more affluent, more "successful," and more integrated into American society. We have shared in the American dream.

But we have also incurred losses in the generational transitions. Life is not static. Things change. Circumstances change. People change. Whereas most of our family once lived within the same neighborhood in Seattle, now we are spread out all over the country. Whereas most of our family once felt a strong sense of belonging to the Sephardic Jewish tradition, now we are much more diverse in our religious and cultural patterns of life.

While we can't go back to the "old days" and the "old country" way of life, we can draw meaningful lessons for ourselves and our next generations. In assembling the memoirs for this book, I have chosen people and events that have left a lasting impression on me...and that I think can leave a lasting impression on many others. This book is one man's record of an era which is rapidly coming to a close. I acknowledge that memoirs are subjective; each person experiences life through his or her own eyes and each remembers things differently.

I thank my wife, Gilda, for her wisdom, enthusiasm...and love. She read the manuscript of this book with great insight and made important editorial contributions to it. I express my gratitude to Netanel Miles-Yépez of Albion-Andalus Books for believing in this book and seeing it to publication. And I thank the Almighty for having brought me to this day.

Part I

Beginnings

My mother used to say that we could learn almost everything we need to know about human nature from our own extended family. Some relatives were wise, some foolish; some were successful, some failures; some optimistic, some morose; some pious, some rebellious. Our family included intellectuals and people of very limited intelligence. We had courageous and outspoken individuals, and we had timid, quiet types. Some had phenomenal senses of humor, and some would hardly ever laugh. In the family, one could experience love, hatred, selflessness, jealousy, greed, generosity, spirituality, materialism, seriousness, humor.

The family included people of great mind and heart, people who were handsome and beautiful, people of striking personality. It also included, without embarrassment, people who were quite ordinary, as well as individuals who had various physical, emotional and mental disabilities.

My grandfather Angel had a shoeshine stand. My grandfather Romey was a barber. My father was a grocer. Among my uncles were a butcher, fish salesman, rabbi, printer, storekeeper, bartender, college professor, and assorted unskilled laborers. Various relatives were real estate speculators, never-do-wells, while others were employees of Boeing. In the days of my childhood, most of the women of our family did not work outside the home.

By the next generation, the extended family came to include

rabbis, teachers, attorneys, insurance and real estate agents, a political scientist, skilled employees in various companies, a merchant marine, salespeople, athletes, a nurse, and several authors of books.

My mother saw the family as something of a microcosm of humanity in general and society in particular. We could understand the world around us if we could understand ourselves.

In those days, the family was large, diverse and whole. We mostly lived in the same neighborhood; we got together often; we recognized a strong vital sense of kinship among ourselves.

One of the focal points of my childhood was the home of my maternal grandparents at 214 15th Avenue in Seattle, Washington. Even now, so many years after their deaths, I often find myself reminiscing about that house, remembering so many details about it. It has stood as a symbol in my mind of our family together. It calls to mind a simpler time, a time when life seemed whole and connected.

A number of years ago, my wife and children and I were visiting Seattle. Whenever we were in town, we took a drive through the "old neighborhood," including a stop at my grandparents' house. But this time, as we pulled up in front of 214 15th Avenue, we found the windows of the house boarded up. The grass in the large yard had not been cut in months. A sign on the front door stated that the house had been condemned.

It struck me that the house might be torn down. It also struck me that the family togetherness which that house had symbolized for me was also in the process of coming apart. Indeed, our family now had members living in different parts of the country (my own family lived in New York City). We had divorced people; we had individuals who had forsaken our family religious traditions. Even the family members who still lived in Seattle were spread out in different neighborhoods of the city and suburbs. If my grandparents' house had become a ghostlike edifice, so the image of our family during the years of my childhood also had become a ghostlike memory.

Fortunately, as I learned some time later, my grandparents'

house was not destroyed after all. A family bought it and restored it.

And fortunately, our extended family still exists on some level. From time to time, family members make an effort to bring back bits of the feelings from the old days.

But neither the old house nor our family are really the same anymore. And no one can put the pieces together again. A civilization has passed forever.

I decided to put down a few memories and observations as a way of conveying the spirit of that civilization. I share Mom's belief that the extended family was a microcosm of society. Although this book talks about my extended family during the years of my childhood in Seattle (1945-1963), it in fact is speaking about a facet of immigrant American society that a great many American families shared. And lost.

This book is a collection of my memories. It is the past sifted through the prism of my own mind. So in a real sense, this book is my personal story. At the same time, though, it is a story that has relevance to a great many people who are rooted in traditional societies, and who strive to adapt to an ever-changing modern world. The story is unique…and universal.

My father, Victor Angel, was born in Seattle, April 1, 1913. My mother, Rachel Romey Angel, was born in Seattle, December 28, 1914.

But even these seemingly straightforward facts are embroiled in controversy.

Dad was born at home, not in a hospital. His parents, immigrants from the Island of Rhodes, were not too fussy about registering his birth and obtaining a birth certificate for him. He was definitely born, that was a fact; what difference would it make if his birth were recorded in the government files?

My grandfather, Bohor Yehudah Angel, had come to Seattle in 1908, following his eldest son Moshe who had come a bit earlier. The two of them operated a shoeshine stand and saved enough money to send for the rest of the family. My grandmother, Bulissa Huniu Angel, arrived in the United States in 1911 with her children Ralph, Victoria, Luna, Avner, Joseph and Rahamim. Joseph, who was then about nine or ten years old, was turned away by immigration officials since he had a contagious scalp disease (tinias). He was sent back to Rhodes and lived with relatives there. Although I never knew Uncle Joseph, his life's story hovered over our family's collective memory.

My father was the first and only American-born child in the family.

Like the rest of his family, he spoke Judeo-Spanish as his mother tongue. This was the language of Sephardic Jews whose ancestors had been expelled from Catholic Spain in 1492. Though born in the United States, my father did not learn English until he went to public school at age five.

When registering him for school, his parents were asked for his birth date. In the old country, birth dates were not that important. Generally, people would know that they were born in "the year of the big flood," of "the year of the drought," or by some other unusual phenomenon. As to the month in the year, they would know that they were born "around Rosh haShanah," or "before Purim," or in connection with some other Jewish holy day.

My grandparents told the school officials that my father's birthday was April 1. Who could refute them? Many years later, when Dad applied for a passport, he had to demonstrate proof of birth. I was then a student in college and decided to confront the bureaucracy by obtaining a genuine birth certificate for him. We first asked the birth certificate office in Olympia (Washington's State Capital) to search for a record of Dad's birth. None turned up. We then provided various documents in which Dad had listed his birth date as April 1, 1913. We also obtained testimonial letters from two elders who would swear that April 1, 1913 was the correct date. After submitting this material, we waited patiently. It was not long before my father received a real birth certificate. We congratulated him on obtaining proof that he had been born. His existence was now official.

My mother's birth date was tied to a different sort of problem.

Her parents had come to Seattle as teenagers. My grandfather, Marco Romey, born in Tekirdag, Turkey, arrived in Seattle in 1908. My grandmother, Sultana Policar Romey, arrived in 1911. She had been born on the Island of Marmara, a Turkish island in the Sea of Marmara. She had come to Seattle at the request of her older sister, Calo, who had settled in Seattle several years earlier. Calo was sure that her younger sister would have a better life in America than in her poverty stricken village of Marmara.

My grandparents Romey were married in Seattle in May 1912. My mother was the second of their seven children. As she grew up, they told her that her birthday was January 7. That is the date she celebrated throughout her childhood and for many years thereafter. When she grew older and applied for her passport, she wrote away to get a copy of her birth certificate. When she received it, she was surprised to find that her birthday was not listed as January 7, 1915, but as December 28, 1914. Mom solved the discrepancy by declaring that she no longer had a birthday— but rather a birthday week. After her birth certificate came in, we celebrated her birthday every year from December 28 to January 7.

Mom died on May 28, 1983. Dad died on July 28, 1991. They are buried side by side in the Sephardic cemetery in Seattle. There are no controversies about the dates of their deaths.

My parents often told us that they were members of a transition generation. Their parents had been born and raised in the old country, having come to Seattle as immigrants. Although the newcomers had certainly made efforts to Americanize, they were very much steeped in the old world culture. My grandfather Romey learned to read and write English; he spoke English uncomfortably, much preferring his mother tongue, Judeo-Spanish. He became an American citizen. My other grandparents only learned enough English to understand what their grandchildren said to them. They spoke English poorly, and never became United States citizens. My grandmother Romey would say that although she had arrived in Seattle as a teenager, she was never able to give up feeling that her real home was in Marmara, that she was in Seattle only on a temporary basis. She made as few concessions to American culture as she could.

As immigrants, my grandparents brought with them the memories and traditions of their families in Rhodes and Turkey. They conducted their households and family life along the models that they had experienced in the old country. My mother used to say: "I might just as well have been born in Turkey. I feel that I, too, am a sort of immigrant in the United States even though I was born here."

But my parents' children were the other side of the transition. We were English-speaking, full-blooded Americans. We went on to become college educated, professional, mobile, and modern. We were two generations removed from the old world. We were part of the generation that was totally comfortable in America, without a sense of being immigrants or foreigners.

Mom and Dad spoke Judeo-Spanish to their parents and to their parents' generation. They spoke English to their children and their children's generation. To each other, they used both languages, a blend of the languages, a jumping from one language to the other; but English predominated.

In the last months of Mom's life, I found that she was speaking to me more and more in Judeo-Spanish. She sang some of the old songs, used some of the old proverbs and expressions. I think she died in Judeo-Spanish. In the last months of Dad's life, I don't recall him reverting to Judeo-Spanish. He had survived my mother's death by eight years and had few people with whom he could use the old language. He died in English.

My parents, both born in Seattle, still had living memories and connections with the old world. Their minds and spirits were animated by the civilization of their parents and ancestors. They spoke the same language, ate the same foods, and shared the same cultural and religious patterns. They were thoroughly proud Americans; but their souls were nurtured in the Sephardic civilization of Turkey and Rhodes.

My grandparents' generation, the generation of immigrants, has passed away. My parents' generation, the generation of transition, has almost completely died out.

And my generation, the generation of pure Americans, is still trying to understand its connection with its past. We also have an old country. We also have memories that inspirit our lives. We also hear the voices of ancestors. But the old country is different for us.

My old country is Seattle.

I was born July 25, 1945, the second of four children born to my parents.

According to the practice of the Sephardic Jews of Turkey and Rhodes, children are named according to a traditional pattern: the first-born boy and girl are named after the father's parents, and the second-born boy and girl are named after the mother's parents. Subsequent children are named for other relatives, alternating from the father's to the mother's side of the family.

This custom underscores the strong family ties inculcated by Sephardic culture. Each child, by his and her very name, is placed into a context. The newborn already has a history, a tradition. Often enough, he or she is named after a grandparent who is still alive. The grandparents witness their continuity in the persons of their grandchildren. They see little children carrying their own names, marching the family into the future. And the namesakes feel a special bond to the grandparents after whom they were named.

My older brother, the first born, was named Leon Bill. As was proper, he was named after my father's father. My grandfather Angel's name was Yehudah. He was called Bohor Yehudah. (Among Sephardim the first-born child was called by the honorific title "Bohor" for males, and "Bohora" for females.) When it came to naming my brother, my parents chose the name Leon—a commonly used equivalent for Yehudah. Yehudah (Judah) was described in the Bible as a lion. Sephardim used the Judeo-Spanish word for lion i.e. Leon. Since my grandfather was known by the appellation Bohor, that name also had to be included in my brother's name. What was a good, modern American name that began with a "b"? Bill!

So my brother's name tells a story of the new generation in the old country of Seattle. It was faithful to the tradition. He was named after his paternal grandfather. Yet, the names were put into an American framework. After all, it would be much easier for this little Yankee to go through life as Leon Bill than as Bohor Yehudah.

Seven years later, I was born. Being the second-born son, I was named after my maternal grandfather, Marco Romey. My parents thought that Marco sounded too old-fashioned, so they called me Marc. When my third grade teacher asked me why my name was spelled "wrong," since Marc should really end with a "k," I blushed when I told her I had been named after my grandfather Marco. From that day on, and to my youthful embarrassment, she called me Marco.

Of course, I was a full-blooded American so I needed a middle name, even though my grandfather did not have one. Mom decided to distinguish me with the name Dwight, after General Dwight D. Eisenhower. General Eisenhower was then a great hero in the United States, having ended World War II with a striking victory for the allies. In her patriotic fervor, Mom went beyond her Sephardic tradition by naming me for an American war hero. She used to tell me that I was named after two great men: my grandfather Marco Romey and General Dwight Eisenhower. With this combination, I was surely destined for wonderful things!

My sister was born about eighteen months later. As first-born daughter, she was named after her paternal grandmother: Bulissa Esther. Bulissa is a beautiful name but it is definitely not American. My sister became Bernice Esther. In Hebrew, she was called Esther, the "Bulissa" being dropped from this American generation. Certain aspects of a culture can remain intact in the United States; other aspects can be adapted; but some things simply had to be left behind. "Bulissa" was one of those things left behind.

About five and a half years later, my mother gave birth to her fourth and last child. If it had been a girl, she would have been named after my mother's mother, Sultana. Mom had already picked a suitable American version of the name, Sheila. None of us was especially fond of the name Sheila, so we were glad that she gave birth to a boy.

By accepted tradition, the third son should have been named after someone on my father's side. The Angel relatives were aware of this fact and devoted considerable effort lobbying my parents concerning the new child's name. They wanted the boy to be called Joseph, after my father's older brother who had never made it to Seattle and whose family members were murdered by the Nazis in 1944. Mom would not hear of it. She said that Uncle Joseph had been an unfortunate soul "always behind the eight ball." The relatives reversed Mom's logic. They argued that since Joseph had such a miserable life, he deserved at least a posthumous reward—that a child of the family should carry his name.

Who was Uncle Joseph? Why was Mom adamant about not naming her son after him?

In 1911, my grandmother Angel travelled from the Island of Rhodes to America to join her husband and eldest son who had come to Seattle several years earlier. The two men had worked hard to save enough money to bring the rest of the family to America. My grandmother Bulissa undertook the incredibly difficult voyage with six of her children. She also took responsibility to bring a neighbor's daughter to Seattle. She figured that this young lady, Bohora Rosa Capelluto, would be a good wife for her eldest son. And if he did not want to marry her, then perhaps the second son would! (The first-born son, Moshe, did marry her.)

When they arrived in New York, they had to pass through the immigration officials. My grandmother was told that little Joseph could not be admitted into the United States because he had an infectious scalp disease.

What was she to do? She had come half way across the world at great effort and expense. She and her young ones were still three thousand miles away from Seattle. To take them back to Rhodes with Joseph was unthinkable. It would be years before enough money could be raised to again bring them to America. On the other hand, what was she supposed to do with Joseph? How could she abandon her son?

As things turned out, several other Jewish immigrants from Rhodes were also rejected by immigration officials. They told my grandmother that since they were returning to Rhodes, they would bring Joseph back with them. He could be raised temporarily in the home of relatives. When his health improved, he could then be sent on to Seattle.

So my grandmother took five children and a future daughter-in-law to Seattle, tearfully sending her little Joseph back to Rhodes. The separation was heart-rending and never left the consciousness of my grandmother and the rest of the family.

Joseph never did make it to Seattle. He grew up in Rhodes, eventually married and had four children. He stayed in touch with his Seattle family by mail. They sent him money and gifts from time to time. But they never saw each other again.

Among the victims of the barbaric Nazis were almost all of the two thousand Jews living in the Island of Rhodes. My Uncle Joseph's family perished. No one of his family in Rhodes survived. Memorial plaques erected after the war at the Jewish cemetery and on the front wall of the synagogue in Rhodes list the family "Angel" among the victims of the brutal Nazis.

Uncle Joseph's scalp disease that led to his being denied entry into the United States ultimately cost his family their lives. Could the immigration officials who turned him away, separating him from his mother and family, have any idea how much grief they caused the family at that time? And did they ever come to realize that their decision ultimately played a role in the death of that little boy's family?

So, as far as my mother was concerned, the name Joseph was out.

One of Dad's relatives did her best, though, to win this child for the name Joseph. She visited my mother shortly after the baby was born, before he was to be named at the circumcision on the eighth day. With great solemnity and reverence, she told my mother of a vision she had received in a dream the previous night. She was told in the dream that the son of Victor and Rachel Angel would be named Joseph. How could anyone do battle against a vision that came in a dream?

My mother was undaunted. She replied quickly and forcefully. "I also had a dream last night. A vision came to me that this baby should be named David."

"Is that the truth?" asked the elderly relative.

"Yes it is," said my mother with confidence. She had won.

"But David? David? Who is the child being named after? We don't have any David in the Angel family."

My mother said proudly: "I am naming him after King David. I love the name David. He is being named for King David."

Family members were stunned at this unprecedented decision. Children were to be named in a specific pattern, and King David—for all his greatness—was not part of that pattern. My father, in his devotion to my mother, defended her decision. The son would be called David.

To pacify the indignant relatives, my parents agreed to name the child David Victor Joseph Angel. In due course, though, the Joseph was dropped.

The names of my parents' four children are an indication of the immense cultural forces that were sweeping through the Sephardic community of Seattle in our generation. Names describe context. And the family's context was in transition.

Our family lived at 511 28th Avenue, between Jefferson and East Cherry until the fall of 1958. Then we moved to the "new neighborhood" in Seward Park, where we lived at 5602 Wilson Avenue South.

Our house on 28th Avenue was in the central district of Seattle. In those days, it was a fairly mixed area. Most of the city's Jewish population lived in this neighborhood. There were also large numbers of African-Americans, Japanese and Chinese. There were even some WASPs, although few stand out in my memory. By 1958, the neighborhood was in the process of turning into the "Black ghetto."

When we lived on 28th Avenue, before the demographic changes, the neighborhood was a place where we felt a sense of belonging. Almost all of my relatives lived within easy walking distance from our house. Many of the residents of the neighborhood were themselves Sephardic Jews of Turkish and Rhodes origins. I knew I was in a Jewish neighborhood because the language I often heard on the street was Spanish—the unique Spanish of the Sephardic Jews of Turkey and Rhodes.

When I would meet an elder Sephardic Jew who did not know me, I would be asked: "Whose son are you?" I would inform the questioner of my parents' names. Then the person would know exactly who I was, where I came from, how I belonged. We grew up in the community not simply as individuals, but as representatives of a family.

Family was the central factor in our identities in those days. Mom and five of her married siblings and their families all lived in this neighborhood. My grandparents' home at 214 15th Avenue was a focal point of our family life. Most of my father's brothers and sisters—and their children—also lived in the central district. It was difficult to go anywhere in the neighborhood without bumping into a relative or family friend.

The rough boundaries of our world were 31st Avenue to 15th Avenue, from Cherry Street to Yesler Way. Within that area lived dozens of uncles, aunts, cousins, great uncles, great aunts, second cousins, third cousins, people related to us through marriage, people related to our relatives through marriage, people who were not related to us at all but whom we called uncle or aunt out of respect. It seemed to me that we were related to most of the Sephardim in town in one way or another.

The neighborhood included important landmarks: the kosher meat markets, kosher bakeries, the Hebrew Day School, the synagogues, many Jewish businesses. We borrowed books from the Yesler Branch of the Seattle Public Library. We played baseball, flew kites and rode bicycles in the army camp, a big field up the block from our home on 28th Avenue. We went swimming and had picnics at Madrona Park on Lake Washington. Once in a while, we went all the way to Seward Park. Among our favorite outings were trips to Golden Gardens, Salt Water State Park, and Alki.

The neighborhood also had its dangers. First and foremost for us was Pete, the Doberman Pinscher who lived in the lot adjoining our back yard. Pete rarely stopped barking. He often foamed at the mouth. He was chained to his doghouse but had a leeway of about twenty feet. He ran around in circles endlessly, wearing a dirt path in the middle of the yard. The owners obviously did not care. They bought Pete to protect their home from burglars, but how could Pete attack burglars when he was chained to his doghouse in the back yard? I guess they figured that the very sound of Pete's howling would terrify any would-be trespassers.

Pete perpetually appeared to be angry and vicious. From time to time, a ball we were playing with would go over the fence into Pete's territory. If it landed within the dirt circle, we generally gave up on it. No one was willing to invade Pete's province of power. When the ball landed outside the circle, we would venture over the fence to retrieve it. Our logic was that Pete could not go beyond the length of his chain. Even knowing this did not completely remove the terror involved in going into Pete's yard. Usually, one of us would throw dirt bombs in the direction away from where the ball was. Inevitably, Pete would lunge after them. This would give us the chance to send someone—usually we sent my little brother David—to race to the ball and reclaim it.

This system worked for quite a while; but then a flaw developed in our strategy. Pete did what we had never considered possible: he broke his chain. I remember looking out our kitchen window one Sunday morning and not seeing Pete. While puzzling over his absence, we got a call from my Auntie Regina on 27th Avenue that she saw Pete running freely in front of her house. Pete was on the loose.

All our relatives were hastily called and warned. None of us stepped out of our houses in fear of Pete. Later in the day, we saw his owners chaining Pete back to his doghouse. The rumor spread that he had mangled a few dogs during his period of freedom. The fear of Pete increased; rarely would we go into his yard again, even beyond his dirt path circle. Who knew if he would break his chain again?

Shortly before we moved to our new house, Pete once again broke loose. We heard that he tore several dogs to pieces and also attacked some people. The police shot him. Just as our Pete problem came to an end, we moved to our new house in the Seward Park district. We immediately learned that our neighbors, two houses down, owned a dog, Brutus. Brutus was the equal of Pete, only he wasn't kept on a chain!

Homo homini lupus. The old Latin saying describes man as a wolf. The noted psychiatrist, Silvano Arieti, believed that people who feared dogs were actually symbolically expressing a fear of the wolf-like nature of human beings. Perhaps on some level, our experiences with Pete and Brutus reminded us that human society also had its underside, its real dangers.

Even though our old neighborhood was a place where we felt a sense of warmth and belonging, it was also a place where we felt some fears. Not everyone in the neighborhood had nice things to say about Jews. Bigots who didn't even know us would sometimes utter anti-Jewish epithets, reminding us that our security was not complete. We had our share of bullies and trouble makers who kept us on our guard. Some of the hurts that I absorbed in fights in those days continue to hurt me still. The Sephardic author, Elias Canetti, winner of the Nobel Prize for Literature, noted that when a person receives a sting, it stays forever. One may learn to control it and keep it from driving him to revenge, but the sting remains. Always.

And yet, the love and happiness of the old neighborhood were dominant. The stings, when they came, helped to teach the lesson that Pete was not really so different from wolf-like humans. And bad people, like bad dogs, are also part of life.

Part II

The Immigrant Generation

Dad's parents died long before I was born, so the only grandparents I knew were Mom's parents, Marco and Sultana (Policar) Romey. Our family spent much time with them, and I often would sleep over at their house as a special treat.

Through them, my inner life was connected to their old country, Turkey.

Papoo Romey (Papoo is the word for grandfather among speakers of Judeo-Spanish) told of his childhood in Tekirdag. He described the synagogue there which was built right along the sea shore. The Jews of the town were poor, most of them merchants and peddlers. The Romey family worked in the kosher meat business.

"Why did you leave Tekirdag, Papoo? And why did you come all the way to Seattle?"

"Things were very difficult in Tekirdag. Poverty. Families were blessed with many children, but how were the children to be fed and clothed? Word reached us that a few Jews from our town had gone to America. They were making money. They had a better opportunity to advance themselves. Word came that a few Sephardic bachelors had gone to Seattle (See-aht-lee, as the Sephardim pronounced it) and found work in the fishing business. Also, Seattle looked like our part of Turkey—natural waters, abundant trees, mountains, open spaces. Some of our young people became restless. Why stay in Tekirdag where life was so hard, where there was hardly enough food for all of the children in the family? So some of us decided to go to America, to make money, to send back as much as we could to help our parents and families."

Nona Romey (Nona is the Judeo-Spanish word for grandmother) had grown up in a small community on the Island of Marmara. She described one of the landmarks of that place, the casa del pasha, castle of the nobleman. Atop a high hill overlooking the city and the sea, a wealthy Turkish nobleman once decided to build a magnificent palace. He wanted it to be a spectacular testimony to his affluence and importance. The townspeople watched in wonder as the construction commenced and progressed. Apparently the nobleman fell on hard times and could not afford to complete the castle. It remained unfinished, an eternal monument to vanity and arrogance. People used to go to the unfinished castle with picnic lunches and would rejoice in its splendors. Here they were, simple poor people, having picnics in the Pasha's castle—while the pretentious Pasha himself was ruined.

Nona used to tell of the persecution of Jews which took place in Marmara, almost as a ritual. There were many Greek Christians who lived there. Generally, they got along well with the Jews. During the week before Easter, the Greeks would be told by their priests that the Jews were a cursed people who deserved punishment. The masses were inflamed with religious hatred. Nona told us that the Jews of Marmara would stay in their homes during the week of Easter. They boarded up their windows. Crowds of Greeks would beat any Jew they could find. They threw stones at the Jewish homes and stores. Nona never forgot the terror of hiding in her own house, as rocks pounded against the walls, as anti-Jewish taunts were shouted by the mob.

And then, after Easter, everything seemed to revert to "normal." The Greeks greeted the Jews as old friends, as though nothing at all had happened.

The scars and fears remained in the hearts of the Jews. When the opportunity arose to leave Marmara and go to America, many of the young people were encouraged to emigrate.

Nona, then just a teenager, left her parents, knowing full well that she likely would never see them again. Indeed, she never did. Letters were sent back and forth, money was sent to the parents: but they never saw each other again.

"Why did you leave your parents if you knew you would not see them again?"

Nona would cry when she dealt with that question. "We had little choice. Our parents wanted us children to live in a better and safer place. They sacrificed everything for us. They themselves could not come, for many reasons. But they wanted us to have a chance for a better life."

I don't think Nona ever forgave herself for leaving her parents, even though they were the ones who encouraged her and her siblings to go to America. Psychologically and emotionally, Nona was deeply tied to the old country. In many ways, she never really left it.

Even as a youngster, I had a particular fascination with relatives who were born in the old country. They struck me as being people who had experienced great adventure, who were bold enough to take dangerous risks. Even though my grandparents and other relatives who were born in Turkey or Rhodes came to Seattle with little or no formal education, they were endowed with inner strength, courage and common sense. They were pioneers in a new world.

Papoo Romey was a man of sturdy faith. He was serious, but in a happy kind of way. He always seemed to have a Hershey bar in his pocket whenever his grandchildren turned up. He could be formal and dignified; but he could also be a genuine nonconformist. He often wore a seed-cap, with the brim turned over to one side. He could wear baggy pants and bright shirts and still appear to be proper and fashionable.

Before becoming a barber, he worked as a longshoreman. He used to walk back and forth to work, a distance of several miles, in order to save the bus fare. He barely managed to eke out a living to support his wife and children. On one summer day as he was walking home, the heat was so strong that he decided to step into a drugstore which had a soda fountain. He splurged and ordered himself a cold drink. He sat at the counter, tired and overheated, and slowly sipped the soda until he was rested and refreshed. He then put his hand into his pocket to take out some change to pay for the drink. To his mortification, he found that his pockets were absolutely empty. He sat at the counter, trying to figure out how he could get out of this situation without losing honor. Remarkably, a man sitting next to him was sensitive enough to recognize Papoo's predicament. He pulled a dime from his pocket and gave it to my grandfather—and then he left the store without even telling my grandfather who he was. Papoo paid for the soda and continued his walk back home. In recounting this amazing incident to his family, he concluded that the mystery man who had given him the dime was none other than Elijah the Prophet in disguise. Papoo offered prayers of thanks to the Almighty for sending Elijah to look after him and to spare him from shame. The moral: if a person is honest and works hard, the Almighty will find ways to help him.

Honor was an essential element in the life of the old country relatives. A sociologist who studied Sephardic immigrants in early 20th century America concluded that Sephardim saw themselves as a distinctive people with an inordinate pride bordering on stubbornness.

Papoo was a good example of this sociological observation. After working some years as a longshoreman, he decided to attend barber school so as to advance himself to a better job. He opened his barber shop in the Labor Temple located on 6th and University. Since many labor leaders and politicians frequented the Labor Temple, they often had their hair cut by my grandfather. Papoo was proud, for example, that he was the barber of Senator Warren Magnussen. But although he had a distinguished clientele, his income continued to be quite low.

In spite of his challenging economic condition and his lack of formal education, Papoo saw himself as being a nobleman. He held the popular tradition among Sephardic Jews that they descended from the aristocracy of Judea who had been exiled to Spain following the destruction of the ancient Temple in Jerusalem. To outsiders, he may have appeared to be just another semi-literate, financially strapped immigrant laborer. But he viewed himself as an aristocrat—even if temporarily reduced.

This powerful pride and sense of honor inspired the entire family. Papoo set the tone with majestic simplicity.

Papoo believed in things, he had principles. He did not apologize for his beliefs and policies, nor did he show hesitation in making decisions. He lived his life as though he were in control. In those days, the husband/father was the head of the household. He had to live up to the responsibilities of family leadership. Papoo did this with unabashed candor and confidence.

In raising his children, he had a number of old country rules of discipline. First, children had to respect their parents, like it or not. There was no talking back, no raising of voice, no protestations or arguments by the children. That was an axiom of family organization. The parents were in charge and knew what was best and what was right. The children had to remember their status: children!

When one child did something worthy of punishment, Papoo lined up all seven children and spanked them. He explained that all seven were guilty whenever any one of them did something wrong. They were responsible to look out for each other and see to it that everyone behaved. A lapse by one child meant that the other children had been derelict in their responsibility.

Papoo used to roll his own cigarettes. But it was clearly understood that the children, should not smoke. The boys would be allowed to smoke only after they had grown up and were on their own; the girls should never smoke.

The children (and later the grandchildren too) kissed Papoo's hand, after which he placed his hand on their head and gave them a blessing. When he entered a room, the family rose in respect and greeted him appropriately. Papoo structured family life in such a way that he was respected, even venerated, without needing to insist on his honor. He expected to be respected: and he was respected genuinely.

Papoo was a deeply religious man. He attended synagogue services regularly. He was president of the Sephardic Bikur Holim congregation in 1929; it was during his tenure that the congregation undertook to build its first building on 20th and Fir. During the 1930s, a newspaper known as "Progress" was published for the Sephardic community in Seattle. Papoo was featured in one of the issues as a pioneer Sephardic leader and activist.

Although his formal education was minimal, Papoo read and studied on his own. Each Friday night he would sit at a little table overlooking the yard and garden, have a glass of piping hot tea (with four teaspoons of sugar), and read the Torah portion of the week. On Sabbath afternoons, he regularly attended the Talmud class at the synagogue.

I often walked with Papoo from his house on 15th Avenue to the synagogue on 20th and Fir. There was a vacant lot on the way which had a narrow dirt path slashed across it in a diagonal. It was a short-cut. Instead of walking to the corner and then turning right, one could walk on the dirt path and save quite a few steps. Papoo never took the short-cut and never allowed me to do so. He insisted that we take derekh hamelekh, the king's road. Dignified and honorable people walk on proper paths, they do not cut through empty lots to save a little time and energy.

If Papoo conveyed strength and dignity, Nona conveyed these same qualities in a feminine way. She was virtually illiterate. She was afflicted with poor health for most of the years I knew her. Yet, she was idolized by the entire family as the role model of what a woman should and could be.

Nona was ingenious. She could create filling and tasty meals out of the simplest ingredients. Leftovers were converted into feasts. She was a gracious hostess.

Her grandchildren loved to spend time at her home. We always had fun. She had no toys in the house except for several worn out tennis balls. Yet, we were never bored. She played "question" games with us: she would say she was hiding in a color and we had to guess what she was thinking of. She would think of a person, or of an animal, vegetable or mineral—and we would ask her questions to discover the answer. She had a "Shabbat television." According to traditional Jewish law, it is forbidden to turn on electricity, including television, on Shabbat. So she had a hand operated viewmaster with a variety of slide programs. It was through this "Shabbat television" that I first saw Disneyland, and first experienced the sights of many of the cities of the world.

Nona taught us how to blow soap bubbles. We would go out to the back yard and pick a dandelion with as thick a stem as we could find. We cut the stem at both tips. Nona would mix some soap with water. We would use the stems like a straw, sucking in the soapy solution very gently. Sucking too hard resulted in a mouthful of soap, a bitter taste I still remember well. We would then blow softly until a bubble would form at the end of the stem. One needed to be patient and skillful to produce good, big bubbles; the joy of succeeding was one of the true joys of childhood. Other people bought soap bubbles and wands in the store, and their children could produce many more bubbles and with much less effort. But we felt sorry for them. They were missing all the fun.

We played games that required no toys or equipment: Mother May I, Hide and Seek, tag. With the old tennis balls, we spent hours playing Seven Up. With pebbles, we played: Guess Which Hand the Rock is in? We also played Steps. This was a game where the leader hid a pebble in one hand. The players sat on the first step. Each time a player guessed the correct hand that held the pebble, he or she advanced to the next step up. The first one to get to the top won.

When we went on a picnic on the shore of Lake Washington, Nona taught us how to go fishing. We would scour the beach until we could find a long enough stick to serve as a fishing pole. Nona then tied a piece of yarn to the stick and attached a safety pin at the bottom. For bait, she fastened pieces of cantaloupe rind on the safety pin. We fished for hours on end. We never caught anything. When we came back to the picnic table periodically to complain that we weren't catching any fish, Nona would change the bait and tell us to keep trying. Her laughter and joy at our fishing made us all happy.

Nona was a born story teller. She told about an elderly couple in Marmara, Dona and Levi, who were so romantic that they actually held hands in public. In a society that did not approve of public displays of affection, this was startling behavior. It was especially so since the couple were already old. Whenever Nona would see an older couple holding hands, she would say: "Dona con Levi," just like Dona and Levi of Marmara. Thus, this romantic couple of the old country became immortalized in this simple proverb.

She told stories about Joha. One of the heroes of Turkish folklore is Nassredin Hoja, a holy man who lived centuries ago. He was famous for his wit and his practical jokes. It is said that before he died, he instructed his heirs to erect a thick door in front of his gave. The door was to be fortified and locked so that no one could possibly break through it. But he also instructed that the door stand alone, without any walls, so that anyone could walk right past the door to the grave!

Since Nassredin Hoja was a Muslim religious figure, the Jews of the Ottoman Empire refashioned him into a Jewish person, inverting the title Hoja into the name Joha. Joha was associated with odd and humorous behavior. Inappropriate, awkward actions were known as echas de Joha, deeds of Joha. To deprecate someone's opinion, one simply said ya avlo Joha, it is Joha speaking.

Nona told Joha stories, some traditional and some that she improvised on her own. Here are a few examples.

One day, Joha's donkey ran away. He searched the entire city, asking everyone he saw: "Have you seen my donkey?" Each person answered "No. I have not seen your donkey." Joha then replied: "Blessed be the Lord." Someone finally asked Joha why he was blessing the Lord. Joha responded: "I bless the Lord that I was not on my donkey when he got lost. Otherwise I too would be lost now."

One day, Joha's neighbor asked to borrow his donkey. Joha replied: Unfortunately, my donkey has died." At that very moment, though, Joha's donkey brayed. The neighbor asked: "Why do you try to deceive me? I just heard your donkey's voice." Joha answered solemnly, as though deeply insulted. "What a skeptical person you are! You don't believe my voice, when here I am a man with a long white beard; and yet, you would believe the voice of a stupid donkey!"

Joha was walking down the street when he saw something sparkling in a garbage heap. He rushed over and picked it up. It was a mirror. Upon looking at it, Joha said: "What an ugly picture! No wonder its owner threw it into the garbage heap."

Joha's wife washed his pants and hung them on the clothesline outside to dry. The wind blew them off the line onto the ground. Joha exclaimed: "Praise the Lord that I was not wearing them at the time, otherwise I would have been hurt." He rushed to the synagogue to recite the blessing one recites upon having been saved from a possible disaster.

Here is an example of a story that describes Joha's wisdom. Three sages had heard that Joha was famous for his brilliant mind, so they decided to test him. The first sage asked: "Where is the center of the earth?" Joha answered calmly: "The center of the earth is exactly under the front left foot of my donkey." The sage asked how Joha could prove that. Joha answered: "All you have to do is measure the earth and then you will see that I am right."

The second sage then asked: "How many stars are there in the sky?" Joha answered: "There are as many stars as there are hairs on my donkey." When asked to prove this, Joha stated: "If you do not believe me, all you have to do is count them." The sage retorted: "But how can one count all the hairs on a donkey?"

Joha replied: "As easily as one can count all the stars in the sky."

Finally, the third sage tested Joha's wisdom. "How many hairs do I have in my beard?" he asked. Joha said: "You have as many hairs in your beard as my donkey has in its tail." When asked to prove this, Joha stated: "It is really very simple. Let us pluck the hairs from your beard and my donkey's tail, one at a time. In this way, we can count them easily."

All three sages recognized that Joha had defeated them. He indeed was the wisest of men.

My paternal grandfather, Bohor Yehudah Angel, died in 1925 when my father was only twelve years old. My father's mother, Bulissa Esther (Huniu) Angel, died in 1939, a year after my brother Bill was born. Their old country was the Island of Rhodes.

When they left Rhodes early in the 20th century, it was still under the governance of the Turks. For all practical purposes, the Judeo-Spanish civilization of the Jews of Rhodes was part of the mainstream Sephardic culture of the Jews of the Ottoman Empire. Yet, there were relatively minor differences that set the Jews of Rhodes apart—differences in pronunciation, in liturgical customs, and in folk traditions.

Where ever Jews of Rhodes migrated, they tended to stick together. Instead of blending in with other Sephardic communities, their first instinct was to establish their own self-help organizations and synagogues. This was true in Seattle, as in other cities. The Turkish Jews (my mother's family) were based at the Sephardic Bikur Holim synagogue; the Rhodes Jews (my father's family) were at the Congregation Ezra Bessaroth. In the old neighborhood, Bikur Holim was on 20th and Fir while Ezra Bessaroth was on 15th and Fir. Although only five blocks separated them, they functioned in many ways as though they were miles apart. Periodic discussions of merger always ended in failure.

Papoo Angel had a shoeshine stand in downtown Seattle. He was a hardworking, serious person, tall and strong. Because he had some religious education, he taught Hebrew to children in the Ezra Bessaroth religious school. He also served for a period as the synagogue's sexton. His income was small; his untimely death left my grandmother and her dependent children in financial difficulty. My father, although the youngest child, quickly understood that he also had to help provide income for his mother. He worked as a delivery boy for the morning newspaper; he sold boxes for people to sit on whenever there was a parade; after school, he worked in a variety of stores and fruit stands.

Nona Angel, in spite of her weak financial situation, was undaunted. She was a rotund woman with a determined, if somewhat jolly, expression on her face. She was actually a celebrity in the community, receiving visits from the great and small. Why? She was known to be able to perform cures. She could heal physical illnesses, emotional distress, psychological suffering. She even prescribed remedies for all sorts of personal problems. She had mastered the old-world folk wisdom; she knew which herbs to use and in what proportions. She was popularly known in the community as "La Gremma," her own way of pronouncing "the Grandma."

One of her major responsibilities was to help people ward off the evil eye. The belief in the evil eye goes back to antiquity. It was prevalent in the general society in Turkey and Rhodes, and was shared by the Sephardic Jews as well.

A person who was jealous of you or who wished you ill could cast an evil eye by looking at you in a malevolent way. Once a person had put an evil eye on you, you felt yourself under a wicked spell. Things would go wrong. Misfortune would follow misfortune.

People needed to protect themselves from incurring the evil eye. Preventive methods were best. First, people should avoid bragging or evoking envy. If they are praised for wealth, they should respond that they are actually deeply in debt, or that the wealth causes them grief; or they should praise God for His kindness. Wealthy people should be known for generosity to the poor and downtrodden.

Those complimented for their wisdom should play down this virtue by saying they are only using common sense and that so many others are far wiser than they. Indeed, one should never receive praise (or give praise) without saying Mashallah, as God wills. This word conveys humility and resignation, demonstrating that there is no intent to activate an evil eye.

Among believers in the evil eye, it is very bad manners to offer a direct compliment to anyone. I recall the story of a woman who praised a mother on her newborn baby: "what a homely child!" The mother responded with happiness and pride: "thank you, Mashallah."

La Gremma used folkloric methods for warding off the evil eye. Blue beads were effective. A necklace or bracelet of blue beads interspersed with whole cloves was even better. Garlic was especially efficacious. For example, one should always keep a few cloves of garlic in a kitchen drawer and in the glove compartment of one's car. Rutha (rue) was also a proven success against the evil eye. By keeping a sprig of rutha in your pocket or putting it behind your ear, you were defending yourself against the forces of the evil eye.

If a person was already afflicted by the evil eye, then a cure was needed. La Gremma used a traditional method known as enseredura, isolation. Toward the end of a lunar month, the patient was locked alone in a room. Soon after midnight, La Gremma would ask the person to name the one who had cast the evil eye on him or her. Upon receiving this information, she would go to the home of the named person, wash the steps to the house, collect the water from this washing, and bring it back to the patient. She would make the patient drink some, while she recited various phrases and incantations. The result: the person would be cured and would leave La Gremma, thanking her for breaking the wicked spell. La Gremma would beam with joy.

Another method for removing the evil eye also entailed isolation of the patient. At sundown of the first day of isolation, La Gremma gave the patient a concoction made of sweet marjoram, orange blossoms and sugar. This was given again at midnight and at noon of the next day. She also sprinkled some powder on the patient. On the third day, she gave some mocha to drink and then led the patient to a hot bath. The patient was smeared with a cleansing solution, as La Gremma recited the necessary formulae. After the bath, the patient was cured.

My father, who helped his mother in effecting these cures, told me that his mother was remarkably successful. She brought cheer and mental relief to depressed and anxiety-ridden men and women. "She knew her cures alright," Dad said, "but mainly she was a masterly psychologist. She understood peoples' needs, their fears and sorrows. She knew exactly what to do to restore them to health and happiness."

Dad told of the time when one of the young men of the family was about to announce his engagement to a non-Jewish woman. La Gremma was horrified at the idea of a family member marrying out of the faith. She came up with a solution.

First, she found out the name and address of the prospective bride. Then, she made my father go to a store and buy a quantity of lard. At midnight, she had my father—then a teenager—take the lard to the address of the young woman in question. La Gremma instructed him to smear the lard on the steps and porch of the bride's house and then return home immediately. Dad always recalled this incident with some terror, remembering how frightened he was that he would be caught for trespassing and damaging property.

Dad followed La Gremma's instructions even though he thought the whole enterprise was outrageous. But it worked. Within a few days the engagement was broken off. Shortly afterward, the young man became engaged to a Jewish young lady. When they were married, La Gremma beamed with joy that perhaps no one but my father could have fully understood.

Although my grandparents Angel both died before I was born, they have had a strong influence on me. When I chose a topic for my doctoral dissertation at Yeshiva University, it was "The History of the Jews of the Island of Rhodes." This project went on to become my first published book. It was a topic that had been aching within me. In studying the history of the Jews of Rhodes, I was trying to come closer to the world of my own grandparents.

In the summer of 1974, I travelled to Rhodes to complete my doctoral research.

A grandchild visiting the city of his dead grandparents for the first time searches for hidden messages in every street sign and store front. Each winding road whispers secrets that cannot be easily deciphered and memories that can no longer be remembered.

The Jewish community of Rhodes had come to a virtual end on July 24, 1944—a year and one day before my birth. On that day, the Nazis deported the nearly 2000 Jews still living in Rhodes. Very few survived the Nazi death camps. The Sephardic community of Rhodes began as a result of the expulsion of Jews from Spain in 1492. It ended in the ashes of Nazi concentration camps.

During the ten days I spent in Rhodes, I tried to recreate in my mind the Jewish community as it had been when my grandparents had lived there. I wandered through the winding streets of the former Jewish Quarter within the old walled city of Rhodes. I found a few Hebrew inscriptions on some buildings. I located the sites of now destroyed synagogues, as well as the one synagogue that still stands. Only a gate of the Alliance Israelite Universelle school survived the bombings of World War II; the school itself was demolished.

I walked along the Mandraki and observed the bustle and

commotion of the merchants on one side, and the eternal sea on the other side. Out in the distance were los tres molinos, the three windmills dating back to medieval times when the Knights of St. John ruled the island.

The Jewish Quarter was filled with tourists. The main square, that the Jews had called la calle ancha, the broad street, was lined with tourist shops and eateries. The main street in the former Jewish Quarter was renamed after the war: it is called the Street of the Hebrew Martyrs. Except for the street sign and a few other clues that Jews had once lived here, the Jewish presence has been almost entirely wiped out. The homes that Jews had once occupied are now filled with Greek families. The stores that Jews had once owned now cater to tourists. I had the feeling of being at a carnival that had been erected on a cemetery.

On Friday night, I stood at the reader's desk in the Kahal Shalom, the remaining synagogue in the once thriving Jewish Quarter. I conducted the Sabbath services according to the style of the Rhodes Jews, as I had learned it growing up in Seattle among Jews of Rhodes origin. I imagined that my grandparents had prayed in this same synagogue when it had been crowded and alive; they had sung the same melodies, uttered the same words. That Friday night all but four people at the service were tourists. Some of us were of Rhodes descent, searching for shadows and sparks from our past, thinking we had found something but unsure of what it was.

After services, I walked alone through the old Juderia. Although it was bustling with activity, as far as the Jews are concerned it is mainly filled with memories of death.

A plaque is affixed to the synagogue. It lists the family names of the Jews who had been murdered by the Nazis. My eyes immediately, spontaneously, found the name Angel—relatives I had never known, who had been deported to their deaths one year and one day before I was born. This was as close as I had come to meeting Uncle Joseph, his wife Sinyoru, and his four children—my cousins—Leon, Bulissa, Jacob and Sarah.

My grandparents were among the lucky ones to have left

Rhodes in the early 20th century. Even though they died before I was born, they helped create a living memory that they transmitted to the future generations of their family.

Whenever I return to Seattle, I drive through the old neighborhood in the central district. I go to the houses that contain my childhood.

The psychiatrist and philosopher, Viktor Frankl, has noted that the truest and surest aspects of life are in the past. They have already been lived; they are done and can never be changed. While the future is uncertain, the past is fixed. The older one grows, the more of life has been deposited in the secure treasury of history. Looking back, one sees what has been done and accomplished; looking ahead, one can only hope and pray. Being an elder, then, has its genuine virtues and pleasures.

And yet, when one contemplates the past through the prism of memory, the result is not necessarily to find certainty. Rather, memory tends to focus on some things and ignore others. Memory makes some people glow in a halo of greatness, while others are remembered with their many defects. What we remember is not an exact description of the past; it is, for all sorts of reasons, that which made the deepest and most lasting impressions on us. We incorporate those memories into our own lives; the remembered past lives on within us.

When I go through the old neighborhood, I sometimes feel that I am once again a little boy who belongs there. But then I shake my head and realize that I am only a stranger to the people who now fill the houses and the neighborhood.

On a summer day many years ago, my wife Gilda and I drove to my childhood home at 511 28th Avenue. Listening to me reminisce, Gilda asked me if we could knock on the door of the house and find out if the owner would let us take a quick look through. I told her that I did not want to do that. She hesitated for a moment and then got out of the car. She went up the front steps of the house and knocked on the door.

A jovial African-American woman appeared at the entrance. My wife told her that I had grown up in this house. Could we take a quick look at it and perhaps snap a few photographs? The owner smiled and told Gilda that this would be fine with her. Gilda waved to me to come upstairs. I came out of the car but said I didn't really want to bother anyone, that I was happy just to see the house from the outside.

Gilda thanked the owner of the house and then came back down the steps of the front porch. She took a few pictures of the house from the front and then went up the long driveway to the back of the house where she took several more photographs in the backyard.

When she returned to the car, she put the camera in her purse and looked at me in wonderment. As we drove off, I told her about the backyard of the house…the old tree I used to climb, the little patch of dirt where we used to grow parsley and mint, the white picket fence that separated us from our neighbor's dog, Pete.

"Why didn't you go look at the back yard again now that you had the opportunity? And why didn't you go into the house when the lady said we could take a look around?"

"I guess I would rather leave the past in my mind the way I remember it. This house is not the thing I want; it's the house in my mind that I want to keep."

When Gilda had the roll of film developed, we found that only one of her photographs of the old house had been developed successfully. The only picture that came out was a shot of the outside front of the house, the house as we saw it from the car, the house as I wanted to keep it in my memory.

On our visits to Seattle, we not only would visit the old neighborhood. We also would visit the Sephardic cemetery. My mother and father are buried side by side. Mom had died in 1983, and Dad passed away in 1991. Walking through the cemetery, we would visit the graves of my parents, grandparents, uncles and aunts, and so many relatives and friends.

For me, a visit to the Sephardic cemetery of Seattle proves the wisdom of the ancient Jewish sages who referred to a cemetery as beth hahayyim, the home of the living. Though this term is a euphemism, it also is--in a significant sense—true. Those who are laid to rest in the cemetery have indeed died; yet, their lives continue to influence those who loved and knew them. They have died; but their memories live on, at least for the next generation or two.

The rows of neatly-kept tombstones remind me of many lives, many stories. Part of my own life is safely deposited in this beth hahayyim.

Bits and pieces of lives, bits and pieces of memories.

Not far from the grave of my Nona Romey is the grave of Uncle Moshe, my father's oldest brother. Uncle Moshe and his wife, Aunty Bohora, lived just around the block from our house. Their red brick home was on the corner of Jefferson and Temple Place (later to be called Empire Way, and now Martin Luther King Jr. Way).

Uncle Moshe spoke in a loud voice. Everything about him conveyed strength and determination. My Uncle Avner told us that Uncle Moshe had to flee from Rhodes to America early in the 20th century. When he had been a worker in a bakery in Rhodes, someone had come into the store and had made some nasty comments to him. Uncle Moshe lifted a large iron pan and smashed the man's head open. No one could insult him and get away with it!

When his parents learned what their first-born son had done, they quickly arranged for him to leave for Seattle, where several Rhodes Jews had already settled.

Whether or not this story is actually true, it left a special aura on the character of Uncle Moshe. We all knew that it could have been true. We all learned reverence for him; no one wanted to raise his ire.

He was loud, energetic and tough. He took chances. He feared no one.

Uncle Moshe used to call me by a series of nicknames: Marconi, Macaroni, Markooch, Markoocho. Even in his toughness, he could be soft and gentle. When I remember him, I envision him with a wan smile on his face. But his advice to me was consistent: don't let anyone push you around; don't be afraid to take risks; stand up for your rights.

In the mid-1950s, the city planners decided to widen Temple Place in order to create Empire Way, a much larger road that could handle a lot more traffic. A problem arose, though, when it became clear that the road would cut right through Uncle Moshe's house.

The city officials approached Uncle Moshe and informed him of the plans. They offered to buy his house at an attractive price.

"What will you do to my house if you buy it?" Uncle asked.

"We will demolish it so that the highway can run through the lot."

"It's not for sale," said Uncle Moshe defiantly.

No amount of persuasion or financial incentives could budge him. It was his house, he liked it, no one could tell him what to do. He was not about to sell his home only to have it destroyed. Certain things in life were worth fighting for, and one's own home was one of them.

Dad tried to point out the advantages of selling the house. "Listen, Moshe, this is a great opportunity for you. You can make a nice profit and buy a new house, a better one. In any case, you can't win this time. The city will build its highway whether you like it or not."

"You don't understand," explained Uncle Moshe. "This is

America, not a tyranny. In America people are free, we have rights. We can't let ourselves be thrown out of our own house. The government will defend my rights."

The planners were able to settle with all other home owners whose property would be affected by the construction of Empire Way. Uncle Moshe was the last holdout.

Finally, one of the city officials came up with an idea and made a suggestion to Uncle Moshe. "The city will not buy your house and will not demolish it. Instead, the city will move your house a few yards back so that it will be out of the way of the highway. It will pay you for the land it expropriates as well as for the inconvenience to you and your family."

Uncle Moshe was exuberant. "Who said I couldn't beat City Hall?" he gloated.

And so it was. A construction company came, picked up the house on huge beams, and moved it out of the path of the new road. Uncle Moshe had won.

The victory was short lived. The house was moved only a few yards back, but somehow that changed everything. Uncle Moshe felt that the house had been damaged in the moving process. As he looked out his window at the construction of the highway, he began to realize that the world outside his house was changing. More people, more cars, more noise, more air pollution. In the end, he had wanted to live in his home as it had been, on the quiet corner of Jefferson and Temple Place. Now there was to be a steady stream of traffic on the highway that ran right by his house.

It was not too long before Uncle Moshe died.

The first funeral I attended was the funeral of Uncle Moshe. I was eleven or twelve years old. We went into the Jewish chapel on twelfth and Alder. A large gathering of family and friends had come to pay their final respects.

I saw the casket in front of the room but did not know what it was. I asked Dad what was in the box. "Uncle Moshe is in there," he answered simply.

I remember my perplexity. "How did Uncle Moshe let anyone

36

put him in a box?"

"He can't fight anymore," Dad said somberly.

That is when I first started to understand what death was.

If Uncle Moshe was loud, his younger brother Ralph was every bit his equal. When Uncle Moshe and Uncle Ralph were together, the volume of their conversations was truly awesome. As a newly-wed, Mom had been terrified to have these brothers-in-law in her home. Dad reassured her that they were both good men, but they tended to speak in loud voices. Mom never entirely lost her fear of Uncle Moshe and Uncle Ralph.

Uncle Ralph's wife, Aunty Hanulah, was a really lovely, sweet woman, with a ready smile on her face. She and Mom had a warm relationship. So as long as Aunty Hanulah was with Uncle Ralph, Mom was not nervous.

After the death of Uncle Moshe, Uncle Ralph's voice became softer, his manner somewhat more reserved. He, too, was getting old. His eldest brother had died; he saw himself as being next in line.

One day—after we had already moved to the new neighborhood in Seward Park—Uncle Ralph (who was still living in the old neighborhood) telephoned my father. He was planning to attend synagogue services the next morning at the new Ezra Bessaroth building. He told Dad that he wanted to come to our home for breakfast after services. Being a request from an elder brother, Dad was obliged to comply. This situation was mainly of concern to Mom. After all, Dad left for work early in the morning and he would not be home for breakfast with Uncle Ralph.

Mom prepared a breakfast of hard boiled eggs, sliced tomatoes, sweet rolls, homemade white cheese swimming in oil, and raki (a strong anise-flavored alcoholic beverage favored by Turkish and Greek people). I was surprised by this menu. How could anyone eat this kind of food so early in the morning? What was wrong with toast, cereal and a cup of coffee? Mom smiled. "Uncle Ralph will like this much better."

And so it was. He arrived at our home and ate his breakfast as though it was the most normal morning meal in the world; and he drank several shots of raki without blinking an eye. After he had eaten to his satisfaction, Mom told him politely that she had to get to her household chores. Uncle Ralph was unperturbed. He had travelled all the way to the Seward Park neighborhood and he wanted to stay longer. He said that he would be quite content to sit in the dining room near the window that overlooked the street. He sat there for several hours, quietly, meditatively. He didn't yell, didn't raise his voice, didn't make any demands. He just sat gazing at the passing cars, lost in his thoughts. He had changed; perhaps he was preparing himself for his forthcoming death.

I tried to make small talk with Uncle Ralph. He nodded politely but kept his eyes focused out the window. "So many cars," he said softly. "So many cars. Where are they coming from? Where are they going? Why is everyone in such a rush?" He nodded his head slowly and sipped raki. "It is time for quiet and rest. Too much traffic, too much noise. What does it all mean and where does it get you?"

Several months after his breakfast at our house, Uncle Ralph died. He was buried in the Sephardic cemetery in a grave adjoining that of Papoo Romey who had died a week earlier. They were buried in a new row of graves against the back fence of the cemetery.

And just beyond the fence was the highway, cars rushing by in an endless procession.

Uncle Avner was caught in the middle. His two older brothers, Moshe and Ralph, demanded his obedient loyalty; and he gave it to them. It was his duty to respect his older brothers and he would do so even to his own detriment.

But his two younger brothers, Ray and Victor (my father), made their own way in life. While respectful of their older brothers, Ray and Victor were part of the new Americanized generation. They strove for independence. Ray and Victor started their own businesses, and Avner found himself—more than once—working for his younger brothers. For Uncle Avner, this seemed to be an inversion of the normal order of things. He should have been the boss, not the employee.

Uncle Avner, the middle son of the family, was consumed with his need to be honored and respected. He was stubborn, hot tempered and demanding. He felt that no one adequately appreciated him; so he often reminded people of their obligation to honor him. This tactic only served to exacerbate his problem; the more honor he demanded, the less he received.

One of my early memories of Uncle Avner was an incident that occurred on a Sabbath morning in the old Ezra Bessaroth synagogue building on 15th and Fir. Following services, there was a memorial service for a deceased parent of one of the members. It was customary on such occasions for families to provide refreshments in the vestry room adjoining the sanctuary. The usual fare included sweet rolls, hard boiled eggs, Greek olives, raisins, pickles, sliced tomatoes, whiskey and raki. On this particular Sabbath, the family provided the refreshments—but not enough to go around. By the time Uncle Avner got to the table, there were no more hard boiled eggs. His face flushed, Uncle Avner loudly demanded a hard boiled egg. He was told that there were none left. This infuriated him. He started to shout: "Why don't I get an egg? Am I not important enough? Do only bigshots get eggs? Why is the family so cheap that they can't provide enough eggs for all the members? I'm entitled to an egg just like everyone else." Dad tried to calm his brother down but it was no use. Uncle Avner kept on shouting until people edged their way out of the room; soon, there was no one left to listen to his grievances. I clung to my father in terror. He told me: "Don't be afraid. Uncle Avner has a bad temper. In truth, he is right. There should have been enough eggs for everyone. But once he lost his temper, he lost his argument. Once he started to shout, he was wrong."

That event was typical of Uncle Avner's attitude. No one could slight his feelings without hearing about it from him. At a buffet reception, Mom once made the mistake of inviting Uncle Avner to the table to help himself to some food. He raged at her: "What do you mean by that? I don't go to any table for food! My wife serves me my food! I don't stand on line for anyone." At a memorial service, the reader asked Uncle Avner to be quiet so that services could begin. Uncle Avner responded in a fury: "No one tells me to be quiet! I tell others when to be quiet!" He kept on talking for a few minutes until he had proved his point. Only after he was ready did the service begin.

If Uncle Avner was ornery and willful, his wife—Aunty Suzie—was his equal. She did not put up with his outbursts. She kept him in line, and together they raised a really fine group of children.

Uncle Avner's quest for respect got him nowhere. His older brothers looked down on him as a younger brother. His younger brothers did not have patience to constantly appease him. His wife was not subservient to him. His relatives and the community at large did not appreciate his temper tantrums.

Yet Uncle Avner had his virtues. He was genuinely loyal and straightforward. He was devoted to Rabbi Isidore Kahan, rabbi of Ezra Bessaroth, and often drove Rabbi Kahan where ever he needed to go.

As he grew older, Uncle Avner mellowed somewhat. He and Aunty Suzie became active in the Golden Age Club sponsored by the Jewish Community Center. They helped out at the Kline Galland Home for the Aged. Uncle Avner, now an old man, apparently gave up his lifelong quest for honor. It didn't matter much anymore if people gave him the respect he thought he deserved or if they ignored. Him. He would just do what he liked, try to get along, help others to enjoy their golden years.

Amazingly enough, in his last years, he actually became well liked and respected. As soon as he had given up his life's battle for respect, that is when he started to win respect. Only when he admitted his own defeat did he achieve victory.

Aunty Victoria made us laugh.

She was my father's eldest sister. I never knew her husband. Whenever I asked about him, my parents became very serious and said he was at Sedro-Woolley. It took me a while before I dared to ask what Sedro-Woolly was.

I eventually learned that Sedro-Woolley is a town in upstate Washington, the location of a mental institution. Aunty Victoria's husband had been hurt in a serious automobile accident, leaving him with permanent injury to his brain.

In her husband's absence, Aunty Victoria had to raise her family. Being poor did not make things any easier. She worked hard. In spite of her many problems, she was optimistic and full of fun. Although she was highly intelligent, her playful spirit led her sometimes to play the role of a scatterbrain. She enjoyed leading people on, teasing them a bit.

Aunty Victoria had her own way of understanding things. Mom once told her of a telephone call she had received from a distant relative in South Africa. The relative was a young lady whose grandparents had emigrated from Rhodes to Rhodesia (now Zimbabwe). The family later moved to Capetown. She called my mother to ask if she could stay at our home during a projected visit to Seattle. The problem was that she intended this visit to last for six months to a year. Mom politely declined.

Aunty Victoria was intrigued with this story. "And how old is she?" she asked.

"About nineteen or twenty."

"1920? If she was born in 1920, she's already well on in years. Why isn't she married?"

"No, Victoria," Mom explained, "I said she is nineteen or twenty years old."

"Es wad I say, (That's what I said)," Aunty Victoria insisted. "If she was born in 1920, she should already be married."

After several more attempts to clarify the facts, Mom gave up. "You're right, Victoria. If she calls again, I'll tell her that she should have already gotten married since she was born in 1920."

"Es wad I say," nodded Aunty Victoria with a big smile, proud of her victory.

When Mom was in the hospital for the birth of my brother David, Aunty Victoria moved into our house to help keep things in order. Each morning she would come into the kitchen as though in a daze. She would say nothing, respond to no greeting or question. She went to the refrigerator, poured herself a glass of orange juice, puckered up her face, opened her eyes wide and then sang out: Good morning! For Aunty Victoria, the day did not start until she had her orange juice.

But then, she shook off her languor and became a knot of energy. She cleaned, cooked, rushed around. She sent my father to work after having packed him a huge lunch. She dressed up the children. She never negotiated with us: just instructed us.

One of the severest trials of her stay in our house was bath time. It was her considered opinion that the hot water from the tap was not really hot. A real bath required heating a pot of water on the stove and then pouring it into the tub—when we were in the tub! We dreaded taking baths. We pleaded with her, begged her. It made no difference. To bathe properly required hot water; only hot water can make one clean; and hot water is obtained by heating it on the stove. That's it. Period.

When we later complained to Mom about these scalding baths, she said: "Well, at least you know you got clean and killed all the germs." Aunty Victoria was vindicated.

Whenever she heard a car honking outside, Aunty Victoria

would get up and call out, "I comee (I'm coming)." I once asked her why she did that., "Well, maybe the car is coming to pick me up to take me someplace."

"But Aunty, people honk the horns of their cars all the time. They aren't coming here to pick you up."

"But how do you know? Can you be so sure? Maybe this time it is someone coming for me."

"But you know the truth, Aunty."

"I do know the truth, little Markito, but you don't know the truth." And that is where the conversation ended. I never raised the question again. Nor did anyone else.

Aunty Victoria often called me cusuegroo, in-law, in the Rhodes pronunciation of Judeo-Spanish. Of course, I was her nephew not her in-law. Aunty Victoria followed her own logic. I was named after my mother's father. My grandfather was an in-law to the Angel family. By simple transference, I (who carried my grandfather's name) became a personification of my grand-father.

She was consistent in this practice. She called my sister, Bernice "Mommy," since Bernice was named after Bulissa Es-ther, mother of Aunty Victoria. She once scolded a young child for not having greeted her respectfully enough. He was named after his grandfather who owned a grocery store that Aunty Vic-toria patronized. She told the bewildered child: "Bension, why don't you treat me better? After all, I am a good customer. I pay my bills. I never give your trouble." The child had no idea what was going on; but the rest of us had a good laugh.

In following her own rule of conservation of characters, those who shared the same name became, in some special sense, one person. The grandparents and grandchildren, linked together by their names, became identical in Aunty Victoria's playful version of reality. We laughed at this quirk of hers; but in her humorous way, she was articulating a very profound understanding of the nature of a family, of the mystery of the generations.

Aunty Victoria, through her understanding of the role of names, was apt to integrate new acquaintances into her world-view by making their names more familiar to her. In so doing, she changed a person from being a stranger to being a long-time friend. When I came to Seattle for Passover in 1967 with my wife-to-be Gilda, Aunty Victoria was quick to change Gilda's name to Zimbul, a popular name among Sephardic women from Turkey.

"No," my mother explained. "Her name is Gilda, not Zimbul."

Aunty's eyes squinted a bit; her brain seemed to be processing this information. "Es wad I say, Zimbul." She gave Gilda a warm hug. Gilda became Zimbul and was happy to go along with her new name. Gilda, who was 100% Ashkenazic, liked the idea of having a Sephardic name. So everyone was happy.

Aunty Victoria was a patriotic American. She decided to become a citizen. She learned to read English. She studied the various facts that one must know in order to pass the citizenship test. When the day of the test came, we all wished her well…but never expected that she would pass.

"Don't worry," she assured us. "I will pass. I love America."

After the test, she gleefully gave us a report. She had indeed passed.

"They asked me questions and I gave them answers. I kept telling them how much I love America. I am not sure if I understood them or if they understood me. Finally, they asked me the name of the President of the United States. I told them I was proud to be in America, in a free country, where a Jew can be President. Our President is Isaac Hower. We call him Ike." (For Aunty Victoria, the names Isaac and Ike were exclusively Jewish names!)

"But Aunty," I protested, "the President's name is Eisenhower."

"Es wad I say, Isaac Hower."

"No, it's Eisenhower. Dwight David Eisenhower."

"Es wad I say, Isaac Hower. God bless him."

I looked at Aunty Victoria's face and she was red with suppressed laughter.

"You're right, Aunty. You're always right."

"Es wad I say."

In her old age, Aunty Victoria never lost her sense of humor. But her face was serious more often, and her laughing eyes started to show glints of sadness, tiredness. She had lived long enough to see one husband die at a young age, one husband institutionalized, some of her children and grandchildren marry out of the faith. She was traumatized when she had to move from the old neighborhood in the central district to the new neighborhood in Seward Park. She had lived in the old neighborhood for over fifty years and was at home there.

One Saturday night, our family went to visit Aunty Victoria. We found her sitting on her front porch staring into the dark, cloudy sky. The lights of her house were off.

"Buenas semanas," we called to her with the traditional greeting at the conclusion of the Sabbath on Saturday night.

Aunty Victoria waved her hands. "No, Shabbat is not over. I don't see three stars yet." (According to tradition, the Sabbath is deemed to have ended once it is night. Seeing three stars is an indication that it is truly night and that the Sabbath has concluded.)

"But, Victoria," Dad responded with a smile, "it's very cloudy tonight. Of course you can't see three stars. Sunset was long ago! Shabbat is over."

"No," said Aunty Victoria adamantly. "If I don't see three stars, Shabbat is not over. I am going to wait here until Shabbat ends."

"Don't be silly," Dad prodded. "You will be staying on the porch all night. It's too cloudy to see stars tonight."

Aunty Victoria did not budge. We stayed with her for an hour or so, but she would not concede that Shabbat was over. On the way home, Dad was in a somber mood. "Aunty Victoria doesn't want Shabbat to be over. She doesn't want anything to change. She knows that Shabbat is over and she knows that everything is changing."

I don't know how late she sat on her porch waiting to see three stars.

Uncle Marco and Aunty Luna were an interesting pair. Uncle Marco was a perpetual joker. He loved a good time, loved to laugh. Aunty Luna, my father's sister, was serious and devout. Uncle Marco enjoyed smoking cigars and playing pinochle; Aunty Luna found happiness in prayer and religious devotion. Uncle Marco didn't mind cutting corners; Aunty Luna was a stickler for detail.

They had unusual quarrels. Uncle Marco was once recounting a car trip they took to California. He indicated that he got a speeding ticket in San Francisco. "No," said Aunty Luna solemnly, "we got the ticket near Sacramento." Uncle Marco strenuously maintained that the ticket was received in San Francisco. Aunty Luna was adamant that it was received near Sacramento. The disagreement continued for the better part of an hour, until another relative arrived who had been in the car with them. "Now," said Uncle Marco with glee, "now we have an eye witness. Tell us: where did we receive the speeding ticket?" The witness answered promptly: "Just outside Los Angeles." And of course this generated a three way controversy that went on for another half hour.

"What difference does it make where you got the ticket?" Mom asked innocently.

Then all three combatants shouted my mother down. "What do you mean what difference does it make? Aren't you interested in truth? Isn't it important to establish fact from falsehood?"

As things turned out, Aunty Luna was correct; she usually was. Uncle Marco was forced to admit it. "So who cares where I got the ticket? Why make such a big deal over a trifling detail?" Then he laughed and lit up a cigar.

One time they quarreled about the year of Aunty Luna's birth. Aunty maintained that she was born in 1899. Uncle argued vehemently that she was actually born in 1898.

Aunty: "Don't you think I should know the year I was born?"

Uncle: "You know, but you just don't want to admit the truth."

Aunty: "What are you talking about?"

Uncle: "You just want everyone to think you're a spring chicken, younger than you actually are."

Aunty: "Are you serious?"

Uncle: Laughter.

Uncle Marco told us stories of his childhood in Rhodes. As a teenager, he had been nicknamed palyachi because he was an acrobat. He could do somersaults and handstands; he could juggle; he could outrun his friends. He was known for his sense of humor and for his love of pranks.

He told us that ships bringing merchandise to Rhodes would anchor in the deep water off shore. Workers from Rhodes would row boats to the ships, transfer the merchandise into the boats, and row back to shore.

Some ships brought cargoes of food items, including lemons. Uncle Marco used to swim the long distance to the ship, sneak himself aboard, snatch a sack of lemons, and then swim back to shore with his loot. He would then show off his booty to all the young men and women he happened to meet in the street.

Uncle Marco recounted these exploits with great enthusiasm and joy. "Why would you want to steal lemons?" I asked him. "And why would you brag about stealing them?"

Uncle Marco's face broke into a broad, happy grin. "Hey, I was palyachi, I was a great swimmer, a great athlete. I was faster than anyone. I could snatch lemons right from under their noses and swim away without them catching me. It wasn't lemons I wanted. It was the recognition."

"But what did you prove?"

"Everyone knew that we Jews were smart. Everyone knew that we were good workers. But they used to think that we were weak and cowardly. So I showed them: we are not only smart and industrious; we are also brave and strong. We could beat them at their own game. They had to respect us. My lemons were a badge of honor."

"Are you still proud of what you did?"

Uncle Marco laughed. "Everyone has to do something daring in life. Everyone has to make a statement. It was a great thing to be palyachi. It was a great thing to prove that a Jew could be strong, quick and brave. They never forgot, believe me, they never forgot."

My grandfather Angel's brother, Yosef, was reverentially known as Hermano Yosef or Tio Yosef (brother Yosef or Uncle Yosef). These were terms of respect that Sephardim used for elders, even when they were not actually related to them.

By the time I was born, he was already an old man. Tio Yosef had a light complexion; his hair was white as snow. His head nodded ceaselessly, as though he were constantly saying "no, no, no." I never heard him raise his voice. He was the epitome of gentleness and piety. Tio Yosef enjoyed the respect of our family and the community at large.

His son and daughter-in-law, in whose home he lived, were first cousins. Most of their children were born with physical or mental handicaps. The household in which they lived was not an easy one. Money was scarce; problems were abundant. With all the difficulties, though, Tio Yosef remained a model of calmness and holiness. "All is for the best," he would say. "Praise the Lord for He is good, His mercy endures forever."

Although he was elderly and frail, Tio Yosef found the strength and energy to go to the synagogue often. After the daily prayers had been concluded, he stayed in the synagogue to repair old prayer books and tattered prayer shawls. He made sure that the synagogue was kept neat and clean.

Tio Yosef also cared deeply about the community's cemetery.

He thought that a society could be judged by the way it treated its dead. A properly maintained cemetery showed that the community cared about its departed relatives and friends. It demonstrated that love and respect transcend death.

During the mid-1950s, the Sephardic community of Seattle was in need of new land for a cemetery. The old cemetery was almost filled with graves. Each new death brought sadness not only to the deceased's family, but to the entire community: the cemetery now had one less space for a new grave.

The leaders of the community recognized and acknowledged the problem. Committees were formed, suggestions were made—but little was done. A new cemetery entailed a large expenditure of funds for the land, for a chapel, for maintenance. One of the Sephardic congregations, Ezra Bessaroth, was raising funds in order to build a new sanctuary in the Seward Park district. The other Sephardic congregation, Bikur Holim, was coming to the realization that it too would have to move to Seward Park-- and to raise the money needed for that eventuality. In sum, the community was facing huge expenditures. How would Seattle's Sephardim also be able to pay for a new cemetery?

If the community could not wait long to make its plans, the cemetery also could not wait. People died. They needed to be buried. Families could not be told that a new cemetery would be available some years from now, whenever the money could be raised. There was no negotiating with a dead body.

As community leaders struggled with this dilemma, Tio Yosef decided that he personally would take responsibility for raising the funds for the cemetery. He saw this project as his last mitzvah, a final meritorious deed of pious devotion before he himself would die. Caring for the dead is considered an especially great act of piety since it is done with pure idealism, without expectation of reward. The dead cannot say thank you.

Once he adopted this project, Tio Yosef was infused with newfound energy. He was tireless in his solicitation of funds. "A good name is better than precious oil," he would say. "Contribute generously so that you will share in this great mitzvah."

He went to businesses and homes. He solicited funds from the grocers and fish dealers; from the shoemakers and storekeepers. He solicited from the rich and from the poor. He would not be put off or rejected. "The honor of our community is at stake. We must care for our dead with love and reverence."

Tio Yosef could often be seen walking throughout the neighborhood in search of donations. His head nodded "no, no, no;" but his intensity was "yes, yes, yes." He used his cane as an extra leg, giving him more strength. People marveled at his devotion.

Tio Yosef contributed generously from his own meek assets. "I cannot ask others to do what I won't do myself," he explained. "I am ready to sacrifice. Let everyone else do the same."

I remember my parents discussing the incredible selflessness of Tio Yosef. He had a fire within him. He wanted to accomplish his goal as quickly as possible. He could not be repressed.

At last, the goal was achieved. Enough money was raised to buy the land and build a chapel. Tio Yosef beamed with pride and joy. The cemetery and the chapel were very much his victory. He not only collected funds but inspired others to donate.

The day arrived when the cemetery and chapel were to be dedicated. A large crowd gathered, and Tio Yosef was congratulated and thanked by many. In a special way, this was his day. He had completed his last mitzvah with admirable results.

At the dedication ceremony, it was announced that the chapel would be dedicated in the name of a wealthy couple who had contributed a handsome amount to the cemetery project. The speaker offered profuse praise of this philanthropic couple.

My father was disappointed by the committee's decision. It was Tio Yosef who had rallied the community to support the project. He had given his time and effort; he had contributed of his own meager funds with amazing generosity. The poor make the greatest sacrifices, but the rich are given the honor.

My mother nodded with calm wisdom: "No one said that life is fair."

In the days ahead, Tio Yosef retained his pious demeanor. He showed no frustration, anger or bitterness. Perhaps his head nodded "no, no, no" with a bit more sadness.

"Everything is for the best," he said. "Praise the Lord for He is good, His mercy endures forever."

Uncle Ralph Policar, my Nona's older brother, was the first of his siblings to leave Marmara for Seattle. He arrived in 1906 at the age of 18. He first earned money shining shoes, and later went to work in the fish business, first in Seattle, then in Portland, and even in Boise, Idaho. He married Aunty Sol (Eskenazy) in 1912; they lived in Portland for some time, and then by the 1940s they moved permanently to Seattle.

Uncle Ralph worked hard to earn enough money to bring his sisters to the United States. First he brought his sister, Calo, who married and settled in Portland. Later, he enabled his other sisters—including Nona—to come to Seattle.

I remember Uncle Ralph as a remarkably dignified man. He seemed always to be well dressed. He smoked cigars. He looked like he could have been a president of a bank or a CEO of a big company. He and Aunty Sol bought a home on 31st Avenue with a phenomenal view of Lake Washington. Uncle Ralph would sit on his rocking chair near the window, smoke a cigar, sip a cup of Turkish coffee, and enjoy the view.

He and Aunty Sol planted vegetables in a grass strip in the middle of the driveway to their house. They did not drive, so the driveway was put to good use.

Uncle Ralph was punctual, meticulous and had a strong sense of responsibility for his family. He had a lively sense of humor and often enjoyed a good laugh with his cousin Ike Eskenazy. Ike, also from Marmara, was hilarious when he told stories and laughed uproariously at his own jokes.

With Uncle Ralph's assistance, his sister Sultana travelled to

Seattle with a group of friends from Marmara. Among the group was Bohora Rousso who was going to Seattle to marry a man she had never met. The marriage had been arranged by the parents. The group travelled by ship to New York, and then by train to Seattle.

Bohora's fiancé, Mordecai Coronel, came to meet her at the train station, bringing along his cousin Marco Romey. Bohora met her husband-to-be and both were very pleased. That was also the first time that my grandparents, Marco Romey and Sultana Policar, met. They immediately fell in love and were married on May 23, 1912.

As mentioned earlier, some Sephardim of Seattle had moved to Portland and established a community there. Among the Sephardim of Portland were my Nona's older sister Calo, Calo's husband Isaac, and various relatives.

I remember our family traveling to Portland one summer in order to visit Aunty Calo. I was just a little boy and had never been to her home before. Nor had I ever met her children. As we approached Portland on the highway, Mom turned to the back seat of the car where we children were sitting. She had a serious expression on her face. "We are going to visit Aunty Calo. She has two children living at home with her. I want you to behave yourselves and act natural. The children are midgets."

"Midgets?" I called out in surprise. I didn't know whether to be excited or to be afraid about meeting real midgets.

"They are just like all other human beings, only smaller," Mom continued. "They will feel self-conscious if you treat them in a strange way. Just act natural. Aunty Calo has enough suffering; she doesn't need us to make more problems."

For the remainder of the ride, we were all silent. We each had to think carefully about our forthcoming visit and how we would just act natural.

As Dad drove the car into Aunty Calo's driveway, I felt my heart sink. My older brother Bill had already been to Aunty Calo's house in the past; he was calm. My sister Bernice, being even younger than I, seemed oblivious to the experience before us. I kept repeating Mom's instructions in my mind: act natural.

Aunty Calo greeted us at the door. She was very round—a round face, a round body. To me, even her teeth seemed round. She smiled and laughed with genuine happiness. She hugged each of us and asked us many questions without waiting for answers.

Within a few minutes, we were sitting around her kitchen table. Aunty served Turkish coffee to my parents, and poured glasses of milk for the children. The table was laden with sweets and home-baked pastries like my grandmother baked. I actually started to feel at home and act natural.

But the thought of the midgets lingered in my mind. Where were they? When would we see them? Are they afraid of us? Will I vomit when I first see them? I sat at the table pretending to be natural; but I was filled with dread and confusion.

A few minutes passed. We were stuffing ourselves with Aunty Calo's goodies as she was chatting away and laughing. She was constantly hugging and kissing us. I kept thinking: where are the midgets? Would they hug and kiss me too?

A few more minutes passed. I started to hope that the midgets would not show up. Maybe they were taking a nap, maybe they weren't even home. Maybe Aunty Calo was hiding them away because she was ashamed of them.

After we finished eating, we went into the living room. I tugged at my mother's dress: can we go now? She smiled sternly and told me to behave myself and act natural.

And then it happened. We heard footsteps from the hall staircase. In an instant, David and Esther were in the room with us. In spite of myself, I shuddered.

They were short, wide and bow-legged. They looked as though they had been squashed and compressed by a powerful machine. It was impossible to guess how old they were, although my mother told us they were in their late twenties. When they spoke, they sounded something like Donald Duck. Esther was wearing a lovely party dress and patent leather Mary Jane shoes. David was dressed in slacks and a fashionable V-neck sweater. They were smiling. They came to each of us, shook our hands, and showed real pleasure in welcoming us. I still remember the squeamish feeling I had when I shook their hands.

As Esther and David were greeting us, my eyes shot toward Aunty Calo. She was not ashamed of them at all. She was beaming with pride and happiness.

"Now," Aunty Calo announced, "Esther and David will take the children upstairs to play for a while."

My brother and sister followed right along as the midgets went upstairs. I sidled up to my mother, but she quickly and as inconspicuously as possible shoved me toward the steps. I took a deep breath and followed the others upstairs.

We went into David's room. He showed us some toys and jigsaw puzzles. He really tried hard to be natural. He was a wonderful conversationalist. Both he and Esther were quite intelligent and spent a lot of time reading. We actually were all having a good time together. I thought that I was acting natural; but apparently David sensed my unease. He pulled me aside and whispered into my ear: "Don't worry about us. We are happy. We don't feel sorry for ourselves, so you shouldn't feel sorry for us either." The words pierced through me.

Our visit finally came to a close. We all hugged and kissed Aunty Calo, Esther and David. We got back into the car, and Dad started the engine. We were going to Seaside, Oregon, for a short vacation. It was one of our favorite places. Usually, when we were on the way to Seaside, we children would be singing, fighting, screaming and otherwise expressing our excitement. This time, we were quiet.

"Did I do okay?" I finally asked my mother

"You were all fine," she said to the children. "You were all as natural as you could be."

"It was kind of fun," I said weakly.

"We'll visit them again one day," my mother responded.

I was glad. But I shuddered.

Within the next several years, both Esther and David died. Although I had only met them that one time, I cried when I learned of their deaths. Mom told me that I would get over the sadness.

Many, many years have passed. But the sadness remains.

Nissim was born in Turkey and came to Seattle as a young man. He was short, energetic and had a very loud voice.

Nissim taught me how to tie the tsitsith—ritual fringes placed on four-cornered garments—according to the practice of the Sephardim of Turkey. He showed me how to loop the tsitsith strings in a pattern of ten, five, six, five, the numbers that represent the Hebrew letters constituting the name of God. He also taught me how to tie the knots of the tefillin, leather boxes and straps that men wear during morning daily prayers. The boxes contain parchments with Biblical verses, reminding us to worship God with our mind (intellect), heart (emotion) and arms (actions).

Nissim taught me how to hold my hand over my eyes during the recitation of the Shema prayer. The five fingers of the right hand are so arranged as to form three Hebrew letters that spell Shaddai, one of God's names in Hebrew. One morning, Nissim rushed into synagogue with an extra burst of energy. He pulled out of his pocket a newspaper article about a certain prominent politician. The article was accompanied by a photograph of the politician—a man of impeccable WASP heritage—that caught him at a pensive moment. The photo showed him holding his right hand over his eyes, and his fingers were arranged precisely the way we do when we recite the Shema. Nissim put the photo close to my face: "You see," he told me with delight, "this politician is obviously Jewish. He is saying the Shema. Who would have guessed?" It is unlikely that the politician realized how much hidden meaning there was in this photo of him!

Nissim's religious nature included a profound love for the land of Israel. I remember him telling me how fortunate we were to be living in an era when the holy land had been restored to the Jewish people. He and his wife had travelled to Israel after it had officially been established as a modern state. The memory of that visit stayed with him. It grew into a longing to return to Israel, to live there, and ultimately to die there.

As the years passed, Nissim's yearning for Israel intensified. He told me: "Israel is God's gift to the Jewish people. It is our sacred land since antiquity. We live in a miraculous age when God has given the land back to our people."

Nissim wanted to move to Israel, to live in Jerusalem, to dwell in its holiness. This was a religious ideal that quietly and steadily burned within him. But his wife did not share that dream. Her family and friends lived in Seattle. She had spent most of her life here. How was she now, at her advanced age, to become an immigrant? How could she hope to learn a new language, adapt to a new way of life?

"Nissim," she told him, "Seattle is our home. We have everyone we love here, everything we need here. Let us visit Israel, even stay there for a month or two. But at our age, it makes no sense to leave home and start all over again somewhere else."

To which Nissim would have replied: "Israel is our real home. Seattle has only been a rest stop along the way. Israel is the home of our people and that's where we belong." Instead of offering this reply, he accepted his wife's words with silent resignation. He would not settle in Jerusalem without her; and she was not ready to make the move.

At some point, Nissim and his wife took a car trip to California. They were involved in a serious accident and his wife was injured badly. She never fully recovered; she died some months later. She was buried in the Sephardic cemetery in Seattle.

Nissim was somber and heartbroken. As a sign of mourning, he let his beard grow, white and full. His eyes were deeper, his voice softer. He looked like he could have been one of the ancient prophets of Israel.

Months past. Then Nissim announced that he was going to move to Jerusalem. He arranged to have his wife disinterred from the cemetery in Seattle and transferred to a cemetery in Israel. He suddenly became re-energized. His eyes grew brighter, his voice stronger. He was at last going to fulfill his dream of moving to Jerusalem.

When he left Seattle, he was crying. He had long wanted to settle in Jerusalem with his wife. Now he was going there to bury her. And to spend his last years waiting to join her in the Jerusalem on high.

Among the regular guests at my grandparents' home each Shabbat afternoon were Uncle Morris and Aunty Esther. Aunty was Nona's sister. The two of them were very devoted to each other. When Nona was ill—which was often—Aunty Esther would visit her and try to lift her spirits.

Aunty Esther, like Aunty Calo, was round. Everything about her seemed round—no angles, nothing jarring. She laughed heartily and often. She exuded a spirit of goodwill and honesty.

Uncle Morris was a sturdy, handsome man, born on the Island of Rhodes. He was always at Aunty Esther's side. Papoo used to excuse himself early on Shabbat afternoons in order to go upstairs and take his Sabbath nap. Uncle Morris would then be left as the only adult male in a room full of women and children. He never seemed to mind. He participated actively in the discussions, complained about the many injustices in the world, laughed at funny stories.

My mother and us children would walk to Nona and Papoo's house almost every Saturday after lunch. Occasionally, Dad would join us, although his normal pattern was to devote the afternoon to his Shabbat nap.

I grew up expecting to see Uncle Morris and Aunty Esther together at my grandparents' home on Shabbat afternoons. This is how things were for years.

At some point, though, their attendance at the Shabbat afternoon gatherings began to decline. At first, they missed a Shabbat every now and then; but soon, the absences grew more frequent.

I asked Mom why they did not come to visit Nona as much as before. "Aunty Esther has not been feeling well."

"What's wrong with her?" I asked.

"They don't know."

This information—or lack of information—weighed heavily on me. They didn't know! How could she be cured if they didn't even know what was wrong with her?

When Uncle Morris and Aunty Esther did appear at Nona's house on some Shabbat afternoons, I stared at her as inconspicuously as I could, to see if I could detect what was wrong with her. She looked a bit pale, less round than usual. Her joviality was somewhat diminished. But all in all, she seemed to be mostly alright.

As the weeks proceeded, her condition obviously deteriorated. Her eyes seemed to be gazing at something far away. Her conversation drifted. She started to forget our names. One could see from Uncle Morris's expression that something was seriously amiss. He was as devoted to her as ever; but his face showed the strains of prolonged anguish.

Nona observed with sadness the gradual transformation of her beloved sister. Aunty Esther looked almost the same on the outside. But her mind was going. Day by day, her memory was slipping away. Little by little, she stopped recognizing us.

Aunty Esther's face continued to smile, out of habit. She laughed, but didn't seem to know why she was laughing. Her face was the same, but her mind was not the same.

Nona had stoical tendencies. She tried to accept Aunty Esther's illness with equanimity, hoping that it would be cured. There was to be no cure. As this reality sank into Nona's consciousness, she mourned the loss of her sister. For although Aunty Esther's body was still intact, her memory had died; she was now only an image of who she had been.

Eliyahu and Reyna Romey, photo taken in Tekirdag,
Turkey, late 19th century

Marco and Sultana Romey (author's maternal grandparents) with their
children. left to right, Regina, David (sitting on the stool) Leo, Estreya and
Rachel (author's mother)

Family group, taken in Rhodes c. 1911. Bulissa Esther Angel (author's grand-mother) is at the center of the photo, surrounded by her children, and some neighbor children. On the bottom row, far right, wearing a fez, is Joseph...who wasn't allowed entry into the US and had to return to Rhodes while the rest of the family went on to Seattle.

Rachel and Victor Angel at the time of their engagement

Rachel and Victor Angel, wedding photo

A "visita": left to right: Rachel Altabet, Rachel Angel (standing), Victoria
Franco, Sultana Romey and Marc Angel (the author)

Aunty Esther lived on for a number of years, with Uncle Morris and family devoting themselves to caring for her.

Some people die suddenly. Some die after a protracted illness. Aunty Esther seemed to have died by gradually fading away.

Aunty Kadun, another of Nona's sisters, was beautiful, stately and elegant. She dressed well, tending to the side of formality. She had a very dry sense of humor and would often not laugh at things that seemed funny to everyone else. It became an informal game among us to see if we could get Aunty Kadun to laugh. We usually lost.

Like her sisters, Aunty Kadun was born in Marmara and had come to Seattle as a teenager. She lacked formal education but was highly intelligent. Her mind was alert and retentive. She knew a great many things.

She did not have an easy life. Nevertheless, she would not let herself be crushed by adversity. Her inner pride and grace helped her to overcome many troubles.

Aunty Kadun was a lady of style and moral seriousness. She believed that good people did not use curse words. When she became angry, she would nod her head in perplexity, or would mutter the words "Sacramento California" in a tone of voice that sounded as though she were cursing. As a little boy, I thought "Sacramento California" was a swear word.

She did not approve of women wearing pants, immodest dresses or swim suits. Mothers should behave like mothers; and grandmothers like grandmothers. These were serious roles, requiring modesty and decency. Children who grew up seeing their mothers dressed immodestly would lose respect for their mothers; they would not grow up to be good parents themselves.

Aunty Kadun was very sensitive to breezes. Whenever she

came to our house, we had to close the windows. If she was in the car with us, the windows remained closed no matter how hot and stuffy it became. She usually wore a sweater or long sleeved dress, even in the summer.

She was frequently at our home. It was customary for the ladies in our community to have visitas, little social gatherings, from time to time. They would invite a few of their relatives and friends, and would prepare a wonderful array of baked goods and sweets. My mother invariably would invite Aunty Kadun to the visitas at our house.

Although these gatherings were not held to commemorate any special occasion, they were treated with a certain degree of formality. The hostess baked everything that was to be served; to offer store-bought goods was tactless and disrespectful. The food was served on the best set of dishes. The hostess and guests dressed up nicely and would not think of wearing something casual or informal.

Women would host visitas whenever the mood struck them, or whenever they felt they had to repay social obligations. One of the visitas hosted by my mother came about in an unusual way. Mom received a telephone call from a woman who said she wanted to stop by for a visit. The voice was friendly and warm. It spoke in Spanish, meaning that the caller was someone from the older generation. Spontaneously, Mom invited her to a visita the following week.

After hanging up the phone, Mom started to make up a list of people to invite. The only problem was that she had not recognized the voice of the woman who had called her! She was too embarrassed to ask the caller to identify herself.

Mom called Aunty Kadun. "We are having a visita at my house next week. We have a mystery guest. Will you be able to attend?"

Aunty Kadun, who had little patience with practical jokes, retorted: "Rachel (Rashelle, as she pronounced it), what do you mean 'a mystery guest?' Enough of this nonsense. Who is coming to the visita?"

"I really don't know, Aunty."

"Maybe I don't like your mystery guest. Maybe I won't come unless you tell me who she is."

"Honestly, Aunty, I don't know. It will be a surprise for all of us."

"Asi biva yo (as I live), I think you are playing a game with me. You shouldn't tease your elders."

During the week before the visita, Aunty Kadun called my mother several times to find out the identity of the mystery guest. She was reluctant to attend a social gathering where she might meet someone she did not particularly like.

When the day of the visita came, Aunty Kadun was the first to arrive. My mother told her not to show any surprise when the mystery guest arrived. She wanted the guest to feel remembered and loved. It would be embarrassing if she ever were to find out the real story behind this visita.

As the guests arrived, Aunty Kadun remained a bit distant and ill at ease. Soon enough, though, the mystery guest appeared—an old friend of the family whom Aunty Kadun liked very much. The afternoon turned out to be a great success. When the visita was over, Aunty Kadun remained for a few minutes after the other guests had left.

"I tell you, Rachel, it was a lovely party. But you nearly gave me an ulcer. All week I was torturing myself about whether or not I would know or like your mystery guest, or whether you were just playing a game with me." Then she gave Mom a classic Aunty Kadun compliment: "Even though you almost killed me, it was a nice visita."

This reminded Mom of another compliment she had received from Aunty Kadun: "Rachel, you are very demure, you hardly eat anything. And yet, you are not slender!"

Aunty Kadun's personality showed itself in another episode. Mom had planted squash in a vegetable patch in our back yard. The squash grew amazingly well. One of them reached an exceptionally large size, and Mom took a snapshot of it with her Brownie camera. When the film was developed, Mom placed the photograph on the mantle over the fireplace in the living room, next to an assortment of family photographs.

On one of her visits to our home, Aunty Kadun found herself in the living room looking at the pictures on the mantle. Being a bit nearsighted, she gazed wonderingly at the picture of the squash, not quite able to recognize who it was.

"Rachel, who is in this picture?"

My mother laughed. "It's my calavasa (squash), Aunty."

Aunty Kadun gave my mother one of her famous cynical glances. "Why are you teasing me? I asked you a simple question, so you should answer me. Who is the baby in the picture?"

"Really, Aunty. It's my calavasa."

"Don't be silly. No one takes pictures of a calavasa and puts it on the mantle among family photos."

"But that is exactly what I did. The calavasa grew so large, I wanted to take a picture of it. I'm very proud of it."

Aunty Kadun removed her glasses and held the photograph close to her eyes. "Asi biva yo, Rachel, this is a picture of a calavasa!"

She looked at Mom who had begun to laugh. And then even Aunty Kadun had a good laugh.

As the years passed, Aunty Kadun retained her vigorous health, energy and dignity. She seemed timeless, changeless. She gave the impression of being immune to aging and dying. However, this illusion finally gave way. Her health declined and she felt she could no longer care for herself in her own apartment. Arrangements were made for her to become a resident of the Kline Galland Home for the Aged, the Jewish community's nursing home. She still would come out from time to time for visits; but these occasions grew less frequent.

When Aunty Kadun died in 1975, this marked the end of a generation in our family. She was the last of Nona's siblings to pass away. I somehow thought that Aunty Kadun's funeral would be marked by a dramatic public ceremony marking the end of a generation. But there was only a simple funeral for a good woman.

Part III

The First American-Born Generation

Mom was the second-born child of her parents. The first-born was her sister Regina. The third-born was her brother Leo, followed later by Estreya, David, Sarah and Esther. Mom's position in the family was to influence her entire life.

In those days, parents (or at least fathers) wanted to have sons. While sons were welcomed with joy and pride, daughters were accepted with resignation. Mom once told me that her sister Regina, even though "only" a girl, had the advantage of being first-born. But when Mom was born, the second consecutive daughter, this was somehow unforgivable. When Leo came along, parental affection went to the new son.

Being second-born and a girl, Mom was sandwiched between two siblings whose births had elicited greater enthusiasm than hers. While very much loved and well-treated by her parents, she started life by feeling that she was not special.

We have a family photograph of my grandparents and their first five children. Mom, at the time, was about ten years old. Papoo is standing in the center of the picture holding Leo's hand. Regina is next to her mother. Estreya is standing at the left corner of the picture. David, who is just a child of two or three years old, sits on a highchair in the foreground. Off to the right stands Mom. She is not smiling. She does not look angry or upset, but neither does she appear to be happy. In her eyes, one sees a kind of youthful melancholy, an introspectiveness. She learned the philosophy of resignation and acceptance. One of her pet phrases throughout life was: "No one said that life is fair. You have to make the best of things."

The family was poor. It was not possible for Papoo to buy fashionable new clothes for his children. Their wardrobes were simple—a few plain things for during the week, and a fancier outfit for the Sabbath. Used clothes, like used furniture for the house, were not unusual.

When Mom needed a new pair of shoes, Papoo would put his hand against her foot to get an idea as to her size. He would then find a peddler who sold shoes and would pick out a pair that he calculated would fit Mom. Whether they fit or not—and they usually did not—those became Mom's shoes until she wore them out completely. When the soles of the shoes had holes, she learned to stuff the shoes with pieces of newspaper in order to keep out the wet and cold.

In recollecting the agony of her feet during childhood, Mom generally laughed about her past suffering. "We were poor. I had no right to expect a fine pair of shoes. I was lucky to have anything at all to protect my feet. That's how life was in those days."

When Mom was enrolled in public school at age five, she did not know how to speak English. The language at home and in the society in which she lived was Judeo-Spanish. When she went to school, she was like an immigrant although she had been born and raised in Seattle.

While struggling to adapt to public school, she had other trials to face. She was a red-head. Some classmates teased her, calling her "carrot top." She became self-conscious about her hair and felt the excruciating pain of being ridiculed by peers.

She was an extremely bright student, quickly mastering English and all her subjects. She loved to read. Her budding academic skills received little encouragement at home. After all, she was "only" a girl; girls did not need formal education. They needed to learn how to be good wives and mothers, things that could be best learned at home. Sending girls to school was simply a concession to life in America.

Mom did well in school. My grandparents had also enrolled her in an afterschool religious program where she learned to read Hebrew and studied Bible.

At home, she learned important skills from her mother: how to sew, embroider, crochet and knit. She learned cooking and the laws of keeping a kosher home. She helped Nona make jams and preserves. She memorized the prayers and blessings that women needed to know.

On Friday afternoons, before the onset of the Sabbath, she helped Nona make wicks for the lampara (oil lamp) that was lit in honor of Shabbat. This was done by breaking small pieces of straw from the bottom of a broom, and wrapping them in a thin layer of cotton. These wicks were then inserted into a round metal holder that was placed in a large glass bowl. The bowl would be filled about half way with water, and above the water would be a layer of several inches of vegetable oil. The wicks were lit about twenty minutes before sunset each Friday afternoon, and this is when the women of the house began their observance of the Sabbath.

During her school years, Mom and her siblings were responsible for household chores. They helped clean the house; bring in the wood and coal for the stove; do the laundry by hand and then hang it on clotheslines in the backyard or basement to dry; tend the yard and vegetable garden. Nona was not blessed with vigorous strength or robust health; she relied on her children, especially her older daughters, to help.

Mom was called upon to assist in caring for her younger siblings. One night, she and her sister Regina were babysitting for the five younger children. The youngest—and most troublesome—was Esther. Somehow, little Esther managed to get hold of a pin. She carried it to her older sisters, threatening to swallow it if they did not accede to one of her demands. They screamed at her to drop the pin, but within an instant Esther put it into her mouth and swallowed it. This was followed by her howls of pain. The older sisters did not know what to do. They shook her, slapped her back, tried to get her to vomit. Crying Esther told them: "If I die it will be your fault."

While Regina was on the phone calling for help, Mom solemnly warned Esther: "Don't you dare die until Mama gets home." Miraculously, Esther survived and continued to give her sisters much excitement for years to come.

Leo could be a problem at times. One day, he hammered a bunch of nails into the wall alongside the staircase, and left the nails protruding from the wall. As it happened, Papoo, who made his own wine in those days, needed to carry a tub of wine down the steps. His pants caught onto the nails; he lost balance and fell down the stairs. Fortunately, he was not hurt too badly…but the wine had spilled and was ruined.

When Nona wanted a reprieve from her children, she would send them on an errand to the home of a relative or friend. She would tell them go and get a teneme aki (keep me here). When the woman to whose house they were sent heard this message, she would tell the children to sit down for a while until she could find it. Then a stall tactic ensued in which the children were kept waiting for an hour or two. At last, they were given a closed bag and told to return home. They were also given some candy as a reward for their patience.

Mom never had a store-bought doll as a child, since dolls were an unnecessary expense. She and her sisters made their own dolls by stringing together empty spools of thread. As a special diversion, the children went to the movies, walking downtown to the Florence or Gem theater. For five cents admission, they would spend the day at the movies. Nona would pack them a lunch, and off they went.

As she grew older, Mom's formal education continued at Garfield High School. She excelled in her studies; she loved her classes. Her social life revolved around her relatives and Sephardic friends; but the public school experience enabled her to develop a broader range of acquaintances.

She once reminisced: "In those days it didn't matter if you were Jewish or Christian or black or Japanese or anything else. Everyone got along, everyone tried to blend in. When the Jewish kids stayed home for Jewish holidays, a lot of our non-Jewish friends would also take the day off school. In those days there was no militancy, no radicalism in our school."

Shortly before she reached her sixteenth birthday, Papoo told her that she would have to leave school once she turned sixteen so that she could get a job and help with the family expenses. Her older sister, Regina, had already left school to go to work. Mom was deeply pained, but she accepted her father's decree with a sense of fatalism. There was really no choice for her, so why fight or struggle against the inevitable?

She notified the school administration and her teachers that she would be leaving school once she turned sixteen. Many of them sought to convince her not to drop out. Mom remembered with fondness that one of her teachers, Mrs. Ryan, called Papoo to plead with him to leave his daughter in school. She was an excellent student with a bright future. But this request made no sense in the context of my grandfather's life. He was a poor man. He had a wife and seven children to support. The family needed every dollar that could be brought in. Education for girls was a frivolous luxury that he could not afford.

So Mom left Garfield and went to work at the Parisian Candy Factory with her sister Regina. They earned 32 cents per hour, almost all of which they contributed to the family income. Although Mom regretted having to leave school, she never expressed resentment against her father. "It was not his fault. It was the way he was raised, the way he was taught to deal with life. We were poor. We needed my income."

I once began a conversation with Mom wondering what her life would have been like had she been born a generation or two later. "You would have had the chance to receive a university education. You could have become a great writer or teacher or public figure or…"

She cut off my line of conversation with a smile. "It is a waste of time to imagine what would have been. I can only live my life as it has been given to me. All in all, it has been a good and happy life. I am grateful to God."

Throughout her life, she was a voracious reader. Her literary interests were broad and eclectic. In spite of her lack of a high school diploma or university degree, she was a highly educated person.

After Mom's death, I was discussing her life with one of my cousins. I mentioned that Mom had never graduated high school. My cousin, who knew my mother well, was stunned. "I had always thought that your mother was a college graduate."

Mom would have blushed.

Dad was the only American-born child of his parents. Although he did not visit the Island of Rhodes until he was in his sixties, he was raised in many ways as though he had been born there. The language of his home and society was Judeo-Spanish, with the distinctive pronunciation of Rhodes Jews.

His mother was a forward-looking woman who wanted her children to adapt well to life in America. She was especially eager for her American-born baby to be modern and progressive. Yet, even in this regard, modernity was supposed to go hand in hand with traditional cultural patterns. For example, Nona Angel was under the impression that American children were supposed to learn to play a musical instrument. Even though there was little money to spare, she arranged for Dad to take violin lessons. He was only nine or ten at the time but was enthusiastic about this special opportunity.

He took his lessons seriously and practiced conscientiously.

His mother was proud of her young musical prodigy. Whenever she had guests at her home, she would call on him to give a recital on his violin. He played the pieces he had learned from his music teacher. The guests were impressed; but then they would ask him to play some Turkish or Judeo-Spanish songs. Of course, Dad could not play well enough to meet these requests; he became embarrassed and frustrated. My grandmother came to think of the lessons as a waste of money; if her son could not play the Turkish and Sephardic songs, what was the point of learning to play the violin? The music teacher told her that it would take years before Dad would gain the proficiency to play the music she wanted. That settled the matter: no more money wasted on violin lessons!

Dad was thin and frail as a child and was susceptible to colds. To protect him, his mother dressed him warmly. He wore her hand-knitted sweaters all year long, even in the warm weather. When Dad grew older, he rebelled. For many years, he refused to wear sweaters. He preferred to wear short sleeved shirts, even in winter.

The calamity of his childhood was the death of his father. At the time, Dad was twelve years old. Only his brother Ray and he were still living at home with their mother; the older brothers and sisters were already married and on their own. Ray was about four years older than Dad.

Papoo Angel left very little in the way of financial assets. The house still had a mortgage. My grandmother earned a bit from those who came to her for cures, but this was not nearly enough to meet the ongoing expenses of the household. Her married children had problems of their own and were not able to add much to her income. Thus, the responsibility fell mainly on Dad and Ray. In spite of their youth, they had no choice but to rise to the challenge. They did.

Dad was proud of the fact that he and Ray were able to earn enough to buy a radio for their mother in 1927. Nona Angel thus became one of the few people in the community who had a real radio, not just a crystal set with earphones.

We have a photograph of my father taken when he was thirteen years old, on the day his mother made a luncheon in honor of his Bar Mitzvah. That morning, she had sent him to synagogue and told him to tell the sexton that this was the day of his Bar Mitzvah. Dad's religious instruction up to that point had been rudimentary. He hardly knew what it meant to be Bar Mitzvah, to have come of age to be responsible for fulfilling the laws and traditions of Judaism. Some old men at the synagogue congratulated him on his Bar Mitzvah. They wrapped him in a prayer shawl and tefillin, and had him called to the Torah. After the services, they again congratulated him, removed the prayer shawl and tefillin...and that was it. Dad left for home without having understood what had transpired.

Later that morning, relatives and friends of the family came to the luncheon his mother had prepared in his honor. He received a few presents, a few hugs and kisses. His mother made a fuss over him, praising his virtues.

In the Bar Mitzvah photograph, Dad is—of course—wearing a heavy knit sweater, even though it was a nice spring day in April. He also is sporting a wrist watch that had been given to him in honor of the occasion. Looking at the photograph many years later, Dad commented that the day of his Bar Mitzvah had mystified him. He had no preparation for it and did not know exactly what it was supposed to mean. He was grateful to his mother for having gone to the trouble of making a luncheon for him and for allowing him to skip school that day. And yet, he long felt that he had not had a real Bar Mitzvah. When his own sons and grandsons had their Bar Mitzvah ceremonies, Dad enjoyed those events as though he himself were finally celebrating his own Bar Mitzvah.

When it was time for High School, Dad was enrolled in Garfield. He was a good student and managed to find time to participate as a writer for the school newspaper. All in all, he was an affable, popular student, known for his lively sense of humor. Throughout his life, he retained pride and loyalty for Garfield and was an avid fan of its sports teams.

Upon graduation from Garfield, Dad sought a full time job.

Going to college was out of the question. There was neither money nor time for such a luxury. He had been working part time for relatives who owned a fruit stand. He decided to seek work in that occupation since he had some experience in it.

This was the era of the great economic depression in the United States. Money and jobs were scarce. Poverty was rampant. For people who were already poor, the depression made matters even worse.

Dad was determined not to be poor. He would work as long and as hard as necessary to be able to live at a good standard of living. While he would not have minded becoming rich, his goal was always to be self-sufficient and independent.

Dad joined his brother Ray and several cousins in operating a fruit stand in the old Broadway Market. Dad and Ray did well enough to buy a car. Dad liked the food business, because people always had to eat...even during depressions.

Within several years, Dad opened a new fruit and vegetable stand with one of his cousins. He was working hard, earning money, and was turning his thoughts to getting married and starting a family of his own.

Meeting Mom was the great turning point in his life.

Mom had a very close relationship with her mother and considered her to be the epitome of goodness, wisdom, gracefulness and compassion. Even though Nona had been born in Turkey, had received little formal education and could not even speak English, she was strikingly alert to the modern trends and to the concerns and needs of her American-born children.

Mom sought her mother's advice on a matter that was to determine the course of her life.

While attending one of the dances sponsored by the Sephardic community, Mom met a young man named Victor Angel. Although he lived only about seven blocks from her, the two of them were not acquainted with each other. He was part of the community of Rhodes Jews and she was part of the community of Turkish Jews; in those days, the two groups did not often intermingle. On that night, though, he asked her to dance. They immediately liked each other and had a nice evening together. When Mom returned home, she told Nona that she had met a very nice young man. Nona obviously saw from my mother's expression that she was very taken with him. She advised her to go to the next dance also, and to get to know the young man a bit better.

Mom did go to the next dance; but Victor was not there. She was crestfallen. Perhaps he didn't really like her; perhaps he already had a girlfriend; perhaps he did not want to see her again. Mustering as much courage as she could, she went across the dance floor to a young man who was a friend of Victor. As casually as possible—and pretending not to be really interested—she inquired about Victor's whereabouts. The friend responded: "Victor is extremely ill; he may even die. He's in the hospital."

Badly shaken, Mom struggled to maintain a calm veneer. "I'm so sorry to hear that. I hope he feels better soon."

She left the dance shortly thereafter and came home crying. She went to her mother to have a confidential conversation.

Mom told Nona that she had learned about Victor's being hospitalized with a serious illness. Nona commiserated with her. Then my mother made a strange request: "Would it be alright if I visited him in the hospital?"

Even as she asked the question, she knew that she was requesting something that was not proper. A young woman simply did not visit a young man, certainly not one whom she hardly even knew. Such an act would be considered to be brazen, immodest. Propriety demanded that the man go after the woman, not vice versa. Mom, a shy and modest young lady, knew this all too well. And yet she asked.

Nona was perceptive enough to understand that if Mom asked

such a question—so much out of character for her—then she must indeed have had deep feelings for the young man. Nona responded: "You go to see him in the hospital tomorrow."

Mom was heartened, but still afraid. "But it is not really proper. And what will Pa say if he learns about this?"

Nona hugged her daughter. "Rachel, you go visit the young man in the hospital tomorrow. Don't worry about what anyone else will say. And don't worry about your father, I'll see to it that he understands the situation."

The next day, after work at the candy factory, Mom went to Providence Hospital to visit a young man she hardly knew. She had learned that he was suffering from a bad case of pneumonia. He was having difficulty breathing. The prognosis for his recovery was uncertain.

She entered his hospital room and saw him lying on his back, looking miserable and forlorn. Upon hearing footsteps in the room, he painfully turned toward the door. He saw the young lady he had recently met at the dance. He broke into a broad smile.

She apologized for intruding. He reassured her and thanked her. The visit lasted for only a few minutes; but it changed both of their lives forever.

Within a few days, Victor Angel made an amazing recovery from his illness. Within a few weeks, he was released from the hospital. Within a few months, he and Mom were engaged to be married. As long as he lived, Dad maintained that Mom's visit to him had cured him from his illness; he owed her his life.

For all his dash and charm, Dad was shy when it came to proposing marriage. He decided to write her a letter in which he proposed to Mom. He mailed the letter to her, care of the Parisian Candy Factory. On the day he assumed the letter would have arrived, he met her as she was leaving work. They smiled. She told him that she had received his letter...and the answer was yes. Happiness!

When Dad first met my Mom's parents, there were a few moments of tension. My grandparents did not know my father's family. Papoo suspected that my father might have been an Americano, a word used to designate a non-Jewish young man. My father teased my grandfather by agreeing that he was an Americano, since he was in fact born in America. But once Mom's parents met Dad's mother, everything was set straight. A wedding date was set—May 23, 1937. That date also was the twenty-fifth anniversary of my Mom's parents.

Papoo took my father aside for a confidential talk. He told his future son-in-law that he was a poor barber and could not afford to give his daughter a dowry. Dad, who had not at all expected a dowry, reassured Papoo that he wanted nothing from him except permission to marry his daughter Rachel. The two men shook hands and became wonderful friends.

Among the Sephardim of that generation, it was customary for the groom's side to arrange and pay for the wedding. Thus, the wedding took place in the synagogue of Dad's family, Ezra Bessaroth. Papoo, who was a staunch leader of the Sephardic Bikur Holim, was less than enthusiastic about his daughter being married at Ezra Bessaroth. Wisely, though, he deferred to the prevailing custom without objection. To maintain his Turkish Sephardic honor, he saw to it that the two witnesses for the marriage contract were members of the Bikur Holim.

Shortly after my parents' engagement, Dad's older brother Ray became engaged. His fiancée felt that it would be appropriate if she and Ray were married before my parents, since Ray was older than Victor. My parents, though, felt that they had priority since they had been engaged first and had already set the date for their wedding. The matter was settled by Nona Angel.

La Gremma knew the traditions well, and she knew that older siblings were given priority to their younger siblings. In this case, Ray's engagement came only a bit later than Victor's and by normal rules of tradition, Ray should have precedence. But La Gremma had a strong sense of justice. She decided that Victor was engaged first, so Victor should be married first. The tradition would have to bend to the dictates of fairness. Perhaps she also had a special appreciation for my mother, whose boldness had saved her son's life. La Gremma decided: and so it was.

In those days, wedding invitations were not printed and mailed to invitees. Rather, the families of the bride and groom made up a list of people they wished to invite. They then hired the synagogue's sexton who would go from house to house to invite the guests. "Mrs. Bulissa Esther Angel and Mr. and Mrs. Marco Romey will be honored if you would join them for the wedding of their children Victor Angel and Rachel Romey, to take place on May 23 at Ezra Bessaroth." The guests responded on the spot—no need for RSVP's.

While the groom's family had the responsibility of arranging the wedding and reception, the bride's family also had obligations. The main one was providing the ashugar, the trousseau. Daughters began preparing their ashugar almost as soon as they learned to sew and crochet. Mothers started preparing from the moment they gave birth to a daughter.

The ashugar included linens, bedding, and articles of clothing. The items were crocheted, embroidered and knitted. Families took pride in the elegance of the daughter's trousseau—the quality of the materials, the craftsmanship of the embroidery, the decorativeness of the patterns. The week before Mom's wedding, relatives and friends came to my grandparents' home where the items of the ashugar were on display. The guests expressed their praise and approval, and were treated to sweets and Turkish coffee. Every day during that week was filled with guests and partying.

Gifts of food were sent from the family of the groom to the family of the bride. These gifts were reciprocated. Each side tried to provide wonderful baked goods and sweets that would be enjoyed by their soon-to-be-joined families.

The night before the wedding, Mom was brought to the banyo, the ritual bath. She was accompanied by her mother, sisters, aunties and other female relatives and friends. As she emerged from her immersion in the water, Nona gently broke a rosca (a round baked pastry) over Mom's head as a sign of blessing. The women expressed their good wishes, sang traditional Judeo-Spanish wedding songs, and enjoyed refreshments that Nona had provided.

The wedding was, of course, conducted according to the Sephardic traditions. As the participants in the wedding procession walked down the aisle, a group of men sang Hebrew songs, accompanied by an oud. Following the ceremony, the guests were served a home-made meal, topped off with a vast array of Sephardic sweets and deserts prepared by the women of both families. People sang and danced to Judeo-Spanish and Turkish music.

What could be happier than a wedding? And yet, sometimes people cry at weddings. From where do these tears stem? Are they merely tears of joy?

Certainly, the tears come from the wellsprings of happiness. But they also derive from other sources: melancholy at the passing of time; fear of change and transition; anxiety about the future. Mom had her set of concerns. She and Dad, in spite of the similarity of their cultural backgrounds, belonged to two different communities. Mom grew up among Turkish Jews, Dad among Jews from Rhodes. These two communities in Seattle maintained separate identities, with each group feeling a certain aloofness from the other.

This fact created tensions in both families. The problems, though, mainly fell on Mom's shoulders. It was customary for the wife to follow the husband's lead. Mom would now have to leave the synagogue of the Turkish Jews and become part of the Rhodes community, where she was a virtual stranger. She got a taste of the impact of this impending transition at her wedding. One of Dad's older relatives, a woman who had been born in Rhodes, made a point of introducing herself to my mother. In the course of her conversation, she referred to my mother as an ajena, a foreigner. (This was a term used by Jews of Rhodes to designate anyone not of Rhodes ancestry.) My mother promptly and uncharacteristically responded with anger. "I am no ajena; I was born right here in America. You are the ajena." The relative was undaunted. She smiled back at Mom with a haughty expression on her face.

Already at her wedding, she could foresee problems she would face as she adjusted to her new life. Holidays, formerly observed in her parents' home, would now be observed with her husband's family. All of her husband's relatives were now her relatives as well; in those days, relatives had claims on your hospitality and generosity. Mom would have to integrate a whole new set of people into her life.

If Mom and her parents cried at the wedding, at least some of the tears stemmed from the fear that their relationship would be hurt in the transition. On one level, my grandparents were gaining a son. But on another level, they feared they were losing a daughter.

As things ultimately turned out, Mom did her best to become part of my Dad's family. But her ties to her own family were so strong that she gradually succeeded in moving Dad into her family's orbit. Dad came to love Mom's parents. As the years passed, our family became part of the extended family of my Mom's parents. We were together with them on Sabbaths and holidays, we went on vacation together, we were at their home often. Mom's sisters and brothers and their children were at the center of our family's life.

So Mom, in her own quiet and steady way, had brought Dad into her family. She was most certainly not an ajena in her own family life and friendships.

After a short honeymoon, my parents moved into a small cold water flat at 20th and Alder. The following year, they moved into an apartment in a duplex owned by an elderly Sephardic couple, at 23rd and Cherry. Dad was earning $22.50 per week at his fruit stand in the Broadway Market. Although this was a good income in those days, he was still burdened by debts accrued during his illness and hospitalization the year before he and Mom were married.

Dad held the traditional attitude that a married woman should not work out of the home. It was the husband's role to provide for his wife and family. So Mom quit her job at the candy factory and started a new life as a homemaker. (She resented the term "housewife.")

Within a year, my brother Bill was born. Although he grew up to be a calm, soft-spoken gentleman, he was a noisy baby. He cried day and night. Mom used all her ingenuity to keep her new baby quiet and happy but Bill was not easily pacified. Dad brought home a book on how to raise children and insisted that Mom follow the advice faithfully. Mom would feed Bill according to the schedule listed in the book; she would put him to sleep at the times recommended in the book. But Bill continued to be a difficult baby.

On a visit to the pediatrician, Mom told the doctor of her troubles. Her patience was wearing thin; she was exhausted and frustrated. The doctor asked: "Are you following instructions from a book?"

"Yes, of course."

"Throw out the book," the doctor ordered. "Just follow your own common sense. Your baby is a human being like you. Are you hungry according to a schedule in a book? Are you sleepy every day at the exact same time? Why should the baby want to follow a schedule from a book?"

Mom broke out in a smile at this sensible advice. She felt much relieved. When Dad came home from work that night, Mom informed him of the doctor's instructions: throw out the book. Dad was not pleased with the doctor; only a quack would advise a parent to throw out such a famous book on child rearing. After another noisy week with Bill, Mom gathered the courage to actually toss out the book. Dad had no choice but to go along with the decision.

A problem arose with the landlord and his wife. They were elderly and they liked peace and tranquility. They did not like to hear crying babies. The landlord asked my parents to find another place to live and to find it quickly.

Dad, in one of his characteristic strokes of boldness, determined that it was time to buy a house rather than to rent another apartment. So the search for a house began.

To the extent that Dad was bold and determined, so Mom was nervous and afraid. How would they be able to pay for a house? Wasn't a house too great a responsibility for them at such a young age?

The two of them found time to visit homes that were for sale. Mom would examine each house from top to bottom, carefully noting every detail. In each instance, she found something wrong. One house was too large, another was too small. One needed too much work, one was too ostentatious. Some were too far from her parents' home on 15th Avenue. All were too expensive.

As the house search dragged on, the landlord was becoming more and more impatient. He wanted them to move out immediately. The more pressure he put on my parents, the more Mom stalled for time.

Dad, whose patience during this process was remarkable, explained to Mom that they really had no choice: they had to move as soon as possible. She could not expect to find a perfect house but she would have to settle for the best she could find. Mom finally accepted the inevitability of their moving, regardless of the expenses and risks involved.

One Sunday, a real estate man by the name of Mr. Bloomer called my parents and told them he had a house to show them. It was a nice house; but the owner was an eccentric and mean-spirited man. Sometimes he would allow prospective buyers into the house and sometimes he would not. The house had been for sale for a long time, but the owner managed to scare off all the potential buyers.

Mr. Bloomer drove my parents to the house—511 28th Avenue, between Jefferson and East Cherry. Mom looked at the house from the car. Spontaneously she said: "This is the house. We'll buy it."

Dad was even more surprised than Mr. Bloomer. He asked: "You haven't even seen the inside of the house. How can you be sure this is the one we should buy?"

Mom responded that she was sure. She fell in love with it on sight.

Meanwhile, Mr. Bloomer had gone up the front steps to ask the owner to let my parents take a look at the house. The owner was in one of his bad moods; he slammed the door and said no one would be allowed inside.

Mr. Bloomer discussed the situation with my parents. Mom's confidence was so overwhelming that Dad agreed to make an offer to purchase the house. Mr. Bloomer felt that the owner would take an offer of $2000. Dad told him that he would like to make the offer but that he did not have enough available money for a down payment. Amazingly, Mr. Bloomer told my parents that he himself would make the down payment, two hundred dollars; they could pay him back a little at a time.

And that is what happened. Mr. Bloomer made the down payment, my parents got a mortgage for the rest, and they made a schedule for repaying Mr. Bloomer for his interest-free loan. They bought the house without having seen the inside of it. In a short time, they moved in; Mom's love for the house only deepened when she first entered it. She had an almost mystical affection for it throughout the eighteen years (1940-1958) in which she lived in it. She was broken-hearted when we had to move to a new neighborhood, and never fully overcame her sense of loss at leaving it.

While my parents were busy buying and moving into 511 28th Avenue, the world was facing a war of massive proportions. The Germans had already established their nefarious concentration camps in which they murdered millions of people. Hitler's anti-Jewish propaganda and his incarceration of vast numbers of Jews sent shudders through the hearts of Jews throughout the world—including Seattle. While the European allies were quivering before the power of the Nazis, the American public was worrying whether our country would be drawn into the war. As millions of Jews were murdered in Nazi death camps, the United States pursued a policy of staying out of the fray. Moreover, the U.S. sealed its borders to all but a few refugees. The anti-immigrant mood directly resulted in the deaths of many thousands of victims of the Germans. They simply had nowhere to flee for safety; they were left to perish.

When Japan attacked Pearl Harbor, it became clear that the United States could not avoid war. The entire country was mobilized to fight the Japanese threat. The U.S. also sent troops to Europe to help the allies fight the Germans and their accomplices.

Patriotic fervor ran high in America. The Sephardic community of Seattle was no exception. Young men volunteered or were drafted into the military service. Dad was exempted since he was head of a family that was dependent on him for support. Moreover, his history of having had pneumonia and his chronic bronchial problems factored into the decision not to draft him.

My Uncle Vic, though, was drafted even though he, too, was the head of a family that depended on him. Being younger and in better health than my father, Uncle Vic was sent to the Far East where he served in battle. Due to his poor eyesight and his dependence on his glasses, he asked to be stationed in a position where his life would not be endangered if his glasses would be broken. He was sent to the front lines!

During his absence from Seattle, his wife Estreya (my mother's sister) moved into our home together with her baby daughter Esther Lee. The anxieties of war reverberated in 511 28th Avenue, as in so many American homes. Mom's role expanded as she became a matriarch and source of strength to her sister and baby niece.

Mom got together with a group of Sephardic women to help the American war effort. They formed a group under the umbrella of the American Red Cross, sewing and knitting garments for American soldiers stationed abroad. They worked long hours

and made numerous items. In order to underscore the seriousness of their efforts, they made themselves special uniforms and
established membership dues. At their early meetings, they struggled to find a suitable name for their group. My Uncle Dave suggested "Knit Wits," but the women, understandably, rejected it.
They finally settled on the name: "Sephardic Do-Our-Bit Club."
After the war, Mom and the other women in the club each received a certificate of merit from the American Red Cross that
included the stamped signature of President Truman.

In July 1944, the Jews of the Island of Rhodes were deported
to Auschwitz. Nearly every family of Congregation Ezra Bessaroth had relatives still living in Rhodes at the time. Communica-
tion between Rhodes and Seattle was all but non-existent during
the war years. As news of the deportation gradually reached
Seattle, a wave of despair and mourning swept the community.
Only after the war did our family learn that my father's brother
Joseph had died in 1943. His wife, Sinyoru, and their children—
Leon, Bulissa, Jacob and Sarah-- were among those deported to
and murdered in Auschwitz.

In July 1945, one year after the destruction of the Jewish community of Rhodes, my parents had a new baby. As indicated earlier, I was that baby.

Now that the war had ended with victory, a spirit of optimism
arose in America. Dad and his brother Ray opened a fruit stand
in the Broadway Market. Patriotically, they named it "Victory
Fruit Market."

Their entrepreneurship led them to soon start out on a new
business venture. They bought a number of pinball and shuf-
fleboard machines, as well as juke boxes, for which they leased
space in taverns. Customers paid to play games and listen to records; Dad and Uncle Ray would keep the profits. They were
busy day and night trying to lease spaces; checking up on the
machines that were in service; collecting the money; arranging
for the repair of machines that broke down. Moreover, they had
to spend much of their time in taverns. They sometimes got into
scuffles with men who had drunk more beer than they could
handle. Mom hated the business from the outset, urging Dad to

go back to his roots in the food business.

While Dad and Uncle Ray were in their new venture, we children enjoyed a fringe benefit. Every now and then, Dad would bring home a large box of 45 rpm records that had been almost completely worn out in the juke boxes. As far as we were concerned, they were still playable, and we played them with tremendous enjoyment. We were the envy of many friends and neighbors who were not so fortunate to have such a fabulous collection of popular records.

After a year or two in this business, Dad gave in to Mom and returned to his original occupation. He opened a grocery store at 621 Broadway East, and named it Angel's Food Center. He proudly stated that he always wanted to have his name in lights on Broadway…and now he succeeded in doing so! He found a partner—Al Israel—and they maintained the business until Dad's decision to retire in 1975.

Angel's Food Center flourished in spite of serious handicaps. It was too small to be called a supermarket; yet it was too large to be a little family store that could operate without employees. It had no parking lot. It had to compete with much larger supermarkets within the same vicinity. The odds were against my father making a success of this business.

But Dad did make his store into a success. He firmly believed that small businesses could thrive in America; that hard work is always rewarded. He could succeed by providing personal service, by greeting his regular customers by name, by delivering groceries to their homes, by taking orders by telephone. His remarkable sense of humor and his basic optimism won the affection and respect of his customers. He was constantly smiling, cracking jokes, making puns. He used to say: "The little guy can succeed in America if he works hard…and knows how to accept life with a good sense of humor."

Dad explained to me some of the secrets of his success. He insisted on selling only the best merchandise. His specialty was having the highest quality fruits and vegetables, and presenting them in an appealing display. He trained his employees to put out only the best produce, properly trimmed. Whatever was not aesthetically up to grade—he brought home for us!

I was once in the store when a woman came in and asked for a bottle of soda. I offered to run back and get it. Dad held me back, and told her the number of the aisle where the soda could be found. When she went to find the soda, Dad told me that it was best to let the customer go through the store when searching for a particular item. More often than not, he or she would find other items to purchase. And so it was. The woman came back with the soda...plus quite a few other groceries. "You have to understand psychology to be in business," Dad often would say.

He once had a customer who asked to buy a copy of yesterday's newspaper. Dad told him that he only had today's edition. The customer left. The next day, the same thing happened: the customer asked for yesterday's paper. Again Dad told him that he only had today's paper. The next day, the customer again came in with the same request. This time Dad gave him a copy of today's paper, told him to buy it and put it away in a drawer so he would have it for tomorrow morning. The customer liked this suggestion and bought the paper.

One of the ongoing problems of the grocery business is dealing with shoplifters. Dad had mirrors installed on the ceiling throughout the store and had signs posted to indicate that shoplifters would be prosecuted to the full extent of the law. These precautions did not deter everyone. Some shoppers would pick up a handful of cherries and eat them while they were doing their shopping. Others would open boxes of cookies or packages of candies and eat them on the spot. Generally, such people were caught and were told in a nice way that they had to pay for what they took. In the case of repeat offenders, Dad would tell them that they should do their shopping elsewhere.

On one occasion, a man attempted to steal a cantaloupe by putting it down the front of his shirt. Dad detected this crime in one of the store's mirrors. When the fellow came up to the check-out stand, Dad rang up the few items the criminal had brought to the counter. Then Dad rang up another charge of $10. The man asked what the extra $10 charge was for. Dad told him it was for the cantaloupe that he had dropped down the front of his shirt. The man did not blush or seem perturbed; rather, he immediately took the offensive. "Cantaloupes only cost one dollar, so why are you charging me ten dollars? That's not legal."

Dad replied calmly. "The price of a cantaloupe is one dollar if you bring it to the counter in a shopping cart. But if you bring a cantaloupe hidden in your shirt, the price is ten dollars." The man threatened to call the police. Dad handed him the telephone. Flustered and angry, the man paid for his groceries including the ten dollar surcharge. Dad told him to do his shopping in the future at the big supermarket a few blocks away.

Angel's Food Center had four large rolling stands on which fruits and berries would be displayed. The stands were rolled out onto the sidewalk in front of the store. By-passers would be attracted to the items and would often buy some. This was a very successful aspect of the business, especially during the summer months.

The big supermarkets nearby, that did vastly more business than Angel's Food Center, nevertheless did their best to destroy Dad's business. A manager of one of these supermarkets called the police and insisted that Dad be fined for putting displays on the sidewalk, in public space. When the policeman gave Dad a summons, Dad was stupefied. He had been placing these stands on the sidewalk for years. They were pushed up right against the store. They bothered no one, nor did they interfere in any way with pedestrian traffic. Many other stores did the same thing. The police officer was apologetic, but he issued the summons. Dad was forced to have the stands rolled back into the store so that no part of them rested on the sidewalk. Some of his optimism about American business faded on that day. He was outraged that the big supermarkets didn't want 90% of the trade; they wanted all of it. As long as Dad lived, he never could understand that attitude. And as long as he lived, he never became a wealthy man.

The big supermarkets tried other strategies to undermine Angel's Food Center. They began to open seven days a week, 24 hours a day. How could a small grocery store compete? It was impossible and impractical for Dad's store to stay open at all times.

One day, someone from the Teamsters union came to the store and told Dad that he had to join the union. Since the store had a delivery truck, he was obligated to pay the Teamsters. Dad did not wish to join the union and didn't see why he should. The union sent a group of noisy picketers in front of Angel's Food Center, scaring customers away. After holding out about a week, Dad joined the union. He saw this as paying protection money.

Some years after Dad had joined the Teamsters, a union representative showed up at the store and told Dad that he was no longer eligible to be a member of the union. Dad was very pleased to learn this news. He came home from work that night with a broad smile on his face.

"Once in a while, the little guy gets a break in America," he quipped. "Usually it's a break of the head, but once in a while it's a real break."

Dad never became a wealthy man, but he lived as though he were rich. He subscribed to the philosophy that wealth is what you spend. What you have in the bank is only potential wealth.

We always lived nicely. We had a nice home, a nice car, and nice clothes. Although we lived relatively simply, we did not feel that we were deprived. We had an idea of our financial limits and we lived comfortably within the boundaries.

My parents' sense of pride demanded that we live at a proper economic level, without going into debt. Mom was especially eager that we not appear to be poor.

Mom's pride caused me some discomfort as a child. Most of my school friends had "taps"—metal strips—attached to the soles and heels of their shoes. The taps were meant to preserve the bottom of the shoes so that the soles and heels would not wear out. This, of course, saved money. But children did not wear taps because of the economic concern, but because taps were fun. They made neat sounds. They clicked on the floors of the halls in school. They made grinding noises on the concrete playground.

I also wanted to have taps put on my shoes. Mom was adamantly opposed: "Poor people wear taps." I explained to her that taps were fun, that all the children had them. Mom responded: "You will not have taps on your shoes. Taps are for poor people."

That ended the matter.

Mom had a similar attitude about jeans. Jeans were sturdy and rugged. They were fashionable among my friends. Cowboys wore them, so what could be wrong with jeans?

Mom generally got me corduroy pants. I liked them but I also wanted jeans. Mom told me pointedly: "Poor people wear jeans." I reminded her that cowboys wore jeans and cowboys weren't poor. Mom was not impressed with my argument. "You are not a cowboy, you are not going to wear jeans."

On my twelfth birthday, one of my uncles bought me a pair of jeans for a present. This was a special pair that had reinforced knees so it could endure a lot of wear and tear. I was delighted. Mom was not.

After several days of my nagging her, she finally gave in. Mom said I could wear them, but only on Sundays for playing outside. I was not allowed to wear them to school. I remember my glee when first putting on the new jeans. As things turned out, I managed to wear holes into them in a relatively short period of time in spite of the reinforced knees. As soon as I did, Mom gave the jeans to an organization that collected clothes for poor people.

This brings us to another of Mom's policies: we could not

wear clothes that had been repaired with patches. Mom sewed quite well. She repaired torn garments and made them look like new. But if any tear was so bad as to require a patch, the garment was given away or converted into canimazos, rags. Why? "Poor people wear clothes with patches."

Mom had nothing against poor people. She had known first-hand what it meant to be poor. She simply did not want poverty or the stigma of poverty to hang over her family. Taps, jeans and patches were symbols of a station in life that she was trying to move beyond.

Dad shared the same attitude. It manifested itself, for example, in the cars he bought. He did not believe in buying used cars. Used cars were for people who could not afford better or who were too tight with their money to buy a new car. Dad did not look down on those who bought used cars; but he would not buy one himself.

The first car I remember was our 1950 Buick Roadmaster. It was a two-tone blue, four door sedan that was built like a tank. The car cost $3000—this was $1000 more than our house had cost only ten years earlier.

Dad named the car "Old Faithful" and it lived up to its name. It gave six years of excellent service. It was a symbol of Dad's success.

"Old Faithful" was a unique vehicle among our extended family. It was new, expensive, and fashionable—and it worked. Most of our relatives had cars of a different genre: used, inexpensive, downscale and temperamental.

Uncle Jack had a jalopy that he named "Geraldine." He used to park the car on the top of hills, with the car facing downhill. The reason for this strategy was that Geraldine did not always start when the ignition was turned on. When this occurred, as I myself witnessed on various occasions, he would have someone push the car from behind so that it started rolling down the hill. Once the car was rolling, Uncle Jack would turn on the ignition and floor the gas pedal. This usually got the car started.

Uncle Solomon had a car of comparable character. I remember a Friday afternoon when he called to offer me a ride to synagogue. He told me to meet him at his house on 26th Avenue. I was glad for the ride, since I usually would walk the mile or so to synagogue. When I arrived, I found my uncle and several of my cousins waiting for me. We got into the car, but Uncle Solomon could not get the automobile to start. He asked us to get out and push the car until the ignition caught. We pushed the car for several blocks but its motor remained silent. We asked my uncle what we should do. He answered: keep pushing. And we did. We ended up pushing the car all the way to the synagogue without its engine ever having started. We pushed it to the top of a hill a block away from the synagogue where Uncle Solomon parked it before Shabbat.

On Saturday night, he offered us a ride home, and we were foolish enough to accept. We pushed the car out of its parking spot and watched it roll down the hill. The ignition did not catch. We ended up pushing the car all the way home.

We deserved it.

After a few years with our two-tone blue Old Faithful, Mom thought the car needed to be refinished. Dad obliged and had the car colors changed: gray on top, white on the bottom. With its fresh look, the car seemed to be new again.

In 1956, Dad decided it was time for a new car. He bought a Chevrolet, with a cream color top and a red body. This car he also named "Old Faithful" and it, too, provided years of good service. Future "Old Faithfuls" were purchased in 1962, 1972 and 1981. In all cases, Dad followed his basic philosophy in buying cars: the cars had to be new, American made, good looking and comfortable.

We were not only in the forefront of our extended family when it came to cars; we also were leaders when it came to home entertainment machines. Before the introduction of television, we had a fashionable mahogany console. On one side was a radio and on the other side was a phonograph. This impressive piece of furniture and modern technology was at the vanguard of fashion in those years. Relatives and friends would come to our house to enjoy the radio and to hear the records on the phonograph.

When televisions came out, our console was destined to become obsolete. Everyone wanted to watch T.V. However, since televisions were quite expensive, not everyone could afford to buy one.

The first ones in our extended family to have a television set were Uncle Solomon and Aunty Sarah (my mother's sister). They had entered a raffle and were the lucky ones to win a new T.V. It only had a ten inch screen, surrounded by a huge light brown console. A rabbit ear antenna sat atop it.

The first time I saw television was at Uncle Solomon and Aunty Sarah's house. Shortly after they had received the television, they invited dozens of family members to come to their home to watch programs on this amazing new invention. We arrived with a great sense of anticipation.

Uncle Solomon had perched the television console on a high case in the living room, and had set up rows of folding chairs for the audience. Aunty Sarah made a huge batch of popcorn. As we excitedly found seats and chatted about the wonders of modern technology, Uncle Solomon called for silence. With a great dramatic flair, he turned the set on.

All of us strained to get a good view of the ten inch screen. We saw some light, then some darkness, sounds of static. Black lines flashed across the screen. Soon, the T.V. warmed up and a picture appeared on the screen. It was very blurry. Uncle Solomon fiddled with the antenna ears until the picture cleared up a bit. The sound was gravelly, the picture was jumbled. In spite of these factors, we watched the program in awe. It was as though we were witnessing an incredible miracle.

When the program ended, Uncle Solomon proudly went to the front of the room and turned off the set. We were clapping with delight. We had entered a new era.

After that sensational evening, Dad decided that our family ought to have a television too. Within a short time, he ordered a Sylvania with a sixteen inch screen. To ensure good reception, we had an antenna attached to the roof of our house. We did not have the first television set in the family, but for the moment we certainly had the most impressive.

My parents' philosophy was to buy the best item one could afford. Owning nice things gives a sense of pride and pleasure. Moreover, it is practical: good quality merchandise lasts longer and works better.

Dad was a stickler for paying bills on time. When he had to make mortgage payments on our house, he made advance payments as frequently as he could in order to retire the debt at the soonest possible moment. He considered it a matter of personal pride that his credit was excellent, that he was a respectable and honorable businessman. When expenses posed problems for him, he found creative ways to deal with them.

For example, our family's teeth were cared for by an excellent—and very expensive—dentist. Dad was loyal to this dentist because they had grown up together as children and had lived across the street from one another. As long as the dentist did not have to do too much work on our teeth, Dad managed to pay the bills without any trouble. Often enough, though, we needed fillings or other expensive work. In those cases, the bills came to a considerable amount, more than Dad could pay at one time. On the other hand, Dad could not rest when he owed money, feeling that it was a disgrace to be in debt. How could he pay the dentist's bills if he did not have enough money available?

Dad came up with a solution: he paid with groceries. The dentist bought groceries at Angel's Food Center. The amount of the groceries was deducted from the amount owed for his dental services. The old-fashioned barter system worked, and the two of them got along fine.

Dad had a notion that a properly brought up young lady must know how to play the piano. He arranged for my sister to take piano lessons with a teacher who lived not far from his store. Usually, he had no problem paying for the lessons; but when he was under extreme financial pressure, he paid with groceries. This was a fair exchange: food for culture.

My parents both stressed the importance of having a good reputation-- being honest, decent, generous and imbued with self-respect. It also meant being true to yourself, not pretending to be what you were not. Mom used to tell me: "Always try your best. It is no shame to fail; it is a shame to give up, to lie, to cheat, to be dishonest." And she would add: "Be good at whatever you do. If you are going to be a bum, be a good bum!"

Mom and Dad believed in living according to one's means. On the one hand, this entailed not going into debt to buy things beyond one's economic level. On the other hand, it meant not living at a lower level than one could afford. They had little sympathy for nouveaux riches types or for people who were meticulously frugal.

Dad always bought nice cars, but not "luxury" cars. Mom always wore a nice coat, but not a mink coat. They found a good balance between being comfortable and maintaining simplicity.

Mom lauded the greatness of the simple, working people whom she called "the salt of the earth." She quoted the Judeo-Spanish proverb, el rey es con la gente, the king is with the people. True nobility of character demanded a close relationship with the common folk. One who stands aloof from or looks down on the working classes is not only a snob but is ignoble. Along with all our relatives, my parents voted for Democrats, believing that the Democrats stood for the working classes.

In the 1952 presidential campaign, the candidates were General Dwight David Eisenhower for the Republicans and Adlai Stevenson for the Democrats. I asked Mom if she was going to vote for Eisenhower, since she had named me after him. She responded: "General Eisenhower is a great man. But I'm voting for Stevenson, the Democrat."

I was only seven years old at the time and I felt insulted that she would vote against the man whose name she had given me. Seeing my consternation, she re-assured me that Eisenhower was a wonderful general and fine person. However, he had been brainwashed to become a Republican. The Republicans looked out mainly for the rich. Only the Democrats cared about the working people. Adlai Stevenson was the Democratic candidate, so he was on our side.

I was still not assuaged.

At school, our teacher assigned us to make a campaign poster either for Eisenhower or Stevenson. My instincts were all for Eisenhower. I started on several posters for Ike, but made various mistakes leading me to discard them. I liked Ike but I was having trouble making a poster in his support. So I decided to make a Stevenson poster. Everything fell into place easily. I concluded that I, too, must really have been for the Democrats.

I brought the poster home to show Mom. She was so pleased with it that she mailed it to the Stevenson campaign headquarters. Some weeks later, I received a letter from the Stevenson committee thanking me for my support. Mom put the letter on the mantle in the living room. It was a proud moment for us.

Although I was glad to be identified with the Stevenson campaign, in my heart of hearts I still felt a tugging toward Dwight Eisenhower, my namesake. When the election results came in and Eisenhower was declared the victor, my parents were downcast. I offered them some consolation: "At least we have a President named Dwight!"

"Yes," Mom responded, "and he is a great man even if he is a Republican.

Part IV

Transitions of The Next Generation

I grew up as part of an extended family that had a clear sense of the role of each member. The men were the breadwinners. They worked to support the women and children. In return for their labor, the men were considered to be the head of their families and were accorded certain privileges.

In our family, for example, Dad had his own place at the head of the table. He had his own place on the living room couch. Neither my mother nor any of the children would sit in his place. Likewise, although we were free to express our opinions, Dad's opinion was authoritative. In fact, he often deferred to Mom's opinion. Even then, Mom would make it appear that the decision had really been Dad's.

Women were expected to care for the family and the home. In our extended family, the women were excellent cooks. They kept their homes in good order and taught their children proper manners. In return, they also were entitled to respect. Mom had her own honored place at the table as well as her own designated armchair in the living room.

Mom had a rule: the children could not ask Dad any questions nor make any requests of him until he first finished eating his dinner. He put in long hours at the store, usually not arriving home until after 9:30 pm. He would be exhausted and hungry.

We developed a routine. When Dad drove the car (or sometimes the truck from the store) up the driveway, he would honk the horn a few times. The older children would run out to greet him and would carry in the groceries he had brought home. He entered the house where he was greeted warmly by Mom. He then would wash up and come to the dinner table. By the time he sat down, Mom had already put his hot dinner at his place. She would overload the plate with meat and a variety of side dishes and would also have a salad of lettuce and tomatoes ready for him.

When we were very young, we often were sleeping before Dad got home. As we grew older, we were allowed the privilege of sitting down with him when he ate his dinner. He ate with such gusto that we would become hungry, even though we had eaten dinner earlier. More often than not, Mom would end up feeding us again "to keep Dad company." Although she also ate dinner earlier, she would fix herself a plate with a few things so she could eat something with Dad. She did not think it was proper to let him eat alone.

Mom prepared elaborate meals every night. She cooked the traditional foods of the Turkish and Rhodes Jews, many of which required considerable preparation. Dad did not consider it dinner if he did not have meat. Fish meals, thus, were ruled out. If Mom wanted to make fish, it could only be served before the "real" dinner. Dad also did not consider a vegetarian or dairy meal to be dinner. Chinese food also did not count. Mom accepted these basic premises and cooked accordingly. Her philosophy was simple: her husband worked hard all day, so he was entitled to a good dinner that would satisfy him.

After Dad had eaten his dinner, we would have time for our family conversations. He would tell us about the various happenings of the day at his store; we would tell him of our activities. The length of the conversation would be determined by the degree of Dad's tiredness or his patience.

We learned from Mom that Dad deserved all the respect we could give him in light of his overwhelming sacrifices on our behalf. When he was thirsty, one of us children would run to bring him a glass of water with ice cubes—his most refreshing drink. When he sat down in the living room, one of us would bring him pillows or a footrest to make him more comfortable.

Dad enjoyed telling jokes and making puns. Each Friday, one of the children would be responsible for going down the block to Sam's Drugstore to buy two comic books. Dad preferred comics such as Archie, Dagwood and Blondie, Sad Sack, and Beatle Baily. Since he took the day off on Saturday in observance of the Sabbath, he enjoyed reading the comics on Shabbat afternoons. He would invariably read some of the jokes to us and we would laugh together uncontrollably. Dad was especially jovial on the Sabbaths, when he was more relaxed, and when he had a captive audience with his family. When he would tell a joke on Friday night, Mom would announce: "Shabbat is officially here!"

Not only were we taught to respect our parents, we also learned to show honor to all elders. We were not to look elders directly in the eye. Rather, the eyes should be aimed downward as a sign of respect. To look an elder in the eye was brazen; it was as if to imply that we were the equal of the elder—which of course we were not.

This particular mannerism eventually caused me some difficulty later in life. When I first began serving my congregation, I was a twenty-four year old rabbinical student. I was, naturally, eager to succeed in my position. It is customary to have a gathering following Sabbath morning services at which Kiddush is recited, refreshments are served, and congregants socialize with each other. In following the pattern of the senior clergy, I used this opportunity to chat with congregants.

One of the elder ladies of the congregation, a woman of great influence in the community, called the president of the congregation to complain about me. She said I was aloof and cold, not at all friendly. When the president conveyed these criticisms to me, I was surprised. I had greeted this woman warmly and enthusiastically when I had seen her on Shabbat.

The following Shabbat, I made a special point of paying my respects to her. But the next day, I received another call from the president in which he once again repeated the woman's criticisms. I assured him that I had been friendly and respectful to her, but he told me to try harder!

In discussing this problem with my wife, she asked me if I looked the woman in the eye when I spoke with her. "Of course not," I replied. Gilda then advised: "This Shabbat, look her straight in the eye when you greet her." I was jolted. "That would be rude on my part. She would become even more hostile to me." Gilda insisted that I follow her advice.

The next Shabbat morning after services, I went over to the woman, looked her right in the eye, and wished her a good Sabbath. I felt discomfited by this show of arrogance on my part.

The next day, the president called me. "She loves you," he said. "She is so pleased that you are friendly and sociable after all."

I still did not understand how to interpret this strange episode. Gilda clarified the matter for me. I was raised to think that it was disrespectful to look an elder in the eye. However, American culture generally teaches that it is disrespectful not to look someone in the eye. A lack of eye contact implies a lack of interest and concern. What I had considered a gesture of respect, the elderly congregant had taken as a sign of disinterest and aloofness.

I learned an important life lesson. If people do not understand each other's cultural signals, they might very well misinterpret those signals and thereby come into conflict. I also learned the importance of looking others in the eye when speaking with them!

Another thing we learned as children was not to ask for seconds of food when we were guests in anyone's home. No matter how hungry we still felt and no matter how much we desired a particular item of food, we could not ask for seconds. If the hostess offered seconds, we were obliged to decline. If she asked again and was insistent, then we could take seconds. In fact, if the hostess insisted on giving us seconds, then we had to accept even if we did not like or want the food. To reject her hospitality would be an insult.

In our community, children learned to kiss the hand of parents and grandparents in order to receive a blessing. This was generally done on Friday nights, but it was also practiced on holidays and other special occasions. I remember when my grandfather Romey would be called to the Torah during Sabbath morning services, all of his children, grandchildren and younger relatives would stand in his honor. When he returned to his seat, we would form a line in order of age, and we would kiss his hand and receive his blessing.

In those days, the family had a definite structure. Respect for elders was deeply inculcated in the young. Good manners were required. Those days were not without problems; but life had a clear context and meaning.

The Talmud instructs: do not disdain anything, for everything has its place. It also teaches that it is a sin to be wasteful. In short, things have value and should be respected.

In our family, we learned the value of things in various ways. Before eating, we were taught to recite the appropriate blessing to thank God for our food. Papoo would say the blessing over bread and then would kiss the loaf before cutting it into pieces and distributing it to the family. It was considered a sin to throw bread or even to let it drop to the floor.

Leftover food was not thrown away. Nona had taught her daughters how to "recycle" leftovers, turning them into healthy and tasty meals. Leftover chicken and vegetables would become chicken pot pie or stew; or they could become the basis of a hearty soup. Leftover baked goods would become toast, stuffing, or crunchy snacks known as parmakes. Stale bread was soaked in water and then squeezed. Eggs and cheese were mixed into the bread pulp, and patties were formed from this mixture. They were fried until brown on both sides and were a special treat known as boyos de pan. When there were too many vegetables at home and there was a fear that they would begin to rot, we would have a meal called quartos, fourths; this was a stew made by cutting all the vegetables into quarters and simmering them in a pot. Ripening fruit would become homemade jam. When there was no way to save the food for human consumption, it was fed to the neighbors' dogs. Inedible bread was fed to the ducks along the shore of Lake Washington.

Delicious side dishes were made from celery roots (apyo), spinach stems (ravicos), and zucchini peels (cashcaricas). Coffee grounds and onion skins were placed in the water in which hard boiled eggs were cooked. The egg shells turned brown, and the flavors were absorbed by the eggs themselves. Known as huevos haminados, these eggs were a specialty for Sabbath and festival meals.

Orange peels could be made into candy or added to baked goods for flavoring. Nona would sometimes place pieces of orange peel and cloves on the burners of her stove in order to give the house a nice fragrance. When Mom peeled apples for baking pies, we would eat the apple peels as a snack.

This heartfelt concern for food was symbolic of a philosophy of life that valued things. Indeed, a society might be evaluated by its garbage. If it discards edible and usable things, it is extravagant. A wasteful society shows disrespect for God's blessings. Long before environmentalism and conservation became fashionable, our culture fostered a deep and abiding connection with the natural resources we enjoyed.

Clothes were kept until they were worn out. If they were outgrown but still wearable, they were given to another family member who could use them. For years, I wore shirts handed down to me from my older brother Bill. For years, my younger brother David wore hand me downs from me. If no one in our immediate family needed or wanted the used clothes, Mom would have the clothing picked up by an agency that provided clothes for the poor.

Without realizing it, our extended family was avant garde when it came to recycling. We used juice bottles as vases for flowers. Jars from peanut butter and jam were used as drinking glasses; or as containers for buttons and sundry items. Cardboard boxes were used as storage bins, receptacles for the family photographs, even as luggage. When we went on vacation, we packed cardboard boxes with pots and pans, meat, bread and other kosher groceries that we would not be able to find at our vacation destination.

And of course we had collections.

We collected rocks, sea shells, sand dollars, sticks, bottle caps, baseball cards, books, knick-knacks, marbles, coins, stamps, jack-knives. None of our collections was scientific; all were spontaneous and fun, without a thought as to future value.

Some of the things we collected had practical uses. For example, we would go to a beach at Deception Pass at the northern tip of Whidbey Island in search of "cheese rocks." Mom used to make white cheese *(queso blanco),* similar to farmer's cheese. Part of the process required putting the curdling milk into cheesecloth and placing it in a pan. For the cheese to solidify, it was necessary for the watery part of the milk to drain. This was accomplished by placing a "cheese rock" on top of the cheesecloth. Mom liked "cheese rocks" that were oval, heavy and thick, and about six to eight inches long. A good "cheese rock" was a prize.

My jack-knife collection should also, at least theoretically, belong in the category of "useful" collections. I was careful to buy or trade for jack-knives that had a "personality." I did not like the plain ones that only had one or two blades. Generally, I bought my jack-knives at Mr. Schain's dry goods store on Yesler, between 23rd and 24th Avenues. I favored those with marbleized handles and that had an assortment of attachments. Among the features on my various knives were corkscrews, a screwdriver, scissors, an ice pick, a bottle opener—and of course blades of different sizes. Why did I buy these knives? I thought they were beautiful, strong and useful.

I cannot remember ever making use of them except to sharpen sticks that I never needed. One time I thought I could be helpful to Mom by using a jack-knife to open up a tightly closed pistachio nut. The result of my valor was that I sliced through the top of my thumb; I still have a scar to this day.

Although I was insistent on choosing knives that had cork-screw attachments, we never had bottles with corks that required use of a corkscrew. All the other attachments were equally un-necessary to me; or they simply did not work when they were needed. And still, I continued to collect jack-knives.

I learned that sometimes we collect things for the joy of col-lecting, not because we think the collectibles are really useful or valuable. If we enjoy collecting, that is sufficient reason to be a collector.

Mom was an avid collector of agates that we would find on the beach at Birch Bay, a resort in Northwest Washington State, a few miles from the Canadian border. Whenever we brought a rock to her for inspection, she would inform us if it was a real agate, or a partial agate, or just a plain rock. She liked small, white stones that you could almost see through when they were wet and you held them up to the sun. Mom also liked snail shells, but only if they were unbroken, and only if there were no live snails still inside them. Scouring the beach for agates and snail shells required considerable patience and concentration. It is a wonder that we children enjoyed this activity so much, since it was so time-consuming and meticulous. We never failed to leave Birch Bay without a cardboard box full of rocks and seashells. We generally also found some fine pieces of driftwood to add to the bounty that we brought back with us to Seattle.

What did we do with all those rocks, shells and sticks? Some of the rocks found a home in our goldfish bowl. Some of the more unusual pieces of driftwood ornamented the patio or garage. The rest stayed in boxes until somehow they just disappeared. The main fun and excitement had been in the finding and collecting.

One of the characteristic features of the homes in our ex-tended family was the display of halintrankas, dust catchers. This included all sorts of knick-knacks—glass fish, little statuettes, salt and pepper shakers etc. They generally were placed on the window sills in the kitchen. Where did these halintrankas come from? What purpose did they serve?

Most of them were won by us children as prizes when playing carnival games at Birch Bay. We would throw darts at balloons or at a moving disc with numbers on it; we would throw baseballs at bowling pins; we would throw dimes onto a table with numbers painted inside circles. Depending on how lucky we were, we won prizes. Generally, the prizes were fairly worthless halintrankas that no reasonable person would ever want or need. On the other hand, since we won the prizes, we were very proud of them.

Needless to say, these prizes could not be cast away. Rather, they had to be displayed proudly. The luckier we children were, the more halintrankas had to be accommodated in our homes. Whenever we won, we never failed to bring some of our best prizes to our grandparents so that they too could share in the joy.

After Nona died in 1959, Papoo kept the halintrankas in their places of honor on the kitchen window sills. When he died several years later, it became necessary to sell the house and dispose of the furnishings. I remember visiting the house for the last time. Everything was in turmoil. Mom and her siblings were going through the rooms, deciding who should take what; and what should be given away or sold. I drifted into the kitchen and my eyes fixed on the rows of halintrankas, covered with a thin layer of dust. They were so many useless things that had given so much pleasure over the years. There was a direct correlation between my grandparents' pleasure in them and our pleasure in them. Once my grandparents were gone, the halintrankas became ghosts of satisfactions long past. I asked Mom to take one of the halintrankas home as a memento. She did. I do not know what happened to the rest of them. It does not matter anymore.

Another category of collectibles were things that had no claim to intrinsic value but that stimulated our imagination. Whenever we received letters from abroad (not too often), we would cut the stamps off the envelopes and keep them in a cigar box. There was a certain awe that went with holding a stamp that had come from a faraway land. In some mysterious way, the stamp connected us with foreign civilizations. Each stamp, whether from Israel, Spain, Turkey or elsewhere, was received with enthusiasm.

Baseball cards also opened new worlds for us. Each card was not only a history of a particular player; it was also a window into another world, the world of major league baseball. In those days, players were loyal to their teams. A Yankee was a Yankee; a Dodger was a Dodger. Teams held together. Rapport developed between fans and the team for which they rooted. Trades, certainly involving the elite players, were not too common. As a little boy growing up in Seattle, where we only had a Triple A team back then, baseball cards symbolized a bigger world, a world where greatness could be achieved. Through the cards, we became part of greater America.

I collected things that had no apparent value or purpose at all. They were not useful, nor beautiful, nor did they stimulate imagination. In this category, I refer to my collection of bottle caps.

I do not remember why I started this collection. Somewhere around the time when I was nine years old, I was well into this project. I kept each type of bottle cap in a separate cigar box. Since Dad drank beer and we drank soft drinks fairly often, I was able to add a steady stream of caps to my collection. To get bottle caps from a wider variety of sources, I searched on sidewalks, beaches, neighbors' yards, or anywhere else I suspected I might find something to add to my collection. It was easy enough to obtain caps from Coca Cola, Seven Up, Budweiser and other popular brands. It was more difficult to find caps from foreign made beers and from less popular soft drinks. However, my collection was developing nicely, cap by cap.

One day I happened to mention my collection to my Uncle Dave Amon, a bartender at a tavern by the waterfront in downtown Seattle. His eyes brightened. "Do you like bottle caps?" he asked in wonderment. I proceeded to show him my cigar boxes containing the bottle caps I had collected.

Within a few days, Uncle Dave appeared at our back door with five or six bushel baskets of bottle caps. With glee and pride, he turned over this prize to me, patting me lovingly on the head. "In the tavern, we get an endless amount of bottle caps. I had all of them put into baskets for you. Now you have a really fantastic collection. And I'll keep bringing you lots more."

I hugged my uncle and thanked him. Together, we lugged the baskets down to the basement where I kept my collection. "Go ahead," he laughed once we had the baskets downstairs, "start sorting them out. You'll have a great time."

I started going through the baskets and fingering the caps, but somehow I felt a lack of enthusiasm and interest. My uncle had to leave fairly soon to get back to work. As he left, he assured me he'd be bringing me many more baskets of bottle caps in the weeks ahead.

From the moment I received this generous gift of many hundreds of bottle caps, I lost interest in my collection. I never bothered to sort through the baskets, I never placed the caps in their proper cigar boxes, and I stopped saving bottle caps from our dinner table. I scoured no more streets, yards or beaches.

When my uncle brought me another huge shipment of caps, I again thanked him…but without enthusiasm. He wasn't insulted, but he didn't seem pleased with my tepid response. After another few deliveries, he finally gave up on me. I thanked him profusely and told him that I already had all the bottle caps I would ever want and that I was no longer collecting them.

I later realized that the reason I had been collecting bottle caps was because it was fun to find things and categorize them. The rarer they were, the more challenging it was to find them, and the more thrilling to add them to the collection. Once the joy of collecting was removed due to the overabundant supply of bottle caps, the collection lost its meaning. It wasn't owning the collection that was important; it was the process of collecting.

Mom noticed my sudden abandonment of my bottle cap collection. She told me that collecting things provided a good lesson in life. Happiness is often found in the process of seeking a goal rather than in achieving it. Searching is more rewarding than finding. Self-reliance is more fulfilling than receiving gifts from others. We appreciate those things that have cost us time and effort more than things that have been given to us.

My bottle cap collection apparently had not been useless after all. It provided me with more useful insights than I had learned from many teachers and books.

French historian, Fernand Braudel, observed that "the mere smell of cooking can evoke a whole civilization." The aromas of foods contain within them the power to draw us back to the kitchens of our grandmothers, mother and aunties. We inhale the fragrance of freshly baked bread and we are children again.

The women in our family were excellent cooks, each expert in the cuisine of the Sephardic Jews of the Turkey and Rhodes. Although the American influence was apparent in our meals, the basic Mediterranean Sephardic cooking style prevailed.

Styles of food preparation separated one group from another. Mom told us that during her childhood years, palpable tensions would arise between the Sephardim and Ashkenazim of Seattle. One of the ways in which this rivalry manifested itself related to food. Ashkenazic youngsters would taunt their Sephardic peers by calling them "Mazola," since Sephardim traditionally cooked with vegetable oil such as Mazola brand oil. As a retort, the Sephardim called the Ashkenazim "schmaltz," the Yiddish word for chicken fat, a staple in Ashkenazic cooking.

It has long been a source of annoyance to Sephardim that Ashkenazim assume that their cooking is traditional Jewish cuisine, while that of the Sephardim falls into the category of exotica. It has been fairly common for people to write "Jewish" cookbooks that feature only Ashkenazic recipes; and write articles on "Jewish" cooking that ignored or misrepresented Sephardic cuisine. As a child attending the Jewish Day School in Seattle, I was taught that Jews eat latkes on Hanukkah and hamentaschen on Purim; yet, in our homes these foods were unknown. We ate bourmuelos on Hanukkah and foulares for Purim.

I vividly recall the first Shabbat I spent in the dormitory as a freshman at Yeshiva College in New York. After Friday evening services, we went to the cafeteria for dinner. At each place was a plate with a little brown round glob. I asked a classmate what this item was. He looked at me in disbelief. "Aren't you Jewish?" he asked me. Seeing my consternation, he finally told me that this glob was chopped liver, a dish eaten in honor of Shabbat. I had never seen, let alone eaten, chopped liver in my life. I went through the same culture shock that Shabbat when being served gefilte fish, matzah ball soup, cholent and kugel. While all of these foods were standard fare for Ashkenazim, they were entirely new to me. My classmates were stunned that I had been raised in such a "non-Jewish" fashion as not to have eaten these foods each Sabbath. While I learned to eat and enjoy most of the Ashkenazic foods, I have never completely gotten over the original pain I felt at the scorn of my classmates. They defined Jewishness according to their own pattern, without considering that there were other valid, traditional and vibrant patterns among other groups of Jews.

One of the main differences I found between the standard Ashkenazic and Sephardic cuisines relates to appearance. A plate of Ashkenazic food is typically brown, beige and orange. To dress up the color, sometimes they toss on a sprig of parsley. In contrast, a plate of Sephardic food is typically colorful and full of variety. Ashkenazim were big on potatoes, carrots and pasta. Sephardim, while also using these ingredients, drew on a wide repertoire of vegetables stemming from their Mediterranean cooking traditions.

When my wife, Gilda, first came to Seattle for our engagement, Passover 1967, she was amazed by the incredible variety of foods that she was served. Having been raised in an Ashkenazic home where the cuisine was brown and where vegetables came from cans, she was delighted to discover a whole new world of cooking. She was so pleased that she eventually went on to become an extraordinary cook and an author of a marvelous Sephardic cookbook, Sephardic Holiday Cooking.

As a child, I could tell what holiday was approaching by knowing what foods were being prepared. Before Rosh haShanah, Dad would bring home a large quantity of leeks, from which Mom would make leek patties (keftes de prasa). These were served as part of a pre-dinner ceremonial on the two nights of Rosh haShanah. Various foods were eaten on these occasions, each of which was symbolic of a good blessing for the New Year. Mom would make pumpkin-filled pastries; pastries with a filling that included beetroots; black-eyed beans cooked in a light tomato sauce. Uncooked symbolic foods included apples dipped in honey, dates and pomegranates.

On Succoth, we ate foods made with the autumn vegetables e.g. pumpkin, squash, zucchini, and leek. On Hanukkah we ate bourmuelos, deep fried doughnuts dipped in honey or powdered sugar. The fifteenth day of the Hebrew month of Shevat is known as the "New Year of Trees;" it is traditional to eat fruits, especially those grown in the land of Israel. A specialty of this holiday, known among us as fruticas, was a sweet pudding made from cracked wheat (prehito or mustrahana). In celebration of Purim, we ate foulares, a pastry made of a flat piece of dough with a hard-boiled egg wrapped in strips of dough. It looked vaguely like a foot—the flat dough being the foot, the egg being the ankle. It reminded us of the villain of the Purim story, Haman, who was defeated by Mordecai and Esther. Haman was hanged as punishment, possibly from his ankles.

Passover featured a vast assortment of foods made without bread or any leavened dough. We had special Passover bourmuelos, deep fried delicacies made of crushed matzah and egg; fritadas, a sort of quiche made of spinach and matzah; reshas fritas, strips of matzah soaked in egg and fried, and then eaten sprinkled with honey, sugar or jam. For breakfast, we broke matzah into little pieces and added sugar and milk. For drinks, we had shurup, which is made by mixing several spoonfuls of jam into a glass of cold water. On Shavuot we had foods featuring the available spring fruits and vegetables.

Each Sabbath was an occasion for festive meals. Mom used to

begin cooking on Thursday night and would be in the kitchen all day Friday. When we came home from school on Friday afternoons, we would find the kitchen counters loaded with things my mother had cooked: boulemas (yeast-dough pastries with various fillings such as spinach, potato, eggplant and cheese); bourekas, (pie-dough pastries, usually filled with a mixture of spinach or eggplant and cheese); pitas (round, flat cheese breads); soutlach (a pudding made of rice flour); panizicos (sweet rolls). Mom would also make cakes, pies, cookies, rice pudding and other sweets for the Shabbat meals.

I well remember the intoxicating fragrances of Mom's kitchen on Friday afternoons. When we came home from school, we went straight for the kitchen counters. Although it took much work and many hours to make all these foods, and although Mom had prepared them specifically for our Sabbath meals— she never once told us to limit our intake on Friday afternoons. Rather, she beamed with pleasure at our enthusiasm. She would say: "salud y beraha," eat with health and blessing.

Years later, when Gilda and I started to cook these foods ourselves, we realized how painstaking and time-consuming it was to prepare them. Gilda once worked for hours to make two dozen spinach boulemas for Shabbat lunch. As soon as she took them out of the oven, we and our children rushed for them. It took little time for us to finish them all off; we had none left for Shabbat lunch!

I called Mom and told her our experience. I asked: "how did you ever let us eat our fill on Friday afternoons, and still have enough for Shabbat?" She answered simply: "I always made twice as much of everything that I thought we would need for Shabbat. That way, you could eat to your heart's content on Friday and there would still be plenty for Shabbat. Salud y beraha."

For Friday night dinner, Mom would normally prepare a first course of fish—usually salmon, fixed in a sweet and sour tomato sauce or in a white sauce made of egg and lemon. The main course would include roasted chicken and many side dishes such as stuffed tomatoes, onions and/or green peppers; a baked dish made of macaroni and chopped meat; string beans; Spanish rice;

113

okra or cauliflower cooked in a sweet and sour tomato sauce; baked potatoes and sweet potatoes; stuffed grape leaves. Mom also would serve a large fresh salad, dressed simply with mayonnaise, and sometimes also flavored with parsley or mint freshly picked from our garden.

This general menu was followed each week without fail. Who could complain? The food was delicious and plentiful. It contained a wide variety of textures, colors and tastes. Who could become bored with it? No one in our family, least of all Mom, ever considered the need to vary the Friday night Sabbath dinner menu. If it had worked well for so long, why experiment with change?

But the crisis was bound to come. And it did.

One Friday night, my brother Bill suddenly raised a previously unthinkable question: "Why are we in a rut? Why do we have to eat the same thing every Friday night? Why can't we eat regular food like everyone else?"

A profound, brooding silence followed. We were shocked.

At the time of this eventful Friday night dinner, Bill was attending University of Washington. In his educational and cultural progress, he came to the conclusion that our family was old-fashioned. We did not adapt enough to modern American society. Rather, we continued to live in many ways as though we were still residing in Turkey, or as though we were new immigrants in Seattle. The food on Friday night was only a symbol of a deep-rooted traditionalism, an inability or reluctance to change or to experiment with new ways of doing things. Bill's complaint about the menu was really a reflection of a much bigger problem that was troubling him.

Mom understood the import of Bill's question. Very diplomatically, and without appearing the least bit hurt, she asked him what he would prefer to eat for Shabbat dinner. He answered: "Why can't we have steaks and potatoes? Why do we have to be in a rut?"

Before anyone could say a thing, Mom said enthusiastically: "Bill, you are right. Next week, we'll have steaks and potatoes on Friday night. There's no sin in changing our menu once in a while."

The next Friday evening, Mom kept her word. After the first course of fish, she served a wonderful dinner of steaks and potatoes. All of us loved steaks and potatoes. But on Friday night, the dinner seemed all wrong. Bill ate with gusto, whether real or feigned I do not know. The rest of us were unenthusiastic about dinner. I remember sitting at my place playing with the steak with my knife and fork. Finally, Dad said: "steaks and potatoes are delicious—but not on Friday nights. Steaks and potatoes taste like weekdays, not Shabbat."

Bill was flustered. "What can I say? You're all in a rut. You can't shake old habits." Finally, with a sense of resignation, he said: "I guess it's okay to have the regular Shabbat food if that's what everyone likes. At least we did try an experiment."

Next Friday night, and for all the Friday nights thereafter as long as Mom was well enough to cook, the traditional foods were served. No more steaks and potatoes; no other innovations; and no more complaints.

Papoo and Nona liked Birch Bay, a lazy resort town in upstate Washington. The beach was rocky, the water ice cold. The one road that ran through town had a speed limit of 10 miles per hour and there was very little traffic.

Birch Bay was a place where there was not that much to do. That was the way Papoo and Nona liked it. It was quiet, scenic, and peaceful.

Each summer, they rented a waterfront cabin for one or two weeks. Uncle Dave Romey, who usually returned to Seattle for summers, did the driving for them and stayed with them in their cabin. Our family rented a cabin next door. Uncle Dave and

Aunty Esther Amon and family rented in the same cabin complex. Sometimes, others of the extended family also arranged to spend their vacation in Birch Bay at the same time. Uncle Jack and Aunty Regina eventually bought one of the cabins and enjoyed it for many years.

As a child, I thought Birch Bay was very distant from Seattle. (It is actually only about 110 miles away.) Our trips there used to take six hours and more.

We left early Sunday morning, all the cars meeting at my grandparents' house on 15th Avenue. The car trunks were checked to be sure that nothing had been forgotten. Aside from clothes, we also packed kosher meat, bread and other kosher food items that were not available in Birch Bay. Each family also brought two sets of pots and pans, silverware, dishes—one set for meat foods and one for dairy, as is prescribed by the Jewish laws of kashrut.

Of course, everyone brought food for lunch. Since we also would make various road stops along the way, and since each stop entailed having cahve (pronounced kah-veh)—we also had provisions of thermoses of coffee and lots of home-baked pastries. Although we generally took these vacation trips in August, we also had to pack warm clothes and winter jackets; the weather in Birch Bay could turn cold or rainy. Papoo insisted that the trunk of each car had to be equipped with a rope, as well as with a warm sweater for each member of the family. Papoo followed the motto: "Be prepared."

Uncle Dave Romey, driving his 1949 Nash, led the caravan. The other cars lined up behind and our procession began. The trip to Birch Bay was not just a way to get from one place to another. It was also a reflection of a philosophy of life. The family viewed the trip as an integral part of the vacation. Uncle Dave was forever studying maps. Whenever he found what might be a "scenic spot," he had no hesitation to pull off the main road and travel many miles out of the way in order to discover this natural wonder.

We hardly traveled thirty miles and we already were at our first rest stop for cahve: Forest Park in Everett. We visited the zoo, played in the park, admired the scenery, ate a snack, and then returned to our traveling. Uncle Dave might also take another detour to Wenberg State Park. This was also just a "rest stop," although we had only traveled another twenty miles or so from Everett. Even though Wenberg was well off the main road, we did not mind; we enjoyed a quick swim, more refreshments, and then got back on the road.

No trip to Birch Bay would be complete unless we drove on the "world famous Chuckanut Drive," a marvelously scenic mountain road. We stopped along the way at Rosario Park, and perhaps one or two other picnic areas. We played baseball, ran races, threw rocks into the water, and ate a late lunch. Then we continued our voyage to Birch Bay, where we generally arrived toward evening.

No sooner had we settled in our cabins than it was dinner time. The fact that we had eaten five or six times on the road did not factor into our appetites. We were always starving upon arrival at Birch Bay. The men set up the barbeque grills as the women unpacked the food and utensils. We ate in the back yard of the cabins, right along the beach. We watched the sun set as we ate our fill.

During the week or two of vacation, we enjoyed swimming, bicycle riding, scouring the beach for snail shells, rocks and driftwood. Some of the family went horseback riding, renting horses from a nearby stable. On Shabbat, we all dressed up in nice Sabbath clothes. We gathered in Nona and Papoo's cabin for the prayer services. Our Shabbat activities consisted of long walks and long naps.

Uncle Dave felt that it was important to explore whatever scenic sites were in the vicinity. We would drive to Peace Arch Park in Blaine, right on the border between the United States and Canada. Papoo would only refer to this park by its original name, Sam Hill Park. He did not accept the designation of Peace Arch Park, feeling that it did an injustice to the memory of Sam Hill about whom Papoo knew nothing. "I don't care who Sam Hill was. If they named this park after him, then they can't take it away from him."

We would also often venture up to Vancouver for a day, being sure to stop at several "scenic spots" that Uncle Dave wanted us to see. His explorer instincts enabled us to visit the Indian reservation on Lummi Island, an Air Force base, a giant tree with a massive hole in the middle of its trunk, large enough for a car to drive through…and many other interesting sites.

In the evenings, we would go to the amusement park in the center of town. We went on rides, played games of chance where we tried to win halintrankas. Another evening activity was to search for crickets that were chirping away inside our cabin. Crickets are fine ventriloquists and it took time to learn how to outsmart them. We caught them in jars and tossed them outside. Undoubtedly, they found their way right back into the cabin because the sound of the crickets continued unabated.

Uncle Dave took it upon himself to take home movies of our travels in order to preserve our adventures for posterity. Mom used to say that he was "creative" since many of the movies turned out to be a series of blurs, flashes and bright colors. He was also known to photograph argyle socks in order to add color to the movies; he sometimes held his camera sideways or upside down, a technique that certainly added to our enjoyment when viewing the films later.

On some years, our family would spend one week in Birch Bay and another week at Seaside, Oregon. Sometimes Uncle Dave and Aunty Esther Amon and family would join us there as well. In 1956, Dad took his longest vacation from work—three weeks. We drove to Los Angeles and spent time with our relatives there, also taking in all the major tourist attractions.

One summer, while we were in Birch Bay, someone in the family said something remarkable: why do we come to Birch Bay every year? Why can't we think of other places to go on vacation? The general response was: why shouldn't we come to Birch Bay each summer? We enjoy it. The dissident was silenced for the moment, but the challenge seeped into the minds of the family. After so many happy years at Birch Bay, we started to find fault with it. The seeds of discontent had been planted.

Papoo was a traditionalist but he had a remarkably open spirit. He was not afraid to face challenges. Before the next summer arrived, Papoo asked Uncle Dave to find another location for our vacation.

Uncle Dave came up with a suggestion: Orcas Island. He pointed out the resort on his well-worn map. Orcas Island, one of the San Juan Islands in Puget Sound, could be reached by taking a ferry from Anacortes. Uncle Dave assured us that Orcas Island was "scenic and quiet." Papoo gave the go ahead; reservations were made.

The Sunday morning of vacation arrived and our caravan began in front of Nona and Papoo's house. Uncle Dave proudly led the procession and reassured us that we were in for a special adventure. Some family members were growling that we should have gone to Birch Bay; others were excited at trying a new place.

Uncle Dave kept us on schedule since we had to catch a ferry to Orcas Island. Our traditional rest stops for cahve were curtailed to two or three. We did catch the ferry and we arrived in Orcas Island for the first time in our lives. Indeed, it was scenic. And it was quiet. Uncle Dave beamed with satisfaction.

We then arrived at the complex of cabins where we were to stay for the week. When we entered our cabin, the first thing that struck us was a very pungent odor. The second thing that struck us was that the cabin did not have a bathroom. After some searching, we found an outhouse in the back of the cabin. It smelled so bad that I refused to enter it. Dad told me: "I don't blame you for not wanting to go in to the outhouse. But when you've got to go you've got to go." I pursed my lips and assured him that I was not going into that outhouse for the entire week, no matter what.

Mom realized that things had not gotten off to a great start. She decided that a cup of coffee would help set things straight. She put the coffee pot on the gas burner and turned the flame to its highest setting. The flames were so high that they literally reached the handle of the coffee pot. In spite of the prodigious fire, after a half hour the water in the coffee pot was still cold.

All the other families in our group had similar experiences. Dad told Uncle Dave that Orcas Island was not for us, that we ought to head for Birch Bay. Why waste the precious week of vacation in such unpleasant conditions? Uncle Dave smiled knowingly. He assured Dad and the rest of us that Orcas Island was a paradise, a splendid, scenic and quiet resort. Dad was not to be convinced: "Maybe it's good for fishermen, but it is not good for us." Papoo interjected: "Some people got tired of Birch Bay and wanted to try something new. So this is something new. No one should complain."

We all went back to our cabins and sulked.

By dinner time, Mom and Dad had decided that our family was not going to stay the week in Orcas Island. The facilities were primitive, the stench was palpable, the stove didn't heat up the food, and I would not use the outhouse under any circumstances. We didn't even unpack our things. Dad assured us that we would leave on the 9 am ferry the next morning and find a cabin in Birch Bay.

This decision having been made, Dad went to Papoo's cabin to inform him of our plans to leave in the morning. Papoo called a family meeting and announced our decision. Everyone else immediately agreed with us—let's leave as soon as possible! Papoo turned to Uncle Dave: "What do you say, Dave? Orcas Island was your discovery." Uncle Dave, ever the gentleman, announced that he was prepared to follow the decision of the majority, though he felt we had not given Orcas Island enough of a chance. Papoo stated: "It is decided. We will leave for Birch Bay on the morning ferry. Everyone be ready on time. If we miss that ferry, there is not another one until the next day."

A glow of happiness burst out among all the family. We were leaving. We were going to our beloved Birch Bay.

The next morning, we put our things in the trunk of the car and prepared to leave. Mom noticed that the meat that had been stored in the freezer compartment of the refrigerator had not frozen. The freezer obviously did not work. This meant that our entire week's supply of kosher meat was in danger of spoiling—

and it was only Monday.

Well, if worse came to worse, we could share the meat that the other families had brought. We soon learned, though, that all their meat had also thawed out overnight.

"Don't worry," Uncle Dave wisely suggested, "we'll stop at a state park on the way to Birch Bay and we can barbeque all the meat. That way it won't spoil." No one could come up with a better idea, so Uncle Dave's plan was adopted.

Our cars started on the way to the ferry boat. We already were running a bit late, and everyone was anxious not to miss the ferry. Surprisingly, Uncle Dave—driving the lead car—pulled off the road into the parking lot of a grocery store. Dad, who was driving the car right behind Uncle Dave, called out the window. "Dave, what's the problem? We're got to hurry to catch the ferry otherwise we'll be stuck here another day."

Smiling, Uncle Dave raised three coke bottles. "I bought these yesterday, and I want to return the bottles for the deposit."

"Get back into your car," Dad hollered. "I'll pay you for the bottle deposits myself."

So Uncle Dave returned to his driver's seat and we were off. We arrived at the ferry with about thirty seconds to spare.

The ferry landed at Anacortes, and Uncle Dave suggested that the best place for our barbeque was Deception Pass, not far away. Once we arrived, all the meat was unpacked and barbeques were set up. The women and girls brought the meat to the grills, and the men and boys watched it cook. No sooner had the grills been cleared of one batch of meat, the next batch was put on. We ate to contentment—and then some. Amazingly, the entire week's supply of meat was barbequed that day, and all of it was eaten right then. The women were worried that if all the meat were eaten now, there would be none left for the rest of the week including Shabbat. But seeing that everyone was having such a good time, the women agreed with Nona who said "salud y beraha, let everyone eat in good health and blessing." And we did.

The only meat that remained after our picnic were a few salamis. These were saved for Sabbath meals. The rest of the week we ate fish and vegetable dishes.

When we arrived in Birch Bay, we were fortunate to find enough cabins for all of our families and we enjoyed the rest of vacation together. As we sat on the beach that night watching the glorious sunset, Dad asked Uncle Dave: "So, Dave, what did we learn from our adventure in Orcas Island?" Uncle Dave replied with a wan smile on his face: "If you have something you like, you should stick with it. You shouldn't feel dissatisfied." Papoo added: "That's true. But a person has to be ready to try new things too. Sometimes they work out, and sometimes they don't."

But we never again veered from Birch Bay for vacation with Papoo and Nona.

Mom used to say somewhat in jest: "I don't have friends, I only have relatives." The fact was that life did revolve around the extended family. Most of our relatives lived in the same neighborhood, within easy walking distance of each other. It was usual for us to visit the homes of our uncles and aunties and for them to visit us. No invitations were necessary.

Nona and Papoo firmly believed that the family had to stay together. They had both come to Seattle as teenagers, uprooted from their parents' homes in Turkey. They knew what family life had been in the old country and they wanted to transplant the old traditions in Seattle. On one level, their lives in Seattle represented a radical break with their past; yet, in their own minds, they were symbols of continuity.

A basic feature of their traditionalism was religion. They maintained a kosher home and expected their children to do likewise when they married. They observed the Sabbath and holidays without fail, and expected their children to follow their pattern.

We were together with family on happy occasions. We grew up

with the feeling that life is good, that religion is joyful, that family is dependable. Papoo could see, though, that the hold of religion within the community was weakening.

Men of his generation struggled to make their livings; many found it necessary to work on the Sabbath. At first, they felt guilty about desecrating the Sabbath. Soon, though, they came to justify their behavior: this is America, not Turkey. The rules of life have changed and we must change too. Should we starve ourselves and our families by not working on Saturday? Many of the immigrant generation learned to violate the Sabbath; they even learned to overcome feelings of guilt about it. If the immigrants who had grown up as Sabbath observers were now abandoning Sabbath observance, what could be expected of their children and grandchildren who never saw the Sabbath properly observed?

One Shabbat morning, we began our walk home after synagogue services. It was raining heavily. One of the older men of the community drove by in his car and saw our family group getting drenched in the rain. He certainly knew that it was forbidden to ride in a car on Shabbat, and he also knew that our family observed Shabbat as carefully as we could. Yet, he pulled his car next to us, opened his window, and called out: "Can I give you a lift home?"

We thought he was brazen. It was bad enough that he was transgressing the laws of Shabbat. Didn't he at least have enough shame not to flaunt his sin before us?

Papoo's countenance was stern. He tried not to look the man in the face. He pulled his raincoat closer around his neck and continued to walk. We all followed him. The man in the car honked at us as he drove off. He shouted: "I pity you."

Papoo huddled our family together as we stood in the hard rain. "I pity him," Papoo said. "We will get wet today but we will remain pure in the eyes of God." The Talmud teaches that it is better to be thought a fool in this world than ever to do anything foolish in the eyes of God.

We didn't mind getting soaked that Shabbat. Papoo had made

us feel proud.

Papoo cared about our religious upbringing and sought to convey his strong feelings to us on various occasions. I was once invited to a friend's Bar Mitzvah that was taking place at Herzl, a Conservative synagogue just a few blocks from the Sephardic Bikur Holim building. My parents allowed me to attend, as a courtesy to my friend. Papoo was not pleased. I explained to him that I was only going to Herzl this one time in honor of my friend; no harm would come to me if I went there just this once.

"That is what everyone thinks," said Papoo. "They imagine they will do something only once and no harm will come to pass. Sometimes this is true. But often enough, one time leads to another, one sin drags another behind. It is the beginning of unravelling the rope."

I assured Papoo I would not allow myself to be tainted by the experience. He put out his hand; I kissed it. He blessed me and sent me on my way. "Remember," he told me, "stay faithful to our tradition. Those who break with tradition destroy themselves and their families."

I attended the Bar Mitzvah. After services at Herzl, I went to the Sephrdic Bikur Holim where services ended at about the same time. I met Papoo as he was leaving the synagogue. He looked me in the eye: "Remember," he said.

"I will," I responded. And I did.

Growing up in our family and community, our lives were strongly impacted by the rhythms of the Jewish holy days. Many of those childhood memories have remained with me to this day.

On the Sunday mornings before Rosh haShanah, the New Year, it was customary to hold penitential services known as selihot. These services, which began at 4 a.m., were usually held in the homes of various members of the community.

Dad used to take my brother Bill and me to selihot at the home of Uncle Solomon and Aunty Sarah. A group of twenty or thirty men gathered there, crowding into the living room. As the men chanted the penitential prayers in Hebrew and Ladino, Aunty Sarah was busy in the kitchen preparing breakfast for all who attended. To this day, when I hear a melody from the selihot service, I can smell the aroma of sweet rolls being baked, and the fragrance of strong percolated coffee.

At one of the selihot breakfasts, the conversation turned to the language of our prayers. One of the "progressive" men suggested that some of the prayers should be recited in English. After all, many of the men did not understand Hebrew. Many of the younger men and children did not understand Ladino. Why not say some of the prayers in English so that everyone can understand?

This suggestion led to a heated controversy. Some agreed with the suggestion, others just nodded their heads as they ate their sweet rolls and drank their coffee. Others were outraged by the suggestion and let everyone know it. Papoo listened to everyone patiently and then made his own comments. Hebrew is our sacred language. Ladino has acquired a kind of sanctity by virtue of its being used for prayer by generations of our ancestors. English has no holiness for us. It is better to recite prayers in Hebrew without understanding them, rather than to say them in English. Prayers mean more than their words. Prayers are sacred, they link us with God and with our ancestors. If anyone wants to know what the Hebrew words mean, he can read the English translation on his own. If we do not pray in the language of our ancestors, it is not real prayer.

With Papoo's remarks, the "progressives" became silent.

On Rosh haShana and Passover, our extended family was too large to meet in one place. Uncle Solomon and Aunty Sarah and family would be together with Uncle Jack and Aunty Regina and family. (Aunty Sarah and Aunty Regina, my mother's sisters, married two brothers, Jack and Solomon Maimon.) Aunty Estreya and Uncle Vic and family would be with members of Uncle Vic's family. Our family, Uncle Leo and Aunty Florence and family, Uncle Dave and Aunty Esther and family, and Uncle Daye Romey would be at Nona and Papoo's.

Papoo presided at these meals. On Rosh haShana he led in the special yehi ratsones, blessings over symbolic foods, praying for a sweet and happy year filled with abundance, peace and security. On Pessah, he presided over the Seder on both nights. Papoo insisted that each member of the family participate in the recitation of the Haggada, whether in Hebrew, Ladino or English. Papoo allowed English since the Haggadah is not in the category of prayer. Rather, it is a study text recounting the Exodus from Egypt. When it comes to study, Papoo felt that people should use a language that they understood. Yet, most of the men stayed with Hebrew and Ladino.

On the night when the Passover festival ended, Papoo and the men of the family remained in the synagogue for a few minutes after services. The children were home with Nona and the women. Nona gave each of the children a brown paper bag. And then the wait began.

All of us children were in a state of heightened anticipation. The older ones teased the younger ones. The younger ones peered out the windows to see if Papoo and the men were coming. There would inevitably be knocks on the back door. All of us would run excitedly to the kitchen. There was no one there; it was only a trick on us. Then there would be knocking at the front door and we rushed to the front hall. Another false alarm. At last the knocking on the door would really be Papoo and the men. The door would be opened quickly, and Papoo tossed a fistful of coins onto the floor. The children scrambled to get the money. Then the other men threw coins and candy, mixed with long blades of grass. The money throw continued throughout the living room and dining room area. The older children went for the coins, the younger ones went for the candies. The women saw to it that all the children succeeded. If the older children were blocking out the younger ones, the women would drop coins right in front of the younger ones so they could not miss getting some for themselves.

This custom symbolized the Israelites crossing the Red Sea during their exodus from Egypt. The grass was reminiscent of the reeds the Israelites experienced at the sea. The coins were reminders that the Egyptians had given gold and silver to the Israelites when the slaves left their servitude; the candies symbolized the manna that the Israelites ate upon entering the wilderness.

During the course of the "money throw," the men sang a traditional song in Ladino. Afterwards, the children counted up their loot. Every face was filled with joy. Every heart was glad. Judaism was a happy, joyous way of life.

Our lives were marked by the regular rhythms of Shabbat and holidays; but also by the events of the life cycle. In a large extended family, there were many occasions that entailed a religious or communal component i.e. circumcisions, baby namings, Bar Mitzvahs (there were no Bat Mitzvahs in our synagogues in those days), birthdays, graduations, engagements, weddings, anniversaries…and on the other end of the pendulum, funerals, mourning periods, death anniversaries. The common denominator of these observances was food.

During the early years of my childhood, the women of the family would get together to cook and bake for these special occasions. The older women, born in the old country, taught their daughters and nieces the traditional recipes and manner of preparation. They showed how to make fila dough, stretching it paper thin over tables, working quickly so the dough would not become brittle. They assigned children the task of grinding the nuts that would be part of the filling for the baklava, a honey-drenched pastry made with the fila dough. While some women worked on the baklava, others were preparing a variety of cookies and pastries. Another group would be making marzipan cookies, using home-prepared almond paste. Depending on the nature of the occasion to be celebrated and the number of people who were expected to attend, these baking sessions might take a day or two, or be spread over several weeks.

During these cooking sessions, the generations of women in the family worked together, gossiped, and sang traditional Ladino songs. They personified the continuity and vitality of the old-world culture brought to Seattle from Turkey and Rhodes.

In the early 1960s, commercially made fila dough and almond paste became available at some of the specialty stores. Most of the women quickly switched to the store-bought ingredients, saving themselves numerous hours of labor. Although everyone agreed that the commercially produced ingredients were not as good as the home made, expedience prevailed over traditionalism. It now became less necessary for the women to get together for cooperative baking. One woman could now make baklava and marzipan pastries on her own, without needing help from anyone else. Time was gained; but an element of family solidarity was lost in the process.

Mothers taught their daughters how to run a kosher home. They also added some traditions that they had learned from their own mothers. For example, it was not permitted to cook meat in its own juices; oil had to be put in the pan before placing the meat in it. Also, it was mandatory for a cook to give a sample of the food to one who had smelled it while it was cooking and expressed a desire to taste it. Otherwise, the person would have an unfulfilled longing in the soul. When a person ate to contentment, the hostess should say salud y beraha, health and blessing.

While most of the family observances centered around joyful events, some were related to sad times. After funerals, the mourners would return home from the cemetery and eat a traditional mourners' meal of bread and hard boiled eggs. Family members, neighbors and friends prepared all the meals for the mourners during the seven-day mourning period. They not only prepared enough for the mourners, but they cooked enough for guests who would be paying visits during meal times.

Among our Sephardic customs is the meldado, a study session held on the anniversary of the death of a loved one. I well remember the meldados observed in my childhood home and in the homes of relatives. Family and friends would gather in the hosts' homes. Prayer services were held. Passages from the Talmud (Mishnayot) were read. The rabbi would share words of Torah. The event evoked a spirit of family and communal solidarity, solemnity, reminiscing. But meldados were not sad occasions! After the prayers and study, there was an abundance of food prepared by the hostess. People ate, and chatted, and laughed. People would remember stories about the deceased person whose meldado was being observed, drawing on the good and happy memories. The memorialized person would have wanted family and friends to celebrate, to remember him or her with happiness and laughter.

Once people began to move out of the old neighborhood, things changed. People moved to bigger homes in nicer districts. The family and community was spread out over a wider area. Many of the observances that used to take place in homes were gradually relocated to the synagogues. Some of the traditionalists insisted on keeping these observances at home; but the tide was turning, and could not be reversed.

Progress came at a cost.

Part V

Changing Neighborhoods, Changing Lives

Uncle Dave Romey was the only one of my parents' siblings to have attended college. He had served in the American armed forces during World War II and was one of the many who benefitted from the government's programs to subsidize college expenses for veterans. He studied Spanish language and literature at the University of Washington, and was especially interested in the Spanish roots of the Sephardic Jews in Seattle. His Master's dissertation on the culture of Seattle's Sephardim was a significant scholarly contribution, making him one of the pioneers in the field of Sephardic studies in the United States. Several other Sephardic university students in Seattle—Albert Adatto and Emma Adatto—also wrote dissertations on the history and culture of Seattle's Sephardim. These dissertations by American-born Sephardim reflected love for their tradition, but also an awareness that the old Sephardic culture was undergoing a serious and permanent transformation.

Nona and Papoo and their generation spoke Judeo-Spanish naturally and unselfconsciously. They saw no need to analyze or study their language or civilization. The young people of the next generation, though deeply steeped in the Ladino traditions, were already becoming Americanized. Their main language was English. They sang American songs, danced to American music, told American stories. Ladino was used almost exclusively in their conversations with members of the immigrant generation.

Uncle Dave realized that a cultural transformation was underway. The more he devoted himself to Ladino, the more he recognized that the culture was slipping away. He never wanted to admit the inevitability of this process; but he was far too insightful not to understand what was happening. He was a staunch traditionalist; yet he wanted to find ways of keeping the tradition alive among the new generations for whom Ladino was no longer the mother-tongue.

One of Uncle Dave's distinctive contributions to our family's life was his use of Ladino proverbs in English form. For example, if he ate something delicious, he complimented the cook by saying: "one b. one d." This was short for the Ladino saying, un bocado un ducado, one bite of the food is worth one gold ducat. To describe an individual whose personality traits never seemed to improve, Uncle Dave would say: "from eight to eighty." This was the English translation of the Ladino proverb, de los ocho fina los ochenta. A person's traits are established by age eight and do not change even by age eighty. A snoopy person was described as a spoon, cuchara, since a spoon stirs up the pot and checks on all the ingredients. A bland person was one "who did not go down with salad," no basha ni con salata, i.e. was unpalatable even when accompanied by something good. People who were on uneasy terms were "friends like a cat and dog," amigos como el perro y el gato. If Uncle Dave said that he had parsley growing on his nose, he was alluding to the proverb fuyi del prexil me crecio en la nariz, I ran from the parsley, it grew on my nose. This meant that one did not escape that which he was trying to escape. We all came to use Uncle Dave's Anglicized Ladino sayings. In one sense, we were maintaining the old traditions; but in another sense we were transforming those traditions into American terms.

Most Sephardim of Uncle Dave's generation could not afford the luxury of attending college. He was the first member of our community to become a teacher in a university, and his intellectual achievements were a source of pride to our family. He taught Spanish at the University of Vermont, Temple University, Drew University, and then spent many years teaching at Portland State University. Much of his early career was spent "back East," much to the distress of Nona. Whenever he was returning to Seattle for Passover or for summer vacation, our entire family gathered at Nona and Papoo's house for a party. Whenever he had to return to his college, we all met again at their house for a somber farewell gathering. Nona was terrified of airplanes (and never traveled on one), and she dreaded Uncle Dave's need to travel by air. After Uncle Dave had left for the airport, Nona would sob for hours until she received a call from him informing her that he had landed safely.

Mom spoke of Uncle Dave with love and reverence, seeing in him an educational fulfillment that she herself had never experienced. Although Mom was quite well-read and an intellectual in her own right, she always deferred to her brother Dave since he was a "genuine scholar."

Whereas only a few Sephardim were able to attend university in Uncle Dave's generation, by the 1950s almost all Sephardim of college age were attending college. Most attended the University of Washington in Seattle. My cousin Al was one of the few Sephardim who went to school out of town, attending Yeshiva College in New York City. After receiving his BA degree, he attended law school at the University of Washington. Al was the first born of Mom's older sister Regina. He, like Uncle Dave, was a religious loyalist, and brought pride to the family as our first attorney.

Al and a number of others of similar traditionalist bent were in the minority. Most Sephardic college students of his generation were moving away from the old patterns of Sephardic life. The process of acculturation that had already begun in the immigrant generation began to accelerate. Even those who grew up in the more traditionalist families were changing their ways. Sabbath observance declined. The dietary laws were compromised or abandoned altogether.

No longer was it assumed that the wisdom of the older generations was valid for the new generation in America. College professors became the new authorities; peer pressure became a major molder of values. Some parents, who were themselves not college educated, began to defer authority to their college trained children. Some parents battled with their children, trying to keep them in line. Others looked the other way, hoping that the rebelliousness of their children was just a passing phase, and that they would return to the normal patterns once they married and had families of their own.

Many of the young Sephardim were marrying spouses who were not Sephardic, or who were not Jewish. It could no longer be assumed that wedding receptions would be kosher, nor that the young couples would maintain kosher homes. Young couples now started to move to the suburbs, especially Mercer Island and Bellevue.

The community was showing signs of breakdown. No oppressor forced the people to give up their traditions. No one threatened them to leave the Jewish neighborhood. They were doing it to themselves of their own free will.

They had a name for their behavior: progress. Uncle Dave also had a name for it: spiritual and cultural suicide.

Russell, our next door neighbor on 28th Avenue, moved away in 1957. The neighborhood was already in the midst of change. More and more blacks were moving in; more and more whites were moving out.

Russell, a hard-working and dignified man, was himself a black. He had been our neighbor for many years. His son, Jerome, was our friend. Russell insisted that his son be called Jerome, not Jerry. Jerome was kept neatly dressed and was taught to be respectful and courteous.

When Jerome was old enough to be enrolled in school, Russell did not want him to go to Horace Mann, the elementary public school on 25th Avenue, just across the street from the Jewish Day School. Horace Mann was a troubled "inner city" school and Russell wanted his son in a more genteel setting with a proper educational atmosphere. Russell enrolled Jerome in the elementary school in the neighboring Madrona district, believing that this would be a better place for him.

The first months at Madrona were terrifying for Jerome. He came home crying each day. Kids picked on him, beat him up. He was frightened to go to school. Seeing Jerome's distress, Russell managed to get him transferred to a school in another district, Leschi. Jerome stopped complaining about school; but he also changed. He insisted on being called Jerry. His face hardened. He started to use foul language. He refused to dress neatly. He talked back to his father. At Leschi, Jerry had become a tough, ill-mannered boy. My brother David and I spent less and less time with Jerry.

In 1957, Russell sold his house and moved to the other side of town. "They drove me out," he told Dad. "They're destroying my son. I've got to get away from here before it's too late."

Russell was not the first of our neighbors to move out. Some said they were leaving because they had more money now and they wanted to live in nicer areas. Others said they were moving to get away from the deterioration that was engulfing our neighborhood. Some said they had to move because they were afraid to stay.

Our old neighborhood was changing for the worse. The house across the street from us was now occupied by several women with numerous little children. Different men showed up from time to time, but never seemed to stay very long. The noise level in the neighborhood went up. Some of the new neighbors did not tend their lawns or keep their houses painted properly. Crime increased. Neighborhood store owners were experiencing vandalism and theft. Our world was coming apart in front of our eyes. Inexorably. Without anyone able to reverse the trend.

Our synagogue, Ezra Bessaroth, came to the conclusion that the congregation would have to sell its building on 15th Avenue and build a new synagogue in the Seward Park area where some members had already relocated. A vocal minority of traditionalists argued against the move. We had been praying in our synagogue building for many years and we liked it here. If we all decided not to move out of this neighborhood, we could maintain our present building and keep our congregation going here. Our families have been living in this neighborhood since the Sephardic immigrants had first arrived from Turkey and Rhodes. We had a lot of good memories here, a sense of togetherness and continuity.

But the move to Seward Park was necessary. The synagogue on 15th Avenue would be unable to sustain itself much longer. The congregation voted to sell the current building and erect a new one on the corner of Wilson Avenue South and South Brandon Street. There was a gap of over a year between the time of the sale of the old synagogue and the building of a new facility. During the interim, members of Ezra Bessaroth worshipped at Sephardic Bikur Holim on 20th and Fir or at other synagogues. For the High Holy Days, the congregation rented a hall where services were conducted according to its custom. Meanwhile, members who were still living in the old neighborhood made plans to move to the area where the new synagogue was being built.

Dad accepted the inevitability of the move to Seward Park. In fact, he was eager to relocate our family there. Homes in Seward Park were newer and larger. Since the old neighborhood was declining seriously, it was surely time to move a better, safer neighborhood.

Mom, though, had a different point of view. Under no circumstances did she want to move from 511 28th Avenue. This was the home where she had lived since 1940, where she had raised her children. This home was in walking distance of her parents' home and her sisters' homes. Even if Ezra Bessaroth had decided to move, Sephardic Bikur Holim was staying in the neighborhood. There was still a group of traditionalists who resisted moving to the new area.

Dad thought that he could persuade Mom by offering reasonable arguments: our family deserves to be in a better home in a better neighborhood; moving to Seward Park won't prevent you from visiting your parents and sisters and other relatives. He convinced her to take driving lessons so she would be able to drive to the old neighborhood whenever she wanted.

Mom was deeply distraught. Why should we allow others to drive us out of our own home, out of our own neighborhood? If we all stay, we can keep things stable.

But everyone was not staying. Many were selling their homes as soon as they could. Like it or not, the neighborhood as we had known it was coming apart. Friends and relatives moved away; strangers moved in. Well-established stores closed. The streets became increasingly dangerous and crime-ridden.

A gang of hoodlums got into a knife fight in front of Aunty Sarah's house on 26th Avenue. One of the victims bled on her front steps and porch. The sons of new neighbors climbed into Aunty Regina's yard and stole cherries from her trees. Cousins playing baseball in a public field were accosted by a group of teenagers who hit them and made anti-Jewish comments. A man walked into Uncle Jack's butcher shop and took a chicken for which he refused to pay. Gangs of students from Horace Mann intimidated the children of the Jewish Day School, taunting, threatening, fighting. Almost every day, there was another unpleasant incident. How much patience could we have? How much longer should we allow ourselves to be subjected to the violence and immorality all around us?

Dad convinced Mom that they should at least look at homes in the Seward Park area. Maybe she would like one of them. Mom reluctantly agreed but found fault with every home they saw. "We are better off where we are," she insisted. "Why should we move so far away?"

Dad hoped we would be living in Seward Park no later than early summer of 1958. My Bar Mitzvah was scheduled for August 2, 1958, and Dad wanted this event to be celebrated in our own synagogue, Ezra Bessaroth. Mom reminded him that the new building in Seward Park might not even be completed by that time; and even if it was, we could not have the Bar Mitzvah there because many relatives would be unable to attend. They were religiously observant and did not travel by car on the Sabbath. How were they to get to Seward Park? They could not be expected to walk the five or six miles from the old neighborhood. She thought that my Bar Mitzvah should be held at the Sephardic Bikur Holim, where her father had been a pioneer and leader, and where most of her relatives prayed.

So it was settled. I would be Bar Mitzvah at the Sephardic Bikur Holim. I began lessons with my Uncle Solomon, who was the rabbi of the Bikur Holim. Dad arranged that I prepare a speech under the direction of Rabbi Isidore Kahan of the Ezra Bessaroth. He also arranged that we would have a special celebration at the new building of Ezra Bessaroth on Sunday morning, August 3, when I would don my tefillin and make a short talk. This would be followed by a breakfast for all the guests. And so it was. I was the first boy to celebrate his Bar Mitzvah in the new building of the Ezra Bessaroth, albeit on a Sunday morning rather than on a Shabbat.

The Shabbat of my Bar Mitzvah was celebrated at the Sephardic Bikur Holim. After services, our family went to Nona and Papoo's house for lunch. Nona, whose health had been declining, was too ill to walk all the way to synagogue. When we had lunch with her, I recited some of my Bar Mitzvah speech, and she cheered me on with glee. On Saturday night, my parents arranged a reception in my honor at the Norway Center, the only hall in those days that had facilities for kosher catering. On Sunday morning, we all went to the new Ezra Bessaroth building where I participated in the services. We then had a festive breakfast for family and friends who had come to synagogue in honor of the occasion.

After my Bar Mitzvah, Dad continued to discuss with Mom the need for us to move to Seward Park. He was very sensitive to her fears and anxieties, but he was determined to win her consent. She finally liked a house that was shown to her, a block away from Ezra Bessaroth; but she was still hesitant. Finally Dad convinced her to agree to have our house on 28th Avenue put up for sale.

When the real estate agent planted a "for sale" sign in our front yard, Mom pulled it out and tossed it in the garbage. When potential buyers came to see the house, she would tell them that the house wasn't actually for sale yet. Dad was very patient, but also very persistent.

Mom was desperately trying to hold onto something. It wasn't just the house that was at risk; it was the world that the house represented. You don't just pick up a family and move away to a strange new house in a new neighborhood. You don't just leave behind relatives and friends, and the whole fabric of life of which the house was part. A house wasn't just a physical structure, it was a way of life.

Mom did not want to break with that way of life.

Mom was a stoic, self-styled martyr. Her philosophy was to accept life as it came and to make the best of things. Nevertheless, she did have a stubborn streak and did find ways to assert her ideas and interests.

She almost never cried. I remember a few times seeing her cry when she was in extreme physical pain. These displays of tears were rare, and she usually forced herself to recover quickly. The tears seemed to leave no trace on her once she overcame them.

I remember her crying deeply and uncontrollably only three times. In each of these cases, the tears never really went away. All her inner strength could not totally wash away the introduction of a new shade of melancholy.

The first time occurred when Mom had finally agreed to put

our house up for sale. A real estate agent brought a respectable looking and very cheerful husband and wife. They went from room to room and at each stop the woman expressed her satisfaction: she just loved the house, she just loved the wallpaper, she just loved the kitchen, she just loved the yard, she just loved everything about 511 28th Avenue. After their tour of our home, they were jubilant. They told the agent that they wanted to make an offer to buy the house. Mom's face stiffened and she could scarcely get words out of her mouth.

Once the agent and buyers left, Mom calmly went into her bedroom and closed the door behind her. Then she cried with all the anguish of her soul; she cried without holding anything back. I was in the living room and overheard her crying. Terrified, I went to her room to see what was wrong. I peeked in and saw her weeping. I walked in and tried to comfort her, but I found myself crying right along with her. "What's wrong, Mommy?" I sobbed.

She hugged me tightly. "We're going to have to move away from here. We're going to have to leave our house."

"But aren't we moving to a better house?" I asked.

She nodded, but kept crying.

She was crying for the end of an era. She was crying for the past that was gone, for the future that was uncertain. She was mourning a great loss in her life, in our lives.

By the time Dad got home from work that night, Mom had tried to recover her usual composure. There was a profound sadness in her eyes that she could not hide, a sadness that never fully went away.

Our house was sold. Mom and Dad had found a nice house in the Seward Park neighborhood at 5602 Wilson Avenue South. It was a large white stucco home, dramatically nicer than our home at 511 28th Avenue. Given the choice of living in either of these houses, almost anyone would choose the one on Wilson Avenue South. But Mom still had her reservations.

She had lived in the home on 28th Avenue for eighteen years. She was to live in the home on Wilson Avenue South for twenty-five years; yet, she would refer to the home in Seward Park as "the new house."

We moved to our new home in the summer of 1959. Mom took driving lessons and received her license. She would not allow herself to feel isolated from her parents and the rest of the family still living in the old neighborhood.

We knew that Mom was adjusting to the new house when she planted parsley, mint and tomatoes, just as she had done in the backyard of our old house. She also planted flowers that had grown on 28th Avenue—silver dollars and Chinese lanterns. She had Uncle Dave Amon, who was a very able gardener, transplant a plum tree from the old yard into the new one.

Mom was eager to have our rutha bush (rue) from 28th Avenue transplanted in the front yard of our house on Wilson Avenue South. The rutha bush in our old garden had grown from a cutting from the rutha bush in the yard of Nona and Papoo on 15th Avenue. Aside from giving off a strikingly pleasant fragrance, rutha was considered to be "good luck," a sure deflector of the evil eye.

Uncle Dave Amon brought cuttings from the old rutha bush and re-planted them in our new yard. He could not get the rutha to take. It would remain green for a week or so and then would fade into grey and brown as it died out. He tried to get the rutha bush going several times, but each attempt ended in failure. Mom took this as a bad omen. Uncle Dave assured her that he would try again in the spring.

Mom had other things to worry about aside from the rutha bush. Nona, whose health had been declining, had fallen seriously ill. For a while, she had been hospitalized but then was brought back home. I asked Mom if I could visit Nona. She replied: "She isn't the same Nona that you knew. She's very sick. She has tubes sticking into her. It's better for you not to see her this way. You should remember her as she was, not the way she is now."

As November approached, Mom considered what to do about the Thanksgiving holiday. For many years, she had invited the entire family to our house for Thanksgiving dinner. She felt she should do so again this year; and yet, how could we have a festive holiday meal while Nona was deathly ill? Mom concluded that we would have a small Thanksgiving dinner ourselves; she could not emotionally handle a large family gathering.

On the Saturday before Thanksgiving 1959, Nona died.

On Sunday, family and friends gathered at the Jewish funeral chapel on 12th and Alder. Our ride to the chapel had been long and quiet. Mom sat in the front seat with a stoic expression, seemingly in control of her emotions. Dad parked the car near the chapel and got out to open the door for Mom. As soon as he opened the door, Mom started to cry uncontrollably. Dad, face solemn and grieved, hugged her and tried to comfort her. She was beyond consolation. In an instant, we were all crying, not just in mourning for Nona but for the horrible grief suffered by Mom.

I have never forgotten that eternal instant of grief. Nona's death was an ending, not just of her life but of our family's pattern of life.

Mom had been adjusting slowly to the recent move to Seward Park. Now, a few months later, she was confronted with the death of her mother. Mom, the usually restrained martyr, could not withstand these cataclysmic events without crying helplessly.

The seven days of mourning passed. Autumn was ending, the Seattle winter was beginning.

In the spring, Uncle Dave Amon planted a rutha cutting in our front yard, as he had promised to do. This time it took. The cutting soon grew into a large healthy bush. Mom took this as an omen that the transition to our new lives in Seward Park would also take hold.

The third time I saw Mom cry helplessly was in February 1983 when I came in from New York to visit her in the Group Health hospital in Seattle. As I entered her room, I found her sitting on a chair in the corner. Before I could say a word, before she could say a word—she cried with the fullness of anguish that I had seen in her only twice before.

As she was crying, she reached out her hand to me: "I'm dying, Marc. I'm going to die."

My grandparents and their generation have passed away.

My parents and all their siblings have passed away.

My generation is getting on in years. Some of my cousins have died or are in declining health. Some still live in Seattle, but some live in Portland, Los Angeles, Sioux Falls, New York, Jerusalem...and other places. Some are religiously traditional, and some have moved far from Jewish religious observance.

Our children and grandchildren live in a world much removed from the "old neighborhood" in Seattle where I was born and raised. They have little contact with the children and grandchildren of the cousins of my generation. They have hardly heard (or never heard) Judeo-Spanish as a living language. They have no first hand memories of the lives of the pioneer Sephardic immigrants who came to America in the early 20th century.

Peter Berger, an eminent scholar of modern American civilization, has noted that moderns suffer from a deepening condition of spiritual "homelessness." The old anchors and moorings have not held.

The old days are gone forever. Looking back can be pleasant; but it cannot create a new framework for society. It is not enough to have a "home" in the past. We need to be at home in the present and to create homes for our children and grandchildren.

The "old country of Seattle" cannot be put back together. It is gone, never to return. But values can live on; attitudes can be transmitted; ideas can transcend time and space. Moderns need not be spiritually homeless if they can create a society based on love, trust, shared values and ideals. Our sense of being at home will come from inner strength, from our immediate family and friends, from our communal structures. For our future generations to feel that life is whole, meaningful and secure, we will need to create frameworks where they feel "at home," comfortable with themselves, comfortable with the world in which they live.

Our grandparents and parents and their generations left us a powerful legacy of memories, values and ideals. As we draw strength and wisdom from their lives, we face the present and the future with increasing confidence. We can't go home again, but neither can we ever really leave home.

Biography

Rabbi Marc D. Angel is Founder and Director of the Institute for Jewish Ideas and Ideals (jewishideas.org), fostering an intellectually vibrant, compassionate and inclusive Orthodox Judaism. He is Rabbi Emeritus of the historic Congregation Shearith Israel, the Spanish and Portuguese Synagogue of New York City (founded 1654), where he began serving in 1969.

Born and raised in the Sephardic community of Seattle, Washington, he went to New York for his higher education at Yeshiva University where he earned his B.A., M.S., Ph.D. and Rabbinic Ordination. He also earned an M.A. in English Literature from the City College of New York.

Author and editor of 36 books, he has written and lectured extensively on various aspects of Jewish law, history and culture. Among his books is a collection of short stories, *The Crown of Solomon and Other Stories*, published by Albion-Andalus in 2014.

Rabbi Angel is married to Gilda Angel. Their children and grandchildren live in New York, Baltimore and Teaneck.

CPSIA information can be obtained
at www.ICGtesting.com
Printed in the USA
LVHW091816230819
628744LV00003B/482/P

9 781733 658928